LEVITTOWN PUBLIC LIBRARY
P9-DBJ-330

PRAISE FOR *I Love You So Much It's Killing Us Both*

"You know Khaki Oliver: the dorm-mate with the punk-poster-plastered wall, the quiet kid muttering withering put-downs across the aisle, the solo Black girl at the show with her defenses understandably up, your best friend if you could just say the right thing. *I Love You So Much It's Killing Us Both* is a glow-in-the-dark switchblade: illuminating, cutting, and unsettlingly comical. In this tale of the obsessions that consume suburban misfits, Mariah Stovall has layered in sneaky-funny one-liners, Easter eggs for punks, and irrefutable truths about the queasy isolation of being the Black friend, the Black girl at the gig, and merely middle-class around rich people."

—Chris L. Terry, author of *Black Card* and *Zero Fade* and coeditor of *Black Punk Now*

"Mariah Stovall's prose sounds like driving in a car with your best friend, volume up high on your favorite song. *I Love You So Much It's Killing Us Both* resurrected feelings I had almost forgotten about what it means to be young in a hard, and nonetheless beautiful, world."

—Vauhini Vara, author of Pulitzer Prize finalist *The Immortal King Rao*

"Mariah Stovall's heady debut plays an addictive game of connect-the-dots between two estranged friends through a galaxy of shared pop-culture references and personal history. *I Love You So Much It's Killing Us Both* is a spiraling meditation on the porousness of music and memory, the blurred lines between obsession and friendship, and the hearts we must break in order to grow—including our own."

—Emma Brodie, author of *Songs in Ursa Major*

"You don't need a prior relationship to the sounds and saints of punk, emo, and hardcore to get swept into the currents of Stovall's pulsing storytelling. Her debut artfully dilates the cruel intimacy of one teenage friendship into a dark but tender treatise on hunger, compulsion, and identity. If you've ever loved—a person, a hobby, a song—so intensely it hurt, this mosh pit of a novel will offer you both sanctuary and feedback."

—Stephen Kearse, music critic and author of *Liquid Snakes*

"A ferocious debut that vibrates with music, insight, and the electric torment of youth. *I Love You So Much It's Killing Us Both* is a story of shared—and shed—trauma that lays bare the power of friendship to make, or break, a life." —Cecilia Rabess, author *Everything's Fine*

"Mariah Stovall's *I Love You So Much It's Killing Us Both* turns up the volume on contemporary literary fiction in the best, most mesmerizing way. This book is a blazing riff, completely on fire from the first propulsive chord. Khaki Oliver leads us on a captivating ride; she is, simply put, one of the most compelling narrators we have seen in quite some time." —Jordy Rosenberg, author of *Confessions of the Fox*

"Lyrical, musical, and brilliantly offbeat, this debut traces the aches and pains of young adulthood with such clarity I couldn't help but be transported back to my own adolescence. Our narrator, Khaki Oliver, is angry and lonely, brimming with nostalgia, and laugh-out-loud funny. She yearns, longs, hurts, and turns alive on the page; I feel lucky to have spent the duration of this book with her."

—Diana Clarke, author of *The Hop* and *Thin Girls*

"*I Love You So Much It's Killing Us Both* is a funny, biting, and big-hearted coming of age story. Enter these pages for Mariah Stovall's witty renderings of the contradictions of millennial youth and for her lovingly excavated cultural artifacts; stay for her poignant reflections on what it means to grow into an adult, to be a friend, and to belong to our moment in history."

—Sanjena Sathian, author of *Gold Diggers*

"With a gift for mapping the inner lives of her characters with precision and intensity, Stovall captures the chaos and confusion of not-quite-adulthood. Like the punk rock anthems we refuse to outgrow, *I Love You So Much It's Killing Us Both* is the soundtrack to the damage we do to ourselves. It's a raw nerve, a meticulously coded manifesto, the coming-of-agency novel we've been waiting for."

—Jim Ruland, author of *Make It Stop* and *Corporate Rock Sucks: The Rise and Fall of SST Records*

I Love You So Much It's Killing Us Both

a novel, or an annotated mixtape

mariah stovall

soft skull new york

I Love You So Much It's Killing Us Both

This is a work of fiction. All of the characters, organizations, and events portrayed in this novel are either products of the author's imagination or are used fictitiously.

First Soft Skull edition: 2024

Library of Congress Cataloging-in-Publication Data
Names: Stovall, Mariah, author.
Title: I love you so much it's killing us both : a novel, or an annotated mixtape / Mariah Stovall.
Description: First Soft Skull edition | New York : Soft Skull, 2024.
Identifiers: LCCN 2023034908 | ISBN 9781593767600 (hardcover) | ISBN 9781593767617 (ebook)
Subjects: LCGFT: Novels.
Classification: LCC PS3619.T6985 2024 | DDC 813/.6—dc23/eng/20230905
LC record available at https://lccn.loc.gov/2023034908

Jacket design by Jack Smyth
Jacket images of flowers © plainpicture / Kathrin Anthean Leisch;
clouds © shutterstock / Flas100
Book design by Laura Berry

Published by Soft Skull Press
New York, NY
www.softskull.com

Printed in the United States of America

10 9 8 7 6 5 4 3 2 1

For ——, who didn't need my urgency

—

For Colin, who I'm glad exists

—

For Jeremy, who said I had too many Jawbreaker shirts

For the kids

PART ONE

You painted my entire world
But I don't have the turpentine to clean what
you have soiled

—Bad Religion, "You"

I'M ENCLOSED NOW

JANUARY 2022

I wanted to be a slut when I grew up. *Slut.* Heavy on the tongue and practically lust, it was wanting I wanted. I was desperate to be desperate and unashamed. But someone told me smart girls weren't sluts. A young woman's intelligence was mutually exclusive with everything else I found remotely appealing. Allegedly. Even my mother said so: one's sexuality was beautiful, granted one was neither hoochie nor fast little heifer, and granted one was on the honor roll. I looked in the mirror, then at my report card. Promiscuity was not on my horizon. That didn't stop me from searching for it in the clouds. They held only rain and occasional lightning. Close enough, but I couldn't get a bolt to strike me. I was wound too tight to be loose. Scholastic aptitude had nothing to do with it.

Then I lost faith in my brain. I'd thought so much, and at a certain point it seemed wise to stop. I willed my brain to cease its folding. Or to fold better. But the sulci and gyri colluded with the axons in their stupid sheaths. I couldn't dissuade them. They went on storing, sharing, and resurfacing troubling information: at Christmas dinner, my aunt was pleased to see my body was getting bigger; Charlie C. said I had hairy ears; one could become pregnant the first time they had intercourse; Charlie C. did not want to have intercourse with me. I was furious. My lower half became my scapegoat, for no good reason. I didn't have a textbook for retaliation.

On the bus to summer camp, I grew a grievance with the human thigh. I might as well have discovered the thigh itself, for all the importance I ascribed to it. The thigh: a sinister trope, a tragic hero from knee to hip. No matter how little its circumference, it balloons when you take a seat. Flesh spreads against a park bench, an office chair, the back of your calf as you bend down to dab at a fleck of vomit on the wall behind the toilet. I thought this was wrong and thought I could right it. This was profligate, pedestrian rage. I ran faster across the emerald fields of day camp, endeavoring to make the thighs allies in their defeat. I swam deeper in the spume-laden lake. My reward? Bottomless hunger.

My thighs were brown, speckled. Bread. Toast, piping hot, and the rest of me melted, helpless as a cool pat of butter, each time I sat down. I wanted to eat myself for breakfast. I spent my mornings on the very edge of my bed, my feet flat on the floor. My father packed my lunch downstairs. I contemplated limbs. My legs were hot dogs begging to be slapped on a grill. I closed my eyes and intoned, *Don't look down*. I was growing, and unaccustomed to appetite, unable to stomach the body's potential to change. Its insistence upon it. Hunger was not the wanting I had in mind.

In retrospect, it was ridiculous. But this was a single summer in my youth. There were entire years during which I forgot all this. I softened and criticized my body with the same tame fire as anyone else.

Now I sit on the ledge of my bed every morning and anticipate the disembodied voice of a mechanical woman. She's suspended in the hollows of a train car. I'm entering, or exiting, the platform of another day. Her words are stern and wrought with warning, though the danger itself is cloaked in static. *Look down*, she cautions. *Watch the gap*. I still don't know where to fix my eyes. My feet? My attention strays from finding my footing. It snags on the slick of sweat on my toes, the angle of my ankles, the length of the hair on my shins, the shapes of the stretch marks on the backs of my knees, those little bolts of light. I chose wrong, I always choose wrong, but I keep moving.

*

Thursday afternoon bleeds into evening. I was supposed to have today off. Sunset seeps through the windows in the lobby of my building. The glare from the glass cuts my vision. I'm exhausted from an uneventful shift at the museum. I key open my mailbox, expecting nothing, ready to abandon the task if a chatty neighbor appears. I find an envelope with something stiff inside. A spam postcard, I presume. A greeting card to mark a meaningless occasion. I leave it on top of the block of mailboxes, where misplaced mail gets placed.

Sweat skates down my skin. I move the single braid of my hair from my left shoulder to my right. The bulb overhead highlights my neck for an audience of none. I double-check that I've closed my mailbox, then walk up three flights of stairs, only to realize I've left my keys behind. I return for them, and for the envelope. Now I take the steps two at a time. The envelope's in the waistband of my tights, like it's paraphernalia and I'm expecting a raid. When I close the door to my apartment, I have my heart in my throat.

A girl named Fiona used to send me mail. She used to pull my shoulders back when I slouched. She read me literature from the Southern Gothic tradition while we walked my dog. She never took her eyes off the page and she never tripped over the cracks in the sidewalk, which is good because if she did, she might have fractured something. She said she loved me. She left without saying goodbye, but if you were to ask her, she'd say I left her. She would be right. But that was a very long time ago and we are women now.

She wrote me letters, wrote me into existence. I returned the favor. We made magnets of whomever would accept us for what we were. We attracted only each other. Without her, there is no me, at least not in this configuration. It's not a question of whether I would be different if our paths hadn't crossed but a question of degree. How many more friends would I have were it not for the bar she set, then failed to clear? How many more plant species would I be able to name if I still stayed up late listening to her contour Latin around the edges of her teeth? With how much more ease would I be able to define *amare*? *Fides*? *Proditione*?

I make the envelope into hope by waiting to open it. I leave my shoes at the door and hang my backpack on a hook. I straighten the leash on the adjacent hook; there's no dog here to greet me. I turn the lights on, and then off, and then on, counting each time, up and up from a random number. In the kitchen, I press a glass of cool water to my face. I boil water for tea, because when I calm down, my body will remember that it's January and my radiator is capricious. I've apparently thrown the envelope on the floor. I wash and dry my hands and retrieve it. I try to remember what Fiona is. A full-body rush. A cursed experiment in collaboration. Someone to share things—a piece of gum; life—with.

The envelope is a rectangle askew, like a dollhouse welcome mat in the most subtle shade of pink. I almost think it reeks of her, even from across the room. I go to it, bring it to my nose. No tobacco. No bright green leaves. Vanilla and burnt sugar, which she would have hated ten years and one month ago. It's addressed to *Khaki Oliver.* The sight of my government name stings. My mother must have told her where I live. There's no return address. A rose gold sticker embossed with a golden rose seals the flap. I open it with my paring knife, a clean slit from end to end.

My presence is requested. In six weeks, we'll celebrate the adoption of Flannery Davies by Fiona Davies. The event will take place in a city I can reach in a few hours by bus or train. I can RSVP to Sam? There's a photograph on the other side of the invitation. A blond white woman, amber-eyed. This is Fiona—there's that dimple in her chin that's like God's stamp of approval—but I don't recognize her. Or her chubby, brown-skinned infant. Their outfits, in so far as a child this young can wear an outfit, are complementary without matching. The bronze stitching in one brings out the copper trim in the other. The girl's eyes are closed and surely the same dark brown as mine. For a moment, I think I've given birth and given her up, soft curls and all.

I wonder who the first person Fiona tells her good news to is, and what that person has heard about me. If Fiona keeps me like a secret or shares me with anyone who will listen. I keep her to myself. I reread the details. If there is another parent involved, their name has been omitted. Unless . . . Sam? I invent a story I can stand: Sam is a casual acquaintance, nothing more. Sam is black. Fiona's neighbors and coworkers and dentist and accountant are black, hence the child. Fiona has done the reading. The work. She's not an ally; she's a co-conspirator. Her relatives die; she redistributes her inheritances. She can recite the Combahee River Collective statement in her sleep. Her praxis is perfect.

I laugh at my fiction until the boiling kettle interrupts me. I turn it off and forget to pour the water into something. Even Fiona's mother thought Fiona was unfit to raise children, and I assume she assumed said hypothetical children would be white. I have no reason to remember this. A chill scales my spine. I'm still sweating. I think about Fiona only when I think about my body. She's always on my mind. But I'm not supposed to think about my body, so it's more like she's always on the cusp, and when she threatens to cross over, I try to remember what I learned when I still went to therapy, and I rationalize those thoughts, that girl, away. Then voilà, I'm lonelier than science can account for.

Because of her, I've trained myself not to develop attachments to human beings. This seems to have improved my health. The stability is hard-won and precarious. I'm better without her. Tears of joy douse my chin as I remember being worse with her. I weigh the likely risks and rewards of accepting or ignoring her invitation. One scenario inspires desire. One sparks fear.

I don't make up my mind, I expel her from it. Taking her out takes so much out of me. Now the sun has long since set. It's halfway to rising. I should eat something. It is difficult, though, so I don't. I flip the invitation back and forth in bed, counting each time, *373, 374, 375*. The colors blur. The air outside cackles with scraps of wind and shallow conversation. I fall asleep and I can hear her voice. There's the steam of her breath as she whispers every thought she's ever had directly into my ear.

—

[2] I wake up early to return the invitation to its envelope, which I then carefully position in my backpack. I'll need to feel it through my coat as I walk. I reach the bus stop and pass right by. I want to wander. I silently greet each dog I pass. There, of course, is the brindled Great Dane with the overgrown toenails. Others are surprises. I try not to smile at them, in case their owners take stock of my face. My headphones aren't connected to anything. I'm sure the dogs can hear the silence but will keep my secret safe. I count my steps—there are worse things to count. Slush makes hideous hills along the curb. Soon my mind is blank, and in this sense, I am beautiful.

At eleven, I bypass the museum's revolving door in favor of the hinged one with heavy handles. The rug at the entrance only catches so much grime from my shoes. I take my seat behind the front desk. For just above minimum wage, I hand out maps. I point to the bathrooms, which I consider open to the public. Business—the hoarding and subjective narrativization of cultural artifacts—is slow this time of year. I'm supposed to deliver a standard greeting to guests as they arrive. Only those lucky enough to come in during the first five minutes of the hour receive a full-throated *Welcome to the Jefferson Museum of American . . .*

People-watching is my true calling. It's been less fulfilling since the powers that be abolished donation-based admissions. I figured out how to print tickets for people who can't or don't want to pay the newly mandated entry fee. In between busy-work, I write, or used to write, field notes. Lately, I can barely bring myself to tally the members of whatever category pops into my head. *Singles wearing necklaces. Identical twins on field trips.* My data collection ends there. It could be worse. If my contentedness becomes restlessness, I could be in trouble. I don't trust myself to try anything, anyone, anywhere new.

The security guards are stationed far enough away that I'd have to raise my voice to chat. We rarely chat. They call me Moody. I think it's fair and quite funny, but not funny enough to laugh at, so they also call me a bitch. This is common, though who am I to say whether it's a misconception? I don't say much, which makes the talkative project. I'm difficult to connect with. Not them. They're normal. It's abnormal to fantasize about, for instance, asking someone who cheers upon receiving good news why they behave that way. I can't ask. I'd be accused of mocking or jealousy, not praised for wanting to understand. I've felt like a sociopath, an extraterrestrial, a man, though I'm certain I'm none of those things.

There was a brief period in which my curiosity had value. I was supposed to be an anthropologist. I have the bachelor's but not much else. I once won a fellowship to travel to New Zealand and do linguistic fieldwork in a Maori community. Something about the legacy of colonialism. I panicked when it came time to commit to the program. How might the food differ from what I was used to? I couldn't sleep for wondering what I might be expected to politely eat during a professional gathering or culturally meaningful event. What if food poisoning resulted in weight loss? I withdrew my application as soon as it was accepted. My moral reservations factored in as well. Seven classes into the major, the word *ethnography* started to sound like *eggnog* to me. It turned my stomach. It was too late to start over.

My professors acknowledged their forebearers' sins, but come graduation day, a thought looped in my brain: *Curiosity, once acted upon, can quickly become violent.* I was fresh out of room for nuance. Now, I'm staring at a clock in a museum owned by the distant descendant of a founding father who had quite the theory about black people. *Love seems with them to be more an eager desire, than a tender delicate mixture of sentiment and sensation . . . In general, their existence appears to participate more of sensation than reflection.* If only our third president had lived to see me in action. I was eager to love Fiona, yes. She made my heart sail. I reflected. Yes, my thoughts were existent and relentless and reckless.

Infrequent footsteps slap the tile floor. Sometimes, this is the only sound for hours, three of which have come and gone since my arrival. It's time for my break. I can't continue the walk I started this morning. The skies are no longer clear. An inside-out umbrella bag caught in the revolving door spits sibilance into the soundscape.

I go to the basement and tap on the door to Stuart's workshop. It's already open. Our most senior employee is hunched, slicing the skin off a dead baby fox. He either nods at me or cracks his neck. I go in and stand next to an empty stool.

"A kit," I say.

His head twitches again before he speaks. "Not to be confused with the kit fox species." Once the cut is complete, he turns to me. "*Vulpes macrotis.*"

He removes every creature's skin with the same reverence. It's a privilege to catch him laying cured hides over sculpted molds. His craft is impeccable. I like the look of it but would not be able to abide the work itself, the materiality of death against my skin. Sometimes when his back is turned, I try to peel the citrus fruits from my lunch bag in that same perfect motion, but my hands are inelegant, and I can get so excited—not hungry—that I give in to imprecision. I'm not supposed to eat in here anyway. And Stuart's not supposed to be here at all. *Taxidermy is the past; virtual reality is the future.* The powers that be tried to fire him last year. He took the directive as a suggestion and kept showing up.

Half his workspace is overrun with other departments' miscellany. An old stack of object labels here. Irreparable pottery shards there. If I try to move a fireproof box, no matter how lightweight, he stops me. It isn't fair. The lavender-haired high school girl who made herself his part-time unpaid apprentice is allowed to touch things! Once, when Stuart stepped out for coffee, I cautioned her against falling for him. She laughed. I pretended to be in on the joke. Thankfully, he and I are alone today. When we first met, I tried love and lust—privately, of course—to no avail. He didn't suspect a thing. Now his thin lips remind me of a slender mail slot. One no envelope would fit through. I almost ask him what to do about Fiona's invitation. If he thinks she might have changed. At sixtysomething, he must know something about people. He doesn't know her. Only I do.

He's peeling the kit's skin back now, cutting tight against the bone. It hangs from her neck like a scarf. He doesn't like when I name them, but I decide to call her Eartha. She's splayed:

her muscles the same lifeless purplish-grey as my favorite pair of socks, her fat a rosy white. I understand the science, but it never ceases to surprise me that the specimens don't bleed. The more of her he peels away, the more prehistoric she looks.

"Stuart?" He doesn't hear me. I stand behind his good ear and repeat his name. "Do people change?" The glass eyes he set aside for Eartha bore into me.

"Well, you know . . ."

I pace and wait for him to say more. He pivots to a conversation with himself about the powers' involvement in a high-level political conspiracy. There aren't windows down here. He runs the air conditioning year round, to keep the dead cold. The lights hurt my head. His preservation potions beget a haze. It could be toxic. His knife makes a different hand and blade flash in my mind. There is Fiona with a box cutter to her bone, and I am not there to stop her, and it is time for me to go. I'm back upstairs before the full picture forms. I think of nothing for the rest of the day. *Nothing, nothing, nothing.* The guests trickle in and out. A text from Georgia tells me to meet her at the bar. A squeal escapes from me without my permission. The security guards snicker. I smile. The surprise of my teeth shuts them up.

*

Six fifty-nine; the sky is blank again. I walk the long way. Happy hour's ending when I arrive, and Georgia wastes no time berating me. We proceed to order as many drinks as we can for the friends we swear are freshening up in the bathroom. I don't think Georgia has ever worn the same piece of jewelry twice.

Tonight, a cigar ring hangs from a chain around her neck. It's reflecting light back at the bartender, who knows how well Georgia tips, even on my cheap drinks, which he slyly makes into virgin versions of whatever she's having. Georgia doesn't notice because Georgia is Georgia's primary concern. I like it quite a lot. She has all the magnetism of Fiona and none of the required maintenance.

Some muscle in my torso twitches. Georgia pops both our olives into in her mouth and goes on about her problems and victories. With so many friends and beaus and coworkers and family members and enemies and patrons, constant conflict is unavoidable. She's all over this city. She's inevitable. I don't remember how I met her, but no conflict was involved. I'd been going weeks without face-to-face conversations with anyone, let alone anyone my age. Georgia appeared just as my psyche was dipping into a desolate place. I have another friend, but he lives in California, and one can throw a lifeline only so far.

Georgia's talking, I'm nodding. I'm the soundboard against which she confirms her opposite intuitions. I tell her to cut ties with everyone who's ever caused her any stress, no matter how much joy is on the other side of the current spat. Drop the dead weight. Live preventively. It's all about the future.

"You're right," she concludes after we debate the case of her manicurist, who'd been charging two dollars more than the advertised price all last year. "Everyone deserves a second chance."

"Sure!"

I know what she'd say about Fiona's invitation. Georgia doesn't skip events. She couldn't fathom the gravity of the situation, of having a single friend and one decade of estrangement between you. I slide an empty glass back and forth. Georgia swipes between apps, planning her next activity. Our allotted hour together is almost up. She puts her phone away and pulls me into a sideways hug. Roses and oud, undercut by cocoa butter. I don't let anyone else touch me. She asks me how I am. I say something just to say it. I never know how to answer that question.

Before Georgia leaves, she has to pee, and no, I may not join her in the bathroom. I must instead guard her spread of half-empty drinks. I do what's asked of me. A man approaches. He nearly knocks her coat off her chair.

I look familiar, he says. He's attractive, with neat fingernails and inflated biceps beneath a broken-in fisherman's sweater. He asks where I'm from.

"All over." I realize my mistake. The ceiling fan above us whirs. If only I could float upward to drape myself over its blades.

"Where are your people from?" he tries again.

"Same place as yours," I shrug. I too once wanted an answer to that question, and thus, at ten years old, wasted a month's worth of Sundays hunting through family photos. I was hankering for a distant relative to blame for my anomalous appearance: my mother's nose, her great-uncle's smile, my father's eyes and ears, all arranged on skin that literally paled in comparison theirs. At family get-togethers, questions, comments, and concerns were expressed in good humor. It was a cut-and-dry case of recessive genetics, vis-à-vis a few generations of chattel slavery and its requisite rapes. I never found the photograph I was looking for; there wasn't one. I don't tell him any of this.

He calls me beautiful. Maybe it's a stand-in for my name. I don't tell him that either. Now he wants to buy me a drink. I want to want one, and a ring, and his undying love. Maybe he'd let me have a black picket fence. I hide my hands in my hair. Unbraiding, rebraiding. He interprets my lack of response as a plea for more admiration. I've stupidly called attention to my hair, and he calls that beautiful too. I'm sure it's the only reason he's here. My hair has always preceded me. Ten out of ten teachers, grocery baggers, crossing guards agree: *Don't you dare cut it. Don't even think about ironing it straight.* My hair was good, they said, with no mention of my moral standing. They petted. Praised and appraised—told me, hand to Jesus, while their other fingers pried around my roots, how much money they'd part with in exchange for my curls. Pretty happened, I realized, when someone grabbed part of you and obscured it with an invisible piece of herself. I didn't like to be grabbed, but the obscuration was pleasant.

I should really tell this man something. If nothing else, I can tell him my name. It's just a name. It's just that my mother took one look at me under the cruel hospital lights and, with Ebony off the table, anointed me Khaki. It was right there on my nose, where the melanin was meager. It was better than the alternatives. I imagine introducing myself as Band-Aid. Cashew. Rubber Band. The Inside Of A Pencil. Iced Chai Latte. A Herd Of Sprinting Deer. Pie Crust On The Verge Of Burning. Sawdust In Sunlight. Cardboard On The Curb. A Paper Lunch Bag On A Bed Of Wet Sand. *Hello, pleased to meet you, I'm An Apple Slice Left Out On The Counter.*

I am preparing to speak when— "You deaf or something?" He leaves just as Georgia returns.

"What's wrong?" she asks between her last sips of everything. She tosses ample cash on the bar.

A little web of hair is wrapped around my thumb. I let the shed strands fall to the floor. They drown in spilled spirits. "Just tired."

I help her put on her coat, then leave her at the nearest train station, where she hugs me again. I walk in a different direction. Hours pass and extremities go numb, even though I'm wearing my best pair of mittens, the ones my father gave me. I duck into an artisanal grocery store to defrost. This is a mistake. Grocery stores are distressing. At least someone else is here, contemplating a small pot of European yogurt. I uncover my hands and explore a nonrefrigerated aisle. A jar of olives catches my eye, with its handwritten label and the black gloss of the oily fruit. I'm trying to calculate the number of calories in an individual olive and how many cents each calorie costs, when I hear Fiona's voice call my name. The glass explodes at my feet. I bend down to fix it. The pieces stutter around the brine. I can't rake them.

"Just stop." An employee looks down his nose at me. "You're bleeding. And I'm not about to get sued." I don't think I look litigious, but I hide my cut hands in my mittens and whisper an apology. He checks his watch and says I don't have to pay for it. I should, however, be gone when he gets back with the mop. I place a ten-dollar bill on the unattended checkout counter on my way out. The paper's torn at the corner. Hamilton's forehead is puckered with a scribble.

On the sidewalk, I spin. Which way is north? By the time I get home, it's after midnight, but I've only counted thirty-three steps. I check the mail. There's more waiting: an envelope full of something substantial. Three stamps are aligned in one corner. There's a uniform *F* where the return address should be. *F* as in *Forgive me.* It's addressed to me. To Olive. I soar upstairs and kick off my boots and shake my hands until the feeling returns. My excitement feels animate enough to open the envelope itself. But I'm the one to do it.

Olive my love,

I meant for this to arrive before the invitation but Sam insists that I not worry myself with the details. Ha. As if it isn't my party!

Please say you'll come, back for good, into my life, I mean! Though I have an extra room—with the softest sheets and loveliest baseboard molding—in case you want to stay a little longer.

I'll tell you now and I'll tell you when I see you: thank you for leaving when you did. Have you noticed how the people who keep their old friends too close are sort of . . . off? It seems like a surefire way to stunt your development. And I'd already done enough of that. Ha.

Her voice has graduated from calling my name from the ether to sending proper sentences to echo off the walls. I can't be too quick to absolve her. I stop reading and remind myself where I am. Here and now. Alone. I put the pages down. I want to sit. I want to sleep for a very long time. I stare at white walls. I have an emptiness infestation.

Minimalism feels inevitable in so few square feet. Comely used napkins, stained with caffeine or the carotenoids of a good peach, litter the kitchen counter for weeks at a time. But my record collection is the only perennial decoration. That and my record player, which was my father's record player when he was my age. The four four-cube shelves that house my music are the only furniture I bought new. Each cube fits forty-eight albums, which I count more often than I play. Seven hundred and sixty-eight sleeves—I know, it's not much—dusty from years of neglect. Seven years and some months without going to a show, and almost as long without listening to a new release.

I can't bring myself to do to the vinyl what I did to my band shirts and concert flyers and unstuck stickers and hand-sewn and hand-stapled zines. I've packed the records into boxes and milk crates, walked them to the curb, set them down, and come back for them five minutes later. I've completed the tedious task of listing each one for sale online, for just a penny and with free shipping to anywhere in the world, so that anyone who wanted them would be able to have them—and canceled the auctions before any bids could come in. I've inquired about donating them to a youth recreational center and ghosted those poor kids.

I pull one from the shelf. Something loud, fast, and familiar enough to drown out Fiona. I pull a splinter of glass from my thumb and flick it away. Dead skin and dirt tickle my eyes. I lift the needle. It seems to leap into a groove. I suck the blood from my frantic index finger and turn the volume up. The instruments have furor. Up. Ian has more. Up. He hollers.

What happened to you?

Honestly, I can't remember. It's possible I never knew. I prefer not to engage with questions I can't easily answer. Therapy is not for me. In it, I learned that I was fixated on the wrong thing. Actually, I wasn't supposed to fixate on anything at all, but that isn't possible, and so I kept my absolute focus on identifying the catalyst of the condition that landed me there. There was more to it than Fiona. But that's as far as I got. The doctor said *why* was the wrong place to start. She said that in the beginning, re-everything-ing was what mattered. Refeeding. Restructuring habits. Resisting my own resistance. She said the rest could wait. I disagreed. I stopped being a patient. It wasn't fair. Fiona found her reason easily. There it is. I'm jealous again.

—

[3]Music is the only thing that wanted me instead of her. The upset occurred soon after we met. She couldn't stand the love music and I shared. I wore that love like a stone around my neck. I fidgeted with it, brought it to my lips, sucked and swallowed. My anxious energy turned to love turned to anxious energy trapped inside me. It caused painful bloating. It was a gas I would unleash in crowded rooms, general admission standing room only. I was invisible until someone caught a whiff. Then there he was, disgusted. I too feigned shock and revulsion. Then I did it all again. Chemical warfare was my newest compulsion. My victims: boys. Men. Not the ones who made the music. The ones who listened to, lived, and died by it.

They sometimes appeared in the wild. Fiona showed no respect when one cruised past. I had no choice. Just an evolutionary imperative to chuck my gaze toward the kissing breeze that trailed him and his skateboard. I didn't care who was attached to the scabbed legs whipping the body through the stagnancy surrounding me. Fiona told me to keep my distance. But what was the worst that could happen when one—tall socks sheathing his rancid feet—carved and smoothed out space so near to the very ground I was standing on? He could untie the world in a moment, with a kickflip, or whatever. I don't understand the mechanics—the paradoxical slackness of limbs hanging listlessly, or crouching, flexed and determined to land a trick. I would've rather died than understood; I couldn't risk falling for myself. I imagined they all laughed the little laugh Kevin Seconds unleashes at the very end of that "99 Red Balloons" cover. (I think it's him. It could be anyone who was there, anyone who now has my undying love.)

My appreciation peaked in the hours I spent on trains and walks, wending between Manhattan and Brooklyn and then back to the western side of the Hudson River, while Fiona was a hostage in a hospital turret. Every so often, the telltale scrape of my only desire would penetrate the music in my headphones and drown out the city's every other sound. It was even better when they came in droves. My only preference was for the brunettes, for brown as close to black as possible. Nothing made for more seductive fear than a succession of adolescence floating on rabid wood and plastic, sporting stupidly cut or aggressively uncut hair. I will never replicate the urgency with which my heart seized when one of them reached out and grabbed—not me, but the driver's side door handle on a taxi gliding through a yellow light. It had no choice. It carried him along.

Now I keep my distance. If I'm not careful, my heart can

still break at first sight. Skateboards, faded band shirts, Sambas and Vans, tattoos verging on generic, black jeans, and scruff scrawled on slack jaws. Now I avert my eyes. Tall goddamn socks. Those were the objects of my affection. Their wearers were secondary, and I was sure they couldn't see me. If only I could have beckoned them without having to speak. If only I had social skills to speak of. They could have held me, maybe, but not while we listened to playlists painstakingly crafted to capture something inherently fleeting. If only they'd been more than mannequins adorned in aesthetics. I played with punk Ken dolls in my head for years. The music seemed to belong on their bodies, so I kept them naked save for the Bad Religion stickers I smoothed across their crotches and chests. I peeled back the corners, pressed them back down. I didn't want to see what was underneath, until I did.

Now I'm crawling back to sound, begging it to take me back. Better it than her. There's a song that will tell me if I can see her again. I figure it won't take too long to find, but night becomes day and I text my manager that I won't be able to make my shift. In fact, I tell her the next afternoon, I have the flu and don't know how long it'll take to shake it. I draw my blackout curtain.

—

PART TWO

To be a fan is to know that loving trumps being beloved.

—Carrie Brownstein,
Hunger Makes Me a Modern Girl

WHAT I MIGHT DO IF I WERE LET LOOSE

SEPTEMBER–OCTOBER 2011

JUST EAST OF LOS ANGELES

4

hen we graduated from high school, I dropped out of the East Coast. I left Fiona for a place in the desert, barely inside Los Angeles's eastern border, where all the girls had their noses pierced, or they were pretty, or both. Where Angela Davis had once taught in secret. In the five-college consortium, mine was the youngest. The one stoned out of its mind. Shaggy in the Scooby-Doo analogy. I wasn't there, at least not primarily, for the student body's reputation or the faculty's credentials. I was there to get kicked in the head.

My first West Coast show had a New England lineup, in Anaheim, by Disney World, Disneyland, whichever one was thirty-something miles from campus. I tried to get a ride from a classmate. I couldn't find a kindred spirit. I put together a roll of quarters and a wedge of dollar bills and reminded myself I liked buses, like I liked suffering for the honor of being reciprocally knocked around in a very hot room. Afterward, I'd find somewhere to close my eyes until bus service resumed. The longer the better; the more albums I could get through.

I'd studied the timetables for my three-hour sojourn. The

neat columns soothed me, but I still got lost. I had to ask for directions twice, once in stilted Spanish, and always after mentally rehearsing how to speak before I spoke, always relying on lessons from a life spent scrutinizing people. In a mall parking lot, I caught a transfer and wondered if it was true that dry heat could turn curly hair straight, as I'd heard from a girl in my orientation group. She was from Arizona. They didn't participate in daylight saving time there. I'd learned so much already. I'd forgotten how to ride a bus. Before I knew it, I was at the end of the line.

The driver looked me up and down and made his face full of mercy. I'd taken the right route in the wrong direction. He told me to wait there while he took his break. I smiled and nodded, with two-thirds of a mind to get out and walk however long it was back to campus, more as consequence than punishment for fumbling a simple task. The empty bus entombed me. My face made an oil print on the window. I noted my place in the landscape, among a smog inspection station, takeout restaurants, apartment complexes, and an unemployment center. My orientation group had passed through a similar area on our way to an interactive presentation about the life and times of César Chávez. One of the group leaders had turned to me, blue eyes engorged with pity, and asked if it reminded me of where I grew up. It did not.

The driver came back and demanded, kindly, that I tell him where I was going. After my answer, he started the engine. *You should make conversation, Khaki. Talk. How? Small. No!* I put my earbuds back in. *Why not? He already knows there's something wrong with you. He doesn't want to talk to me. He's busy. Not that he's incapable of speaking and driving at the same time.*

It's too late, here come the other passengers. They're already staring at me. No one is paying attention to you. I turned up the music and drew my legs to my chest, pulled my sweater around them, and pretended to sleep. Every few minutes, I opened an eye. The driver's promised cue came half an hour later.

Tentative were my steps into the street. It was without crosswalks. It had wide highway-like lanes. Palm trees aside, there was little scenery, but three buses, three and a half hours, and there was the venue and there were the kids huddled outside it, and there was the person selling me a ticket without offering me a chance to supply ID for the wristband that would allow me to drink. I was undeniably underage. I went inside. I was home.

Chain Reaction is just a long room with a bar in the corner, flyers on the walls, and a stage overlooking a scuffed floor. It was somewhere between Madison Square Garden and a New Brunswick basement show, and I'd missed the first band. The next one was setting up, so I scanned the congregation, found him near a wall, and said, "I like your Cobra Skulls patch" to the kid in black denim. He was always there.

I tried not to stare at the semiotics of which he was composed: beet-colored hair cut so short you might argue the color was natural; a steel ring in his septum; Xs, wide and declarative, drawn on his hands for the night, even though, or precisely because, he was old enough to drink. Permanent ink on his forearms. I focused on the song coming from the speakers. I could have shed a tear for every song that had ever been relegated to background music. This one was by The Smiths.

"You know them?" he asked. His eyebrows—not magenta but cast-iron black—climbed higher on his forehead. He turned toward me. I flattened against the wall and forgave his disrespectful question. "I haven't seen you around," he said, his breath plaque and mint. He was short and slender and he was not a menace.

He laughed when I told him where I was from. Well, at least it wasn't Florida. I should have said I was Oregonian, could have said anything and he would have believed it. I put one hand on his shoulder and touched his ear with the other. I stretched the pinky-sized hole in his lobe a little looser. He looked down at his phone. Perhaps I'd misjudged our potential. Perhaps I had to continue speaking. *Say anything, Khaki. Spill speech on space!* I could only think to tell him about how Fiona once mistook her cat's nipple for a tick and tried to rip it off.

He cocked his head. The man was happy to talk about his cats. Three seemed excessive, but I let that thought pass. He put his phone away. I let him talk until he decided to tell me his name.

"I'm Matty. And you're . . .?"

The air left my lungs, the room, the Golden State. I made a beeline for the bathroom before his mouth closed. I tried to be reasonable. Matty was a common name. *Khaki, no one you know is in this time zone, waiting to grab you by the hand— or was it your waist? A hand over, or in, a mouth, fingers that didn't flinch when bitten— Khaki, can you please calm down? It's called a coincidence.*

Graffiti and stickers garnished the empty bathroom's every inch. I turned the faucet on and pressed my hips against the ledge of the sink basin. My exhaustive research into panic attacks suggested that my fits lacked the urgency of true panic. I did not feel the terrifying certainty that my death was imminent. Instead: overwhelming evidence that I was very much alive and would remain as such for the foreseeable future. I resigned myself to a muffled sort of suffering. It turned more uncomfortable than painful once the initial shock wore off.

My phone buzzed. My roommate was reminding me to be careful. But I shouldn't have had to be; the world should've been safe. *I heard you get straight As for the semester if your roommate dies*, I typed. He'd loaned me all those quarters for the bus. *Lol*, I added, *I'm fine. Thanks, Dad!* A sound check shook the walls. I wanted to call Fiona and ask if Matty was malignant or a cosmic joke. But it was late where she was and we weren't on the best terms. I'd shed the person who knew me best; I'd relinquished the responsibility of knowing her back.

Matty's name was a good sign. He was a fresh start I shouldn't keep waiting. I stopped at the merch table on my way back. Another ten dollars, another black shirt, and sure, I could have that sticker for free. All was right in the world. Matty smiled at me from the floor's perimeter. He was fine standing at the back, he said, when I returned to his side. He was just there with some friends. This wasn't really his scene. I left him.

The first note rang out. Guitars gushed. I forgot he existed. Two hundred bodies rushed forward. Jon's nasal voice droned around the room. Heads banged and necks nodded. Some act of physics sucked me toward the stage. I was close enough to push the pedals. If I stayed there, the force behind me would bend me forward. My elbows would have to prop me up; I'd have to balance one leg on the floor and bend the other to join my arms on the stage. I retreated slightly. We slowed and swayed and sped up and toppled over and were surfed over by bodies. I wasn't tall enough to help carry their weight, I was just tall enough to get kicked in the neck. A wave of stage divers was incoming. One offered to boost me up whence they'd just fallen. Others mouthed *You okay?* Men made minor contortions to tame what I'd spent so much time preparing to face. *You sure?* So many men apologizing for what I was preparing my thanks. Yes, there were some girls, but mostly there were men apologizing for my relief upon receiving confirmation that we batter each other the same from coast to coast. Shin to forehead, shoulder upon shoulder, watching out for each other, percussive concussions, knuckle to ear to busted lip, crying *And that's when I knew you were dead.* This was safer than the sudden onslaught of strangers on a bus. We repeated without rinsing, seeped more with every song and set. Clapped. Howled. Demanded. *Lose your voice and make it hurt.* I forgot she existed.

Soon my ears were ringing and it was over and Matty was surrounded by his friends. I picked at my arms, the skin newly soft from incidental exfoliation. Many deep breaths made me able to cut into their circle. I said hi to the others, hooked my finger back in Matty's gaping ear. I whispered that I wasn't tired, but I couldn't hear myself, so it's entirely possible that I was screaming. I convinced him to go on a walk.

The streetlights were sporadic. The stars sputtered on. He was four or five years my senior, depending on the time of year, and we were practically neighbors. My school made him bristle. Even after I reminded him that very few students paid the full tuition. Submitting standardized test scores was optional, though not in my case, as my grades plummeted at the end of high school, in tandem with Fiona's attendance. I couldn't tell him why she couldn't go to class, but I satisfied him with the fact that my admission hinged on my SAT score and personal essay alone, as if that made me more proletarian.

He was ready to head back, he said.

We were walking in a circle. The end was inevitable, but maybe delayable. There was a playground across the street. "Wouldn't it be fun to sleep there?" I ran to it and scaled the fence. He made no haste, but he followed and unlatched the gate to join me.

We nestled at the bottom of a school bus–colored slide. I gave him one of my earbuds and told him not to judge me for their cheapness—I kept my good headphones far away from shows. He said he understood, and with that, we took turns playing God. He chose a Kid Dynamite song after my Lifetime, and each rare passing car spat a breeze that slapped the wire fence without rhythm. We were utterly alone. Six songs later, he freed himself from our yellow temple. I started to shiver. The desert sun dragged the temperature down with it each night as it set. August days gave way to November nights. Who knew California could be so cold? I was still learning. He was walking away and yelled over his shoulder to make sure I was coming.

I was unbearably thirsty and so full of pee. I went to quickly squat in the bushes. When I caught up to him, we did not hold hands on the way to his car, which was black, of course, the last one in the lot. I blanched at my reflection in the side mirror and then again when I saw myself in the napkin holder at the Denny's he took me to. My mascara had smeared and redried like wet sugar. His Xs were immaculate.

We sat side by side in a burgundy booth. I collapsed into

him and felt the machinations of his body. Eggs: chewed. Coffee: drunk. Everything sucked down by gravity, muscled through all fifteen or so feet of his intestines. I told him caffeine was a drug, just to hear him fill in the rest of the lore.

Hey, Ian, my friend says caffeine is a drug.

Tell your friend 'Fuck you.'

We kept talking about my school, laughing at the kids who wore Birkenstocks and pierced their nostrils rather than the cartilage in between. Their guitars were acoustic. They levitated in tired hammocks that clung to broiled trees. Presumably, his band seethed electric, heels digging into concrete in abandoned warehouses and half-paved backyards. Stumpgrinder, they were called.

"Fucking hippies," he said of my peers, for the third time, shaking his head. Had he not been straightedge there would have been a cigarette tucked behind his ear. He wasn't a cartoon character, exactly. There was something rudimentary about him, like a comic book sketch. "You're hella weird too, by the way. Could've waited until we got here to use the bathroom. We're in a drought or whatever but there's still indoor plumbing."

I twisted my neck to lock eyes with the convex Matty in the napkin dispenser. "How was I supposed to know where we were going?" He went back to his breakfast. I sat up to escape the vibrations of his jaw. The restaurant's lighting was somehow worse than the venue's. I looked at him anyway. His skin was lighter than mine, but the angle of the cheekbones on his otherwise flat face gave me hope. Surely he wasn't white. Surely this time could be different. He pressed a greasy kiss to my forehead, where an invisible bruise was forming. I assumed I was in love.

It was almost two when we left. I offered to drive. He laughed at that, and many other wrong things. On 57 North—like the song, though I suspected he didn't like that band either—he turned the radio to a country show and left it undisturbed. Something classical came on at the top of the hour. Sleep caught and released me. When we were off the freeway, I asked if it was called that because there weren't any tolls. He snorted without answering, so I asked him to tell me more about him.

A Riverside childhood. Four years at CalArts. I pretended to be familiar with these things. I pictured a house on the bank of river. I pictured surfers maneuvering watercolors between waves. The car lurched as a coyote crossed the road. He braked and reached across the car to keep me in place. It was beautiful, I said. He warned me that they eat people's dogs.

"A million years ago, they were people's dogs," I said, to see if he'd correct me, then ask me if I liked dogs, then ask to see a picture of mine. *Khaki, no. He's a cat person.*

We idled in the parking lot outside my dorm. Rather than chide him about the pollution, I pulled my seatback more upright. I smelled terrible. His ears had me smitten. I turned to him. He graced my mouth with his. It was a languid, bitter kiss. It was the realization that something horrible was going to happen next.

"Are you chewing gum?" I held out my hand. "Someone could choke."

His face twisted into itself as he stuck out his tongue. The wintergreen nugget rolled into my palm. It looked like a little brain. If a tea leaf could think, I thought, it would do so via this.

He cleared his throat and handed me his phone. I typed my number with my empty hand. He could choose what name to attach to it.

"Are you a slut, by the way?" I asked.

He was aghast. No, he told me. That would make him impure.

"Impure," I repeated. He was serious. "Me too—I mean me neither," I admitted. At least not yet. I had a whole life ahead of me. I kept that part to myself.

"Cool," he yawned, shifting into reverse. "Good night."

I was in love. I let the door to my dorm room slam. Cameron was a good sleeper. I wrapped Matty's gum in a tissue and shoved it into a drawer. It had good company: my dog's favorite toy and a corner of the blanket from his dingy bed. They were not wrapped in Kleenex but in vacuum-sealed bags. I contemplated my treasures, I showered, I slept, I cut my new T-shirt into a more exiguous silhouette before I put it on. I nodded off in the class it didn't occur to me to skip.

—

[5]On the housing form I'd filled out over the summer, the question about which gender I wanted my roommate to be—male, female, nonbinary, no preference—perplexed me. I didn't care. I ended up sleeping next to a Coloradan male. Cameron planned to major in philosophy, politics, and economics at the Scooby school. His love of weed explained his Shaggy enrollment. I should have hated him, his permanent smile, his questions

about why I needed to wear sunscreen. But I yielded when he said it was his girlfriend Jane's idea for him to live with a girl. It would prepare him, she reasoned, for their future together. Their past stretched back to elementary school. Four years apart would be easy to weather. That made me trust him. He, like me, knew love. Except he recoiled when I told him what I'd written where the housing questionnaire asked which fictional character you related to most. *Humbert Humbert, ladies and gentlemen of the jury.*

Fiona and I didn't go back as far as Jane and him, but I suspected we'd outlast them. I told him what I could about her. Unclassified information. We used to skip class together. A whole day of school to go to the zoo, where we burst into tears at the first exhibit because the marriage of captivity and sanctuary was more than we could handle. Once we pulled ourselves together, she howled at the wolves and cackled at the hyenas. I moved my lips in time with her sounds and she never thought less of me for it—for the part of me that preferred to look and listen. We were the oldest kids there, or we were very young adults.

Before classes started, Cameron looked Fiona up online. He wanted a face for the stories. I thought he could wait. She'd be visiting soon. I watched expectantly while he clicked. He went back and forth between two photos on her neglected profile: the oldest image and the most recent. The former was three and a half years old, the latter from a few weeks ago. I was in both, though as slightly different versions of myself. Fiona seemed eternally the same. Her face disappeared as he zoomed in on her body. And mine. We were immortalized on her back porch, July legs and arms bare and awkwardly knotted, feeling indistinguishable. Anyone could see where she ended and I began. I steeled myself. He was going to ask why she looked the way she did. No, he just wanted to know why she wasn't wearing a band shirt.

We then left for yet another orientation week activity. On the Mounds, our lumpy rendition of a quad, we were instructed to form a horizontal row. Our RAs and peer mentors read the instructions. *Take one step forward if there are people who work for your family as servants, gardeners, nannies, et cetera. If you are male. White. Forward if you are cisgender.* "If you are Cameron," I muttered. He shot me a conciliatory smirk, as if to say he was well aware of where this was going and had accepted the journey ahead. *Take one step back if your ancestors did not come to the United States by choice. If you were raised in an area where there was prostitution, drug activity, et cetera. If you were ever ashamed or embarrassed about your clothes, house, car, et cetera. Take one step back.* We were teenagers; everything embarrassed us. *If there were more than fifty books in your house when you grew up, take one step forward.* I didn't even keep count of that. *If you have health insurance.* Didn't the school require it? *If you have a disability, take one step backward. If you have or expect to inherit money or property, forward. If you had to rely primarily on public transportation, take one step back.* What about New Yorkers? *If you were ever stopped or questioned by the police because of your race, ethnicity, gender, or sexual orientation. If you were raised in a single-parent household.* Most of us stared at our feet, but the nearby shuffling was impossible to ignore. *If your family owned the house where you grew up. If you attended private school at any point in your life, take one step forward.* Present location excluded? *If you were ever the victim of violence related to your race, ethnicity, gender, or sexual orientation, take one step back. If you and your significant other can show affection in public without fear of harassment or violence. If you are a survivor of any type of physical or mental abuse.* I couldn't move. The temperature was exactly half of boiling. I tied my hair up off my neck. The sweat vaporized in an instant. *If most of your friends are the same race as you.* I only had Fiona. *If anyone in your family has suffered from drug or alcohol addiction. If you are a person of color. If your parents did not grow up in the United States.* Surely there was minor European royalty among us. *Step forward if your parents attended college. If your parents told you that you could be anything you wanted to be.*

I ended up very far away from Cameron. Maybe he was far away from me, his nonroyal European eyes nearly piercing the tree trunk in front of him. I missed his glassy stare, which was strangely keen for someone who was constantly high. I tried to compel him, psychically, to smirk at me again. I'd expire if he didn't. There was no one else on campus with whom I'd been able to complete a conversation, no one else who didn't ask why I looked sad all the time despite the fact that I didn't, no one else who didn't mind me calling things funny more often than I laughed, though I often laughed until tears fell and refused to call it crying.

Our activity ended. The ozone felt worryingly thin. The sunshine was—I cannot emphasize this enough—absurd. Cameron tied with someone for what would have been first place had it been a normal game. His cowinner Gabriel was a sore one, a Connecticuter in a too-tight white T-shirt and unbranded selvedge jeans. After learning I was from New Jersey, he asked me on three separate occasions if I was from Camden.

No, my home was suburban and my parents had college degrees and yet there I was in the bottom three, sandwiched between Danny, a half-Tongva first generation student with acting aspirations and heterochromia, and Daisy, a Vietnamese American lesbian with six siblings and a motorcycle license. *No*, I wanted to cry out, *but I have never truly suffered! I have never doubted that I belong here! That I was destined for greatness! That I could achieve anything I wanted!* We were released. Gabriel stormed off to roll a cigarette. According to him, smokers were a marginalized group.

A weight on my shoulder stunned me. I was almost sick from the touch and its suddenness, but it was only Cameron, unfazed by his triumph and eager to go get a snack. He was salmon tinged. The way that his blood couldn't resist announcing itself constantly from beneath his skin, the way that people couldn't resist a good white boy—these things became a boon to me. The attention lavished upon him made it easier for me to exist in peace. The poor thing always had a sunburn.

I followed him, that afternoon, and on countless other occasions, to the dining hall. It was the only place on campus where shoes were required. I was livid each time someone walked barefoot, and it's not punk, I know, but I like certain rules, and I don't know why but Fiona always thought that was funny. Our other on-campus food options were two student-run cafés, one of which was bought for a dollar and moved across the country board by board years earlier, both of which were always playing "Wagon Wheel," whether in its original Dylan form or as a live impromptu cover. But Cameron preferred the dining halls. Every meal was made a marathon. Our bevy of free time split randomly between our dining hall and the other colleges'. We came of age at buffets. His stomach could hold food like his lungs could hold smoke, whereas Fiona stretched appetizers out for ages. I tried to forget her other features.

As Cameron and I passed the days over chilaquiles and chicken tenders, I watched it occur to increasingly familiar, hungry faces that the two of us would always be there—before they realized it was time to eat and after they arbitrarily sorted their waste into garbage, compost, and recycling and put their dishes on the conveyor belts that led back to the kitchen. Some kids tried to turn us into an asylum when they didn't want to sit alone or needed a break from their friends. I didn't blame them. Their flip-flops were repellent, as were the comments that came with them, like Lyle's suggestion that his family would gladly pay off the national debt of a certain Caribbean island if only they knew to whom they should cut the check. I texted Cameron under the table for confirmation that Lyle, with his water polo tan on his wagyu-fed deltoids, really lived on our floor and did not in fact go to the Fred college. He had his mother's last name, and every Baby Boomer in his immediate family had a Wikipedia page. There was a study room named after his father. Cameron's family preferred environmental philanthropy over educational philanthropy and Fiona's family—I was moving on. Perhaps Cameron couldn't take me totally over because he wasn't a girl.

Vera mistakenly spoke Spanish to me at the salad bar at Daphne, the women's college she called home. I'd been circling the local kale to stretch my legs. Cameron and I were two and a half hours into dinner. I confessed my monolingualism to her and segued into telling her about holding my breath every time someone afraid to call me black stumbled instead over *African*

American. She told me how her mother and nanny, both whose sienna skin she shared, taught her and her brothers mercurial Spanish. The romance of it sailed above their father/husband/employer's Irish-German-whatever head. Now Vera woke up early five days a week to take high-level Spanish classes and chase them with three-hour naps. She took pride in having tits of slightly different sizes. She ripped herself to shreds if she got less than 97 percent on a school assignment. She didn't like that I thought of her, of us, as girls, not women.

One Tuesday, while I waited for Cameron to get out of class and join me for the second leg of lunch, I confessed another thing to Vera. Something was wrong with Matty. After ninety-four text messages, it was undeniable: he was too nice. Vera was more interested in singing the praises of her panini than in psychoanalyzing someone she'd never met. Matty and his hamartia were my only concern. I wanted to overlook his flaw. I wanted to care less. I said his name out loud once for every ten times I thought it. I could not breach sluthood's border. As always, I was singularly obsessed. Fiona would have dropped everything, let a batch of homemade croissants burn to ash, to come pore over Matty's latest punctuation mark with me. I would never ask her to.

"He never asks for nudes. And he's always in a good mood. Like, he got blamed for someone else's mistake at work the other day and had no interest in plotting his revenge. The only negative things I can get him to say are about the kids who go here. Oh, and he hates ska. Even—what kind of monster doesn't like Op Ivy?"

"Tragic!" Vera mussed her hair. *Ennui* was tattooed in delicate script on the crescent of skin behind her ear. "Who hurt you?" I didn't say anything. A widow's peak marked her small forehead. It matched her first initial. "What are we going to do?" she asked. I didn't know her well enough to parse her tone. I picked at a sandwich I'd lost interest in. "And why are you in such a rush to get wifed up? Please tell me you aren't saving yourself for marriage." She nudged my side.

"Saving myself? That's funny, Vera."

"Is it?"

I reread her one of Matty's texts. It was one-fifth smiley faces. A notification reminded me I'd missed a call from Fiona. Ignored a call was more accurate. I was waiting for her apology, or I owed her one. August had been a bickering fog: sentiment, separation anxiety, illogical nostalgia for something not yet lost. I opened my thread of texts with her and deleted random messages.

Vera started a one-sided discussion of the follies and triumphs of a reality television show about teenage mothers. I ripped up the crust on my plate. She declared that it was past time for society to admit that virginity is an unproductive social construct. She was very animated. I considered my cup of water. My nails raked the grooves in the saffron-colored plastic. I ran my knuckles across my chest. *Does Vera want me to talk?*

She exhausted her tirade and looked at me for a full minute before announcing she'd help me get over Matty.

"How fluid is your sexuality?"

The sip I'd just taken went down wrong.

"Okay then." She went to get two forks and a piece of chocolate cake.

The plate she placed between us was blazing white. The skin

over her closed eyes shook with joy as she chewed. A gilded cross cast a shadow on her throat. Fiona had the same necklace. I dragged my fork around. Every meal at every college was all you can eat. At least six entrees could be cooked to order. It was preposterous. I'd had quinoa before, but not the red kind. You could walk out with an entire pie and no one would bat an eye. Salted butter was the secret ingredient in the chocolate chip cookies available at every brunch, lunch, and dinner, and I had lost my appetite.

—

[6]Like sustenance, new information became difficult to absorb. The exception was something I'd read online about how many calories chess grandmasters burn during tournaments. Sitting. Thinking. In class, I sat and scribbled. I did not consider my stomach's relationship with my hypothalamus or prefrontal cortex. History of Anthropological Theory, American Anarchists, and The Mathematics of Patterns did not require much of me. But I spent most of Intro to Linguistics thinking. Muscularly. I was taken with my professor's gravel voice and pesky bangs; she blew puffs of air upward, redistributing her hair in newly bothersome arrangements. Years of postgraduate education had calcified behind her eyes.

If nothing else, I understood the international phonetic alphabet. It alone seemed worth the price of the course. It was a pleasure to memorize. It gave me something to translate lyrics into, and I wondered if there was a career that would allow me to do only that for the rest of my life. Once we settled into the semester, Wendy moved on to more complex matters. She, and seemingly everyone else in the room, began doing math and advanced logic problems with adverb phrases and invisible vowel pronunciation rules. My notes became impossible to untangle from errant verses and ideas for the next mix I would give to Cameron. He'd caught a case of aural Stockholm syndrome after his ill-advised insistence that I could blast music in our room whenever I wanted to.

I could not raise my hand and admit to Wendy that I was lost. She cold-called; I looked down. I had no friends from whom to seek counsel. This was a Scooby class, mostly populated by its students and Velma's.

The air conditioning amplified my confusion. It was too hot outside and too cold inside and it was impossible to assimilate. The lights were always off but the window brought in light. Wendy's curriculum was taxing. Squirrel watching was easy. I saw one little rodent drag another's corpse across the pale grass. I could taste where the dead one's neck crumpled between the live one's lips. How did you diagram a sentence? Quizzes came and went. Rather than be the last to finish, I left large portions blank. Time muddled itself. Someone had begun pulling my strings, orchestrating temporal loops—playing the same scenes of my life back again and again with slight variations.

Wendy graded in green ink. *Come see me please,* read a note barely contained in a corner of my latest problem set. Beside it were her office hours. Below it was where I'd transcribed the words to a song. Harmless, unserious words about how the girl you want will come to her senses one day. Get sick of that jerk's cock and finally love you back. If anything, I deserved extra credit; it was in perfect IPA.

I went to the office hours as requested. Wendy rushed through an elementary explanation of the material, then revealed her real agenda. She wanted me to "say more" about the "coded message" I'd left for her.

"It's just an old song," I mumbled. I hadn't realized I'd written it on something I was going to turn in. "I didn't write it, I just wrote it down." The sentiment it contained was so salient it must have overtaken me. I'd become sure that Matty had a girlfriend. He rarely responded to me during daylight hours and never invited me anywhere. She wanted to know how a young woman could enjoy something so misogynistic. "Something what?" I didn't raise my voice. "He was a kid when he wrote it and there are really sweet songs on the album too."

She could not have been more unimpressed. I abandoned my plan to explain the band's legacy to her. I decided not to recommend she listen to their cover of the Beach Boys song with which she shared a name, which was now stuck in my head and was probably also inappropriate for young women. Any and all mentions of jealousy and heartbreak and unrequited love were probably off limits. I tapped my sternum as she rummaged around the folders on her desk. She extended a double-sided sheet of paper to me.

"I teach a class on language, gender, and power every other semester. Older students usually fill it up, but I can make room for you in the spring. I think you'd really get something out of it." I took the syllabus. "For the final project, it would be fascinating for you to do a quantitative analysis of the syntax in songs like this."

I nodded and thanked her so she'd forget I existed.

"You can enjoy something and be critical of it at the same

time," she called as I retreated. My misogynistic fingers found every object in my bag except my headphones.

*

A junior had told Cameron that Velma's annual Foam Party was taking place that night, that it was "literally white excess" and not to be missed, as long as you got there early, before you'd get stuck bearing witness to the commencement of a threesome that only two participants had been planning for weeks. It was sound advice. The occasion inspired every tenth person we knew to drink until they went dead behind the eyes.

An hour before the party started, Cameron and I looked on in horror as a boy on our floor whistled Skrillex louder than should have been anatomically possible. With a zombie's determination, he jammed his key card into a dozen wrong doors. Phones were left in their owners' rooms to avoid water damage. When the time came, we walked the eight minutes to Velma's campus. We passed two girls squatting to pee. They fell backward into a bed of cacti, pinky fingers locked in solidarity. Cameron averted his eyes. They didn't care who saw their underwear. They, and plenty of others, hung their clothes to dry in the sun to save electricity. He quoted Kant when I told him he was too polite.

We arrived at the same time as a platoon of Fred brethren. Two wore matching tank tops, which proclaimed our nation UNDEFEATED SINCE 1776. Vera and her friend Natalie were already there, in bikini tops and bandage skirts. Natalie greeted Cameron with an approximation of a shimmy. Vera grabbed my wrist and insisted on deconstructing my disinterest in dancing with her. She thought I was self-conscious because I didn't know the song playing. I did know the song playing and I liked it, but dancing to it in this environment, where everyone was on display, would have made me uncomfortable—but that fact itself didn't make me uncomfortable. I accepted my natural inclinations, where others were determined to change them, and maybe I avoided telling people how I felt because when I tried to, they didn't believe me, as if I had nothing better to do than invent multilayered fictions beneath which to hide my true feelings, which wouldn't make sense because if I were lying about my feelings, I would lie toward normalcy, not away from it. I didn't tell Vera this; I didn't understand why Cameron was allowed to not want to dance. She gave up and released my carpal bones.

The last party I'd attended took place in a high school classmate's mansion on New Year's Eve and primarily involved shielding Fiona from suitors in whom she had no interest, as well as from people she'd harmed—allegedly—physically and psychologically in elementary and middle school. I whispered wicked insults about them to her. She batted her eyelashes. When someone obliterated on Four Lokos broke our host's father's priceless Scandinavian sculpture, Fiona withdrew her arm from the hook of mine. She flitted across the room and knelt to pick up the pieces. The debris disintegrated further with each attempt. The audience dispersed. I sat and waited for her to tire of her self-induced trance so we could walk the long way back to one of our houses and share one of our beds. As usual, I would have no man to kiss when the ball dropped at midnight, no one to sing "100 Resolutions" with, and she wouldn't be able to sleep.

The dorm courtyard writhed with urgency. Bodies were difficult to differentiate. They were covered in alabaster bubbles; they'd been invited to the White House because of the nonprofits they'd started at fifteen, or they were undocumented immigrants with successful fashion blogs, or the reigning Miss Teen Taiwan. I shuddered to imagine the curt tidbit the admissions counselors had used to identify me. The prodigious hooked up in the stew of hormones where they stood. Pulses of occasional light clashed with the music's unchanging tempo. I was dizzy but still not hungry, and I wanted to ask someone why—if I had broken one of the few parts of my emotional circuit that functioned correctly, if hunger was even an emotion.

The Jenga tower of pizza boxes on a nearby folding table haunted me. The provisions were administrative attempts to slow down the alcohol sprinting toward our still-developing brains. Natalie, or one of her many doppelgangers—one in ten white women looked like Natalie from afar—reached for a slice. She waved pepperoni to the heavens. I took a slice for myself, a bite of tangy rubber. I threw the crust in the grass.

"I'm ready to leave," I said. Cameron couldn't hear me. I pulled his shoulder. He leaned down. I repeated myself. I hated having to repeat myself. Natalie was heading back to the dance floor. She motioned for us to join her. Vera's earrings ricocheted off her jaw every other beat. "Stay with them," I told him. He did.

The walk back was the long way. I clutched my stomach every few feet. That pizza had been abominable. I implored my surroundings to distract me. The campus stereotypes were starting to crystallize in my head. After leaving Velma (800 engineers with explicit instructions not to cook meth just to see if they could, whose salaries at twenty-two would be more than I would make at sixty), I passed through Daphne (950 young ladies; 475 madonnas and 475 whores), then Scooby himself (1,500 people for whom the cachet of an actual Ivy was too gauche and/or too unattainable), then Fred (1,300 future war and white-collar criminals), and home to Shaggy (1,200 fucking hippies). I texted Matty and received no response.

Lauren, a moon-faced girl from Wendy's class, stopped me outside my dorm. She was dying to know if Cameron and I were a thing. "A lot of girls like him, but they're afraid of you."

Her phone was tucked into her bra.

My laughter walloped the light post she was leaning against. "What if—maybe I'm afraid of them?" She thought that was funny. I wanted to strangle her. I sighed. I tried to understand. "I don't know why he calls me Bub, but it's Bub, it's not babe." I turned my back toward her. "Anyway, I have to go. I'm meeting someone," I lied.

She adjusted her bra strap and skipped toward the party. Hopefully, her phone was without a case to protect it and by foam or clumsy blind-stepping foot would be broken by the morning.

I thought Matty's name many times during the last minute of my journey. I thought his name as I unlocked the door to my room and as I stared at the room's contents. I had no idea what I wanted to do. I could go for a longer walk, in another direction, maybe without headphones, even though I really wanted to listen to "Wendy," if for no other reason than to get it unstuck from my head. I got in bed with my laptop and searched. *punk sexist girls women emo romantic*. The most promising result was from an eight-year-old issue of a zine that I knew was important but hadn't read much of, because at a certain point I did have to do my homework. The writer posited that her generation was largely immune to the menace of early 2000s emo masculinity because they'd come up on Babes in Toyland and SDRE, not Dashboard and NFG. I was essentially immune. I only liked one and a half of the bands she indicted by name. I too knew women were more than life-ruining, heartless, monstrous sluts. I liked Laura Stevenson and Jeff Rosenstock equally. I could write a dissertation on the inner workings of Fiona's brain. And anyway, I liked sluts. I thought sluts were very cool. My head dropped to the keyboard. My smug eyes shut. I had a terrible dream.

I woke up desperate to move. Cameron wasn't there. I changed my clothes and slipped out into the dark. I ran to the sound of my breathing. Just beyond our single square mile of campuses, Route 66 welcomed me. The public space had turned gorgeously private by virtue of virtually everyone else being home asleep. I wondered how long it would take to reach Fiona by foot, if she'd meet me halfway, if I'd ever trust her again. I put my faith in the unyielding pavement. Of course, I couldn't really run fifteen hundred miles. I moved more slowly on my way back.

Cameron twitched in his sleep when I returned. I kept the lights off, not wanting to wake him. He stirred but stayed quiet when I tripped over, then onto, the scale that Jane had packed for him. My heels made a red number appear on the digital display. Before I took a shower, I stepped on and off and on and off and on and off until the digits, and the rhythm of summoning them, stuck in my head. I wondered what distance I'd run. Once I was clean, I resumed mounting and dismounting the platform. Sometimes the number changed slightly. A pattern refused to emerge. I had time to crack the code. I moved the scale over an inch and got on and off and so on. I must have stopped to sleep.

A warm wave ripped me from a nightmare. An imagined tower of pizza had left me in a puddle of actual piss. I had eaten so much at the party. I had gorged myself on entire floors' worth of dough. Ceilings of sauce. Columns of cheese. They'd regenerated. I'd eaten them again in hopes of revealing an end or exit. There was none. I might have died in there. No, you can't die in your dreams. I came to my senses, gathered my dirty bedding, and money from Cameron's desk. On the way to the laundry room, I saw Lauren taking a selfie as she stumbled back to her room.

*

At brunch, Cameron wanted to know where I'd gone in the middle of the night. I told him the truth: I'd gotten food poisoning from the pizza (asbestos in the garlic? Shrapnel in the Parmesan?) and gone out for fresh air.

"I don't think the one bite you spit out on my foot was enough to make you sick, Bub."

"Hmm." I didn't have the heart to tell him he was wrong. "Did anything happen at the party after I left?"

He reported that an ambiguous, ominous "they" had sprayed tear gas into the crowd when it was over. To get them to go home. It was that or a fire extinguisher he was pretty sure. How else to account for the rashes, or were those hickeys and bruises, lighting up everyone's inner thighs and necks? My skin was unmarred.

My stomach was, by then, unbothered. I proceeded with caution lest I upset it again. I was a dog, let loose to sniff out the perfect patch of grass on which to relieve myself, finding nothing, nowhere, then holding it in until I broke and made a mess. But I didn't break. I didn't make a mess because I didn't really eat. I felt nothing at the next nonmeal I picked at, or the one after that. The bare minimum in my body left next to nothing in my mind. I found relief so total I almost cried in the middle of the dining hall, almost tapped a butter knife against a glass to call the whole place to attention as I climbed on top of the espresso machine to proclaim the good news. My feelings were vanquished, my problems extinct. I would never be uncomfortable—I would never be anything again. I finally knew what it was like to pray and be answered. I finally knew what it was like to have faith, to be like Fiona. These were not things I was sure I wanted.

—

[7]I perched on an empty bench, waiting for a bus to take me a few miles away, to a place two or three times bigger than where I'd met Matty. Just another room with a stage and a ceiling high enough to accommodate all our feelings. He wasn't there. But he was kind enough to text me about the venue's sound quality and lighting costs. I hung on his every excruciating detail until the music started. Into It. Over It. was plaintive and intimate, and somehow not the worst band name Evan had ever come up with. When he was done strumming, I managed to speak four sentences to him, about ABC No Rio and the state we were both from, and I bought his newest record to

make up for already having pirated it online. Then AJJ plucked out a crowd-pleasing set that was essentially the same as the last one I'd seen them perform, culminating with the same frenzied sing-along. *Hey everything, fuck you!* This was the one thing I still wanted to feel, and so I would continue eating, just enough for it and it alone. While Frank Turner played, I tried to clock which of his tattoos were new, until some guys got rowdy during "Long Live the Queen" and the girl in front of me kept looking at me when I bumped into her, like she'd never been to a show before, like it was my fault that the song about the dying girl made me miss Fiona, who, unfathomably, had not visited me yet. She lost her balance when I shoved her two feet in the other direction. I left as soon as the music stopped. The lights went up and the people with souls ostensibly like mine turned back into inscrutable strangers—except for a group of guys I recognized from the dining hall, who showed no evidence of recognizing me.

That sustained me until the next one. Its roster (Duke Nukem Forever/Tension/Burn Idols/HOY PINOY/Get Greens) was entirely novel to me. Five bands sludged together, in the best possible way, in the back room of an Arabic restaurant. The night was silly, animalistic, borderline inhumane. I did not feel endangered. I felt strangely feeling and unfeeling, and all of this was what I imagined it felt like to be fucked. The place was full of the most beautiful men you've ever seen, glowing while they glowered. The lucky ones would be off to Discord Fest that weekend. Matty wasn't there that night, which made absolutely no sense. Actually, it was hard to see. He was probably there and taking pains to skirt me.

The next one was in a warehouse, *the* warehouse, its address an open secret if you knew who to ask. I didn't want Matty to think I was needy. I found the street name deep online and hoped he'd think I was a pleasant and resourceful surprise. Cobra Skulls were playing. I knew he'd be there.

The woman in charge of the door was more proof for Wendy: our collective gender politics were fine. This girl was literally wearing an ONSIND beanie. I told her I liked it as I gave her five dollars and she Sharpied my proof of payment on the back of my hand. I went inside and joined the few dozen others. Cobra Skulls were starting. On the side of the room opposite where I stood, the garage door closed, cutting off the outside air. There Matty was, with his friends. Of course he was wearing a Coke Bust shirt. There weren't more than twenty people between us. The only other obstacle was a couch against the back wall, which, as I'd soon learn, sunk more than you expected, no matter how many times you sat on it. Opposite the couch, the band played.

Devin flip-flopped between shouting diatribes against the military industrial complex and belting broken-hearted love songs with a twang. Meanwhile, I couldn't say anything that wasn't prompted by a very direct question, or ask Wendy what semantics meant in the context of her class, or tell Fiona I was sorry for what I'd done. For all Fiona's histrionics, she'd forgive me if I apologized, and I'd apologize if I could piece together the end of the summer. Unless we'd been fighting since winter or spring? Someone nudged my shoulder. I jumped. A sloppy drunk man was looking for a fight. (Not with me; in the scene, violence against women was discouraged.) The band had to stop and remind us we were all supposed to deeply love and respect each other in some untenable way. Someone walked the agitator out. The cops were not an option, because they weren't to know, or be reminded, about the venue's lack of permits and licenses, and also because they were bastards.

Matty, also a bastard, was looking straight past me. Maybe he was looking at the sound booth. Maybe he hated me and wanted to pretend our eyes, and other body parts, hadn't met before. I could do that. I didn't want to embarrass him. I didn't want anyone there to know that with a gun to my head, I couldn't tell you what a guitar pedal was for. He scratched his chin and flipped a switch in me. I didn't know how he could do this. He could deign to drag his five o'clock shadow across my neck in his car, but now he couldn't tilt his chin up at me in one millimeter's worth of acknowledgment? I twisted each earring that snaked up my cartilage. I wanted to ram each metal post into a different one of his fingertips. Silver scissors to stab his pinky. A hoop through the middle one. A wolf to shred his thumb. I wanted one of my hands to protect him from the other. I did not want to reconcile my conflicting desires. I did not want to have desires. Cobra Skulls finished, and I composed and scrapped texts to Fiona until Nothington was up. Then I felt a little better. *Whoa-oh-oh* was a panacea and "This Time Last Year" let me think of her without having to think of her, but then it was over, and the bands went back to Reno and San Francisco or to the next stop on the tour. I walked the three miles back to school.

*

About an hour later, I checked my phone in the dorm parking lot. The only other people outside were going to or returning from parties on the other campuses. I had a missed call from Fiona. Nothing from Matty. I clicked on her number and counted the rings.

"Dear?" The transatlantic accent she slipped into when she was tired was in full effect. The effort of maintaining it helped keep her awake. She'd spent her childhood studying black-and-white films, deconstructing their artifice with the passion of a covertly staunch believer. It's not as pretentious as it sounds. She was very charming. I held my breath to hear her breathing.

"Yeah, hi." I lowered myself to the ground. Pebbles sank into my skin, carving temporary craters.

"Can I tell you something funny? You actually woke me up." She sounded so steady. No longer prone to pacing. It was news to me that she did things like sleep. She said, "I've been doing well. My bad dreams stopped and now I sleep so heavy, like I'm at the bottom of the ocean and, somehow, I've found air."

That sounded like the side effect of a new medication. "Is that healthy—not dreaming? What if there's something important you can only learn in a dream?"

She didn't know what I was talking about. She must have said that to me before, but it felt like the first time. It felt like a sword between each segment of my spine. We used to be able to count on communication: letters, notes in novel margins, hieroglyphs doodled on each other's skin, Morse code, options for any wild or mundane situation we might find ourselves in.

"Why did you call?" I asked. "You keep calling. Are we not fighting anymore?" I tilted my head as far to the left as it would go. Silent tears cut across my nose. I waited for her to ask what was wrong.

"I don't know, Olive. Why did you answer? Why does anyone call anyone? What does everyone call us?"

"Codependent." I regretted the miles I'd put between us. I resented the technology bridging them. "But we aren't anymore. I have to have a new life here. I can't do both."

"If you say so."

"I do. And don't you?"

"I do. And do you miss me?"

"Yes." I required her. Her wordplay. The fingernails she kept so short she couldn't feel them against her palm when she made a fist. I waited for her next word. She asked if I missed anyone else. I put my weight into my palm and winced. "No. There's another one now. I fell in love again."

"What took you so long?" She sounded dreamy, not with wonder but gutted from fatigue. I wanted her to guess his name, but she was drifting. She asked me to spin whatever I wanted to tell her into a story that would put her to sleep.

What could I say? That every afternoon when the temperature sat at three digits, I could suppress only so many visions of Matty, I could only pine and perspire and wait to be texted back. I snapped, "Why can't you tell me a story? You're the one who was so desperate to talk to me."

"I suppose we are still fighting, then. Call me tomorrow, when the sun is up, please? When we're in a better mood. I love you."

She hung up like she didn't need to hear me say it back to her. I deleted her number.

I lay down and made a noise like a trash compactor. From somewhere farther than I could see, a voice I didn't recognize asked if I needed help or was just having fun. I had no idea. I set a timer and cried for fifteen minutes, because, like Fiona's mother always said, anything longer than that and you're just being dramatic. I wiped my face on my knee before I went inside and went to bed. I fell asleep telling myself the story Fiona wouldn't have wanted to hear.

Once upon a time, I learned to be suspicious of Fiona's unending offers to make me a sandwich. Once upon a time, I said only if she ate one too. We ate at her pace, which was so slow it tasted like nothing, and when we finished I ran up the stairs behind her and barged into the bathroom before she could lock the door. I think she slowed down on purpose. We sat in silence until it was too late for her to bother throwing up and I understood that she didn't love me enough, or perhaps loved me too much, to do it in front of me. I held her ugly hand. I didn't know what else to do. Once upon a time, I didn't know that it hurts to have food inside you once you've made your middle adapt to near-constant vacancy. Didn't know dinner feels like bombs bashing into sand banks on the ocean floor, like displaced sediment and seaweed forming fireworks that swirl back together, while your intestines stutter, unable to remember what their cells were programmed for.

A text from Matty woke me up. He said he'd been busy with work lately. It was nice seeing me at the warehouse, though it'd seemed like I was in my own world, so he'd left me alone. And by the way, I could come to his place any time.

I told myself a better story. I'd soon know the thread count of his sheets, whether the lock on his bathroom door was built into the handle or screwed higher up on the doorframe, if he had a proper saltshaker or poured it straight from the carton. I passed out again.

[8]It was afternoon, early October, and I probably should have been in class, but I was on my way to the mailroom to pick up a care package from my mother. The scenery was almost enough to seduce me into lounging outside, among the smart, cheery people. But I'd been turned off picking figs from the tree by the chicken coops after overhearing an argument over whether a fig was still vegan if a wasp flew inside it and died.

"Hey, Jasmine!" someone called to me. This only happened when I wasn't with Cameron. Jasmine and I were roughly the same height and, if I'm being generous, color.

After obtaining my cardboard box, I went right back to my room. Thinking myself too good for the elevator, I struggled up the stairs. The altitude gave me the opportunity to survey the whole dorm. The paranoid among us derided the panopticon design: three three-story halls that formed a square, with the student center as the fourth side. In the center courtyard, the pool compelled people to lounge like they were in a satire of Southern California. I preferred killing time in bed, where I was fairly confident I wasn't being watched.

I attacked the box. Fingerprints mottled the transparent tape Eleanor had used to seal it. She'd sent jojoba oil, snacks that were both off-brand and non-GMO, and my childhood copy of *Where the Sidewalk Ends*. The book fell open. I skimmed the poem about the king whose love of peanut butter sandwiches nearly kills him. It felt like a threat. Eating, as a concept, was approaching nonsense. It was not like riding a bike.

There were days I was less afraid of upsetting my stomach; I'd intend to eat more and try to eat more and find I couldn't quite remember how to eat more. I'd been ditching class to stay in bed after running. The panting and tongue lolling, the chest rising and collapsing, made other movements difficult. I was free, in those hours, from the shackles of self-reflection. Exhaustion made every aspect of living tolerable, then insurmountable, then tolerable again. On days I could complete my academic engagements, my energy dissipated in the late afternoon. I was numb, save the occasional sharp pain, which the dopamine rushes overshadowed. I mistook this for happiness, which is not the worst thing to feel. I shuffled Eleanor's offerings into the snack collection on Cameron's side of the windowsill. I was halfway through reading each item's ingredient list when a phone call interrupted my work. It was my mother.

She said hello. She didn't need me to say hello before she got into it. I traced her handwriting on the shipping label while she spoke. *From Eleanor and Cedar Oliver.* Like my dog was my father. What had I been up to, she wanted to know. That morning, in the dining hall, I'd gotten caught in the crosshairs of a junior whose voice grew louder with each sentence. He needed someone to commiserate as he enumerated each time he'd had to admit he didn't "fucking speak Chinese" and didn't know what his name meant and refused to look it up or ask whoever'd named him. I'd nodded while he pantomimed punching someone repeatedly, his chin-length hair swinging as he shook.

"Poor baby," Eleanor said. "Tell him to holler at me if he needs someone to talk to. And you haven't sent me a picture of you in front of a palm tree yet."

"I haven't, you're right."

"Well, you have four more years!"

"Yep."

She subdued the pep in her voice to gingerly announce that she'd gotten a new job. In December, she'd move to Oakland. To be closer to me. Already she was packing. Labeling what went in which room. Scattering uncapped permanent markers around her, striping her skin when she made sudden movements. My father and I weren't there to cap them closed for her.

"That's nice," I said.

I'd last seen my father when he helped me move in August. He'd come down from Oregon to delight in doing exactly what was expected of him. The dorm light gave him a halo. He told nervous jokes, every fifth one clever, made me buy one more towel than I thought I needed, and was gone before Cameron and his family arrived. I didn't know how my father would react to Cameron not being a girl. Our understandings of each other were five years out of date. When Eleanor had left him and she and I moved across the country, my visits back on second-rate holidays and four-day weekends were too short to explain the changes in me, at least not without evoking the estrangement neither of us had wanted. Instead, I watched him fry fish and onions. His peach cobblers bubbled. We couldn't talk with our mouths full.

Now, I sat facing the window, thankful no one could see the flakes of dead skin around my hairline. My cuticles fissured. I'd given up on my upkeep. Eleanor asked again how my first semester was going. I didn't know what she wanted me to say. "Good, I guess." She pried inconsequential details about professors out of me. I spared her a report on the video I couldn't stop watching. In it, a cow's corpse was expertly butchered.

Her voice shifted again, to that low mellow register. "You know I'd put Cedar on the phone if I could."

I waited for her whistle and the click of his toenails as he dashed to her side. Every so often, he and I were reunited by a stray piece of fur. I heard a third person breathing on the line and somehow thought he was there.My father greeted me. I did not like surprises. I traced a one-inch line on the back of my hand, connecting the same invisible points again and again. This back and forth, I told myself, was all a conversation was. Had my hand been paper and my finger a pen, I would have ripped through the surface.

"We have good news," he said. He and Eleanor were going to try getting back together.

"Cool." The ring was back on his restless hand, then. The gold had been vanishing and reappearing at random for years, like a cold sore forged from precious metal.

"I'll move and then—" she clarified.

"—we'll see where things go from there," he finished. They were back in sync or they'd rehearsed.

He went on, this time without her. "And I have something else—more important—to tell you. I have to tell you how sorry I am for not being there for you for so long. So long. I should have made more of an effort. I should have gone to visit you. But I want you to know that it was hard—sometimes it's still hard for me to just, well . . . I get the blues."

He used to sing me freeform lullabies, none of which he could ever recreate. He cleared his throat. How did his ring feel against his scalp? I'd grown up watching him tug thousands of hairs from his head. And in my childish way, I'd tried to help by tugging more. I know from old photos that it started when I was born. In one image, he holds me in the crook of one arm and tweezes around his temples with the opposite hand.

"It's called depression, Dad. It's not a big deal." I traced the line harder on my hand. His hair didn't grow anymore. "Wait—you had postpartum depression? You didn't even have to give birth," I said with more malice than intended. "You divorced him over that, Mom? Was 'in sickness and in health' not part of your agreement?" My parents' very existence sometimes offended me; I was literally made out of them. It felt like an invasion of my privacy.

He told me to watch my tone. She was remarkably silent. He came to her defense: she had done her best to take care of him, which wasn't her job—she already had a job—and they both had me, and he should have been there for me, and all those trips they said he took for work were an excuse—sometimes he couldn't feel anything, or do anything except drive a few hours to a hotel and stay for as long as it took to clear his head, and sometimes he forgot to tell her where he was—and he never knew when he'd be back, but the least he could do was tell her that he'd left—and then she'd worry that he'd done something permanent and, regardless of whether he was gone for good or just until next week, she had to come up with something to tell me.

"I know your friend gets sick too sometimes," he said. He'd never met Fiona.

"We aren't friends anymore."

"You know you don't mean that." Eleanor rejoined the conversation, at the helm. "Miss Fiona didn't mention that the last time she came over for dinner." Her voice caught on Fiona's name. "I think she's lonely, sweetie."

"I think it's her fault she's stuck there." My pulse picked up.

Eleanor clicked her tongue. "It's not like you to say it's her fault."

"It's not like her to not tell me something. And she seemed fine the last time I talked to her."

"She said you haven't been in touch at all since you left. I can understand you wanting a little space from me, but she's practically your sister."

"We really aren't that close anymore. But we talked yesterday. She probably forgot. You know how she is," I said, though I apparently didn't.

"She's . . . well," Eleanor said, "healthy."

The room started a slow spin. My phone fell out of my hand. It bounced off a pillow and landed in my lap. I had a rush of revelation. I was fixing Fiona, like no medical professional could. My absence from her life, coupled with the absence of meals from my life, was fixing Fiona. Somehow. We were both better than ever. And even at that distance, I felt close to her. I had brought her to me in spirit without involving the mess of her flesh. I could feel what she felt and erase what I felt. Two birds, I thought. One stone. I thought this with the resolve of someone who has no idea they've gone insane.

I retrieved the phone and asked Eleanor what exactly Fiona had eaten at dinner. Once Eleanor confirmed it, I said I was hanging up to call her. But I got lost revisiting the list of what I'd planned to eat that week. Fiona had suffered so long. I could take a turn, to atone for what I'd done to her. The details were returning. "Fiona!" I said. I looked for my phone. It was nowhere to be found. Good. She was superstitious. She wouldn't want me to jinx this.

*

I picked through meals and slept through parties and waited for the streets to empty so I could run in peace. I knew my route so well I started closing my eyes for seconds, then entire blocks at a time. I imagined Cedar was there, straining to sprint, his blood pressure climbing each time he spotted something to chase, his tail flicking my shins, van Gogh swirls of spit on his tongue. The hues above us were a mess of melting sorbet. I'd heard that pollution painted sunsets orange, sunrises red and pink. That turned out to be another rumor. My insides spasmed. Steps slowed. Weeks passed. I passed through the rest of town, the land of trees and PhDs. I rounded corners without regard for what might be around them. The sun was the only thing ever waiting for me, popping up a little later each day as the days grew shorter. By a small margin, the temperature cooled. The distance grew. I reached adjacent towns, where the average household income seemed to fall along with the white percentage of the population. I didn't investigate. I was my only concern. Joints clicked. Toenails blackened with blood. Contact lenses shriveled in dry eyes. The harder it became to move, the more I had to. The number on Jane's scale changed and changed. My actions were, by then, compulsions. I feared abandoning them. I could have if I'd wanted to. I didn't want to. This was good for me. And for Fiona.

—

[9]I'd come to California to forget her because I couldn't forgive her. No, I'd come to California for a band, and when the time

finally came to see them, Joyce wasn't even headlining. It didn't matter. Nothing else mattered. I hadn't even asked if Matty would be there.

Cameron's car had recently materialized. First-year students weren't allowed to have them on campus, but all of a sudden he had a student parking permit. I felt high and he actually was, so I drove us to LA and stopped on the way for him to get a veggie burrito, then for pitted dates, as if he hadn't spent an hour eating at Velma before we left. The detours made the traffic more tolerable. And I liked that other people were allowed to eat.

I did not like him trying to listen to the band we were going to see. It was bad luck, I told him. I almost totaled the car four different times, reaching for the stereo while he tried to slap me away. "Put on something else right now or their van is going to crash and you'll feel like a fucking asshole. Now, Cameron! I am so fucking serious. They could die. Deadass they *will* die. Let's just listen to Leer or something, okay? Fuck!"

He laughed so hard he coughed—he never coughed—because it was the loudest he'd ever heard me speak. After changing the music, he wanted to tell me about Marx's breakup with Proudhon. I said it would have to wait. I was trying to listen to the song he'd put on.

We passed Skid Row. I parked soon after. I read a sign over and over again until I was sure his car wasn't going to get towed. Cameron hummed a Joyce song and asked if that was also verboten. I punched him very lightly. I looked around. City Hall was an art deco titan stabbing the sky. Cameron kept humming.

We were an hour late, but when we got to The Smell, the

show hadn't started. We turned around and walked in a random direction. At a bus stop, a man without a place to live strummed a guitar to himself. A man with an expensive leather belt sneered as he passed him. The first man accused the second of being a federal agent. Across the street, a pastiche of people and tents filled Grand Park.

Cameron stopped to get a better look. "Who are these . . . these Lords of Dogtown?" He christened the inhabitants we could see, as they were scruffy and serious in a spirited way.

"Did you know that Rise Against played Black Flag in the background for a scene in that movie?"

He did not. He focused on the demands someone was shouting through a megaphone. They were Occupying the park. Soon, our classmates would camp in hammocks and thin tents, wistfully Occupying the Mounds. Cameron started to cross the street. I pulled him in the other direction and, as we walked, began lecturing him about the highs and lows of Rise Against's discography and the relative commercial success they'd achieved after I stopped keeping up with them.

"Sorry," I interrupted myself. "Is this boring?" He shook his head. "Right," I resumed. "So obviously they aren't Green Day. No one will ever blow up like that again. No one will ever have such a strange list of accomplishments." I could have lingered on Green Day, but I didn't want to linger on Green Day. Fame was the real matter at hand. Fame brought me to Fall Out Boy, and maybe—I was simply thinking out loud—*maybe* there was an argument to be made that Fall Out Boy was more punk than Green Day. I explained that we had to account for Racetraitor, and for Arma Angelus, and then I was back to Rise Against, not sure what, if anything, my point was.

Cameron's stomach called again, so we tabled the discussion for the time being. The Mexican restaurant we wandered into was selling water for two dollars. I refused to let him buy me a bottle. I could drink from the bathroom sink once we got back to the venue. Los Angeles tap water was grey with mineral deposits that I had to hope would fortify, rather than diminish, my marrow. When we started walking again, he offered me the first sip of his decidedly uncloudy drink. I said no, and that I'd already said no, and that I didn't like having to repeat myself.

"All right, Bub. I'm sorry. So you've really never gone to a concert with a friend before?" He squinted. His hair was overgrown. Parts of it now fell just below his brow.

"Not never, but habitually, no. Fiona isn't," I searched for the right word, "built for this. You'll see when she visits."

The next four blocks came and went in silence.

"Yo, why is going to see this band more punk than joining the political movement protesting income inequality?" If he narrowed his eyes any more, they'd disappear.

"Oh, you know." I didn't know how to tell him that punks were rarely as meaningfully political as people liked to think.

He closed his empty water bottle, twisted and squeezed it. The pressure sent the cap flying. I waited while he trotted off to retrieve it. He tossed it between his hands until we passed a recycling can.

"Are the Arctic Monkeys punk?" he asked.

"I've only heard that one song, but absolutely not."

"Is something only punk if you like it and I've never heard of it?"

"No one's hiding anything from you!"

"What about Burger Records? Are they punk."

"*I* don't like their bands but—"

"What's the difference between punks with a *ks* and punx with an *x*?"

"Nothing really, but it's hard to explain."

"You like Nirvana. Are they punk?"

"A lot of punks listen to Nirvana, but that doesn't make Nirvana punk. Or not punk. Wait—do you mean me personally, or the collective you? Because I really just like 'Negative Creep.' And do you mean punk to me or to the culture at large? Because if you tell someone you like punk—which you should never, ever do—they don't bring up Nirvana. They don't know what to bring up. Do you know how many people think I listen to "—I lowered my voice—"Slipknot?"

"Slipknot!"

"Sure, I like 'Wait and Bleed' just as much as the next guy, but it's really hard to remain civil in the face of such a massive misunderstanding. You should try it sometime. Please ask Jane to name a contemporary punk band and tell me what she says."

"You're going to make fun of her no matter of what she says."

"Yeah, you're right."

"So, hypothetically, if she says the Arctic Monkeys, I tell her that's wrong because . . .?"

"Again, I don't really know what they sound like. I think they're just an indie band, which used to signal an ethic but now signals an aural style. Whereas punk got more stylistically diverse over time, so you have all these sub-subgenres—crack rock steady, Oi!, I don't know, death rock, whatever—that sound radically different despite their common origins. I can draw you a subgenre flow chart to help you remember all the stupid names. Like I would absolutely love to talk you through the difference between powerviolence and grindcore. If you want. Are you sure this isn't boring?"

"I'm sure, Bub." After a week of nagging, he'd gotten me to loan him a shirt from my oversized clothing phase. I made him look me in the eyes and promise, three times, that he legitimately liked Rancid. And not just . . . *And Out Come the Wolves*.

I brainstormed my chart outline out loud, making sure to emphasize that Kinsella-influenced contemporary Philly emo and Midwest emo were entirely different things. We continued in what we were pretty sure was the right direction. He made a game of stepping on every crack in the largely empty sidewalk. When I got to country punk, he glanced up to object. He insisted the genres were diametrically opposed, like a KKK offshoot of the Black Panther Party.

"No, no, no, no, no. I can't even dignify that with a response. What matters is that country punk is different than folk punk and that these different pockets continue to reflect *and* challenge the homogeneity that naturally arises out of community with a shared set of cultural references, vaguely similar ideologies, and loosely connected social networks. It's less about what you sound like and more about where you play and who you record with. Honestly, the Arctic Monkeys could sound exactly like my favorite band—shut up, no, I'm not choosing a favorite right now—but I'll never know because I'm not going to come across their music. And if I do, it won't be in the right context." I stopped myself from asking again if I should stop. "You know how sometimes you have to hear something a few times before you get into it? Then it hits you and you love it? I think if I listen to anything enough, I'll start to like it. Like an arranged marriage. Isn't that fucked up? Time and love shouldn't have anything to do with each other." I'd never told anyone that before. "But it obviously wouldn't work with the Arctic Monkeys."

We were back at the venue. The entrance was in an alley. Admission was always five dollars. All shows were all ages and alcohol-free. The air always struggled to flow. While Cameron used the bathroom, I wandered back outside. It was a little easier on my lungs, though some intangible quality in the concrete irked me.

A human male came my way. His second lip piercing looked infected and he was quick to tell me about the unaccredited vegan culinary school he'd recently graduated from. The campus was someone's condo in Colorado. A thin strip of reddish hair hung from his chin. It's tricky to explain what my standards were, but he did not meet them. An arm was around my waist. A ribbon of relief. Cameron, acting as an escape hatch. "Hey, man," he said, and walked me inside.

We stood toward the back. The people on stage finished their set. Cameron tapped his left foot and clapped generously. I didn't care about them, or the headliner, and I hadn't heard of the other two bands on the bill—though maybe it was just a matter of time before I was fawning over them. The crowd skewed younger, browner, more feminine, and queerer than I was used to.

Joyce came out and checked their sound. Without a word to Cameron, I went to plant myself in front of them. Anticipation wiped me blank. Then they started to play. They were moons an ocean made to wave. In just over one hundred seconds,

"Call Out" was indignant, then predatory, then desperate, the title phrase finally repeating until the music swallowed it and the next song began. There was no time or room or need to breathe. There was no telling what old ink the newer sleeve of black ink on Barry's arm was hiding. He sang, *Explosions, derailments and screaming children. Oh my god I think I'm in love*, more boisterous than belligerent. Eight more songs tumbled out, two of which were new, none of which were their catchiest (because Cameron just had to hum earlier, or maybe because they were sick of playing it), and one of which was old enough to catch me off guard. These fifteen minutes were why I'd crossed the continent. These fifteen minutes ended fast. Cameron's keys, which I'd recently attached to a carabiner for him, and my Dead to Me pin were missing from my backpack. The front pocket had gotten unzipped. I alternated between kicking around the trash on the floor and glancing up at the random things people were holding up to be claimed by their owners. A girl had the keys. I hugged her after she handed them to me. The pin was a casualty I'd have to accept. I helped Cameron help someone look for a phone. We all knew it was a lost cause but didn't give up until the affected party admitted defeat.

On the drive home, Cameron tilted his seat back and scrolled through my iPod. "Can we to listen to Joyce now?"

If he needed to tempt fate that badly, I said, he could put it on shuffle. Forty minutes later, he needed a fourth dinner. I stopped at a gas station and busied myself with a towering coffee and a text to Matty. Cameron watched his mozzarella sticks be lowered into the fryer. Then he ate them in the parking lot before I finished backing out of the spot.

"Switch seats with me then," I said. "I need you to drop me off in Upland." We rearranged ourselves and proceeded to Matty's.

We got there before I was ready to get out of the car. A new song had just come on.

"Is this shitbird singing about getting his date drunk and raping her?"

This was what happened when you put it on shuffle. I stopped singing along. "No!" My mouth hung open. "Well, yeah, but it's a character he's embodying. It's the poetic voice speaking. Didn't you take AP English?"

"Why would he want to embody that character?" He turned the key to stop the engine's grumbling. The streetlights waited for my answer.

"Again, are you not familiar with the concept of art? Words literally speak quieter than actions. What, do you also think old white people should take rappers to court over their lyrics? Or, like, sue a metal band every time there's a school shooting?"

"This feels different. It feels—"

"Beautiful. The basic riff. The slow burn from meek to savage. The way he lets you in so close that you can hear where his tongue is in his mouth." I took off my seat belt.

He unplugged my iPod, handed it to me, and told me to wait. "Are you happy?"

I was either very hot or very cold. "I think so. Why?" He'd just broken my heart. Once someone asks you that, they've already decided for you. They'll never believe you over themselves.

"How do you not know?"

I sipped my last ounce of coffee. It tasted like sour grass. "I don't know. When I say I am, no one believes me, and when I'm not, no one thinks to ask. But you believe me. Right?"

"I don't know, Bub. You're confusing."

"Everyone's confusing! They're unbelievably confusing and they act like I'm the one who— Whatever. I answered your question. And I'd never lie to you. So can I go now, Dad? Matty's waiting." I flung the door open and slammed it closed. Cameron told me, once again, to be careful.

[10]I knew exactly what I felt: endearment. I endeared this to myself: Matty's living quarters smelled like beef ramen and kitty litter and sun protection factor.

"Hi! Matty! I! Missed! You!"

"Hey." He closed the door behind me and put a black cat into my arms. An identical one yawned at us from the windowsill. The one whose nose was an inch from mine seemed about as happy with the situation as I was. If Matty'd had expectations for this moment, we weren't living up to them. "If you close your eyes," he said, "it's easier for her to trust you."

"Okay?" I blindly patted the creature's small outline. Cedar was utilitarian in comparison—a pillow, a chair, a footstool, a bodyguard. The cat, whose name Matty never told me, squirmed away and sauntered into another room. I tried to laugh. "She doesn't like me," I said. Or I somehow smelled worse than the room I'd just entered. *But I like you,* I waited for him to say.

"Make yourself at home. I'll make you a drink."

"Thanks!" I amplified my ardor. I did not mock his cliché.

I sat in the corner of the couch. A third identical cat watched me from beneath the coffee table. Hockey jerseys and thrifted records were pinned to the walls. Coffee percolated. Matty hummed just loud enough for me to hear. I had almost identified the song when a stream of dull thuds began outside. He half-ran in from the kitchen. I wanted to dissolve into the cushions and watch him for the rest of my life.

"Are you not seeing this?" He yanked me up. I stood behind him at the window. There were no curtains or blinds. It was hailing. Enlarged salt was barreling down on inelaborate ranch homes, seasoning the straw-colored lawns. "This is so cool," he said.

"Yep!" The desert was ridiculous. But maybe Vera was right. Maybe there wasn't something wrong with him, or with unbridled enthusiasm. I'd spent my whole life being droll, being myself, and it wasn't going that well. I inserted myself between him and the spectacle. The weather was a sign. Everything was a sign. He was probably my soulmate, all things considered. I kissed him. Something rippled through me. I kissed him impetuously. My life depended on it. I was fading and he was a warm body and calories are energy, which is simply heat. He pulled away to ask if this, or maybe I, was still okay. I pushed my tongue harder into his, moved hands to hips. It could have been an hour before the front door eked open.

Cold crept between us. I shoved Matty off me. His roommate entered and took his time untying his shoes before adding them to the pile by the door. I wiped my mouth on my hand. As I stuttered an introduction, I forgot to use my exclamation points. My elbow found my rib while the two men agreed on some sort of agreement.

The roommate went away. I heard what I assumed was his bedroom door shut, but I didn't catch a lock clicking. I realized I didn't know if they had locks on their doors. That, for some reason, made me want to die. Matty was hail-gazing again. Part of me wanted to put my head on his shoulder. A larger part of me just wanted to look at his shoulder. I wondered if he could feel my eyes, if my desperation did damage, like ultraviolet rays. If he knew his cheekbones belonged in a gallery, behind bulletproof glass. He turned around and brushed my hair behind my shoulders. He said it was pretty. He asked me what was wrong. I didn't know. I was so, so—something. The butterflies in my stomach were dying off. I was hungry enough to throw up.

Those aren't things you can say, so I said, "Have you ever seen snow?" I put two fingertips to his jaw and turned his head to face back outside. He snapped back around.

"Are you homesick?" He looked at me like I was an idiot, but he did it in his benign way. To him, California was the only place one could want to be. He sat me on the couch with him. Did I want to climb a white-topped mountain together sometime, he asked. I tried to nod. He leaped up. Did that mean we were going right now?

He went to the kitchen and returned with a chipped mug. "This is my favorite cup." His fingers spread, revealing an alligator bent into the shape of an M. He handed it to me.

If air can shrivel, the air shriveled. I told him he was sweet. There must have been a quarter cup of sugar in my drink. The mismatched furniture started to warp. He searched the room and held up a flyer from a stack on the floor. I summoned all my concentration. I needed him to stop moving. His band was playing a show soon and he wanted me to . . . what? My hands shook. He leaned toward me. A cat cried. Black flashed in my peripheral vision.

I twitched hard enough to drop the mug. The ceramic cracked in half on the edge of the coffee table. The carpet drank the liquid. I braced myself for his fury. *He wants you to leave, Khaki. He never wanted you here. He is a nice, normal man and you don't really like nice, normal men, do you? Don't look, but he's staring at you. He knows. I don't know what he knows but he doesn't like it. If he could hear what you were thinking, he would never speak to you again. His roommate can probably hear this too. The cats have been onto you from the jump. Just go. Go!*

The panic should have been gone, because my stomach was empty, but the panic was right there, because I had miscalculated something, because I was very, very dumb.

"I'm sorry," I said. "I should go."

"Why?" he looked up from the spill he was trying to contain.

My voice was gone. I may have spit it into the cup before I dumped it at my feet. He sighed that he would get his keys if that was what I wanted. A cat appeared or reappeared. I forced a sentence out. "I want to walk home." He wouldn't allow it. He cupped his half-wet hand around the back of his neck and asked what he'd done wrong.

It wasn't him, it was me, but I knew how that would sound. It was me, realizing that I might faint soon, and fainting was one of the most embarrassing things I could think of and I was not going to let that happen in front of him. Or anyone. *Khaki, you're fine, stop being so dramatic.*

"Nothing," I said. "You've never done anything wrong."

"Why do you have to say it like that?" He released his neck

from his grip, then reassumed the position, like his head would otherwise come loose.

"Like what?"

"Like you're making fun of me."

"Can we just go lie down?"

He spat his gum onto a shard of mug and led me to his room.

We lay in parallel lines on top of the covers. Skate decks had me surrounded. I was dead and this was heaven. A photo of him with his mother was on his dresser, without a frame. I relaxed. My head belonged on his chest.

I asked him to rate, on a scale of one to ten, how much he hated his father. All straightedge guys hated their fathers. "Ten being the highest," I said, in case that wasn't clear.

"Don't know him. I'm adopted."

I counted that as a ten. I lifted my head and rolled over. My face was just shy of flush with the wall. "You don't know anything about him? Not even—I mean, I don't think you're white. Right?" I had my predictions for what the texture of his hair would be if he let it grow more than an eighth of an inch.

"I said I don't know." He rolled me back over to face him.

Maybe I'd hurt his feelings. I sat up and apologized. "You were right earlier," I said. "I am homesick. There's this girl I miss." I did not say Fiona's name. That would have felt like a violation. He told me to call her tomorrow, send a message, make a video call. I said I couldn't.

"Can she call you?"

I buried my face in his neck. "No," I said when I came up for air. "But neither can my dog."

He laughed. Like I hadn't ruined everything in the living room. He had no fury. He ranted, amiably, about how hard it was to find lighting that didn't make his cell phone cat portraits come out like Rorschach tests.

I tugged at his shirt and nearly fell out of the bed. His top half was stained and flawless. I counted each tattoo. One: a black sheep surging forth from four black bars. Very original. Two: the word *Embrace* flanking a ghostly silhouette. A little more original. Three: Calvin and Hobbes dancing around his arm, beneath the banner of Four: FLEX YOUR HEAD.

"Could I give you one?" I poked an empty space, wanting him to have a use for me.

"Give me what?" He wrapped his hand around mine to still it. He was tacky with spilled coffee and then I was too.

"Give you a tattoo. I've done it before. I'd do a good job. You wouldn't regret it! Do you regret any of these? What if you change and change your mind?"

"Nah. People don't change. How much coffee have you had today, by the way?"

"I don't know," I said. I knew.

Five: a date in roman numerals at the nape of his neck; Six: the bear from the California flag, skateboarding on hind legs. Seven: a washed-out feline curled between two of his fingers. Eight: HELL, but the *l*s were hockey sticks, and they were on fire.

I took off my shirt, the majority of which had been cut off the morning after I bought it. He held the tank top up to his torso. "You wear like . . . doll clothes," he chuckled, looking me up and down. What had Ian said? *Tell your friend 'Fuck you.'*

The taste of vomit clung to the base of my tongue. *Fuck you, fuck—Khaki, wait . . . maybe he's not making fun of you.*

I petted the stubble on his jaw. I had longer hair on my legs. He had moles on one shoulder. Pain shot up the left side of my chest. I leaned in. I began ceasing to exist when we kissed. I was a mouth emancipated from its more troubling functions: speaking; eating. He extinguished what of me he touched; I needed him to continue until he destroyed the worst part of me, whatever, wherever it was. He pulled away a few minutes later. I climbed on top of him and removed more clothes.

"What if we just kept talking?"

I declined. He reminded me he liked to take things slow. He remained indescribably sweet, didn't flinch at the force with which I latched on to him. I could have died for his black jeans, his black Infest shirt now at the foot of the bed, his black shoes out by the front door. The soft of his skin. Of course I was happy.

"Is this okay?"

He closed his eyes. I kept watch.

His body lacked a strong central thesis. He was neither built nor lithe, tall nor short, hirsute nor bare. He just was. I guided him inside me. I was as gone as I could be. Still, my fingers cramped intermittently while I tried not to dwell on the fact that every man who ever saw me naked would likely be a new iteration of him. Palimpsest, pentimento, lines erased with new too-same strokes smudged over before they dried. I was suddenly too tired to move most muscles. Circulation was lost. I closed my eyes. He came and I missed what he said as he slid out of me. I ran my finger through the mess on my thigh.

While he wiped it off with a sock, I put on his shirt—inside out to minimize the chances of him objecting.

"Do you ever wish," I asked, "for seasons?"

"No way," he said. "Endless summer."

He swatted me when I stuck my finger in the hole in one of his ears. Poor Matty. Poor Southern California. Stuck in an amaranthine dream. The farthest east he'd ever been was Boston for a Have Heart show. Otherwise, it was Texas. He thought nothing of New York, but he wanted to take me to the flea market or the Hollywood sign sometime. I siphoned his good attitude for myself. I would go anywhere with him. But for now, he just wanted to cuddle. I felt him fall into slumber.

On my way out, one of the cats tried to escape along with me, though she was probably planning to go in the opposite direction. After much effort, and while singing a Spraynard song, I got her back inside. She was a shadow with eyes. I walked back to campus, hoping they'd all be devastated that I'd gone.

—

[11]I hated Saturday nights—the final hours before Sunday mornings, when I'd have to plan the next seven days of my life around whatever contemptible indulgences I'd let slip the last time around: bovine breast liquid—pasteurized, frozen, flavored, sweetened, churned, swirled into a cone; wheat—harvested, ground, salted, risen, baked, sliced, buttered. Until then, I trailed Vera and Natalie from Daphne's campus to the liquor store and back. They discussed the potential pros and cons of manufacturing their own tequila with agave from the surrounding plants. The sidewalk wasn't big enough for three.

Cameron was on his way back from the airport. He and Jane had spent a few days together in Nashville, even after I'd pointed out to him, map and all, that it did not constitute meeting halfway. He didn't mind. I didn't care about equality either; I just didn't want him to leave.

"I heard you're still hooking up with that townie? How's the D?" Vera shouted over her shoulder. We'd just gotten back to campus. Her timing seemed intentional.

"Comme çi comme ça," I whispered, running my fingers across the nearest inanimate object. Daphne, like Scooby next door to it, had planted non-palm trees everywhere in a desperate attempt to look like lost parts of the East Coast elite.

Vera encouraged me to prioritize my pleasure. Her bracelets, the same color and thickness as the waves in her hair, trilled as she spoke. Any onlookers probably assumed she was talking to Natalie. I was still walking behind them. I contemplated Vera's aroma: crisp floral perfume at her wrists and throat, notes of wax from the candles she made from crayons in her spare time. She once solemnly announced there was no Crayola match for my name. Only Tumbleweed. Desert Sand. Tan.

The white exterior of their dorm was caked in dust. It seemed to gesture, judgmentally, toward chastity abandoned. In their room, Vera plugged in the white Christmas lights she'd hung around three of the walls. Her side of the room was pristine. Creamy but not white, like the inside of an almond or a business card in *American Psycho*. While she and Natalie got ready for the night's party, I tried not to die. I'd forgotten they didn't have air conditioning.

Natalie packed a bowl and they passed it back and forth.

I would not risk sparking an appetite. Something possessed me to put my head on Natalie's shoulder. A few months ago, this girl had never set foot in any ocean. I felt sorry for her. The only time we'd spent alone was five minutes at brunch that we filled by looking up the tuitions at our friends' private high schools. Now she said, unprovoked, that she was terrified of not having the slightest idea what she wanted to do in college, in life, or next week. It seemed everyone around her was so put together; even their mistakes struck her as self-assured. People from Idaho didn't belong in a place like this. She didn't belong in a place like this. My nonreaction invited her to say more.

She told me what she'd learned in class that week, about a tribe in Papua New Guinea in which boys grew up fellating their elders. They believed semen fortified young bodies. When men married, they made deposits in their wives instead.

"Oh?" I wondered if I could hold my breath until Cameron got back.

"Everyone else in the class seemed so accepting. Like who are we to judge? But I—cultural relativism. Cultural relativism, right?" she sing-songed, her jaw stiff. She'd grown up around plenty of fundamentalist Latter-day Saints.

Vera was taking shots and watching a muted makeup tutorial. She smiled and traced the arc of her cheeks with an invisible brush.

"Is this what you thought it'd be like here?" Natalie asked me. "We're in the middle of nowhere, not Hollywood. I miss home. Is that sad? Is this like, you don't know what you've got till it's gone? Vera, put on the parking lot song, por favor!"

Vera ignored her. I removed myself from Natalie and told

her we were meant to keep moving, no matter who we left behind, even if it was someone whose finger you'd once cut open to press her blood into yours.

"You are so hardcore," she gawked. She missed my point entirely. That was the last time I'd forget I was a novelty to her, a peculiar story to pocket and take home to a town that Confederate sympathizers founded, a town that she, sadly, missed.

She tore into a bag of animal crackers, the lions and polar bears frosted like pearls. I wanted to ask her to dump the rest of the bag in me. But then someone knocked on the door.

"Natalie, go get that, por favor!" Vera yelled.

She did, beaming at Cameron. He bypassed her open arms and handed me an enamel pin. *Music City USA*. I pricked my finger in my rush to fasten it to my backpack.

He didn't say anything about Jane, only that he was more than ready for the storied Motherfucker Party. The event was the brainchild of the consortium's only vestige of Greek life. The unofficial group, a gender-neutral fraternity-sorority hybrid had a house off campus, and they felt strongly about a drink that involved vodka, rum, tequila, Bailey's, Kahlúa, ice cream, and Coke.

I convinced our group to walk, rather than drive, the mile there. I promised I'd drink with them. For some reason, this excited Vera and Natalie. Cameron reserved comment. When we arrived, the door was wide open. I was not inspired to enter. Too many people were doing too many different things and producing too many different sounds and smells and potential social interactions. Members of the siblinghood had taken off their shirts or not worn them to begin with. They were charging five dollars to drink. Cameron shepherded me in, then volunteered to get a cup of Motherfucker for us to share. The amateur bartender mistook his five-dollar bill for a twenty and paid him back threefold.

Vera was flung over a Scooby girl and talking to two guys whose schools weren't obvious. I recognized the shorter one from Wendy's class, though he did not attend Wendy's class seminude. He did, though, eat complex carbohydrates during lectures. I had also seen him camped out in the gym with a cadre of free weights. By the windows. In broad daylight! For everyone to see. Once at dinner, I'd overhead him making a big show of saying he was full, only to pull his plate closer and lower his head as he licked it clean. I wanted to be him. Kill him. He sent me down a search engine rabbit hole (*why isn't bodybuilding an eating disorder; bodybuilding delusional; are bodybuilders okay*). Now he had Vera's friend's ass in one hand and a box of cereal in the other. I waited for him to choke. Puke. Cry. But no. He just confessed to the Scooby girl that sometimes he felt like sports played him instead of the other way around.

When Cameron rejoined us, I took the cup. The Motherfucker was effective, if cloying. I texted Matty as my pride receded. He was just chilling, he assured me, doing nothing but keeping that PMA. Yes, literally nothing. I made him confirm: he didn't have a pet research project that occupied his every spare moment. He wasn't mentally cataloging his every inadequacy. He was just existing. I was baffled. I was charmed. While I daydreamed about a perfectly imperfect marriage to him, Cameron procured another cup. I drank that too. Alcohol was an inefficient source of calories, though I couldn't remember how many per gram. I encouraged Cameron back to the bar and counted the seconds he was gone. Natalie was staring. At me. Not at the man in the living room who was wearing the bottom half of a panda costume and literally picking up a suitor in a red thong. I later heard that someone from our year was upstairs taking an oatmeal bath with a girl who was way out of his league. No amount of tequila could make me capable of enjoying such an activity.

The room was spinning. The rooms were always spinning. I looked down. My feet were still. Cameron said he had something to tell me. He took me into the hallway and shouted over the music. I grabbed the half-empty cup from him.

"Jane eats all the time."

"She whats all the time?"

"*Cheats*. Once a year. What do you call it? A roaming holiday. I know what you're going to say. I know what everyone thinks they would do if they were me. But it's not like I've walked in on her, you know? She goes off and she comes back and she tells me and she starts shaking and crying. Like she's the one in shock? It might not even be true. Right? Out of sight, or something. I don't know what she wants from me." The skin between his eyebrows creased like an accordion.

It seemed paramount that I text Matty immediately. *I would never hurt you*. I hit send and saw Cameron narrowing his eyes, waiting for me to do something. What was I supposed to say?

"Sorry your girlfriend's a whore."

He corrected me: no one was paying her, and even if they were, sex work was perfectly legitimate. He cut me off from the drinks.

I tried to convince him to break up with her. "You're so far away from each other. You can't be apart and then together and then apart again. Do you know what you can be, though? Happy. But you have to leave her. Wait—I know! We can count how many bad things she's done and subtract that from how much you love her and figure out if this is worth it because I get it, you know. I left Fiona. She let me do it. Because she loves me too she loves me so much and imagine if she found out what I've been doing here." All the molecules of alcohol chose that moment to band together and pummel my small intestine. "Do you want to know why Fiona's so fucked up? Because she can't remember how not to be. No? Fine. You want the real reason?" He strained to hear me. "Oh my god, I'm not actually going to tell you. It's a secret."

I went to find the bathroom—somewhere quiet to call her. I had to find out exactly what she was doing, everything she'd done since the moment I left. But really, I just threw up. It was for the best. It was a lobotomy by way of my esophagus, so that she would quit my brain.

*

When I woke up, my intractable limbic system was still creating emotions. Outside, it was still too warm. I considered smashing a saguaro into my corneas. Lizards scurried under our heels. They stretched their scales between bouts of baking. I whined to Cameron about the weather and ran my fingers along the walls on our path to an early dinner. The older students' dorms were covered in school-sanctioned murals: a neither fierce nor cowardly lion; a black box filled with white block letters that read SEX INDUSTRY WORKER; that Audre

Lorde quote. Then there were the impromptu additions. HITLER LEARNED IT FROM COLUMBUS.

Cameron squinted at my wrist. "What's going on here, Bub?"

"Here, it appears that I gave myself a tattoo last night. Weren't you supposed to be watching me?"

As it turned out, I'd matched him with a random Daphne girl, found my own way home alone, and failed to arrange a tryst with Matty.

"You've gotta eat more if you're gonna drink like that. Jane did that shit all the time," he said, putting her in the past tense.

"I will."

"Good. So that work of art's supposed to be . . . a boat?" It was. "How wasted were you when you got that *F* on the back of your neck? Is there a theme here I'm missing?"

"Yeah, they're both for Jawbreaker," I lied. "I can teach you how to fill in the other three *F*s for me. Wait, have we talked about how they played the basement of our dining hall in the nineties? Have we talked about Jets to Brazil?"

—

[12]When Halloween fell on a Monday, Tuesday, or Wednesday, the student bodies puzzled over whether to celebrate during the preceding or following weekend. They hedged their bets and declared any night within five business days of the thirty-first fair game for a party. I skipped them all. But the time I spent deciphering costumes from afar helped me see the dining halls for what they were. Each table was an altar to evil. Slimy creatures gathered round to build shrines to slick burgers and grilled cheese, stodgy pasta, soggy heirloom tomatoes,

omelets, smoothies, snug tacos in two-ply layers of soft corn tortillas, and pho—all prepared to our individual whims. These were the bites in which we constructed and realized our wildest dreams. I lost sight of the Halloween cover shows I'd been anticipating for weeks, forgot that "Astro Zombies" was the greatest pop song of all time. Who cared, when here was gluten-free pizza, allergy-free chicken breast, vegan risotto. We puzzled over trays of steaming food, in awe of the bounty that nearly sixty thousand dollars a year could buy. It was not enough to be orange or white—the carrots and cauliflower also came in surreal purples and golds. No matter how thoroughly our studies or socializing depleted us, sturdy bánh mì and silken curries and local grass-fed beef were there for us. We struck riches in the basket of fresh fried potatoes that never ran dry. Gallons of fresh fruit awaited us, already cubed into submission. We beheld hummus and peanut butter for days and built mile-high sandwiches only to flatten them between the sizzling jaws of the panini press. You should have seen the glee it brought to Vera's face, even halfway through the semester. Regal columns dispensed cereal straight into the palettes we cleansed with any number of dairy or nondairy milks. Two, sometimes four, flavors of slow-churned ice cream buttressed the soft-serve in chocolate, vanilla, or swirl. Our sun-kissed thumbs summoned espresso and mocha by way of red buttons. We could choose not to sleep. I could choose not to dream about sleeping with—Matty who? Whole avocados and strawberries, chocolate bread pudding and Cornish game hens were among the rare treats that turned the queues competitive and exposed the greedy among us. Those freshly baked chocolate chip cookies were not a privilege but a right at Velma, every weekday evening at six o'clock sharp. I studied the online menus prior to each would-be feast, to prepare myself for the deluge of rapturous hell in which we spent so many small eternities. I did not dare stray from the arbitrary meals I mentally 188 274 Net prepared and plated days in advance. If only I could have carried an invisible scale and spared myself the uncomfortable freedom of estimating my portion sizes by eye. Upholding these private commitments was my only moral imperative, 500 and one just as arbitrary as anything else we deem sacred. One day a food would calm me; the next it made my blood cold. And so, more rules. Counting turned from a code I thought I'd crack into a dead language unworthy of revival. The orderly arithmetic 877 was more gripping than any assigned reading. The absurd pseudo-calculus I came up with had me forecasting nonsense like *calories per minute*, burned, consumed, or imagined. I got stuck 99 BPM 865 in front of the mirror for hours on end, my appearance as legible to me as the signs in a foreign city. Nothing else interested me, and in turn I was no longer interesting. So considering what mine was, I stopped wanting a reason to get out of bed every morning. My mind emptied. This was all for Fiona, yet I was the only thing I could see—in other people, their bodies, what made its way to their mouths 6 Teaspoons. I became them precisely because I was not like everyone else. The chasms between people had always haunted me. That I did not need to eat 238 (wanted to, but had forgotten how) pushed me further to the outskirts of our species. I couldn't whistle either. I never shed a tear for that quirk. It's just how I was made. I was detached, too defeated to feel anything other than 342 35 19 22 502 my physiology. Resign yourself to anything and before you know it, it isn't aberrant at all. I don't know that illness can be aspirational or how something so banal 122 568 can masquerade as fascinating or 1029 200 399 114 123 40 45 48 Goal Weight 200 499 20 710 3710 Minutes 2048 66 299 33 583 5 25 0 0 0 0 650 200 940 319 399 115 128 116 114 112 0 88 209 0 why I am trying 200 3999 274 710 to 345 561 13 167 40 238 900 110 Current Weight 184 200 60 60 2 Cups 25 205 749 379 0 39 827 402 500 2004 558 43 109 480 2 302 84 455 603 500 0 600 307 128 Oz 22 287 2 Cups 25 205 749 379 0 39 3090 99 100 0 42 123 102 187 6 19 Lost 299 304 60 454 32 18 1 449 1372 559 69 15 d e s c r i b e Snack 15 93 120 34 378 800 800 800 800 800 731 93 Miles 3248 902 4005 0 59 340 666 290 348 108 99 100 103 42 42 30 5 208 804 30 397 108 2994 710 209 810 758 104 Dinner 107 127 1088 400 320 209 200 Lunch 572 520 572 27 307 something 45 4073 500 756 208 479 296 3500 1328 208 27 128 396 602 740 720 1200 80 64 520 759 988 1229 428 145 247 2876 382 193 11 872 706 12 0 82 937 750 Gross 128 777 no 4093 80 45 287 18 1 449 1372 559 69 15 Snack 15 93 120 98 96 99 101 66 443 96 Date 80 0 98 39 840 1209 1340 1560 1800 3200 2100 Hours 0 0 34 45 2073 74 92 808 1372 4152 0 303 407 599 100 203 400 116 114 112 0 88 Calories 622 795 14 25 730 284 84 one 288 505 300 283 256 23 100 Breakfast 123 334 998 1002 should 38 0 7 Miles 207 122 97 872 700 900 1100 45 Goal 2309 8 0 12 149 19 BMI 0 8 211 1038 723 2201 3090 99 100 0 42 123 102 187 6 Teaspoons 19 Lost 299 304 60 454 32 655 709 1235 556 183 906 554 777 1010 2343 2000 97 52 33 have 74 124 0 75 99 98 97 96 95 554 566 400 977 543 1290 539 25 3 97 3200 Inches 411 17 300 66 329 854 706 399 115 128 209 0 200 3999 274 710 Grams

345 561 13 167 40 3226 0 544 34 54 603 479 329 7 503 600 1123 1909 235 609 876 973 208 212 Average 717 719 900 965 8 56 32 0 1372 922 911 11 99 145 6 559 69 15 Snack 15 93 120 104 Remaining 2133 76 0 43 Days 56 60 66 443 96 776 5032 112 432 744 976 900 3200 7 55 678 642 975 330 1654 794 854 76 0 45 112 103 54 90 Current Weight 42 7 14 804 1997 0 3.5 65 155 950 110 to understand. 108 99 805 1200 940 3191 Weeks 14 500 108 45 110 304 495 8 88 6 Tablespoons 4 36 49 24 506 83 Lunch 0 5 5 719 900 965 856 32 0 104 Remaining 2133 76 0 43 Days 56 60 66 443 96 776 5032 112 184 200 60 60 2 Cups 25 205 749 379 0 39 827 402 500 2004 558 43 109 480 2 302 84 3710 Minutes 2048 66 299 33 583 5 116 396 602 740 720 1200 80 64 520 623 967 80 54 33 677 759 1909 235 609 876 973 208 212 Average 717 719 Miles 3248 Maybe if I 9 0 2 4005 0 59 340 666 290 348 108 99 100 103 42 42 30 5 208 804 30 397 0 82 937 750 Gross 128 777 4093 80 45 287 18 1 449 110 304 495 8 88 6 200 60 55 678 642 975 330 1654 794 854 76 0 45 112 103 54 90 Current Weight 42 7 14 804 1997 0 3.5 65 155 950 110 108 99 805 11 Weeks 14 500 108 45 Tablespoons 60 2 Cups 25 205 749 379 0 39 3090 99 100 0 42 123 102 187 make

6 19 Lost 299 304 60 454 32 400 it 97 7 543 1290 539 25 3 97 320 0 6 55 709 1235 556 183 906 554 777 1010 2343 2000 97 52 33 74 124 0 75 99 98 97 96 95 554 566 90 Current Weight 42 720 1200 80 64 520 623 967 80 54 33 677 759 988 1229 428 145 247 2876 382 193 11 Days 56 60 66 443 96 776 5032 112 432 744 976 900 3200 7 55 678 642 975 330 1654 794 25 0 0 0 0 650 200 940 319 399 115 128 76 0 43 Days 56 60 66 443 Net 96 776 5032 112 184 97 872 500 700 Lbs 900 unfathomable enough 1100 45 Goal 2309 8 0 12 149 19 BMI 0 8 211 1038 723 2201 3090 99 100 0 42 123 102 187 6 19

Lost 299 304 it will 60 454 32 655 709 1235 556 183 906 554 777 600 1123 1909 235 609 42 42 30 5 208 804 30 397 0 82 988 1229 428 145 247 2876 382 193 11 872 706 12 BPM 865 54 603 479 329 7 503 600 11 23 937 750 Gross 128 777 4093 80 45 287 18 1 449 200 60 55 678 Net 96 95 554

cease to exist and 566 400 988 1229 428 145 247 2876 382 193 379 0 39 3090 99 100 0 42 123 102 187 6 19 Lost 299 304 60 454 32 18 1 449 1372 559 69 15 200 940 319 399 115 128 76 0 43 Days 56 60 66 443 96 776 5032 112 184 97 872 500 I can 700 Current Weight 42 720 1200 80 64 520 623 967 80 54 33 677 759 988 Grams 1229 428 145 247 2876 382 193 stop 11 Days 56 60 66 443 96 776 5032

it 112 432 744 976 900 3200 7 55 678 642 975 60 66 443 96 776 5032 888 8 88 32 56 640 800 72 160 8 Average 717 719 900 965 8 56 32 0 1372 559 69 15 from Snack 15 93 120 104 ruining Remaining 2133 76 0 43 Days 56 60 66 443 96 776 5032 112 432 744 976 900 3200 7 55 678 642 975 330 1654 794 854 76 0 45 112 103 54 90 anyone

Current Weight 1088 188 88 8 else

32 56 640 800 72 160 8 1654 794 854 76 0 45 14

—

TO SUFFER FOR YOU LIKE I DID

NOVEMBER–DECEMBER 2011

13 I put Fiona's number back in my phone. I was not made for solitude. I typed *I love you*. She took twelve minutes to reply. She was busy, but we could video chat the next day at five thirty, my time. Over dinner. She said she wanted to see me. She meant she wanted me to see her. Twenty-four hours later, there she was.

We took each other in. The connection lagged. Her blinking blurred. My mother had tried to warn me. My friend was holding up just fine beneath her new mass. This was all I'd always wanted. I'd been on the carousel—recover, relapse, repeat—with her so many times. If she had recovered, and a rounder face was no guarantee, but if she had truly recovered, the evidence supported my hypothesis: my presence was the key variable. She was better because she was no longer with me. And I could never tell her.

"Why are you in my bed, Fiona?" I'd stripped the walls of my possessions before leaving. Now I mentally rehung everything in its proper place. She turned around. Maybe her location was news to her.

"Well, I'm here because I sleep better here."

Her hair was longer. It looked thickened with something, like the roux in the soup she'd cook me when the leaves turned and fell. She'd taste it as she went and spit each slurp into the sink while the water was running and I'd pretend to hate what she was doing more than the fact that she was trying to keep it from me.

"Does Lena—she's letting you?" I asked. Eleanor never minded company.

"Lena and I are doing better. I never gave her enough credit before. She's always had good intentions."

"Like when she said it was a blessing you're infertile because you'll never have to deal with a daughter like you?"

Fiona cleared her throat. "We're doing better now that we have more space."

"So you live at my house?" A childhood dream come true, and turned grotesque. And where was Cedar?

"Don't be silly, it's just a day or two a week." She was helping Eleanor pack up our apartment. It was the most physical exertion Fiona was allowed. When we used to rearrange the furniture in her living room out of boredom, no could be bothered to thank us or tell us to put it back. When my mother came home to a remixed apartment, she'd kick off her shoes and laugh. *Girls, I'm glad you're expressing yourselves.*

"Why didn't you ask me if you could live there? Tell me, I mean."

"Why didn't you call me back?" I knew that was rhetorical. "Oh never mind. So tell me, is college everything you dreamed of?"

Fiona's gap year was not spent backpacking on far continents. She was working retail for money she didn't need. Well-paid doctors and consultants meanwhile discussed her probable ability or inability to function independently in the near future.

I told her California was hellish. I relaxed my shoulders and sealed them in a blanket. Her eyes grew, disbelieving. Didn't I remember what I'd texted her a few minutes into my prospective student campus visit? *This is what I want.*

"Only the climate is hellish," I said. "I still want everything else."

"You do have air conditioning, don't you?" She stuck her tongue out.

Yes, and things were cooling to something like spring. The past weekend was clammy, presided over by clouds, I said, though she probably looked up the weather. I angled the computer to show her the land outside. It was being prepared to get paved over to make room for the dorm I'd live in the following year. The students who were protesting the construction, on the grounds that building on top of such a unique ecosystem was wrong, would fail. They didn't want to preserve the land. They wanted to burn it, like Indigenous stewards, I explained to Fiona, though she probably already knew.

She was looking at or beyond me or somewhere else entirely. When she asked about Matty, I said things were peachy keen. She couldn't wait to meet him when she visited, she said, and meant she couldn't wait to criticize him behind his back under the guise of looking out for me, only to be vindicated when he inevitably dumped me, which I would later see was for the best.

With that, we fell into it, gossiped for hours with more curiosity than venom—about the girl two years older than us who was living with a forty-year-old dealer (of exotic fish? Heroin?) in Hawai'i, about the guy our year who'd tried to reinvent himself at MIT by going by his middle name, about the Keystone pipeline. I could spend the rest of my life handcuffed to her. I would do whatever it took to laugh at something unfunny that only we understood, to miss a green light because I was watching her instead of the road.

I asked what her favorite flower was these days; I'd been thinking of sending her some.

"Well, for now, let's say the common poppy. They grow in cornfields, you know. They're so much lovelier than the crop but they're technically the weeds."

Before I could find out if there was a certain color poppy she preferred, she asked if I could believe that our twelfth-grade English teacher had come into the stationery store and not said hello. Fiona rang up her thank-you cards. Her day was ruined until she realized she wasn't being snubbed. She was just unrecognizable.

"It felt amazing to be brand-new."

"Did it? Really?"

"Olive!"

"What? Are you even sure that's what happened? She wouldn't have recognized you either way. You only went to her class like once a week." Not to mention the two-month absence from school altogether that year. But I didn't care about any of that. I whispered in a single breath, "Fiona, can you please tell me why you didn't tell me you were better?"

She leaned away but stayed in frame. A little more space to tack on to the distance. "Because," she matched my cadence, "I didn't want to say it and have it not be true by the time you saw. I'm so different now. What if one day you don't recognize me?"

"That's what you're worried about?" For as long as I'd known her, she'd been tethered to the abusive relationship she was in with herself. If she'd made strides in escaping it, then shirking me would be much easier. It would happen when she went to college next fall. I would be shirked. Forgotten. "I'll recognize you. You're the same to me no matter what. You'll always be my favorite person. I don't care if you change. In the good way or the bad way."

Her smile was off. "It'll stick this time," she said. "This time I might not be a waste of everyone's time. Everyone spends so much money and time on me! There's no time like the present, or the future." Her skin reddened where she pinched her arm. "Am I getting ahead of myself? Do you think maybe that's good?" Before I could reply, she decided it was time for her to go.

"Promise again that you'll visit soon?" I feared we would separate like an egg. In an invisible hand, I, the white, would fall through the fingers. She, the precious yolk, would stay cradled in someone's satin palm.

"A horse is a horse, of course of course," she sang.

That wasn't a promise. I needed the word from her. I wasn't going to ask for it again.

"I love you," we said in sync.

She must have known by then. She might have known before I did. She'd said to meet at five thirty for dinner. We'd both shown up without anything to eat and said nothing of it. All the years I'd spent desperate to understand her, unable to close the gap between sympathy and empathy, had led to this. I left; she lived. I restricted; she restored. It was all for naught, I know that now. I know sympathy and empathy are asymptotes at best, that it's not possible to understand another person.

Cameron came home with a compostable to-go box for me.

I popped the lid open and frowned at the once-distinct food groups. While he walked, they'd smushed into sameness.

"Thanks." I packed my backpack and said I'd eat it at the library.

The food made a splash in the first garbage can I passed. I'd told him I didn't want anything. I went off campus and wasted the night walking, marking new points on my latest pilgrimage on the endless road to Fiona's—my—our salvation.

—

[14]At some point, I returned to Wendy's office. She was pleased, I think, until the third time she had to repeat her point about DP movement. Her bangs were pinned back.

"I'm sorry, what?" I blinked. "One more time?" Everything that had transpired since the last blink eluded me. My finger traversed a set of photocopied notes. She stopped the ineffectual lesson and sat beside me. Her sweat was jasmine. Walks on loosely pebbled paths had left debris on her ankles. She asked how I was feeling.

Hungry. What did she want from me? I couldn't smell her thoughts. "Cold," I said mechanically, knowing it was the wrong answer. She placed her hand on mine, to verify or vilify me. I could tap a message out on her hand in Morse code. For some reason, *iodine* was the only thing Fiona taught me how to say.

Wendy closed the window and sat back down. "And how do you feel psychologically?" Her green pen fit into a burgeoning bruise below the cuticle on her ring finger. She was unmarried. She wouldn't understand why I was trying to use my body to host the thing Fiona had exorcized from herself. I didn't understand either because it didn't make sense.

"You're clearly a very bright young woman, but I'm worried that your work and your behavior are uneven," Wendy ventured. "Are you taking anything? Maybe something that helps you deal with all the stress?"

"Coffee." I rested my palms between the undersides of my thighs and the grey plastic of my chair. She had misread the situation. I was not at risk of exposure. I was safe.

She shot me a sideways glance and began listing people on campus I could speak to in confidence. Who could help me, "professionally." They had advanced degrees in the medical and social sciences. I braided my hair. I wanted to knock on something, to feel the reassurance of a structure, but Wendy might not like that, so I unbraided my hair. She was still talking. "I don't know if you know this, but every student is entitled to a handful of free sessions at the health center. If she needs more time than that, they can refer her out."

"A handful?" If there was something wrong with me, a hand could not contain it. If there was something wrong with me, I would not let it be named or confiscated. There was something wrong with me, but it was actually right, because I needed it, in a primal, inarticulable way. There was nothing wrong with me. I paused as if my confession was imminent, as if I was going to share with her the unhinged spreadsheet in which I kept meticulous track of my energy inputs and expenditures, of the size of my body and my shits. "No, I didn't know that. I'm glad you told me."

She resumed the original lesson at half speed. For twenty minutes, I focused. We'd repeat the exercise in futility every week until the semester ended. What I learned always escaped me as I walked back to my campus, short of breath. I took the same steps on the same stones and sand, passed the same sun-poisoned students, heard the same sounds of the same canons of scholarship, squinted at the sprawl of the same screensaver sky. I'd craved the sameness, and the sameness was defacing me.

*

Later that week, the student center put a welcome wrinkle in things. One of its walls, a single enormous window, overlooked the pool at the center of the first-year dorms. From the courtyard side, Cameron, Vera, and I saw punks aggregating inside the building. Vera said she didn't think I was actually one of them. I pushed past her. They were setting up for a show, alternating between hauling equipment and checking their phones.

"You're too self-aware," she said. "You're a hipster."

"Since when do people play here? Why doesn't anyone tell me anything?" I said with my back to her.

She oohed with sarcasm and aahed with sincerity. "Sketchy, sketchy, sketchy," she finally tsked.

Cameron said we should go help.

Matty entered stage left. I reached for my key card. No one else was supposed to let him past the locked doors.

Vera would not shut up. "If you were actually part of it, you wouldn't be able to be so observant. You're more like an anthropologist. You have all your flyers and those little pictures on your walls and all the bands memorized like it's your job."

Before I could ask what memorizing a band meant, she and Cameron were gone. I was tearing the door open in a trance, my footsteps militaristic. Matty and some guy were sitting on a folding table.

I relaxed what I thought were all my muscles, only to realize I was still more clenched than not. *Just. Calm. Down.* I didn't need to count the days since I'd seen him on my fingers. I didn't need to sprint to the gas station to buy him a dozen roses. I took a deep breath and a stab at a smile. "Hey! Who organized this?"

His friend explained that DAC hosted shows on campus a handful of times a year.

"A handful!" Neither of them gave any indication that they knew who I was. I gave up on trying to make eye contact. "Who's DAC?"

The friend's black ponytail was pulled through the back of a Dodgers hat. He might have been the roommate. "You know? Direct Action Claremont." I did not know.

He introduced himself. His face would continue to crop up over the years. His mustache bounced as he spoke to Matty in Spanish laced with inside jokes I couldn't follow. I would never commit his name to memory.

"That's so weird," I said. "Because I *go here* and I didn't know anyone else was . . . into this."

I texted Matty a question mark. Then an exclamation point. *!!??*, he replied and shoved his phone back in his pocket. Like it would detonate if he exposed it to too much air. He sniffled, caught a loogie in the back of his throat, and swallowed it. I tapped my sternum, trying to think of something normal to say. His hair was freshly trimmed and dyed. His friend wandered off. I took the vacant side of the table.

"Do you ever sit on flights of stairs and cross your arms over your knees and tuck your head into your arms?" I asked.

"You know—like Ian." The pose, I reasoned, might make him feel closer to his reluctant God. "And is it like haram for you to let your hair get any longer than that?"

Matty told me I wasn't as funny as I thought I was. That being mean wasn't cool. I wasn't cool. I was, as Wendy said, increasingly uneven. The unchanging desert had turned me mercurial. My mind was so rigid regarding my physical regimen that it couldn't control anything else. My disposition inverted without warning. I went from agreeable with apathy to frenetic with hysteria, though Wendy wouldn't like me using the *h*-word. Matty was pouting at me. His hands were screaming, in still-wet ink, that he led an unintoxicated existence, flashing the sign that, like every sign, was just a simulacrum of an incidental icon. I hated, at least in that moment, the concept of shorthand and every example of it. But there'd be no scene without it. Maybe when the show started, I'd burn the building down. We could all start fresh.

He stood to stretch. Was I about to lose him? The swath of skin between his ACxDC crewneck and the top of his jeans taunted me. The anger shifted. Was it so hard for him to see that I was good for him? Or could be if he'd let me? I hoped he'd choke on his gum. He inched away. Could he hear what I was thinking? That now I wanted to taste his tongue.

At the podium behind us, another new face fiddled with a computer shackled to a projector. He asked if anyone had an iPod. I jumped at the chance. Never before had I had something to contribute to all the waiting around. Whoever this person was looked over my shoulder as I scrolled through my library. I put something local, but defunct, on. And yes, I felt bad for the only half-listened-to songs. More people poured in to do nothing.

Matty waved me back over and pointed at the ceiling. I didn't see anything. He shook his head and rattled off the exorbitant cost of each light above us. He stated things about LEDs and fluorescence and specialized specs that were beyond me. "There's so much money in this room," he said. "I bet it's usually empty."

"I'm sorry," I offered, unsure of my culpability. I was also sorry for whatever sins of lavishness were being perpetrated in other parts of the building, particularly in the room named for Dolores Huerta, whose importance Vera had explained to me. Mostly, I was sorry for what I'd eaten that day.

He smiled and said it was all right. He said everything happened for a reason. *Yes*, I was tempted to tell him, *things happen because people make them happen*. His friend returned and made me promise to come back when the show started.

"And bring your friends," What's-his-name added, with the slightest curl of his lip. "We're playing third. It's gonna be tight." They left to help move something.

I noticed Cameron hovering in the doorway, wearing one of my shirts. Strangers greeted him warmly. Once he was free, he asked if we could go get a snack at Velma. I obliged, eager to see what he would order, how many crumbs he would create, the napkins he would sully.

Vera rejoined us for the excursion. She sat with me while Cameron got his food. "Please tell me you aren't going back to that 'concert.' That masculine energy was seriously overwhelming. Is it really safe there?"

"Well, I don't know. The floor is a stable surface. It's not like grinding on someone on top of a beer pong table." I didn't know if people actually did things like that.

"But the people I grind on *go here*. What if someone gropes you while you're . . . charging at each other? You wouldn't even have time to process it."

"It's not a jousting tournament, Vera. And there's only infrequent groping. The groping is incredibly infrequent. It's probably statistically insignificant."

"One time is too many times!" She grabbed my chin and made me look straight at her. "Dream bigger," she added. "We don't have to live like this."

Cameron took the seat between us and asked where punks got their flannel shirts from. Vera helped herself to his curly fries. I wondered what Matty's preferred form of potato was. I patiently watched Cameron drink a third diet Sprite. But lines had to be drawn. "Bro, we're taking your next refill to go." He gave me thumbs-up.

I set a brisk pace for the walk back.

A three-piece named Viscera was starting when we arrived. I waited for Vera to declare it too loud and leave. It took her fifty-one seconds, or one song. Spectators' shirts advertised Ruptures, Dangers, Casket, Plagues. I hoped all those things were in Matty's future. He had a blond girl at his side. I wished all the terror in the world upon them. Hoped they were rotting out in real time. Cameron asked why I wasn't in her place. I shook my head, perhaps in a worrying way. He assured me she and Matty were only standing next to each other, the same as us.

"That was definitely a friend hug, Bub."

My eyes welled through a breakdown. If we'd missed Matty's set, I was glad. I did not need to see him and What's-his-name growling on ground level, which—trust me—is where they would have insisted on playing even if we'd had a stage. I either thought that ethos was splendid or I did not fucking care.

The next band was more extreme than the one before. I wanted to thank them for their thickly grating music and apologize for that the fact that I would never buy their records. I couldn't listen to something like that in isolation or on demand. It would birth black holes hungry to abduct me. It would too efficiently diminish my sense of self. It would remove me from reality. One listen wouldn't kill me, but I listened to everything on a loop. A loop of this? Boom. I'd be obliterated.

Cameron shook me out of it when it was Matty's band's turn. Of course, they played the fastest. I'm not ashamed that I swooned. Sweat slinked down his forearms, on pathways I'd kissed. His eyes were closed. What's-his-name made his mouth a cave for the microphone. His vocals were so garbled I could pretend he was saying whatever I wanted. *He loves you. He loves you not. She loves you. She loves you not*, a loop which, at some point, they decided to stop.

Cameron was determined to help clean up afterward. We did, until an In-N-Out craving came over him. It was his idea to walk there. Bypassing the hordes of kids going to and from the parties he'd declined invitations to didn't bother him.

Once we were off campus, the sidewalk became inconsistent, then nonexistent. The marquee outside our neighborhood strip club said OCCUPY MY LAP.

"So what's going on with you and Bro Soda?" he asked.

"Who?"

"Your . . . friend. Matty? Consumer of soda because he denies himself beer."

"Things are going on. Good, good things. We're good."

We continued in silence until tomato, onion, and seared cow spiced the air. The restaurant was sandwiched between a pawn shop and a Popeyes. Two gangly palm trees out front leaned across each other, forming a perfect X. I would have sent Matty a picture, but he would have taken it the wrong way.

At the walk-up window, Cameron doubled his order and paid for "our" food. A picnic bench held us while we waited. On the other side of the four-lane road, a smattering of one-story homes, in soft browns and pale oranges with undecorated yards, provided reprieve from the strip malls.

When Cameron's food was ready, he pried the lid off his shake and dipped a steaming fry in it. I did the same. *It's okay, Khaki, a little bit won't hurt her. Or you. You can eat if you want to. I don't want to. But you* do *want to, don't you?* I pushed my fries toward him. *You can talk to Cameron, Khaki, you trust Cameron, you can tell Cameron—*

"Did you know a bunch of neo-Nazis live around here?" he asked.

"A bunch? Not a handful?"

"No, no. Way more than a handful. A bunch. It's fucked." He opened a packet of ketchup. "Sorry, were you about to say something before, Bub?"

"No." I took the flannel shirt someone had left behind at the student center and balled it into a pillow. Cameron was eating too fast or too slow. My head felt like a construction site.

On the walk home, he started talking about Horkheimer. It took me a disquietingly long time to place the name, to remember that Cameron was, in fact, a serious student of philosophy; he had not gotten into Neue Deutsche Härte without consulting me. When he keyed us into our building, my foot caught on a stair. A few steps later I tripped over a laminated nametag that had fallen off a door. He kept reflexively propping me back up.

I asked if he wanted to hear something funny. "One of my professors thinks I'm a drug addict." I tried to glean his reaction without making eye contact. I tried very hard to laugh.

One of the rare Christian girls on campus was shuffling around the halls, talking on the phone. She scowled at us. He waved.

"You have been looking sort of . . . disheveled," he said to me.

"I have?" I'd all but stopped looking in the mirror.

"And I do get smoke in your stuff sometimes," he added. I'd been wearing my baggiest shirts—the ones I'd never cut. He'd been borrowing them. We grabbed them from the floor between our beds every morning, turning them right side out while we sniffed to see if they'd gone from lightly worn to reeking.

"We should cut your hair," I said when we got to our door. I was exhausted, but sleep was too solitary. "With like clippers?"

There had been a pair on the concrete a few yards down for weeks. Cameron went to get them, and we went calmly into our room. It was not theft. Our peers were trusting. They left laptops unattended in rooms with propped-open doors, practically willing them to vanish. Some bikes had never been locked to a rack in their lives. I left my phone on the tabletop each time I went for a fruitless lap around the dining hall.

Cameron plugged the clippers in by the bathroom sink, then put his desk chair in front of the mirror and shrank himself to meet the height of my hands. His shoulder helped me balance. In it was a pocket of muscle leftover from ten years of tennis lessons. As I moved the clippers, the floor came to resemble a barn teeming with hay. If nothing else, I'd cut it evenly.

He asked how he looked.

"Honestly? Like a fucking Nazi punk." His narrow nose was more prominent. His light eyes sunk deeper into his face. "I am so sorry. Let's maybe get some dye tomorrow?"

He nodded congenially. He hummed something I didn't recognize. My headache continued its cawing. In theory, I knew how to cure it. In reality, the calculus was impossible to put into practice. *What is the most right, very best, perfect thing to eat? You'll never know! The mistake you'll make is not worth making; it will make you sick. Aren't I already sick?*

I focused on Cameron. I didn't recognize him. He said he had something to ask me.

"Okay, ask me."

The worst part would be his concern, the roundness of his eyes, the hoarse whisper when he asked why I hadn't been eating. I would deny everything.

"The DAC guys are graduating this year and they asked me to take over. You'll do it with me, right? I told them they should have asked you in the first place, but they said you were hard to track down. What else? I asked, and you can use some funding to print that zine you were talking about starting. They also do some, uh, actual activism stuff. But I can do that part and you can do the shows."

"You should do everything without me. I don't think I like going to shows anymore."

He took a robust breath. I got a lecture. I was wrong. I was more qualified than he was. I could use it as an excuse to spend more time with Matty. I could handle the finances since I loved numbers. (How did he know that?) A rush of blood darkened his face. "Does it bother you that there aren't a lot of black people at these shows because it makes me kind of uncomfortable, and I heard you talking to Vera about someone touching you so I . . . that must make you feel—"

"I don't feel anything about those things. Those things are not my fault and those things are not my problem, so I don't know what do you want me to do about them?" He started to reply. "Can you shut up for a second?"

My skull was going to crack. I was broken. My mind didn't start spinning a song to calm me down. It started counting the hours until I could go for a run, counting up how many units of energy each unit of distance would require. It did not specify if I would stop at some point or would have to go on like that forever. The inner monologue was by then indistinguishable from my own voice, and far louder than anything that came from an amplifier. Perhaps I could no longer choose what to listen to.

Cameron had gone to sulk on his side of the room. I got in bed with my laptop and my spreadsheet and made my calculations in silence. He started watching *Shrek*.

—

[15]Per my calculations, I'd retained a single shred of autonomy. I was salvageable. My life was still mine, and for it I chose music; Matty. I had done enough suffering for Fiona's sake, and all without acknowledgment. She hadn't planned her visit, and, despite my best efforts, I couldn't choose how I felt about it. It felt, unremittingly, like shit.

Music at least appeared and disappeared when I told it to.

Matty too, more or less. For days, I'd done little besides reread our text thread. Syllables scoured. Plain English treated like Proust. It was actually quite simple. Our conversations strained only when I was too negative. Thus, I couldn't be myself for much longer.

I washed weeks' worth of grime from my hair and tried to summon him. His car, he claimed, was blocked in by his roommate's. I told him I wanted to have sex, meaning it or not meaning it, just wanting to see what would happen. How it might make us feel. He took his time responding. In bed, alone, I reviewed everything I had and hadn't consumed in the last seventy-two hours until I remembered I didn't do that anymore. Canker sores festered inside my lips. I read a comprehensive croissant-making tutorial and, around the second lamination, realized that was probably a bad idea. I stood. Apple seeds spilled from my sheets. I sat. I transcribed an EP's worth of lyrics for a website that cataloged them and told myself archiving was activism.

Matty texted me that he'd arrived. I collected him from the parking lot. Not knowing where Cameron was or when he would return, I led us to a study room. We activated the motion-activated lights. I did not comment on the four-dollar bottle of electrolyte-infused spring water Matty had with him. A paper bag, translucent with oil, wiggled in his other hand. The smell spread like smoke.

"I brought you a doughnut." He unwrapped it, waved it in my face. I was speechless. "You said you were hungry," he explained. That seemed unlikely. The ring of pink glaze was grainy at its edges. The sprinkles hung on for dear life. It would taste like the plastic flotation device it resembled.

"I don't like that you did that."

"What? Everyone likes doughnuts."

No, some girls—some people—don't. I ate a section of it to appease him. Does it matter what it tasted like? I swallowed so I could kiss him, erase myself, or add him to me. I did that for some time, but I was, or we were, quick to tire. We lay still on the couch and whispered about nothing. I wanted to regale him with erudition, without effort. But I had little idea what was going on in my classes. We stayed still for so long that the room went dark again. I started to say something about Boas. The sentence stopped mid-thought. Matty didn't mind the cliffhanger. Nor did he resuscitate the conversation. *Why is he making me talk? What depraved torture is this? What is a thing he would want to talk about? Him, him, him.* I asked what he'd been like in high school.

"A basketball player? I find that hard to believe." He wasn't very tall, and I thought his thing was hockey.

He jerked away. My neck cracked from the sudden shift. "Why are you always trying to tell me about myself?" he said. The lights were back on. "You don't know me."

I hadn't said that I didn't believe him, but it dawned on me that, to him, the distinction was irrelevant. I backtracked. "What position did you play?" I didn't hear his answer. More silence followed it. Was I willing to stay on that couch until I figured out how to talk to him? I tried. I blabbered.

"I've been thinking about your adoption and how you must be worried every girl you kiss is your sister. Or cousin. Or—"

He sat all the way up that time. "What the fuck? Are you drunk?" He didn't make his exit. He resorted to picking up the book half-hanging out of my backpack. The pages rippled under his thumb. I envied the paper's place against his skin.

"It is indecent and filthy for a respectable girl to know anything of the marital relation. Oh, for the inconsistency of respectability, that needs the marriage vow to turn something which is filthy into the purest and most sacred arrangement that none dare question or criticize," he read.

"Of all the words there," I asked, "why that?"

He turned the book toward me. It was the only thing I'd underlined. "The most sacred arrangement," he repeated with reverence, and told me his best friend had just gotten married. If I'd been invited I wouldn't have gone. Chatting up strangers. Cake. Matty had so many friends he probably took them for granted. He didn't have to protect them. *No, Khaki, you don't do that anymore either.*

"I don't want to marry you, by the way," I said. "I don't believe in soulmates. For romance. For friends, I do, but I don't know, maybe you can't be sure, maybe you can't trust anyone. Or yourself."

The room was dark again. He said I worried too much. I told him I couldn't help it. He told me I had to try to get out of my own head. And go where? My head was, at least, familiar. If you fake enough smiles, he swore, happiness follows. I had nothing nice to say to that, so I laid him back down and commenced copulation.

The couch we were crowded on was the color and firmness of unripe avocado flesh. He breathed like he was getting over a cold. He said we could stop if I wanted. I did not want to stop, though it did feel like I was on the wrong end of a halfhearted stabbing. I only wanted wanting. I had it then. I had imploring thrusts and groans. But it would soon be over. His determined smile was tinted grey. He was incandescent.

I held him closer. The lights came on. His heartbeat trampled mine as he finished and loosened my grip and thanked me so tenderly and I wondered why I'd ever wanted to hurt him. I tossed the rest of the doughnut into the trash while he zipped his fly.

"Could I use your shower?"

"Be my guest," I said.

"Why do you have to say it like that!"

"Like what?"

"Never mind."

I walked ahead of him to my room. I followed him into my bathroom. He took his shower like I wasn't there. I sat on the other side of the curtain, which didn't quite reach the wall. Magenta water, like day-old hibiscus tea, rolled down the drain. I ran a finger through it.

"How much do those motion sensor lights cost?"

He didn't hear me. I didn't mind. My desire was gone. Matty was exhaustible. Full of limits, by no fault of his own. He was only human. He was not a spreadsheet whose cells seemed to extend without end. Not a scale whose lower limit I had yet to find.

The water trickled off. He used Cameron's towel without asking whose it was.

"Can you walk yourself out?"

"Did I do something wrong again?"

"Again?"

"The last time we . . . you disappeared on me. Why didn't you say bye? Or ask for a ride. It's dangerous for you to walk around by yourself in the middle of night."

"I couldn't sleep."

"Why didn't you just—I'm sorry to hear that. You know, it'd be cool if you didn't make it so hard to get to know you."

"I don't know what that means."

He shifted his face. Fake smile; real happiness. "I answer all your questions, don't I?" he asked. I nodded. "So you could talk to me like I'm real to you instead of like I'm a social experiment you're running." I asked how to do that. He put his head in his hands. I counted thirty-two seconds before he went on. "Think of it like this: I'm allowed to be as interested in you as are you in me."

"Okay? I've never flossed in my life and I don't really understand how electricity works and I wish I cared enough to wear red lipstick every day but I hate how it smells and I find your kindness borderline pathological and pretty soon you'll realize that I'm straight-up inimical but I'm hoping you won't mind because opposites attract or whatever."

"Um . . ."

"Did I talk to you the right way?" I reached for him. "Did I make you happy?"

He dodged me and got dressed. "I need to think about it," he said. I was so heinous that not even he could find my bright side. "And I don't know what *inimical* means."

I started to define it.

"I understood what you said. From context. It's like, you're not in Bad Religion. So it would make me happy if you could chill with that. All their shit sounds the same anyway."

His mouth curled inward. I couldn't tell what he was humming and I was going to admit it, but the bathroom door slammed and the bedroom door slammed and he was gone.

*

We'd been at the dining hall for two hours. I'd been trying to count every piece of silverware in the room. No. I had to eat. Where was Cedar? I could have been slipping him handfuls of food under the table all along. No. I had to eat. *You can try, but you're going to do it wrong. Don't bother.* I studied nearby meals before taking another walk to inspect the food on offer. *Members of that food group are outside your repertoire.* I went back to our table with something and moved the napkin dispenser to give Cameron a clear path to my plate.

"Don't you hate onions?" he asked.

He'd been going to shows without me. French Exit and Summer Vacation; Ceremony and the Souls; Seahaven and Touché and La Dispute, and I didn't even want to know who else. He was making new friends. My face was falling asleep. It felt like a gift for no occasion, and I cherished my misery because although I couldn't pinpoint its origin, it was all I had. My mood swung every few hours, always further down.

Vera jiggled her arm and told us how much bread she'd eaten that afternoon. "I think I'm getting fat." She flicked through her phone. "I think it's all the flavored vodka . . . banana pancakes . . . rum . . ." I wanted to hold her down and scream at her that it didn't matter.

Natalie made a point of turning her back to me before discussing their plans for the night. Was an alcohol run necessary? That was her top-secret query.

Vera wondered if they should cut back on drinking. "These girls in my Spanish class were talking about how they'd never had sex sober. I realized I haven't either. If you're both drunk, it cancels itself out though?" The last hookup of hers I'd heard about was a Fred senior who earnestly thought himself saintly for making egregious messes in his room in order to give the cleaning staff ("maids") enough work to do.

I zoned out until I heard my name. She was offering to set me up with Jason someone. Natalie said I wouldn't like him. He wasn't white.

"Wow, Natalie. You're out here judging people by the color of the skin and not the content of their character? Does this kid like The Replacements? Vera, does Jason prefer *Tim* or *Pleased to Meet Me*? I think we all know that's all I care about. Jason's a convicted arsonist? Fine. Great. Cool. I'll stick with him until the day the fucking sun goes out."

"Khaki, can you please stop speaking in code for like five minutes? I am begging you to let me have a normal conversation with you."

"Why do you get to decide what a normal conversation is, Vera?"

Cameron tried to defuse the situation. I'd forgotten my promise to dye his hair. I kicked Natalie under the table as I got up to leave for my room.

I needed to throw up. To be hungry. To want again and again and again. For me. Not for Fiona. It was never for her. That was just an excuse because being a martyr was easier than admitting that I needed help existing while everyone else operated with so much ease. The earth turned without effort. The sun made perpetual assault look simple. The succulents carried on without rain, and I could only make it to the bathroom floor.

I was gagging when she called. I coughed and spit and wiped my hand on my shin. She said I sounded weird.

"Yeah I'm just— I have a tickle in my throat. And this bad taste in my mouth."

She told me to try rinsing it out with baking soda. I sat and wedged myself into a corner. "Wow, Fiona." I pulled my knees tighter to my chest and turned to press my forehead into the cool of the door. "I don't need your help." She needed mine. No, she didn't. I couldn't keep it straight. "How much longer until you get here?"

She cracked the joints in her hands one by one. It was November. She'd been saying soon since the summer. Now her doctors had okayed the trip. But her mother had vetoed it. Lena said our relationship was too intense. I brought out the worst in Fiona; I discouraged her independence. No, I wanted Fiona to independently use her own credit card to buy a plane ticket to come see me.

"But next semester," she said. "Promise." She was trying some new things, one of which was being open to the idea that we—she corrected herself—*she* didn't always know what was best for her.

I left the bathroom and got into bed. "Fiona, you're not really going to listen to the woman who told you you were lucky you were cute because otherwise people wouldn't put up with your 'insistence' on being sick? Are you forgetting the time she almost kicked you out of the house because she thought you needed a 'reality check'?"

She went so quiet I had to make sure I hadn't accidentally hung up.

"I don't see what the big deal is, dear. You agree with her, don't you? Do I hold it against you?"

I grabbed Cameron's notebook and wrote. I might be able to say it if I wrote it down first.

Dear You,

I did something bad. Or something bad happened to me. It just happened—I don't know why. I only know it's not your fault.

I'm so scared and I don't want to scare you but I think it's permanent. Except you seem to know how to undo it. I'm scared that if I undo it from me, then you'll do it to you again.

She would kill me. It would kill her if she knew. She was still talking. I traded the paper for the computer screen. The spreadsheet. I'd forgotten the sound of her laugh. Maybe our love wasn't true. It wasn't enough, music was not enough, no man was enough, but someday the numbers would add up to enough nothingness. She said I had to call my mom more often. I didn't. I didn't have to do anything except catalog, calculate, count.

The bathroom wanted me back. I went. I flipped its light on, then off, then on. The last filigrees of sunset filtered in through the window that hung four feet above the toilet. I'd forgotten to flush. I closed the lid and sat on it. I gave up.

"I have something to tell you."

"Something bad?" Fiona cracked her wrists, her spine, all the once jutting, now concealed, things I'd always pretended not to see. "You can say it. It's okay. No matter what."

"I'm tired of taking care of you." I inhaled as I said it, like that would take it back.

"Oh, Olive. I know. You know I know. Gosh, it took you so long to admit it."

"I— I'm— You—"

"You never had to take care of me. I never asked you to."

"But you didn't ask me not to." I tapped my head against the wall behind me. "And I'm starting to think that I'm not that smart after all. A smart person would've figured out another way to love you."

"I tried to stop you. Sometimes. Honest! But I just don't have your talent for being hostile toward affection."

I begged her forgiveness. For what? For leaving. She said she was more concerned with what I'd said before I left. She said I'd meant it.

I had and still did. "And you meant what you said too."

"No!"

"Yes."

"No, I took it back."

The door opened from the other side. I hung up without thinking. Or maybe Fiona and I never got disconnected. Maybe she heard everything. I don't know. She hasn't spoken to me since.

The gasp that Natalie let out must still be stuck on that ceiling. Did I really look that bad? "We didn't know you were here." She walked backward, unwilling to take her eyes off me. Her neck tried to twist away. I went into the bedroom with her. Her hair was a mess.

"Our bad," Cameron said. He wasn't wearing a shirt, mine or otherwise.

Now Natalie's eyes darted around. "Who puked in your trash can?" She tugged her skirt to lay lower on her thighs.

Most likely me. "It was that girl Vera was trying to get with last night," I whispered. I was afraid to look at the vomit for confirmation. How long had it been there? Why hadn't Cameron noticed?

"Bummer," he shrugged.

"Are you cheating on Jane?" I shouted. My phone clattered at my feet. It was a poor explosion, with all the force of one kernel of popping corn. "With *Natalie*? She's so . . . boring. Maybe she's pretty? But you'll never remember her when you're done with her. She's like latte art. The most interesting thing about her is how well she's adapted to the giant crack in her phone screen. And why does she keep saying she needs to get out of this town? What does that mean? Is someone holding her against her will?"

My curiosity, though contentious, was genuine. I couldn't figure out what it was like to be Natalie. Straight hair and people skills and thinking she knew how to dance, even when she just lifted her arm, drink in hand, and flapped her wrist out of sync with the music but on pace with the spirit of things.

"Hello!" she shouted back. "I'm standing right here. I can hear you. What is wrong with everyone at these schools? I . . . I miss Idaho?" Her chin quivered. She balanced on one leg and tried to shove her shoe on. "Cam, can you stand up to her for once?" She tripped into the hall, trusting him to do it or knowing he wouldn't.

He ripped open a pack of Skittles and told me to shut up. I was already quiet. A mass of sugar slopped in his mouth. "I know you're on some fucked-up Heathcliff and Catherine shit or whatever. But art is not real life, Bub. I don't think you understand what a healthy relationship is, and you don't seem willing to figure it out. You've probably pushed away everyone who's ever met you, much less cared about you."

He didn't care about me. He let me lock the bathroom door. He cleaned my plates. He let me lie. No one would ever love me enough to treat me how I wanted, which was not to be loved but to be enabled.

"Is Jane okay? I mean, are you okay without Jane?"

Now his mouth was a little less full. "How many times have you told me to break up with her? How did you end up on her side? No, I'm not cheating on her. I would never do something like that. I dumped her a few weeks ago." He blew his nose into the half-empty candy wrapper and threw it on the floor. "When did you of all people stop paying attention?" He laughed. "And while we're doing this, can you tell me why? Why me? Do you know how many times a week someone asks me why I'm the only person you'll say more than five words to? Why am I so special? Am I a puppet that's fun to control? You're smarter than me! You're cooler than me! Congratulations! You win. And now you hate me and we don't hang out anymore? Is this how Fiona felt when you did whatever unspeakable thing you did to her? Can you explain—without a stupid fucking playlist—how you can be emo when you're so unbelievably insensitive?"

I knelt by the door to pull my shoes on. "You can tell Natalie to come back. She can spend the night. I'm leaving. Isn't that considerate of me?"

I waited until I was off campus to start running.

—

[16]I declined to go home with Cameron for Thanksgiving weekend. Vera called it Thanks-taking; the colonizers were the opposite of generous, except when it came to genocide and biological warfare. She went somewhere to help feed the homeless. I stayed in bed. Eleanor wouldn't stop checking on me. I sneezed once during a phone call and she asked if I had the flu. I played along but downgraded it to a cold. She wanted to send medicine. I wouldn't take it. I'd just google *calories in pills.*

For days, I curled up with what I couldn't convince myself to eat. Yet. I would soon. I would wait for the sun to set, or the local news to come on a TV I didn't have, or for someone to say an obscure word no one would ever say. My mouth was crowded with its own strange taste. I brushed my teeth and drooled and swallowed and felt so incredibly dumb. *Khaki, you're being unreasonable. You can just eat. I cannot!* I clicked between my spreadsheet and my calendar. My parents were going to see me in a few weeks. If forced to deal with this, they'd break up again. I flipped through Cameron's sole notebook and dotted his *i*'s without reading his notes. I did not sleep. I made sloppy work of all my overdue homework. I tried to stream a show Eleanor had said I would like, but all the actors had bodies, and so I had to close the browser.

The free-for-all schoolwide email system seemed like a safe form of entertainment. Thousands of threads had accumulated since school had started. So this was what had been going on around me: someone looking for someone else who was studying abroad in Ecuador the following semester. Someone canceling the Naked Contact Improv club's next meeting. Someone campaigning to make the entire campus clothing optional. Someone planning to dye the water in the Fred fountains red, in protest of Condoleezza Rice's scheduled guest lecture. Someone sharing the funniest video they'd ever seen and someone canceling Guy Fawkes night due to unforeseen conflicts and someone advertising an educational workshop about anal sex. No one was looking for someone to languish with.

I had to get out. I rose and dressed and took buses and trains until I was in the neighborhood Chuck Ragan named an album after, though listening to *Los Feliz* in Los Feliz would've felt unlucky. I made Comadre snarl at me instead. They were too intelligible. I was ready to let a black hole play on a loop. I endeavored. Every album came up short. Each one emitted a measure of light. I settled for silence and walked toward no destination. I heard but didn't hear the noise of the street. When a man turned a corner a few yards ahead of me, I followed, enchanted. He ducked into a bank; I waited outside. My imagination mushroomed until he reappeared. He was not who I wanted. I chose a different direction. Strollers and canvas tote bags slowed down the few people in my path. It was a lifeless, slipshod city. I couldn't count my way up and down tidy, gridded corners or follow Bleecker's bent. Unglamorous anonymity wasn't on offer. I couldn't weep in public in peace or tuck an inconspicuous scream into the rumble of an underground train.

I kept walking. I bought a pack of mixed nuts, found a bench on which to separate them into almonds, cashews, peanuts, pecans, and left the piles for the squirrels. I kept walking. An empty movie theater took me in. A gilded sex addict struggled on the screen. I only had eyes for his teetering sister, crying, gurgling on a ledge. Who was on the other end of her phone? *I love you. I love you. I love you*, she begged. I left before something less perfect could imprint itself upon me. I had to find Griffith Park and take notes on the trees for Fiona. I pressed one joint into another and made sure not to catch myself reflected in any store windows or the backs of passing sedans. *I love you, Fiona. I love you. I love you.* If I thought it hard enough, she'd hear me.

I forgot where I was going, that *pain* was the word for the thing I was in. My heart, not my soul's container but my literal heart, felt fickle. I sat on a curb. I wanted to break the thing that had a hold on me. Wrest the parking meter from the cement. Swing it overhead. I'd settle for breaking anything. I'd bludgeon every window, table, and chair in the empty restaurant across the street. Destroy the world to resurrect me. I'd hotwire a car and speed into a brick wall. The impact would snap me out of it.

Soon the sun was gone. Cameron texted to ask if I had anyone to have dinner with. I had already eaten, I said. And I had, at some point in my life. I found the way back to San Bernardino. It was forty minutes, or maybe miles, spent staring at the other passengers' feet. I tried to guess their top halves, despite knowing knees do not determine heads do not determine worth and a body is a body is a body—I tried so hard to make it meaningless.

The walk from the bus stop to campus required more than I possessed. I stood, stalling. The blue of the street signs was so much darker than the sky. I wondered how many Spanish barrel tiles there were in the state of California. A passing car slowed and the driver shouted something at me. Two girls, arm in arm, shimmered on the other side of the street. Their voices combined and carried as one. Murky, majestic, they cast no shadows on the ground. They could have been us and they were walking quickly away.

Fiona and I could be together if we could be well. I could be well. She could enroll at Daphne. We could live off campus, in a place with a yard for Cedar to dig. In a place with an avocado tree. We would pick up the fruit where it fell, crack the leather skins with our thumbs, and eat the flesh with our hands. Our teeth would scrape the peels. I rushed to my room, opened my spreadsheet, and scrolled. The numbers blurred like falling water until I reached the end. I deleted everything. I stepped on the scale and sobbed over my feet. The number was perfect. It was over. I was free.

*

I began again. After the holiday, I chose a plate. I heaped food on it. I felt every gram. Twenty minutes later, Cameron picked up my fork and trained the tines on the untouched meal. I got up and carried a new plate around. I placed that one on the conveyor belt, sorry for the person who'd have to wash something clean. I tried again: a food that was easier to handle. I let it cool. Seven minutes. Cameron swooped in. He was me and I was Fiona and I had no idea who either of us were anymore.

"I'm going to a Food Not Bombs meeting this week if you want to come, Bub," he said. His hair was growing back. Vera told me about an upcoming LSU-BSU mixer. There was also some feminist thing at the coffee shop on her campus. She said I had to do the training to become a DJ for Scooby's radio station. I said yes to everything. Sunrise yoga, sure.

Natalie asked if anyone else realized how much time we spent together. A few months was nothing, Cameron said. We had three and a half revolutions of the planet left to go. I could still help with DAC. I could book Tiny Lungs. Yes to everything. Eating was a thing. I tried again and ended up with coffee.

I texted Matty. Could he take me somewhere new? Should I tell him that I was showering regularly and shampooing and conditioning my hair and vomit was no longer flecked on the corners of my clothes? Another plate. *This is fine.* A saucer this time. *It's okay if you make a mistake.* Blue plastic. A slice of something. *It doesn't mean anything.* A smear of a condiment. *It's just one time. It's nice. It's aromatic.* Something green. Something hard and orange. *Everyone else is doing it.* Slimy red. Waxy yellow. *You're okay, you're okay, you're okay.* I ate. Nothing happened. *I'm okay? You're okay. Oh. Okay!*

I ate.

Nothing happened.

I ate.

Nothing happened.

I ate.

Nothing happened.

I ate.

Nothing happened for weeks. I pushed myself toward my former normalcy. I felt and felt and felt. At Scooby, there was ice cream. Sugar stung my teeth. I thrice blocked Cameron from encroaching. I did not run. I digested. My bodily functions functioned without intervention or documentation. I licked the remains of something from a knife. I missed a call from Fiona. *I love you. I love you. I love you,* I thought when I saw the notification. She could wait. I needed to catch up to her. She'd had a head start but we'd be the same soon. Out of sickness. In health. Under the avocado tree.

—

[17]Matty wanted to take me to Amoeba, so I put on a dress and made my mouth red and smiled. I'd been practicing. Every morning, he sent a text to wish me a nice day. Every morning, I returned the sentiment. I spent the drive to Sunset trying to hold the hand he kept jerking away. It wasn't personal; he just liked to drum on the steering wheel. I got lost in the apertures stretched into his ears. I loved the way his grey-blue eyes were tainted, dishwater spilled into an overcast sky. I rolled down my window and pretended the 101 had air you'd want to breathe. Filthy as it was, maybe I did want to marry Matty. He didn't recycle, and he drove to places that were well within walking distance, and he left the lights on when he left a room. None of it mattered. I was going to smile until my face was creased beyond repair.

He said my hair looked very pretty. I asked if he ever wished he could text his cats.

"You mean talk to them?"

"No. They can only text. If my dog was a bad speller I would love him a little less."

"What are you majoring in, by the way?" He laughed.

I said I didn't know or think it really mattered. He snorted as he parked. I asked what he'd majored in. Technical theater. I'd probably known that before and forgotten. I was leaning toward anthropology, I said. "Studying subcultures." I exited the car without incident. I'd never be dizzy again.

The building's facade was a carnival of neon, mural, and stone. He held the door open for me. I nodded over his shoulder for hours while he browsed the aisles. He said *Unfun* was okay but he'd never heard *Dear You*. I didn't care. There were more important things. The flakes of dandruff on that patch of his head. Nothing had ever been so cute. He bent down to tie his shoe. He stood with his feet slightly turned out. Adorable. He bought me something I'd never heard of and guaranteed I'd like it. My record player was at home. I would have to listen at his house in his bed in his rarest T-shirt with his glued-together crocodile mug in my hands and my hair on his pillow and the dust of his dead skin mixing with mine.

He held the door open for me. I kissed him on the empty sidewalk. The concrete beneath us was perfectly square. Privacy didn't concern me. He took me to get tacos and I tapped his foot with mine under the wooden table. Our used napkins formed a hill. I choked down slow-cooked beef and ate a churro and sucked sugar from knuckles and drank a soda and he blushed when I burped and I would have kept eating if he'd told me to but the sun had set and it was a long drive home and if a double-decker bus—*Khaki, stop it. Where's your PMA?* Nothing crashed into us.

We sat in traffic. Trash Talk kept us company, which was nice, but I wouldn't have minded like five minutes of Lemuria. I wouldn't have minded if the city around us was contained more clearly. That was it. I didn't allow myself another negative thought. Los Angeles was the perfect size, actually, for him to take me places and tell me how to talk to people, and the sex would improve in proportion to the progress of my disposition and all I had to do was agree when he said *The Twilight Zone* was better than *The X-Files.*

He turned the music down, entered the carpool lane, and put cruise control on. This was good. I could feel it. The opposite of a crash was coming. He chewed a brand-new piece of gum.

"Do you," he said, and I knew I would say yes, no matter the request, but I also knew he wouldn't like being interrupted, so I let him finish, "maybe want to be my girlfriend? I've never had a girl approach me instead of the other way around, so I wasn't sure if I should wait for you to ask me to make things official, but I figure you might be less mean to me if I—"

My phone started ringing. I sent Eleanor to voicemail. She called again. He said I could answer it. I didn't ever want to speak to anyone other than him. He popped his gum and reached for my hand.

It rang again.

"What!"

She asked if I was I alone. Yes, I lied. Sitting down? Yes, I told the truth.

"Lena just called me. Fiona had a heart attack," she said. "Are you still there? Did you hear me?" I caught myself nodding, realized she couldn't see me, still didn't say a word. Matty whispered a question I couldn't make out. My face fell into its natural grimace.

"No," I corrected Eleanor, "a heart attack is caused by a blockage of blood to the heart. Fiona's heart must've failed at sending her blood to her body, and that must have sent her into cardiac arrest." The shock surfaced something that I'd read around the time I'd met her.

A review of nearly fifty years of research confirms that anorexia nervosa has the highest mortality rate of any mental disorder . . . Heart disease is responsible for the deaths of many individuals whose cases are severe . . . In cardiac arrest, the electrical impulses that cause the heart to beat are turned off . . . Metaphorically speaking, a light bulb may flicker for several days or weeks, every time you flip the light switch. One day, the filament in the bulb bursts. Prolonged bradycardia or other conditions known as arrhythmias can work much the same way on the heart. The heart may simply stop beating . . . Suicide is another common cause of death. The surprise was that she hadn't intended it.

She'd gotten so close and thrown it all away again. And she couldn't even tell me about it herself. She sent her mother to send my mother to do it. She promised Fiona wouldn't die.

Was I still there? Eleanor asked. Was I still there? No. The world had ended. I must have seen it coming.

I asked if I could come home. No, that was in boxes. Most of it was already on the truck.

"Are you going to be okay?"

I had the same question for her. When I ruined things with Matty and ended up like Fiona, or when I got caught trying to jump off a bridge, would Eleanor leave me like she left my father? I hung up.

Fiona's number went to voicemail. Mailbox full. If she had just come to visit. If she had come with me to begin with. If she'd gone on one less hike. If I had said no three years earlier, when we sat on my iced-over fire escape and she pawned half her mandatory meal replacement bar off on me. If I could just go back.

Matty had pulled onto the shoulder. He tried to get me to tell him what was going on. The popping of his gum was arrhythmic. His desperation was repulsive. I crossed my legs, uncrossed them, pulled my knees to my chest, stretched them long, crossed them again. Pressed one joint into another. *Khaki, spill speech.*

I croaked. "I'm sorry. But it's private. It's nothing. Go away."

"Hey, chill out. It's going to be okay. You can tell me anything."

"I can't," I gulped. "Don't you think I would if I could?" I surprised us both by screaming, "I can't chill out when the only friend I've ever had is in the hospital and it's my fault and I can't even begin to explain why. Especially not to you. I can only talk to her about it and she's un-fucking-available for the foreseeable future." I recoiled from his hand. "I promise you I cannot chill out. I don't have an off switch. But please, tell me what it's like. I can only imagine how hella fucking fun it is to not constantly nitpick everything you've ever done and overanalyze everything that there's the slightest possibility of you ever doing. How cool is it to be you and have access to peace and quiet whenever you want? Do you have any idea what I would do for one hour of quiet? Is that something you can help me out with? Can you fix my brain?" He reached out again. "Get away from me!"

"Can't help if you don't let me try." He dimmed his grin.

"This isn't about you and I don't want your help and I don't want to be your fucking girlfriend, you posi pussy piece of shit, and if you don't start driving me home right now, I'm going to open this door and run in front of an eighteen-wheeler."

I shouldn't have said that, but if he knew me at all he would have known it was a joke. It was obviously a joke. Fiona wouldn't like it very much if I died on her.

"Are you for real right now? You can't say shit like that. You are so psycho sometimes." He found a beat for the steering wheel.

Had I not just asked for quiet? How difficult would it be, I wondered, for me to gouge his eyes out with his hands?

I thought carefully before I spoke. "I'm sorry but I'm just not like you. I've been trying to out-smile you for the last five hours, but pretending to be good enough for you is only making me feel worse." *She isn't going to die. She's alive, alive, alive.*

"Being a spoiled kid from the suburbs doesn't make you a bad person. You're not running an international drug ring.

Right? How is there even room in your body for so much negativity?" He forced his eyes shut and started humming.

"If it bothers you so much, then why can you still get your dick hard enough to put inside me?"

"You're right. There is something wrong with you. You're not crazy. You're not the devil. You're just a bitch. A cunt, maybe. I don't fucking know."

He wiped his eyes, got back on the road, and sped to our exit. I apologized in the parking lot. He extended a stick of gum. When I reached for it, he wrapped his arms around me. I asked him to stay.

"You need to go to a doctor."

"What kind of doctor?"

He kissed my forehead and drove away.

My room was empty. I chucked my phone at Cameron's wall and found a pen.

Fiona,

This isn't the first letter I'm going to write you. It's the last one. I can't do this again.

I'm glad we never had to see each other at our worst. I understand it now, but it's still incomprehensible. It's terror without an end. I seem to run on fear now and there's always room for more. Capacity is a thing that somehow scares me. Space and waste and wastes of space. I don't think we fit together anymore. By the way, I'm at my worst.

I know you're going to get better. Without me.
You're going to live the rest of your life without me.
Please eat a pear. Take one with you on the Trail.
And I'll love you forever, if ever, more than anyone
before or anyone to come. Even if I'm wrong.

Love,
Olive

I grabbed the trash can by the door and threw up. Half-digested birria and sour cream made more sour by gastric acid, and it's not like I had to force it. You love something, you let it go. Maybe she'd come back on her own.

—

[18]I devoted days to eating. I refused to fail or be like her. Ice cream? I imbibed. Ten minutes later, it was floating in the toilet bowl, still cold. I only threw up in emergencies. Everything was cataclysmic. Five and three and eight times a day, every day. Until the day I couldn't do it. It was an unsanctioned strike. A demand: self-preservation. I inflated. My skin struggled to stretch. For twelve hours, I contemplated hanging from the ceiling. And then I was back at it.

I prepared and discarded plates of identical food. I had to preempt my mistakes. But the worst had already happened. *You still haven't heard a word from her.* What else was I afraid of? *Khaki, this isn't working. You're still feeling. That might not even be a problem. This is not a solution. You might die if you keep doing this. That is not what you want. It's not not what I want.* My disappearances between identical courses went unnoticed or unquestioned or uncared about. *Khaki, you don't have to—* The force of forcing food up pushed one of my contacts into the toilet. *I had to. Way to go, there goes your birth control pill.*

I waited for her call. Time muddled itself. I fell asleep on my homework. Gave up. Woke up to a text from Cameron. Did I want to walk him home from some shitty party? I got in the shower. I heard him come home, open my computer, and scroll through my new spreadsheet. I listened closer. No one was there. My shoulders fell. I made the water colder. I understood Fiona's God in that moment. Just a little more suffering and someday, surely, I would be back to normal and that would be heaven. No, it would never end. God was a place where you were always kept waiting.

I drank from the showerhead. Consumed. Expelled. I shut the water off and stood there until the moisture evaporated from my skin. I weighed myself and went back to bed. Got up to see a number again. Put on another pair of socks and meant to answer Cameron, but the night, or week, got away from me. Matty kept texting me; he was there whenever I was ready to talk. I dialed my dad and hung up before the call connected. A rock of peanut butter sat inside me. I remembered, barely, pushing it down my throat. I could live with it, die from it, head over to the trash can. Routine, routine, routine. A knotted cord of compulsions.

The honeymoon was over. My legs were asleep. *Your blood isn't flowing. That's dangerous. I'm fine. You're fine? Yes, I'm just very cold.* Dinnertime. I texted Cameron that I would meet him at our usual table. I threw away my tooth enamel and emptied the trash into the toilet. There was that small window above the toilet. Someone could have heard me. Good. I was doing well. I was eating again. Days were just numbers. Tomorrow another one full of capsaicin-laden food, as if the threat of it burning on the way back up would deter me. I was undeterred. *I'm fine. I'm just very unhappy.*

I stopped trying to eat, stopped needing to throw up, woke my legs up, went outside, and never stopped moving. On Monday, I closed my eyes while I went downhill. Cedar made sure I didn't fall. On Tuesday morning, I saw stars, couldn't remember what I'd done a few minutes earlier, what I'd meant to do next. *So you* do *want to die now, Khaki, is that it? I just want you to be quiet.* On Wednesday, I tore through the air and into the trunk of a tree. Bark on my forehead. Branches slashed my cheek. I came to with Cedar's wet nose on my temple. He shook his head at me. Not his tail. Fiona pulled me to my feet. I felt the bruise forming. She was gone. I was on a residential street. The windows would light up. The people would emerge from their homes any minute. They'd see me, and what was wrong. Nothing. Good. No one but the dark.

*

Concealer, coffee, finals week. Cookies at Wendy's final exam, like we were in the third grade, and wouldn't that have been nicer than being all grown up and rapidly disintegrating? I chewed mine and spit it into my water bottle, not caring who saw. And if they did, if they understood, if we all took turns licking my teeth like windshield wipers, then eradicating every drop of spit that had mixed with the flour on my tongue, they'd also understand that I would never be able to stop. I threw up in my mouth, swallowed, had nothing but more vomit to wash it down with.

Halfway through the test, I laid my head on my desk. I plugged my fingers under my jaw and counted my pulse. Was Fiona's the same? *No, she is much more alive.* I sat up as straight as my spine would allow. A cramp stiffened and stalled my hand. I sagged like damp cotton candy. There was green scrap paper on which I was to show my work. I wrote down my numbers for the week. No other problems were worth solving.

"Ten more minutes," Wendy announced. Three of us were left at our desks.

I walked my near-blank exam to the front of the room and recycled my scraps. Or I did the opposite. I can't remember. I wasn't really there.

Cameron ran into me between Fred and Shaggy.

"You okay?"

I'd thought he was done asking me that. "No, Cameron. I feel like a landfill no matter what I do."

"You never get wasted and you sleep twelve hours a day. You'd feel better if you just ate something." He rubbed his eyes. "We missed you at lunch."

"One meal doesn't make a difference."

He pulled a rolled-up bag of Takis from his pocket. I couldn't tell when he was high anymore. We didn't talk anymore. He asked me to leave our room at random so Natalie could come over. Now he started walking faster.

"Where are we going?" I asked. He, he pointed out, was going to meet with a professor. "Bye?" I squeaked at his back.

In our room, I dumped the contents of my backpack on the floor. My eyes darted to the door handle every few seconds. How long had I been carrying that tomato around? I held it up to the light, like a gem with so many faces. My thumb depressed the edges of a patch of brown and white mold. How strong was my stomach? I took a bite. It tasted like a globe of snot. But it had been so exquisite before it broke down. I couldn't waste it. The rotten apples didn't crunch. The forgotten grapes weren't wine. I found bread and a jar of peanut butter underneath my pillow. I was going to shit myself, but I couldn't take the few steps to the bathroom until after the last bite.

I did what I had to. I ignored the bouts of blackened vision when my airway was completely obstructed. I focused on the word *surfeit*. What song was it from? It was on the tip on my tongue and Fiona was in a medically induced coma or under doctor's orders to rest or maybe no one was stopping her from picking up the phone.

I got back into bed. Cameron had taken the pictures of Jane down from his wall but there was one left, beneath his bedframe, in a corner on the floor. My wall was a shrine to people I'd spent hours with in stereo, spent hours inches away from, and had no desire to actually meet. Teenage Bottlerocket and Defeater and I couldn't remember when I'd last been to a show or when I had last tried calling Fiona. Eleanor didn't have any news. I fell asleep counting everything I had left to lose. I reduced myself like a fraction, reduced myself like a sauce set to simmer. I had a million words for it, none of which was starving.

In the morning, the bags of Cedar's things that I kept sealed in my desk were open. I stared, refusing to believe that the escaping smell hadn't transported me back to the real world. I panicked. I calmed; I could retrieve the air I'd swallowed. I shoved my fist down my throat. Only carbon dioxide came back out. I took a deep breath. It smelled like bile. No stale dog slobber. No masticated meat.

—

[19]Cameron got invited to a birthday party at one of Matty's friend's houses. He dragged me to the car. While I drove, he and Vera each texted Natalie something, which she then read aloud and guessed if it was a Crayola color or a strain of weed.

It was obvious upon our arrival that this was, more accurately, one of Matty's friend's parents' houses. We wandered into the garage, where some guys were playing Blink covers. Matty appeared, shaking a can of Red Bull but never pulling the tab open. I left and found the kitchen. The urge to take inventory almost overtook me. Strawberries sparkled on the counter, washed and still wet. I ate one. I pressed the ring of its leaves into a ball and swallowed them because I was incapable of asking where the trash can was.

I went into the living room and sat on a couch of confident white leather. One of the guys from Dudes Night struck up a conversation that flowed easily to a central question. Was that one Tim Barry solo song better than Avail's entire discography? My spirits slightly lifted. Just as we were reaching a conclusion, Vera plopped down in between us. She announced that she'd lost Natalie, whom she assumed was jerking Cameron off in the car.

"Do you want a sip of this?" Vera offered me her drink. "Girl, come on. Live a little. No? Whatever. Anyway . . ." She told me some half-formed theory, hers or someone else's, about how food was essential at all points in one's life. Sex, conversely, was firmly nonessential before a certain age. But after the first time, it seemed indispensable.

"What about kids whose parents don't let them eat sugar?" I asked. "They probably can't stop once they finally get to try it." I had accepted the terrible enduring taste in my mouth. Vera talked herself through a tangent. She, or a statistician, had surveyed people, asking: If forced to choose, would you give up food or sex? For the purposes of the hypothetical, one could, in this case, survive without food.

"If you choose food, can you have sex if there's an apocalypse?" the Dude wondered. "If you have to repopulate Earth to save mankind?"

"Humankind," we corrected.

Vera whispered to me, "Are you okay, by the way? You didn't eat at dinner. Natalie said Cameron said you have history with one of these randos. Should we use someone else here to make him jealous?" She started scrunching my hair.

"Yes, I'm okay, Vera. Can you mind your own business?" I had eaten a strawberry. What had the point of that been?

"Wow." She held tight to my hair. "Do you have any idea how hard I tried to be your friend? The only reason Cameron still keeps you around is because it's convenient to have a sober chauffeur."

"Let go of me." *Sober* didn't seem like the right word to describe me. Matty crossed the corner of my eye. I flew toward him and followed him down the hall.

"Matthew," I said, slipping into the bathroom behind him. The roots of his hair were coming in. I locked the door.

"My name is Madison," he grumbled.

I laughed. "What?"

"I gave up correcting you over text because I thought it was autocorrect. Remember when we met? I was introducing myself and you ran off like you were about to barf. You seemed tipsy or coked out or something, but I get it now. Loud and clear. How's that song you like go? *You're so hard you're brittle. You shatter easily.*"

"That's the nicest thing anyone's ever said to me." I smiled. He took a long time to sigh. It seemed to make its way up from his feet. I looked at the toilet. I finally had company, but one strawberry wasn't worth it. I closed the lid and sat down.

"Who else do you know at this party?" he asked.

"I don't. I have no idea why I'm here." *Madison, Madison, Madison.* "Madison?"

"Thank you. Yeah?"

"Do you want me to leave?"

He shook his head and turned off the lights. I pulled him down onto the tile and sat in his lap with my back to him. He said ocupado to the impatient knock on the other side of the door. I wanted to lick the insides of his arms, the strips of skin that never got tan. He'd gotten annoyed when I called plugs gauges. I'd done it every chance I got. What had he done to deserve that? I asked if I could tell him something.

"I know these other guys named Matty and I thought it meant something, but that's not even your name, but one of them is friends with this guy in that Portland band and I know you are too, and I know it's probably not the same guy, and even if it is—" I looked at his hands. I wanted, I wanted— I was not entitled to the affection of everyone I desired. It was not normal to wish death upon him as soon as he upset me. I could not invalidate, appropriate, or exterminate shittiness by hurling it back at a man. "I think I tried to hurt you the way someone else hurt me. Sorry."

"It's all good."

"But you could have been nicer to me too. Like not been so opposed to doing things together in public at first."

He spoke into my neck. “We both know that I asked you to get dinner and coffee and whatever all the time. You said you hated restaurants because you had to talk to the waiters and I said I could order for you and you said that was sexist. So yeah, I gave up on that too. And I invited you to Disney and you said it was stupid.”

“It is stupid.”

“Bro!”

“Okay, I see how that was maybe rude. Sorry! And I’m sorry for wasting your time. I shouldn’t be anything with anyone right now.”

“That really sucks about your friend.” He lifted me gently off him so he could get the lights. I shook out my leg, recuffed my jeans, and flushed the empty toilet. He went to the sink.

“I never made you do anything you didn’t want to do, right?” I asked. No response. Nothing written on his face. “Maddie?”

“I don’t know what to tell you.” He squirted soap into his hands and scrubbed.

“The truth.”

“I don’t know.” The ink barely bled.

“Oh.” I didn’t push for an answer. “Hey, why don’t you just tattoo those on?

“I might get around to it someday. Right now, I—I’m gonna go.”

That was it. I spent the next three and a half years staring at the backs of his hands at shows. It was always too dark to tell if he’d gone through with it. When I ended up shoved against him, I didn’t grab him and see if they smudged. We both just said hey and got on with our lives.

—

[20]I counted each step to the top floor of the library. I fit myself into a corner and stared at a spreadsheet. Cameron found me, sat down, and unpacked. He put a paper cup next to me. I closed my computer and tried to smell the flavor of the tea.

"You see this already?" He turned his screen toward me. The Bouncing Souls had announced the lineups for their annual end of year shows in Asbury Park.

DEC 27

The first night of Home for the Holidays 5 is December 27th, here's who is playing!!!:

The Bouncing Souls

Title Fight

White Wives

Blacktop Kids

DEC 28

The party continues, and in fact RAGES on Dec 28th:

The Bouncing Souls

The Explosion (reunion! OMFG!)

The Holy Mess

Luther

DEC 29

Just when you thought it couldn't get more exciting, the mosh pit opens up for HC on Dec 29th:

The Bouncing Souls

H20

Ensign
Up For Nothing

"Which one are we going to?" he asked. "Do you want to go to all three? I can get my parents to pay for me to fly out. I can even get a hotel if there's not room in your—"

"My mom is moving, remember? I can't actually go."

"Bummer. Well, would she be cool with us flying out together?" His socks didn't match; one of them was mine.

"I don't want to go, Cameron. Just drop it." I stopped him before he could apologize. I asked him if we were best friends.

He sang along every time he walked in on me listening to something. The only words he ever said were *Rise above, we're gonna rise above!* He made them fit every melody, or non-melody, as was often the case. He used to think "I Wanna Be Sedated" was called "I Want a Piece of David." He had a way of finding exactly what I was looking for in a pile of black clothes.

"More like sisters, Bub." He slumped down in his chair and spread his knees. "Have you ever heard of Raymond Carver?"

"I don't know." Carver? Was that a stage name? Was he a drummer?

"No one namedrops him in a song?" he asked.

"Maybe. I'm a little rusty." I looked at our legs, in case something had changed since the last time I compared them. I had habits to break.

"Well, I think you'd like his short stories."

"Why? Is he hot?"

"You bet. Total heartthrob. Multiple mental illnesses, untreated by choice, and no interpersonal communication skills. Great taste, though. Big Blacklisted fan."

"That's the reason," I said.

"What's the what?"

"That's why you're the only person I talk to. Because you aren't afraid to make fun of me. But please, tell me more about Ray."

"I'll just show you. Let me go grab one of his books."

"Cameron!" Someone shushed me from the other side of a shelf. "Please don't leave. I have to ask you something else."

"Shoot."

"If the first time you kissed someone, if she had gum in her mouth, and if you had her spit it out, you would throw it away right? You wouldn't hide it in your desk?"

"If I really liked her, I'd chew it."

We let our laughter loose, at low volume. He used his palm to trap the steam from the tea. After a sip, he handed it to me. There wasn't, he promised, any milk or sugar in it. I tried to drink it at the pace of a person with a normal relationship with food and drink.

"Do you think this is all worth it?" He gestured vaguely at the books and notebooks and computers. "Could we have just gotten library cards and assigned ourselves all this reading?"

"Maybe. I mean, I figured out what my problem is, so I know everything I need to. We can drop out whenever you're ready."

"What's your problem, Bub?"

"It's always like *Holy shit! A Ceremony fan! I guess I'll go pledge my undying love to him no questions asked.* And then it turns out that there are questions I should have asked."

"I'm glad I don't have to date them."

"That's very helpful, thank you."

"Speaking of dating, can you do me a favor and be a little nicer to Natalie for me?"

"That's a very good question."

"Can you try to be a little nicer to Natalie for me?"

"I can."

"Much appreciated. So, on the off chance that we don't drop out just yet, where should we study abroad when we're juniors?"

"You can choose. As long as it isn't too racist."

He buried his hands in his face. I told him it was okay. We had time to figure it out. We could do something else in the meantime. Maybe go start smoking cigarettes.

"No, not yet. My parents would disown me," he said. "Who'd pay for our gas?" Our families were so few days away. He asked if I was happy about it.

"I wouldn't mind never seeing anyone from my past again." I finished the tea. It was chamomile. I felt full, like I might start leaking. "I hate the idea of them seeing me and thinking I've changed. Like they know anything about me from looking at me. Like I'm supposed to stay the same. Like why did my high school yearbook have a superlative for Least Changed?"

"Did you want to win that one?"

"What do you think!" A vein in my leg twitched for lack of sodium.

"I don't know! That's why I asked. Sometimes I feel like I'm supposed to be able to read your mind. And when I can't you hate me for it."

He had no idea how much effort it took to make thoughts into words for someone else's consumption. I'd never tried to tell him. A cloud shifted. Unfamiliar light flared in through the windows. I narrowed my eyes when he did.

"I don't hate you. I just can't do anything anymore. We have to do the same things over and over again, just to undo them and redo them. And not fun things we choose for ourselves! Boring things no one would ever choose. How do you brush your teeth? Twice a day? How does anyone wash the dishes or make their bed or go to work or look at the grading rubric on a syllabus or call their parents or fold their clothes? I'm supposed to check my email for the rest of my life? That's insane. You can't tell me that isn't insane."

He accepted my head on his shoulder. I cried and let the world, or a few encyclopedias, see. When he asked what was wrong, I made his fingers a stress ball in mine. "You have to squeeze back," I told him. He did. He turned bright pink. *You can tell him, Khaki. I know. I will. I just need a little more time.*

My phone lit up. Fiona. Not Fiona. The dean of students needed to meet with me before I left for winter break.

*

The dean was long and reliable. A well-crafted candle—seemingly ornamental but essential in emergencies. I ignored his attempt at a handshake. "Thanks for coming," he said. "I know it's a busy time of year." The flame of his voice didn't rage, it flickered. I sat, as directed, on the couch opposite his standing desk. He closed the door and asked me how things were going.

I said, "It's a busy time of year." SITTING KILLS read a friendly reminder above his computer.

He nodded. "Tell me about it!"

My mind was silent. So this was what it took. I finally had what I'd wished for. I did not want what I'd wished for. I shifted in my seat and conjured noise, any noise. I rolled the stick of an imaginary lollipop between my fingers, imagined the candy clacking on the bone of my teeth. The sound slid across my tongue. Got sucked up from my throat. Smashed between my ears, where it became the puck bouncing off the perimeter of an air hockey table. I shook my head.

The dean was talking about pressure and hard work and the pictures of women in magazines. He shuffled in place in his homely shoes and said, "It's been brought to my attention that you might be struggling with disordered eating, or possibly something more serious. Possibly an eating disorder."

Possibly. Brought to his attention by whom? "Oh," I said. For all I'd built it up to be, my worst nightmare—accusation; exposure—was only a conversation. Not even. It was only his words, and I didn't have to give him mine in return.

"So you agree?"

"No." I tried to gauge how few syllables I could realistically utter. "I don't understand."

I didn't—understand why my nail polish chipped off in my throat in my favorite single-stall bathroom in the basement of a certain academic building every Monday afternoon—understand how to sate a desire that itself was the absence of wanting, or the epitome of it—understand why I wanted to want everything without needing anything, which was obviously impossible—understand how someone could have told him what they'd told him without my consent. Did he understand how it was going to feel when I shoved my foot down that someone's throat? Was it Wendy? Cameron wouldn't do that to me. The last time I'd seen Vera, she flagged me down as she was leaving a Fred dorm and told me to stop looking so "post-traumatic." Natalie could have been angling to free up the other side of Cameron's room.

"We have a wonderful team of specialists right here in town. They specialize in working with students in your situation. They or I can speak with your professors and ask them to give you special extensions on your assignments. Has this interfered with any of your final exams? The offer extends to next semester too. I can get you more time if that's what you need. Do you need more time? I imagine that in this situation it would be very hard to think critically. Do you agree? Your health and safety come first, of course. If you need to take a leave of absence—"

He could not be serious. If I wanted help, I would get help. "Whoever told you that has no idea what they're talking about. I have no idea what you're talking about," I said, and for the first time I heard the flatness everyone was always pointing out in my voice.

Frustration almost found a foothold on his face. He reset it to a friendly neutral and kept talking. His tenor fluctuated. "Self-esteem is tough. Even at my age. I get it. It's hard for guys too. Look, you don't have to tell me anything personal. What if you just tell me how you feel right now? What do you need? How can I help?"

I don't know if he believed those were the right words to say or if he was repeating what he'd learned from a slideshow in grad school or at a professional development retreat. I did not have low self-esteem. I had no particular desire to be looked at and yet I did not mind being seen as long as I was perceived correctly. No one perceived me correctly.

Something came unstuck from my subconscious. *Should I be more ashamed or embarrassed?* It rallied around my head. I couldn't remember where I'd heard it. If it had a tune, it was gone. Albums had come out, shows had gone on without me. But I could still find Fiona's hair in everything I owned. It might as well have sprouted from my scalp.

I had to say something to the dean, but what? *I always turn tea kettles off right before they whistle and stop microwaves before they beep. I stand around getting more and more nervous about not being able to stop them before the screech . . . Don't you also always take the stairs? . . . Do you ever chew water by the gallon? Do you know how long it takes, Bernard? Is anything a better virtue than patience? . . . I thought I'd made it to perfect before. But there's a new number, and I can wait. I'll even let you interrupt me before I go back to it . . .* Patience *is just another word for faith and God is a place I can wait, wait . . . Is there something, someone, you would do anything to protect—who you would call the cops on right before you closed your eyes and let them escape? Who you play dumb for, Bernard? If there's no one, if you have nothing, then I cannot make you understand . . . If I'm willing to die for something, someone, that doesn't mean I'm in love, it means I'm so overwhelmed that all I can do is give in . . . I tried to let noise suffocate me but it always let up. There are rests written into all the songs I've found so far . . . And why do you think you have to protect us? I'm not a hummingbird egg. I'm not sure you aren't just looking out for yourself, Bernard . . . I'm not sure you don't step on the worms that come out in the rain to get something to drink. I'm not sure if you realize that some of them are going to die anyway: the ones who can't stop drinking, who keep drinking, not knowing or caring how much they can hold . . . Did you know eating shrimp turns flamingos pink? Did you know that not everyone is like this? Apparently there's another way. I don't get it. I can't get there.*

I didn't say anything. A new word came unstuck in my head. *Corroboration* dripped down my chest. I didn't care who had reported me. They couldn't prove it and it wasn't a crime.

"Jasmine—Khaki, you're shaking."

"I'm angry," I said. If only every feeling were that easy. "I'm sorry," I said, though I wouldn't say what for. "Thank you so much, but I don't need any help right now." I got up.

"There will always be someone here for you, *Khaki*. Come back before you're ready. Please don't wait until you are." I got let go.

*

It was gold outside in December and it would never snow. I walked until I reached the dirt lot where I'd heard they were building a sixth college. Did Scooby have any heroes left or just rotating villains in masks? The possibilities were endless. Or this was the end.

I went back and submitted.

"Hi, Bernard. I need help now."

I answered his questions. He introduced me to more people like him. I answered their questions. They gave instructions; I followed. I passed tests, completed challenges, and moved on to the next. Time chipped away at their vigilance. They relaxed. They didn't see me relapse.

—

PART THREE

When the Angry Young Man is white, male [. . .] he is a cultural icon [. . .] cheated out of his rightful place in society. Can the Angry Young Man be black? Or a woman?

—Sharmila Sen, *Not Quite Not White: Losing and Finding Race in America*

WE'RE ALL CLOSE TO THE END

FEBRUARY 2022

21 In four weeks: Fiona. I keep my distance until then. I doubt she shares her life online. I'd rather wait for the real thing regardless. From what I understand, she and Eleanor exchange pleasantries twice a year or so. My mother left me a voicemail last night. I listened to it this morning. Have I decided on a gift for the shower? No. By the way, great news, Fiona's asked her to be the *grand-godmother.* As if that's a thing.

The museum is deserted. My hands soil the desk each time I touch it. It is massive and mahogany and I am so safe behind it. Patrick is the only guard working today. A vertical banner behind him announces the newest exhibits. He's trying to perfect a fantasy sports roster. Every few minutes, he yells two names at me.

"Who's going to have a better night?" he asks, tapping his phone screen.

"The first one."

I open my texts and archive incipient conversations with unsaved numbers from fruitless first dates. Fruit, olives, Fiona. I haven't made it past her letter's first page. If I never finish reading it, I never have to know if it gets worse. Hope is my favorite conspiracy theory. I retrieve the envelope from my bag and sit back in my seat. I'm perched oddly high, exposing too much of my torso to the empty lobby. The lever on the side of my chair sticks when I try to adjust it.

> *It hasn't been easy to leave you alone for so long, but I know you didn't need me anymore. You wanted me to learn to live, with or without you, mostly without. I know I can be overwhelming. I know I can be too much.*
>
> *Do you ever feel a jolt in your fingertips and an unpleasant itch in the back of your brain when something reminds you of us? That feels important: that it's unpleasant.*
>
> *I think we've endured enough of our own punishment. Don't you? I forgive you if you forgive me. I forgive myself if you forgive yourself. Promise.*
>
> *Eleanor told me you'd been sick. My heart broke. I'd rather not talk about it again. Let's pretend it never happened. Let's talk about something else . . .*
>
> *Flan! Isn't she perfect? I can tell she's going to outshine me. She is worth all the paperwork and plane rides and Amharic lessons I've been taking so I can teach her her language.*
>
> *Are you going to have babies? If you have to adopt, I can help you—it's not so hard if you*

know the little tricks. Imagine our daughters becoming best friends. We could be single mothers together. I could make sure we always had enough help.

Wouldn't it be funny if you had one that looked like me and I had one that looked like you?

I lick the cracked corners of my lips, fold the letter in on itself, and put it away. I think I still love Fiona. I can't say if I still like her. I scribble with a Jefferson pen on a Jefferson pad of paper. I don't have to respond to her letter. I can pretend I never received it. I can write my own and send it overnight. I'll have the first word.

Fee Fi Fo Fum Fiona,

I got Sam's invitation. You must realize I've been waiting a decade to hear from you. You must realize that it's very upsetting when the person you love most cuts you off. Was I just frostbite on your toe? Did I hurt to sever?

We barely spent four years together and it's taken me fifteen to understand the difference between you and us. I regret, very much, wasting my life on this. And yet sometimes my mind rewrites it all as rosy. It power washes the misery with a silt of perfect pink. I'm writing this down so I don't forget: There's you (miserable) and there's us (miserable) and there's me—without you (to be determined).

Speaking of you, this reminded me of the things you used to be so preoccupied with:

Joyce Burstein began the epitaph project in 1995 on a burial plot in Hollywood Forever, a historic cemetery in Los Angeles. The ongoing project comprises a traditional tombstone carved from slate, finished as a chalkboard, and accompanied by a bronze chalk box for the use of visitors. It exists in other iterations, including cemeteries, exhibitions, parks, and publications.

Maybe you want to come see it? There's not much room in my place but I could sleep on the floor and you and Flannery could have the bed. I guess she needs a crib? Can you rent one of those or . . . We could go visit LA and see the original. Does the baby mind flying? You've probably been out there already. How was the PCT?

If you're wondering what the visitors here write on the blank slate, it's uninspired ~~shit~~ stuff like THE END *and* YOLO *and* GONE FISHING. *There was one deeply earnest plea from a woman with cancer. And a slightly inaccurate rendition of an Eliot stanza.*

What would you have to say for yourself? ***AT LAST!***

Just kidding. You don't want to die anymore. Do you? I felt like dying when— I'm scared to see you. I'm scared to start feeling good. If we start again, we can never end.

How can I love you (I do love you), want to spend the rest of my life with you, and never want to see you again? That isn't rhetorical. I'm really hoping you can explain my feelings to me.

I rip the page from the pad, tear it into very small pieces, arrange them in stacks of four, and throw them away. I could bypass paper altogether. I could text her photos of a different exhibit. Grieving the Immortal: Post-Mortem Mourning Photography in 19th Century America. I've walked the room full of old photographs and daguerreotypes of dead children five times today. Many of them are in their mother's laps, dead of diphtheria or cholera or something that required antibiotics that did not yet exist. Most families couldn't afford portraits. They splurged.

Triplets who died in childbirth are lined up and swaddled in white, bearing an enormous resemblance enormous great northern beans. An eight-year-old boy slumps in a chair, as if after a particularly rousing game of tag. His eyes are closed. Would Fiona prefer a shot of him, or the girl, maybe twelve—curls pressed into her hair, Bible in her lifeless grip? She stares back at you. *Fiona, do you think this was an artistic choice or a quirk of her physiology*? The girl whose image hangs next to hers has fake pupils. Doe eyes painted on closed lids. An unnatural blush colors her cheeks. I have a soft spot for the teenager on his back, in his best shirt and trousers, on a thin blanket on a tidy bed. There's a smudge on the print from sloppy processing—or there's a gunshot wound in his forehead. So many dead white children in beautiful repose. They should work that line into the guided tour. Or I could finally give one. My manager asked me to cover for an absent docent last month. It could have opened doors for me, she said. She didn't want to see me stagnate.

I decide to check on Stuart. The last time I saw him, he was mid-conniption, veins bulging with passion. *What kind of celebration of preserving and honoring the dead doesn't include taxidermy? Frankly, they're embarrassing themselves. Prescient of me to cut my official ties with them. Any self-respecting thinker should be ashamed to associate with this joke of an institution.* His corduroy shirt was misbuttoned. It gathered awkwardly at his stomach. *I'm ashamed,* I'd reassured him. *Get out while you still can, kid.* He went back to making a mold of an otter skull. I tried to memorize his wrinkles in case he really was leaving. I wanted to tuck his greying hair behind his ears. When he dies, will the mortician do him justice?

His office is empty. I assume the worst, then dismiss the thought. The awful lights are on. He's just getting coffee. Or taking a shit. Probably both. I go into the workshop anyway. His desk is bare. Eartha the kit is gone, probably presiding over her purchaser's mantel. A drawer in his desk ekes open. I'm being recorded, but no one ever watches the silent footage. I pull the drawer toward me and push sharps and magnifying glasses aside. A stuffed mouse with cinnamon fur looks at me with four eyes. Two identical heads are crammed onto her neck. I look closer. The seams are sloppy. Who made this? Stuart is steadfastly antichimera. He doesn't believe in playing God. I remember his lavender-haired apprentice. I slip the mouse into the pocket of my cardigan and stroke the V at the bases of her—their—neck with my thumb. I don't assign a name. I wonder if Flan would like to have this as a toy.

—

[22]That night, I walk straight home. The bus and I broke up. The dull soreness in my legs is worst first thing in the morning, but it feels like company. I move the mouse—mice?—to my coat pocket and count the heads until I reach my building. *One, two, one, two.* My knees are worn-out rubber bands.

I bypass the mailbox. Upstairs, my records are mostly as I left them, jumbled around and beneath the bed. A few have newly slipped onto the lawless floor. It's okay. I know where everything is. *Less Talk, More Rock*? Next to my pillow, at the bottom of the tower with *Jane Doe* on top. *Full Collapse*? Bottom corner of the bed, all the way to the left, in the sleeve for *Clarity*. I'm not sure where *Clarity* is. It couldn't have gone far. My search doesn't last. I get distracted. There's so much at which to marvel. Transparent cyan (limited run), marbled marigold and orange wax, none of which can eclipse solid black. This is how I've spent all my free time since the night I reunited with Ian. With all of them. I have hundreds more hours of music to listen to, innumerable associations to trace and rabbit holes to go down. A bridge from 2001 recalls a chorus from 1995; I have heart palpitations until I've heard them back-to-back and can pinpoint where they diverge. A bassline reminds me of sitting smushed against Fiona in the back seat of her father's car on our way to the mall, her behind the driver's seat, talking about the difference between a symphony and an orchestra, me leaning to the left, the muscle down my side acclimated to the pose.

I can run on memories, I think. I'm sure my stomach growls. I don't hear it. The fridge just holds jam and pickles. I pretend I don't live within walking distance of at least three grocery stores with aggressively fresh produce from every hemisphere. It's January, yes, but it's summer somewhere. For the right price I can enjoy fat blueberries from Peru. No, I can't. I keep listening.

The malformed mouse looks nice next to the record player. She gets knocked to the ground when I shake the room—dancing, stomping, flailing around. But for the most part, I focus. I'm here to organize and evoke. To piece my life into a solved puzzle. To see if the soundtrack makes the story or the other way around. When my back starts to spasm, I lie down in the last open space on the floor. My eyes welcome the rest. There's so much to consider.

Of course, only music released before my last day of college is eligible. But can I include more than one song by the same artist? Yes, but only if the songs are either an iconic pair that appear in succession on a record and were always performed together live, or if the songs appeared on different albums and I place them at least eight songs away from each other. How to choose between different versions of the same: a half-illegible demo, an energetic but imperfect live cut, a technically better but emotionally blunted remaster? And am I attempting to capture the moments as I lived them or as I think of them now? From my perspective or someone else's? All to be determined.

There are certain lyrics I should struggle to sing. Instead, I allow myself pleasure. An album is ending. I put another on, and another, and there are so few hours of sunlight. I can't imagine anyone is keeping track of the days of the week. I unearth the iPod and an old USB cable from my closet; I'll need to fill in the gaps in my physical collection. It's Friday? I'm adrift in the agonizing honesty of a voice straining to sustain a note while keeping pace with a snare defying the laws of space and time. I cannot pry myself from the dexterity of a hand curled around a fret, a hand somewhere on a journey from self-taught to professional. And oh my god, the sounds that come from mouths. Defenseless dirges. Crackling threats. Disclosure. Articulation. Undaunted exposure. I renew my vows to this. I can't imagine why I ever broke them.

I lose a day turning a single album over and over. Repeat, repeat, repeat. Never, ever change. I'm dizzy, headachey, and declining. I supplement the sound with an order of a highly engineered, shelf-stable food product. My card doesn't decline at checkout. I am optimizing. I tell Georgia I'm going to visit my parents. I tell my parents Georgia and I are going camping off the grid up the coast. I stop brushing my teeth. My body insists on some basic functions, but I don't have to look in the bathroom mirror. Reflection is dangerous. Pathologizing lends itself to policing. So I pretend. A body? Don't have one. A scale? Haven't weighed myself in years.

I pay the premium for overnight shipping and storm the lobby when it arrives. The carrier blanches when I wordlessly take the box from her hands. The cardboard is open before I'm back at my door. *Khaki, if you start this again, it's going to be very difficult to stop. It's not worth it. Trust me, I already know!* The third-floor hallway is empty save for a few welcome mats and a sneaker waiting to be tripped over. I throw the scale down, next to a dead roach, on what looks like the most level part of the floor. On I go. I say I don't like this, know I don't want it, so why do I—I reenter my apartment, strip, and weigh myself again and again, the saddest call and response. At the very least, this particular sadness is simple. Streamlined. I really understand it now. It's singularity, not starving, that I thrive on. Thoughts tunneled; feelings filtered in avoidance of the emotional entropy for which I still feel unequipped. Fiona would be so disappointed.

Fiona would—I am not Fiona. My treatment was outpatient, never in-. Fiona wanted to die. I've always wanted to live. I don't want a career or a calendar crowded with events. Other people can start families. They can brighten each other's days. I don't want to change the world. I just want to learn how to eat without caring what it means. I tried. I swear I tried to restore myself. To function. The prescriptions I was given didn't make sense. They said my rigidity was a problem, then they tried to replace it with theirs. If I had to be ruled by rigidity, I preferred my own. And the forest. They always wanted to talk about the forest. I was too infatuated with the chloroplasts inside the leaves. A doctor once tried to make me literally embrace my reflection. I did it. I didn't scream *The opposite of hate isn't love, it's indifference!* I didn't get better. I don't even know what food is—how can I eat?

Food is finite. There's always a last bite. Every sinew of stretched mozzarella ends, and I live in fear of the last lick each time I lap at porcelain, always in private and eternally full of shame. It's ephemeral. The smell of oven-melted chocolate chips fades from front-of-mind to forgotten. Sometimes before the first bite. The sting of minced allium subsides, and the tears fall away in pitiful pools. I can't be the only one saddled with the agony of stillness each time my jaw ceases. It's eternal: the unlearning and relearning. I already changed once. That was enough. And Fiona doesn't want to talk about it—the way the things we put in our mouths leave our bodies one way or another—which, fine!—but we still take something tangible from them. How can I capture it? How can I not start a spreadsheet, formulate a plan? Music has to make its way inside again and again; but this is permanent—it can't leave my gut. It's practically inherent in me. I can do as I please. I can live like this. I just have to be very careful to remain hydrated. I just have to call out sick from work when I'm hungover after sober nights on which I eat too much or not enough, regret it, reverse it, feel myself returning to form. I can settle down with this. I have nothing but time now.

I cannot live like this for another minute. A record spins thirty-three rounds, but strength through wounding is bullshit and the masses of humanity don't always have to suffer. I will stop living like this as soon as I find the reason why I started living like this. But I've heard it said that the human brain isn't capable of reason when it comes to its own behavior, that we're only masters of rationalization after the fact. I've heard it said that you might never recover.

How does she feed herself, let alone her child? With the most amazing dinners and birthday cakes. She must feed Flan like she's the only person in the world. That little girl is probably smarter than me. She won't make my mistake of thinking Fiona is too. I fall asleep with intimations of sugar and wax on my tongue. I bolt out of bed to check that the envelopes are in my backpack. Blood stipples the postmarks. My hands are still healing from the olive jar glass. Sleep won't come back.

I hate Fiona. Wholly, for the first time. When I met her, her blond hair was dyed orange, like the dusk. For years, I thought that was how she was born. I still can't unlearn my first impression. When I look at her now, with a buttery ponytail swept high on her head, I stop myself from admiring how natural the illusion looks. Maybe no one who met Fiona after she got sick really knows her. It's possible that she was gone by then, or at the very least irredeemably different. Once I left her, I was too. Once, I wanted my existence to be infinitely bigger. Here I am, ten years later. All grown up and —— pounds down and up and down and up and *Khaki, you have to calm down. Go to her. Go get calmed down. She squeezed your hand as hard as she could when you needed pain and pressure to stop the panic in its tracks. She used her allowance to pay for a not insubstantial portion of your record collection when you wanted to make the switch from CDs and MP3s. She made a very funny face when she was about to sneeze. She could not stand glitter. She was terrible at loading the dishwasher and very good at painting your nails. She had no driver's license and a visceral hatred of people who used the left lane for anything other than passing. She made you improbably, impossibly, unsustainably happy and then simply very sad and you know perfectly well that she was only trying to protect you.*

I grab the mouse and try to behead her. I can't get a good grip. My hand bangs against the corner of the record player. The song skips and sounds, for a moment, like it's underwater. A half-formed scab reopens on my finger. I try to hurt something, someone else; I get damaged. I try to move on. I get pulled back because the thing about the past is that it has a past. Once you begin an exhumation it's hard to know when to stop digging.

—

PART FOUR

We find fulfillment in writing, recording, and performing music . . . Anything beyond that . . . it doesn't really have anything to do with us.

—Jim Adkins

Could you tell me how to grow—
or is it unconveyed—like Melody—or
Witchcraft?

I could not weigh myself—Myself—
My size felt small—to me—

—Emily Dickinson
Letter 261

A LONELY RAGE

JUST WEST OF NEW YORK CITY
DECEMBER 2007–AUGUST 2008

23 When I was a child, things happened to me with no regard for my desires. I went to school at a certain hour and obeyed teachers' whims. At home, I wasn't allowed to watch violent television or chew gum. My parents began treating each other like strangers and I was powerless to intervene.

My father had never been one for idle conversation, but in the months preceding my thirteenth year, he withdrew further into himself. His fidgeting resounded more than his rare utterances. When he wasn't at work, I joined him in listening to worn blues records in the living room. They warbled, rumbled. I narrowed my eyes at Eleanor when she interrupted. I put my feet up on the coffee table. She didn't harangue me. He didn't notice either of us. Then his breathing began to annoy me. Everything did. He'd say "on accident" instead of "by accident" and I'd want to evacuate my skin. He'd skip around albums or stop a song during the bridge. He'd pull out more of his hair. I remembered the disgusting way he and Eleanor used to kiss any time or place. Now they worked longer hours. After school, it was me and Cedar. He needed feeding, walking, brushing. I asked him questions he couldn't answer. At school, I said to my desk mate Charlie C., in passing, that I talked to my dog. The ridicule followed me to the playground. I passed the forty-minute recess with invisible ire.

My discontentment found a mate in my hormone fluctuations. Every day stretched me more sensitive and self-absorbed. I put myself to bed early. I maximized my opportunities to dream. I couldn't sleep. The walls didn't muffle my mother's pleas. *What do I do wrong? How can I fix it? Why aren't we enough?* She demanded to know how nothingness could have such a stronghold on someone who had everything. I almost understood. He didn't seem sad to me, he just seemed elsewhere. Eleanor rose her voice in vain. Cedar howled. Bugs trawled my skin. I turned on the lights and pulled back the blanket to scratch where I itched. My skin was bare. I preferred my parents' older arguments: my father reminding us that Cedar's forebears had a history of being tight with the police; my mother emphasizing that dogs did what they were trained to. They could help uphold oppressive systems or lead the blind or herd sheep. Cedar's primary directive, though unspoken, was to blunt the fact that I was an only child with asocial tendencies. He slept next to, but rarely in, my bed. If hate was a learned behavior, what was love?

There was a weekend morning, toward the end of all this, when my father roused himself. We were going, he announced, out. He held Eleanor's hand as he drove us to the base of a modest mountain. I doubted he could climb it. When we arrived, I ran ahead with Cedar. I wanted to measure the space between each evergreen needle. He wanted me to let him off his leash. At random, he'd spring onto his hind legs to lick my face. Instinct or learned behavior? We went where the land was most clotted with trees.

I realized my parents weren't trailing us. It took a long time to retrace our steps. Cedar came to a stop a hundred yards away from the clearing in which we'd left them. I clutched his leash until I began to purple. She was making her best effort to argue. Every few syllables, her hands cut the air. His eyes were on everything except her. She tore the glove from her hand, the ring from her finger. It fell between their feet. She started approaching us. I shivered, having forgotten I was visible. My father knelt to the damp earth and pocketed the metal. I'd been bleeding for five days each month. I'd just stopped growing. He struck me as small.

The next week, he left in a snowstorm. Overnight, the wind warmed everything. She and Cedar and I woke to tropical rain. A few weeks later, we moved from the West Coast to the other, where puberty continued to collapse and remake me.

*

Eleanor radiated heat in the last days of that December, hoping I'd humor her with the slightest enthusiasm for our new hometown, with its veritable selection of shops and restaurants and its art museum and the new library cards we'd soon possess. She believed there was such a thing as a cosmopolitan suburb. This was it—home to a beloved comedian/political commentator, *New Yorker* writers, the mind behind Dora the Explorer, the guy from *The Wire*, Kumar, Tony Soprano's therapist's office, and the family upon which *Cheaper by the Dozen* was based. This was the premiere destination for Park Slope couples starting families. Her hysterectomy scar had been healed for years.

At least six trees were in front of, behind, and towering over each quaint Tudor cottage and stately colonial and Georgian apartment block. We rented the top half of a duplex. It too was appropriately wooded, branches naked for the time being. Eleanor spent hours on capricious phone calls with various confidantes. I couldn't stand to listen, so Cedar and I left. We weren't used to snow that stuck and piled up on curbs. When a new layer fell, he became possessed. I wanted to let him free to roll around in it, to let him chase the squirrels he lusted after, let him ribbon their meat with his incisors and drink their blood at my feet—but a car might hit him when he dashed to the other side of the street. I suppose my mother felt some similar way about me.

When Cedar shat on the enormous front lawns of houses set hundreds of feet back from the manicured streets, I didn't pick it up. I usually turned a corner afterward, imagining what I'd do if confronted. Sidewalks were compulsory so that people of various ethnicities might jog, walk, and push strollers with ease. Eleanor hadn't befriended anyone local. Her phone calls dwindled. She—who could help a stranger touch up makeup in a movie theater bathroom, or find a new karaoke partner at the DMV—spent evenings with wine and old photo albums.

She'd hiccup reminisces at me while she pried laminated pages apart. *Look at how innocent we were. Hmm, there's a little blur around his fingers in this one. Couldn't keep still! I could have sworn he didn't start doing that until—* She flipped further backward. *Here's the night he proposed.* He did it during a game of Scrabble that progressed at the rate of one turn every twenty minutes—him pulling her away from the party she was hosting in their cramped apartment, her trusting him not to cheat when she wandered off to greet someone or strut to a song. He kept the board from getting jostled. Finally, everyone cleared out. She took off her too-tight bra at dawn and saw the declaration dangling from the row where she'd spelled out *moose. Marry me el.* A record rotated in the other room. He rescued a trampled daisy from the broken vase in the hallway and bent it into a ring.

He wasn't in the picture; he was the one who took it. Her hand on the board. *I never stopped loving him, you know. If I could have hated him, it would have made it easier to leave. I had to—for you.* That last part didn't seem true. I was fine. She'd been dressing entirely in white since we moved, mourning in her own way. Her wedding ring was back on her finger. *I shouldn't drag you into this. Sometimes I forget you're still a kid.* But my age wasn't the problem. There were qualities of mine that I knew were like his. Challenging. Frustrating. Baffling. I was careful to mask them, lest I break her heart too.

*

Only after it was done did Eleanor inform me that she'd enrolled me in the ninth grade instead of the eighth. I muted myself, accidentally, on my first day of high school. I was unsure which of the three double sets of bright blue doors to enter through. The columns abutting them seemed more for show than structural integrity. Keystones sat above the arched first-floor windows. There were three stories of brick. And that was only one of the buildings. And so I could not speak.

Rumor had it that seniors baptized freshmen in the brook. The hazy water ran, partially underground, between the two campus buildings. I soon saw that cliques existed but weren't so insular. Still, I could not speak. According to a hyperbolic Urban Dictionary entry written my sophomore year, this was "Probably the most unique high school in the country," where a fondness for weed and "big butts" promoted racial and social harmony on an open campus with security guards more interested in freestyle rapping than enforcing rules; thus things were "loose" and the students decided how little or how much to get out of their education, when they weren't inventing slang that would "end up coming out in rap songs five years later."

I watched and listened closely. The junior and senior proms were the only dances. Both were poorly attended. Neither crowned royalty. The school also lacked a valedictorian. Such contests were gauche, or they triggered too much competition among the overachievers. But no one was above dumb fun. Even Malik—with supposed ties to a gang one town over and an incontestable Napoleon complex—wasn't too cool to use his backpack to sled down the hill next to the freshman building.

My classmates were, and I would soon be, more arrogant than typical teenagers, due in part to being pampered by parents who thought themselves very hip or who had scarified too much to not give their children everything. Some of said parents might attempt to intimidate or charm teachers and school administrators when their children's grades or class schedules "needed" adjusting. These were very progressive people. They could've chosen private schools—or at least charters—but didn't, partially on principle, partially because they paid very high taxes to buoy public institutions. Resources were abundant, and not. If you lived in the rich zip code, you could ride a school bus. If you lived in the other one, you could ride a public bus.

I intended to go unnoticed by all two thousand of my peers. But there are always questions for the student who appears midyear. I said my name and where I was from. When I wanted to say more, I couldn't. They lost interest. I touched my mouth when they turned away. My neck was intact. My lungs inflated when I inhaled. My speech returned at home. By week two, I was at peace with my affliction. I'd never gone out of my way to make friends. I'd always dreaded repeating myself when someone couldn't hear what I'd said, and one could never hear what I'd said.

Between classes, everyone erupted into laughing and shoving and handholding. I vowed I would not say something just for the sake of saying something. Some teachers gave me the benefit of the doubt. Some thought I was stupid. Meanwhile, Trevor was asking Miss Gilchrist if her pants were a mirror because he could see himself in them. I read aloud if she asked me to; I didn't know why she cared that I never volunteered. We broke into small groups for projects. I did the work and let others present it.

History was worth more of an effort, perhaps because the person teaching it was both black and a man. I didn't want to be responsible for another grey hair cropping up in his waist-length locs. He assigned Howard Zinn, kept our desks arranged in a circle, let us sit on the floor if we wanted, and went by his last name, Shaw, with no *Mr.* tacked on. It was too like *master*. I nodded whenever he, or anyone, asked if I was okay. He was the first one to believe me. I stayed after school to help a few other volunteers update the white butcher paper he hung in his classroom windows. He was keeping track, with hand-painted numbers, of the casualties of the wars in Iraq and Afghanistan. Civilians and combatants. Both sides. Each digit was as tall as me. The count passed 100,000. I tallied the words I capitulated each day. How low could I go? Fifty? Twenty-two? Ten! My project was shallow in comparison, but I couldn't stop.

Every time my Spanish class split into discussion groups, I got appended to the same gaggle of girls. They neither invited me into nor excluded me from their deliberations, all of which were conducted in English. Was it still slutty to wear leggings as pants? Was it slutty to give head when you felt like it? I was deeply jealous of their extracurriculars, exaggerated though they probably were. I could try to mimic my way into their good graces. But I was uninspired. They mostly bored me. Then they brought up Fiona. She'd been in the hospital so long that she might get held back.

"I heard it was cancer."

"I don't feel bad for her."

Two of the girls, both named Alison, recited a story. Three years ago, Fiona stopped getting invited to sleepovers because of the time she wanted something—*What was it again?—Who cares?—Too stupid to even remember*—and her host told her no. Fiona grabbed a zester from the kitchen counter in retaliation and took five swipes at her host's skin.

"She's crazy!"

"At least like use a knife?"

Alison dropped any pretense of discretion and said, "Maybe the new girl will like her." She didn't have the decency to look at me and see how it landed.

"Tengo que orinar," I said to no one. I rushed to the bathroom and locked myself in the stall farthest from the door. I leaned against and away from the graffitied wall until I was gently bashing myself into it. My pulse slowed as I tried to imagine Fiona. If what she did to that girl had even hurt. Probably not. I thought it was sort of funny. *Zest* called to mind a snappy clown. If she did it to me, I could take it. I had a sudden urge to punch and be punched. Maybe Fiona would punch me in the face if I asked her nicely. I had to find her.

I started straining during attendance in case I'd missed something. No, she wasn't supposed to be there. And yet she was missing. The school really was loose. We were allowed to leave campus during lunch, or whenever. I walked home most days to visit Cedar. I never ran into her on the way.

*

A few weeks later, a lunch-hour storm forced me into the school library. Every seat was taken. I waited out a girl with red hair. She seemed on the verge of leaving—the library, and something else. She had a jaw you could cut ribbon on, which was likely how she'd severed the lilac one wrapped around her ponytail. The scrapes escaping the sleeves of her sweater seemed to contradict the ditsy flowers on her yellow dress. I got whiplash trying to get a better look. She glanced over her shoulder. I gasped. Red rimmed, her eyes hemmed in tears. She was scraggy. Rundown. Each part of her threatened to float off in a different direction. Then she was gone.

I took the chair she'd left empty and cold. Maybe I'd seen a ghost. My shoe caught on something. I picked up the paper caught under the chair leg. A months-old lab report. *Fiona Davies*. Her data was flawless, her analysis thin. She'd gotten a B–.

To think now that the first time I saw her she hadn't been crying at all, that her eyes may have been wet because she'd just thrown up or been unable to throw up. But in that moment, I read her melancholy as revolution. My father had suffered in silence. His unhappiness forced him into exile. Fiona was sadness incarnate in a very public package and seemed to be doing just fine.

To think now that my mother thought she could keep woe away from me. She'd raised me to be wary of becoming the Angry Black anything. With that off the table, little else appealed. I pined for all sorts of destruction, all of it out of the question. Not for Eleanor's reasons. I had my own: violence demanded intimacy with something outside myself. I couldn't have anger, so sadness had to suffice.

—

[24]Every day at lunch and after school, I sat in Fiona's library seat. In March, she resurfaced. She settled at an empty table in a far corner of the room. I waited three minutes, then sat diagonally across from her. I tried not to leer. I opened and pretended to read *The Silent Twins*, a true story in stout paperback that I'd found at a used bookstore and already finished three times: June and Jennifer Gibbons, born 1963, were black and they were Welsh and they were twins and they spoke only to each other in a language only they knew. They left school early every afternoon. They spied on boys and set

fires that the police assumed they weren't capable of igniting. They sang. They wrote stories and plays about different, if not better, worlds. They were institutionalized. Medicated. The stories stopped. And the songs. June and Jennifer, Jennifer and June, swore that if one of them died, only then would the other finally speak. Jennifer went shortly thereafter. The autopsy revealed no drugs or poison. *Sudden inflammation of the heart.*

I looked up. Fiona was blatantly reading the back cover of my book. I moved my hands so she might see more clearly.

"What's your name?" she whispered.

Her russet eyes matched her dark orange hair, and she would not stop blinking. I did not know Morse code. I opened my mouth. To my horror, my voice was unavailable. I brought my finger to my lips.

"We can talk," she said. I shook my head. She cocked hers before disappearing into an aisle of books. *Khaki, if you don't get up right now and follow her and say something to her—* I banged my knee on the underside of the table. She came back and dropped an enormous book in front of me. *DSM IV.* In the seat next to me, she turned the pages. When she found what she was looking for, she touched my arm. I followed her fingertip as she underlined *Selective mutism* and the words beneath it.

1. *Consistent failure to speak in specific social situations (in which there is an expectation for speaking, e.g., at school) despite speaking in other situations.*

"Is that like you?" I nodded. We repeated the process for the next three items on the list.

2. *The disturbance interferes with educational or occupational achievement or with social communication.*
3. *The duration of the disturbance is at least 1 month (not limited to the first month of school).*
4. *The failure to speak is not due to a lack of knowledge of, or comfort with, the spoken language required in the social situation.*

She evaluated me with unbelievable authority and nonchalance. And then we reached the end:

5. *The disturbance is not better accounted for by a Communication Disorder (e.g., stuttering) and does not occur exclusively during a Pervasive Developmental Disorder, Schizophrenia, or other Psychotic Disorder.*

"I'm not a psycho," I said. Those were my first words.

"If you say so. But I'd still be your friend if you were."

I waited for her to elaborate but she let us steep in the stillness. She was content to soak until pruned. She turned to the entry on personality disorders. I tried to focus on Jennifer and June's diaries, which contained many descriptions of their vitriolic attempts at destroying each other. Fiona checked the time and sighed. I watched her pack her things. I wished she'd bring me with her.

*

The next day, the library was without her. I counted the windowpanes and considered throwing myself through the glass. I thought better of it. I didn't want to make a scene. The remainder of the day was excruciating. After the last bell, I waited to cross the street. At least Cedar could be counted on for company. I took a step, and someone grabbed me.

I withdrew my knuckles from Fiona's and shielded my nose. The scabbed-over marks on her hand didn't faze me. It was the blooming white-flowered trees diffusing the scent of fish. She copied my movement without mocking. I glanced around to catch the rest of the ninth grade watching its resident freaks coalesce.

Fiona asked if "they" were gaslighting me too.

I wound a strand of my hair around itself and made an ambiguous gesture of the head.

"I'm not a psychopath either, by the way," she assured me. "And not all psychopaths are dangerous anyway. I just have a lot of doctor appointments."

"Do you really have cancer?"

She asked if I could keep a secret.

I got closer to her and gave her a part of myself as collateral. I told her I couldn't deal with new people, present company excluded. She told me she was afraid of food. Her admission was outlandish, each word punctuated with a blink. My face stayed neutral.

"It's irrational," Fiona said. "Like triskaidekaphobia, if you've heard of it."

"Afraid of food?"

"I suppose I'm just afraid of eating it," she clarified. "Well, no, that's not quite it—it's what happens afterward."

Which was to say she was afraid of snacks and the mundane and making decisions, of chewing and tasting and birthdays, of choking and weddings and taking basic care of herself and funerals and burning her tongue. Of comfort and indulgence and guilt and holidays and disgust and home. Which was to say that she had to reckon with evil at least three times a day, though I understood none of that then.

I held her gaze to keep from inspecting her body. "That sucks. You know what else sucks? We don't have any classes together." I didn't care how eager I sounded.

"Conspiracy."

"Gaslighting."

We could laugh, we didn't need to smile.

"See you at lunch tomorrow? Don't be late. I have to leave early to go to the nurse."

"Khaki," I said.

"What?"

"That's my name."

"That's funny."

"I know."

"Fiona."

"I know who you are." She didn't ask how, but she looked both ways before crossing the street. That left me sweating and reeling, watching her return to wherever she came from. Her only visible muscles were in her calves. Chicken breasts straining to escape their cellophane wrappers. I averted my eyes, afraid to stare at the sun.

*

We reinvented our lunch hour. It wasn't like she could eat. One day we guessed, in unread bets on secret scraps of paper, how long it would take everyone to forget we existed. We were a specter and a shade. Or we were witches. We cast spells on each other, and curses were blessings. I wished to be different and feel normal at once. She made it come true. Fiona was not sadness incarnate. She tickled me pink, rained cheer down on me, twisted me giddy, made me want to skip through the streets.

We outgrew the library and claimed a spot in a paved, tree-lined alley a few blocks from school. She would try to braid my hair during the few minutes it took me to finish the uninvolved lunches Eleanor packed me. I didn't bother with Fiona's hair, which was too fine to grip and unraveled as soon as I wove it into anything of note. Her whiteness, which I still tried not to look at for fear of being blinded, was dappled with primary colors. Sickly biological yellows, blues, and reds. When I got a little bruised, I was glad the brown blended in.

"I tried to make myself throw up once," I said. "Before we met." I'd forgotten until that moment. She yanked my hair and stabilized my head before I choked on my sandwich.

She sliced the last letter from my last name, made me something that could scare her. "Olive, swear to me right now that you will never do that again."

That was the first sliver of anger I unearthed from her. "I swear to you that I will never do that again."

I knew I couldn't ask the same of her. She'd already told me everything. Her illness had become serious three years prior. Treatment came at the end of the previous summer. My arrival coincided with the tail end of the bad, and enough of the good, that, for a time, she would credit me with helping cure her.

When she was done poorly doing my hair, we sat side by side to minimize the distance our voices had to travel. I'd stored up so much speech it came out in probing, thoughtless projectiles.

"Is it the number zero that you're chasing after?" I asked. Fiona was lucidity and lunacy. The perfect puzzle. I needed to believe she had rhyme and reason.

"The concept of zero is part of it, but there's more. Zero pounds. Zero everything. Zero me. Even bones are going to weigh too much eventually." Her logic was inscrutable.

"If it's a lost cause, then why not just stop trying?"

"It seems to happen to me, not because of me."

"Well, I think it should stop soon. You seem close enough to zero," I said. The numbers we wanted for her moved in opposite ways.

"No, I'm very far away."

Before I met her, she spent the end of each lunch period with a meal replacement shake in the nurse's office, then tried to compensate with calf raises on the sidewalk around the corner. She bounced up and down, balanced a lit stick of tobacco between her lips, and inhaled the smoke for dessert. Now we walked a few blocks so she could buy me a slice of pizza. I asked her to take the first bite. She tapped off the grease like cigarette ash and set it back down. I ate it in four bites, grabbed a napkin, and erased every trace so that she might hold my hand on the way back to school.

*

Eleanor took it in stride when I informed her that I'd never again walk Cedar with her. I would do it with Fiona. The three of us stuck to alleys and side streets. Tree trunks cushioned our conversations. Fiona rattled off plant nomenclature with a fat grin on her face. She approved of Cedar's name, obsessed as she was with wilderness and survival skills. *Just in case!* The Bradford pear tree, she informed me, was behind the piscine scent overtaking the school grounds.

We traversed the six square miles of town. We liked to hide things. I lifted mascara from the drugstore while she kept disapproving watch. She'd offered first to pay for it, and when I refused, offered to take the fall if we got caught. Loyalty was loyalty. Secrets were secrets. Like how appeasing her doctors was starting to take its toll. After the horror of being discovered and exposed had worn off, exhaustion overtook her. But she wanted to do the right thing. I nodded like I knew what she was going through. But I'd broadcasted my issues. She turned that around and made us the same again.

"I know you not talking at school wasn't a secret, but your mom didn't know. Or your dog. I was hiding from everyone, but you were just lying to the people that matter."

I laughed and scraped an imaginary bug off my neck. I thought her blinking would help shoo it away. But that was not for me. It was to help her stay awake. She had to turn the world on and off to stay in it. I shook the makeup out of my sleeve and placed it back on the shelf. Outside, we reunited with Cedar. I untied his leash from a parking meter. He panted with separation anxiety. I kissed between his ears before we started walking.

On the next block, she lamented, "Even my eyelashes look fat." Then she laughed a dry sound, like flint waiting to ignite. In her therapy session the day before, she'd been reluctant to be introspective. She fretted to me afterward in a text: *How do you know what you'll find? Or if you'll like it?* She would answer the professionals' questions, and mine, but not ask herself any. She always thanked me for staying calm in the face of her confessions. My placidity sprang eternal. But that one made me doubt what we were doing. Introspection seemed important. If Fiona couldn't do that, we should go our separate ways. But the courage behind her confessions made her impossible to abandon.

I clenched my fist as Cedar strained toward invisible prey. Between the two of them, they could smell everything. I often wondered how she even made it through the day.

"I already hate myself to the extent I have to make a daily list of reasons that I deserve or want to live. Pathetic, I know." She pinched my arm. "I don't generally tell people when they make the list, because they don't know how to take the news. You made it."

We were stopped at a red light the first time I told her I loved her. I didn't care who heard. She traced a loop around her wrist. "Are you sure," she asked, "you don't want to change your mind?" As if I had a choice. The next ten lights were green when we reached them, and when she got tired of walking we settled on the edge of someone's lawn. Cedar sat between us. The sun shone off his teeth.

"He and Eleanor made the list too," she said.

When Eleanor had suggested I invite my only friend over for dinner, I'd contemplated telling her that Fiona was on a diet or had life-and-death allergies. For some reason, I told the truth. My mother promised to never say anything to the effect of *Somebody needs to get that baby a sandwich.* Afterward, I texted Fiona, immediately, in a panic. I had unkept a secret.

"It's okay that you told her," she now reassured me. "It was going to come up eventually. I just don't want more people to feel like they have to worry about me."

"It's hard not to," I said, stabbing at the grass.

"I don't do it on purpose," she snapped at me—the first time since my vomiting confession.

That wasn't what I meant, but I didn't need to correct her or apologize. We were volatile in a way I mistook for normal, as if the same thing would happen to any two people trying to converge. As if that were a thing other people were trying to do.

"I think my mom is more annoyed than worried," she said. "We hate each other, but I can't remember who started it. Why must Lena always tell me the sound of my voice annoys her? Or that she loves me, but she doesn't like me? Sometimes I wish we could take back all the things we've said to each other. That might make everything else easier."

"I don't know what I would do if my mom didn't love me. Or if Cedar didn't." I raked the fur on his back as he stood up. "No offense."

"Don't bother being sorry about me and my mother."

She jumped up when Cedar lifted his leg to pee. A cigarette appeared between her lips as he finished. She leaned into the flame, motioning with her free hand for us to go ahead. We did. I prayed for her to yell it—*Olive, wait, I love you too.*

*

Fiona's house was enormous, full of things but uncluttered, and lacking her parents more often than not. I couldn't grasp the difference between the study and the den, the guest room and the spare bedroom, the main oven and the convection oven. She baked brownies whose batter I was not allowed to mix or pour. The week before, it had been apricot-filled crepes.

Rosemary scones soon after. Pecan pie when I told her it was my father's favorite.

I loved watching Fiona's parents, plural, when they did materialize, because I just had the one in my immediate vicinity. Mr. and Mrs. Davies moved around each other from opposite ends of any given room, like they were misremembering an old dance. *What was it like before we had this child?* They hid their fatigue from me at first, perhaps to stave off mine. They kept cheery track of the pounds of flour and perfect prisms of European butter that always needed replacing. They keyed merry shopping lists into their BlackBerries before descending upon the liquor cabinet, the wine cooler, the spirit cart, to unwind. Fiona and I weren't interested in their stashes. She instilled it in me that, like an alcoholic, someone with an eating disorder isn't ever really better. In that case, I could never accuse her of failing. She could never let me down. Another lesson: an anorexic, *anorectic* technically, could be bulimic—and Fiona was—but a bulimic could not be anorexic. It was like squares and rectangles.

At times, our noses would point up the stairs, toward the airborne splinters of her parents' bickering. We discovered that her mother loved her father more than she loved Fiona. It was okay, Fiona assured me, because her father loved her more than he loved her mother.

We tired of them and returned to our places in the kitchen. I asked how she was doing.

"Better. But backsliding is a constant temptation. It's an always debate. Like suicide. I've gotten too comfortable with the ideas."

"You won't get to a point where nothing's worth living for."

What gave me the confidence to make that proclamation? I didn't know. My gut just said I would always have her.

"You can only live for other people for so long," she said, maintaining a measured distance between the brownie batter and her skin.

I was given a spoon to lick, but only once she was sure it wouldn't drip during the handoff. Sugar sanded my gums. I'd long ceased caring about my weight. With Fiona it didn't matter to me; and she cared only about hers. She called me perfect, my shoulder a good one to literally lean on. She would knead it and make me promise I wouldn't start plucking my eyebrows or straightening my hair. But I wanted to do those things. I wanted to do the things that might garner a boyfriend. She'd never broached the subject of romance. I certainly wasn't going to.

"If living for other people is the only way to buy enough time to find your own reasons, then who cares?"

"I can't live my whole life trying not to hurt someone."

The frosting came together. Powdered sugar loitered on her cheeks before she wiped away the white freckles. She set the bowl in the fridge. She held her measuring spoons upside down when she scrubbed them in the sink, so that the divots wouldn't fill with water and splash her face.

"Aren't you someone?"

"Who knows. There are so many debates going on in my head, constantly."

"That's good. It's good to think, I think?"

She put the square glass dish in the oven and slammed the door. "It's so strange that I can be honest with you. With everyone else I have to force things out like I'm punching myself in the stomach, like it's—"

"Puke," I said.

She set the timer and knelt to peer into the oven. "But I think it's okay to be silent sometimes. I think it means more."

We went to the wood-paneled basement. She wanted to watch *Gone with the Wind* on VHS for the fifth time. I rewound one of the two tapes to a random scene: Scarlett was unconscious. Rhett was carrying her up the stairs. We sat on the brocade couch without speaking until I announced that I'd never fainted. It seemed, I said, like it might feel calming.

"It just hurts," Fiona snapped. This was my third strike. "It's just your physicality failing. I could crack my skull open. What if no one found me? It just feels like I'm a weak, helpless female." She seethed and she softened. "Which if I'm being honest, I suppose I am."

"I meant that I wouldn't mind if my body could manifest my emotions. Then I wouldn't have to explain them."

"Well, that's okay," she said. "That I understand." It looked like she wanted to ask me something, but she went back to talking about herself. She knew it drained me to be within striking distance of the center of attention. I knew I was the only person willing to listen to her who wasn't charging her parents by the hour. So I kept asking and she kept answering because that was what friends did.

The timer sounded upstairs. "Wait, you've really never binged?" I asked, but she'd already climbed to the kitchen. Her cat had woken from a nap and was parading her butt in the air. Her orange fur was two shades lighter than Fiona's hair. The tag on her collar said MERRICAT, but Fiona called her Mary Katherine. She did not like me, though she liked to get her claws stuck in my hair. She hissed and went back to sleep.

Fiona came back and placed nine perfect squares in front of me. She hadn't had a crumb. She'd forgotten about or decided against the frosting. She pressed play. I grabbed the center brownie. They were underdone on purpose. I ate without thinking until Mammy appeared on the screen.

I migrated away from Fiona. She asked what was wrong.

"Why do you like this movie so much?"

"I don't like it, exactly. In the place Lena sent me to, this and *Air Bud 2* were the only movies in the rec room. So I suppose that by association Scarlett helps me remember how to take care of myself."

"Right." I finished the ninth brownie while the credits rolled. I'd soon learn she liked all old movies. She found meaning in seeing what one could accomplish under the constraints of rudimentary technology; next thing she'd have a thing for Oulipo.

The next time I came over, I took one meditative bite of shortbread. Three weeks later I crammed cupcakes down. A lemon square. Cinnamon rolls, a pint of rice pudding. She never commented on what I did or didn't consume. She just grabbed hold of anything leftover and scraped it into the trash. Then her head returned to my shoulder. It all evened out. We were steady. Fiona wasn't gaining anything, but she was maintaining the progress she'd made. She wasn't cured, but she was close enough.

*

I was not always calm. I clenched my jaw in the middle of art class to keep from falling to pieces when I read her latest text.

I have this sharp ache in my chest. It's unbearable.
Idk what's making it.

On my front porch the night before, she'd promised me *I don't not eat. I mean, I do eat.* Duh. Otherwise she'd be dead. *Just not as much. And I can't always keep it down. It's not so bad, though. You don't need to be scared for me.* It must have been the hundreds of thousand of sips of coffee keeping her alive. Stray ounces of dairy. The full-fat kind. The brain needs fat to function. She'd told me that.

After that text, I didn't see or hear from her. It took until the next morning to get a real answer about what was happening. It was folded into a note covered in letters barely big enough to read. She tucked the paper into my fingers in the minutes between classes. The blood vessels in her eyes flared like the veins in a leaf. Red maple.

Olive, I was sick in the second-floor bathroom.
Something inside of me might have burst. I'm
disgusting. If I go home my mom will ask why
and if I tell her the truth she will bring me to the
hospital. But I can't stay in the bathroom. I came
back to class. I wish you were here. Everyone is
being too loud and I'm going to get some water or
maybe I might faint, which would be

I connected our initials, F—K, on the lid of the box I keep her letters in now, not meaning to be vulgar but trying to remember how it felt to be anchored to someone, how the fact of the anchor was more important than the fact that the ship was leaking.

For every false alarm, something—me? Not me—kept her in the world. I learned to live with her ups and downs as if they were the seasons. Spring would soon be summer. She was still there, and imperceptibly stronger. My heart skittered the first time the humidity tipped to one hundred percent and ripped open the clouds on an otherwise sunny day. The rain came in sheets, with halts of fleeting thunder. We ran in the water, walked on it, because she was in remission and that was a miracle. I never asked why she got sick in the first place. I waited for her to tell me. Then we never spoke of it again. With that, I thought, I knew everything about her.

—

[25]We did normal things too. At the mall on a Sunday, I watched her scour racks of new clothing for anything she could pass off as vintage. She pressed a floral skirt against her thighs, gave up and asked where I wanted to go. I led us to the store that sold CDs and DVDs. She let go of my hand to roam each aisle. It was clearly meant as exercise. It wasn't worth asking her to stop. I read alien names in Rock backward from Z to A. *The Who. U2. Radiohead. Motörhead. Jane's Addiction. Fleetwood Mac. Blur. Bad Religion.* Fiona's belief in God was the only thing I disliked about her. Bad Religion had at least six albums. That seemed like a testament to talent. I picked one with a text-only cover. Stocky letters, clashing paintball colors.

Fiona was near the checkout counter. I joined her. Her face

labored to refrain from passing judgment on the jewel case in my hand. She snatched it into hers.

"What is this?"

"I don't know. I thought it looked cool."

I handed her all my cash and stood slightly behind her. She made small talk with the cashier while he rang us up. I looked across the hall. When she asked where I wanted to go next, I pointed at Hot Topic.

"I'm not going in there," she scoffed, tapping her foot.

"I can go by myself."

We realized, at the same time, that I was out of money. She handed me some of hers. "I'll wait for you in the food court." I wasn't sure she needed another espresso shock. It wasn't worth asking her to stop.

I crossed the store's threshold alone. The employees' pierced faces and generously lined eyes made them less foreboding than cleaner-cut strangers. My jaw relaxed. My fingers unwound. My blood was at ease. A black tutu hung from a velvet hanger on the wall behind the register. I browsed until something struck me: a bleach kit and a jar of green dye. I picked up one of each, which was enough for only a small section of my hair. I didn't have the resolve to commit completely. I didn't want to spend all Fiona's money.

In line, I folded and unfolded the bills. Soon it would be my turn. I would say hello, place my merchandise on the counter, place the cash in the cashier's hand (*you aren't too good to touch a cashier,* my father had warned me), say thank you, take my change, and place my receipt in the bag (*in case they accuse you of stealing,* my father had warned me). When the time came, I enacted the steps. At the last second, I placed a twenty-pack of black rubber bracelets on the counter. I would wear them all at once. A cast without an injury.

The escalator took an eon to return to me to Fiona. She motioned for me to reveal what I'd done.

The mouth of the black plastic bag was puckered closed with red yarn. I didn't want to show her the contents. I handed her the change. She waved it away and pried the bag open.

"Manic Panic? I suppose that's clever."

"Will you help me dye my hair?"

"I'll do anything for you."

She asked if I wanted anything else before we went home. I shook my head. She called her father to retrieve us, then insisted on carrying my bags to the car.

*

It was only when I was alone that I could listen to the CD. Well, Cedar was there. The triangles of his ears promised to have compassion. *B-A-D-R-E-L-I-G-I-O-N-N-O-C-O-N-T-R-O-L.* I traced the letters without expectations. The crack of the case snapping open was a small, satisfying violence. The disc swirled in my stereo. The first song made me want to punch someone in the head. Or take the blow myself. A broken bone, an altered framework; all I wanted was to never be the same again. Never mind that I had never been on either end of a fist.

I sat on my bed, afraid and impressed. Each song flew by, somehow nimble beneath the heft of its lyrics. Struggling toward subjective notions of sanity. These were the things Fiona and I talked about. This had more force than her. It was wiser about the world, about the pitfalls of tenure and accretion. I wrote down the words I didn't recognize. I'd look them up later. Later came after just twenty-six minutes.

I started the CD again, lay on my back, and tried to match its animus. I'd found something anyone could have but no one else wanted. Cedar draped himself across me like a championship belt. He twitched his tail. He understood the urgency, by dint of the intensity of a single molecule of scent, the overwhelming thrill and umami of chicken bones stolen from the trash, of the crushing relief of a loved one's daily return, of private feelings that threatened to escape your chest. Head over heels; nose over tail. We listened twice more, then danced down to the kitchen. Eleanor was unpacking the last of our boxes. The tape peeled away with a pleasant screech.

Her laptop sat on a white desk in the corner. The window above it overlooked the driveway we shared with our neighbors. I asked her permission to use the computer. I typed *punk* into a search engine. The results were archaic. *Current punk news,* I tried. I clicked on something. It hypnotized me: a website without a message board. But anyone could register an account to comment on the hastily reported stories, the concert—no, for some reason, the correct word was *show*—and album reviews. Not just albums, I learned. EPs. Split seven-inches.

I was, at first, very permeable to the opinions of others. Inevitably, eventually, I thought my knowledge would match theirs. We would be equal, but they would always be opposite to me because Bad Brains, Los Crudos, Poly Styrene, minor list of other minorities aside, it seemed nothing was whiter, more male than this. It didn't occur to me to care. I was listening to them, not looking at them, not trying to be them. I wanted to show my father the beautiful thing I'd discovered but was unsure how to tell someone who'd known since I was in utero that in twenty-six and a half minutes I'd changed and would keep changing. I was fumbling with the drape of my skin, turning it inside out, turning toward a truer self, stumbling through the motions.

I convinced Eleanor to take me back to Hot Topic and made her wait for me outside. I craned at the T-shirt wall. *Linkin Park. Pink Floyd. Gorillaz. Jimi Hendrix.* Screen printed flames. Nine Inch Nails coming from the speakers, though of course I didn't know that then. *Tool. Avenged Sevenfold.* Skulls and wings. *Sublime.* There must have been other colors, but I saw red, black, and white. *Marilyn Manson. Pantera. The Used. HIM. From First to Last.* I resolved to be fluent, even in what I didn't like. But there was so little time. Fifteen minutes until closing, I heard someone say. I grabbed a shirt that was far too large. *Bad*, it read above a crossed-out cross, with *Religion* beneath it. I got in line, and then out, then back in with a second shirt, a Bob Marley one for Eleanor. On the way back, I played *No Control* for her.

"Exuberant," she said.

When we got home, she took Cedar for a walk. I left her shirt on her bed—to surprise her, and to avoid an extraneous interaction. On her laptop, I opened myriad tabs and began unending lists. The Hindenburg could have floated past the window. I wouldn't have noticed. My focus felt almost like an ailment. I knew it would be chronic. There was no limit to how many things I could love, to the album reviews I could counteranalyze, no shortage of Mitch Clem or Cometbus to read. Abbreviations asked to be memorized. SST; MDC. Mundane words—*mineral, orchid, knapsack, heroin, quicksand, seaweed*—had new meanings. I tended to the past and to the present. The recent headlines went:

New Music: Bigwig: "Ashtray Monument" (Jawbreaker cover)

Kerrang! awards enrage Fall Out Boy / My Chemical Romance fans

Review: Citizen Fish by Leftover Crack

Talking Vinyl with Var Thelin of No Idea Records

Review: Channels, *Waiting for the Next End of the World*

New Music: Lemuria: "Pants"

Review: Appleseed Cast, *Lost Songs*

Tours: Converge / 108 / Internal Affairs

I lurked in the comments. I luxuriated in words written by people with no shortage of flannel shirts or tattoos. I thought them exotic. They had cheap whiskey dependencies, driver's licenses, and testicles. I took the time to imagine each one and his hands and the narcissistic undertones of his self-loathing. But my mind stayed, mostly, on the music. The archivists and the contrarians were nothing without the noise itself.

*

Fiona told me my new shirt wasn't very nice. I folded my arms over Bad Religion's logo. "It's just a band, remember? I'm not a fascist or anything."

"I remember."

She did help with my hair the next weekend. The green and black remind her of a bog. She never asked to hear *No Control.*

The hours we couldn't spend together became better. I could no longer live without letting a song play on low volume in the background of my brain. With it, existence was much easier. I didn't have my father's blues. I was ecstatic. I wrote lyrics down my jeans and the across my T-shirt hems. Black on black; invisibly important. I found a record store downtown that sold me a steady supply of Manic Panic. Cedar was allowed inside as long as he steered clear of the hand-sewn leather trench coat on the back wall. Ted, the owner—an egghead, a goth—set a vintage Crass poster aside for me. In Spanish class, the Alisons droned, in English, about Dumbledore's Army; I hid earbuds under my hair and listened to Jodie Foster's. My history teacher let me to listen to Econochrist while I captured the government's latest casualty counts. At home, I cut letters out of camouflage fabric to spell the names of broken-up bands. With floss, I stitched them to one-dollar T-shirts from the Salvation Army where Fiona got cable-knits and tea dresses.

I was walking between buildings, between classes, when a girl in a Weekend Nachos shirt asked me if I had a cigarette—no—or a lighter—yes (Fiona's). Sophie told me she liked to steal silverware from restaurants. That turned out to be the extent of her personality. She and Fiona had gone to middle school together and not spoken since. Fiona said Sophie was uninspired. *She's just sort of there. Doesn't she remind you of a nonflowering houseplant made of silk? No, not silk. Polyester.* But Sophie had three nose rings and she didn't have a doctor's appointment almost every day after school. I helped her leave stacks of the latest showpaper around town. I played fetch with her dachshund in her bedroom and read the embarrassing stories in *Seventeen,* and she did a decent job of giving me a small stick-and-poke of a fly in the crook of my left arm. I tattooed an upside-down cross in between her middle and ring fingers in return.

Fiona was not pleased. She started walking a step ahead of me everywhere we went, spoke in short sentences, ignored my jokes. The plain panic behind her distant expression brought me back to the days I'd waited for her to reappear in the library, to the dread I'd lose her when I'd barely found her. I stopped returning Sophie's texts. I gave Fiona her lighter back. And then she said, "I love you too."

—

[26]I went back to solitary research and listening sessions after school. The first website I'd found was still my epicenter, but I'd branched out to other sites—proper message boards, and though I of course never posted, the commentor I most admired used the same account name across the internet. He was impossible to avoid. I labored for weeks to manufacture enough courage to instant message him. Adrenaline shot through my thumbs, the nape of my neck. My elbows, somehow. I shifted in my seat. He wanted to be found. I typed hello. He typed hello. So it went, almost every day after school.

Matty was one thousand two hundred and forty-eight miles

away. A student of poetry who seemed, at all of nineteen years old, impossibly brilliant, and who possessed, somehow, time to read my description of the frame of a half-built house I'd seen on a walk with Cedar. Christmas lights clung to its corners in March. It made me cry. A house with a birdfeeder made exactly in its own image broke my heart too. He encouraged me to take it easy. I told him about the fake bugs I felt on my skin, and the real one I'd had Sophie tattoo on. He said he had the same ink for the same reason, and it was then that I knew I would marry him. A week later, I begged accounts of his drug and/or alcohol use. I wanted to know what to anticipate when it came time for me to partake. He gently steered the chat back to Revolution Summer. When we couldn't agree on which was the superior acoustic song on *Goddamnit*, or the better side of the Faith/Void split, he was civil. He was, I was sure, impressed by my polemic.

My neck twinged from the poor posture I adopted during our conversations. I was too transfixed to care for comfort. I was trying to enter the screen in my kitchen and exit through the one in his dorm room. I imagined him: average height, without birthmarks, with cavities in molars. As far as I understood, bedroom eyes and tired eyes were one and the same. I assigned him those too. I caught my subconscious painting him with strokes of dark brown, tight spirals of hair on his abdomen, a birth year that matched mine, a threadbare Gorilla Biscuits T-shirt on his shoulders. But a thumbnail I found while searching—he didn't offer; I didn't entreat—revealed he was pasty. And the photo was cut off at the neck, so who knows what he was wearing.

Every night I had the same dream. He drafted dactyls on translucent sheets of paper, then overlaid them on my skin.

Every morning I prayed he'd mail me a ghazal to tuck away until I was old enough to have it tattooed on my stammering heart—not the skin on my chest, but the organ beneath it, and so what if it killed me? That was the point.

No letters arrived. He didn't know where I lived. I persevered.

He contained multitudes: a shellfish allergy and an encyclopedic knowledge of the history of ice hockey and an intense distaste for late-stage capitalism, and if it disappointed him that my understanding of him, of everything, was so simultaneously vast and incomplete, he made no mention of it. Responses were not always instant, but he never left a message unanswered.

The transcripts of our conversations resided in a hidden folder on the computer drive, our words huddling together like I knew we someday would. I deserved a crown for the poise with which I learned to tear myself away from him when Eleanor came around. The rustle of shoes and paws at the foot of the stairs meant I had twenty-six seconds before she and Cedar would arrive in the kitchen to debrief me on their walk. I could not have cared less about the yoga-slash-capoeira instructor she'd just befriended. The remorse Eleanor had about destroying our family was depleted. Miss Congeniality was back. I logged off and slid from the desk chair to the floor.

Cedar lapped water from his bowl, then swiped his nose across my forehead. Eleanor handed me a bowl of raw green beans to eat while she made dinner. She wanted to know what I'd been up to, musically speaking. My last report included the Dead Milkmen, whose name she endorsed. *Okay! What they know about Toni?*

"Any new bands today?" she asked.

"Yeah."

"Have you heard Bruce Springsteen? He's got soul. And a brother on the sax. I'm sure your father can send you something of his."

"Okay." I tossed Cedar a green bean. He liked catching it more than he liked the taste. Eleanor turned her back to us to stir a pot. I arranged my food into the letters in Matty's name. I swallowed him in pieces—*at, my, t*—and waited for the seeds to take root inside me. I had to tell Fiona.

*

"Something magical is happening to me." It was the next afternoon.

"Hmm?" She opened and closed the curtains on her eyes.

"There's this guy I like—"

"Hmm." She kept her eyes closed.

Fiona didn't like anyone. We loved each other but she had never felt like *that*. She called sex *it*. I now realize her pituitary gland may have been so preoccupied pumping the hormone that regulated her blood pressure that it didn't produce as much of the one that would stimulate the growth of her ovarian follicles. It's also possible her psychology, not her physiology, explained it. Or that they were working in tandem. At the time, I just knew the distinction it marked between us felt like a betrayal. I said her name to get her to look at me. To get her to say something.

Being in love like *that*, she declared, sounded like a lot of pressure. No, I explained, it was easy. Imperative. I had to do it. It was much easier than being loved.

She asked who he was, when she could meet him, if the two

of them had gone to elementary school together. "He must be lovely if you love him." She started on her ninth piece of gum without offering me one.

"Matty's . . . far away. But I'm hoping he'll ask me to—maybe I could sort of run away." I'd never said his name out loud. "You could come visit me."

"Would you love Matty if you didn't have to? If it weren't imperative?" Pieces of her nails flaked off when she picked at the polish. There was something in the way she said his name. She breezed through it in a single syllable. Such blithe desecration. I scratched the fly on my skin.

"Of course I would."

I told her everything about him, how I'd found him, how easy he was to talk to, how he'd changed my life, that he was my life. Like her, but not.

Her face was stone. "If you love him so much, then why did you wait so long to tell me about him? Are you sure you aren't ashamed of him? Is he defective?"

My lip shook. I looked up to keep the tears from falling. "Why would you say that?"

"I just want to make sure he's good enough for you. Does he deserve you, dear?" She took my hand with more strength than I knew she could exert. "Who do you love more. Him or me?"

The school year was over. I knew I wouldn't make new friends the next year, or the next one, or the one after that. She needed me and I liked it. She was right in front of me and begging for affection. Matty was just words on a screen. I could leave him behind.

"You, Fiona. I love you."

"Thank you," she said. "I've always needed someone to."

*

She proved me wrong that summer. In July, we played a game of poker with our mothers. It was the four of us, plus Cedar, and for one night we pretended our families were the same. Mine whole; hers happy. I'd spent the night before cleaning, but there were corners I couldn't reach. Certain scuffs refused to shine. Years later, I would be vindicated, and further embarrassed, upon realizing the obvious: her house was scoured weekly by a professional cleaner.

Fiona's mother offered to deal the cards. Eleanor made playful protests that a guest shouldn't bear such a burden. Lena prevailed. *One, two, three, four, five.* I followed the beat as she laid a stack out for each of us. She did it with her c'est la vie smile. Her hair fell to her shoulders in an unbroken wave of sculpted honey. Fiona's mother was doing great, in that she looked like she was doing great. Was she okay? Yes. She was incessantly okay.

I knew because people never stopped asking, as if she were not in fact, could not possibly be, fine. In many ways, the town of forty thousand was small. Everyone we knew knew about Fiona. *Oh, Lena, oh it's so nice to see you, so tell me, how are . . . things?* Her response to the inescapable question was okayness that never wavered. She delivered the non-news with a sneer, but I saw in her each time the exchange occurred—at school functions, at restaurants, at home with her own husband—a relief. To be asked was all that mattered. Her catharsis came not from unrepressing a truth but from having an answer someone else sought.

We reached for our hands and considered our chips.

"We aren't even betting on anything," Fiona said, speaking solely to her mother. "This is silly." I was too riveted to check for Eleanor's reaction. Up to that night, her interactions with Lena stalled at drop-off and pick-up pleasantries.

"What exactly do you have to put up?" Lena looked at her own cards with vicious indifference.

Of course, I couldn't interject. No one was more difficult to speak to than Lena. After the first night I slept at their house, Fiona waited until I was safely home to tell Lena the copper-plated boar-bristle hairbrush we'd borrowed from her had snapped in half after catching on a snarl in my kitchen. Fiona spent the next week mocking the look on her mother's face. I joined in her derision. I felt awful. I didn't know a hairbrush could cost two hundred dollars.

I couldn't fathom why my home had plastic poker chips lying around—why they of all things survived the move. The once-black chips were grey; the red-and-white colored pieces called stale peppermints to mind.

Lena kept her teeth on display while we cycled through our turns. One hand ended; another began. "I was cleaning out the basement the other day," she said. "I found the most precious drawings and little poems Fiona made in kindergarten. She used to be so sweet."

Fiona and I locked eyes from opposite sides of the table. Kindergarten. Six or so years, I calculated, before she got sick.

"I don't know if I want to know what they're up to now. I was quite the wild child at their age," Eleanor said. I imagined my mother's most daring teenage escapades involved a dozen adoring friends and picnics that were abandoned if it began to rain.

"You're bluffing," Fiona said, to no one in particular this

time. She jiggled her legs beneath the table, like a sentient soda can shaking itself up. I was hungry. They each held a glass to their lips. We'd scheduled the date for after dinner. The women drank wine. Fiona sipped coffee from my father's mug.

"We can't all be as good as you." Eleanor's loosened tongue alluded to the lies Fiona's illness required. No, she was taking aim at Lena's maternal instincts. No, she'd discovered the man I was hiding in her laptop. (I couldn't quit him outright; I'd just stopped telling Fiona about him.) I pressed my elbow into my hip and focused on the sensation.

"Who do you mean?" I asked my mother twice, because the sound didn't make it out the first time I tried.

"Did you say something, sweetheart?"

I said no with all the confidence I could muster.

The rules of the game weren't entirely clear to me. Calls? Folds? Bets? I had assumed we were playing poker, but had it been something else, I wouldn't have known the difference. Every time I shifted my stare, I discovered new dust I hadn't swept. It wasn't until Fiona first sat at our kitchen table that I realized it wasn't real wood. She didn't have to say it; her presence made it abruptly obvious. Now Lena must have thought it odd that our only television and our only computer sat on different tables on opposite sides of the kitchen. Eleanor liked to keep the living room as peaceful as possible; it was for couches and candles.

Was Eleanor winning? She turned to Fiona and complimented her dress, then asked if I'd ever wear something like it.

"It is black, Olive," Fiona offered.

"Careful sharing clothes with her," Lena said. "She can be quite the slob."

Fiona scratched at her fingertips. She never missed any vomit when she wiped the toilet down. She hadn't even thrown up in months.

Eleanor asked Lena what their plans were for the rest of the summer.

"We're going to start the Appalachian Trail at the bottom," Fiona said, "and try to make it from Georgia to Virginia in a month."

It was odd; Cedar and I had yet to receive our invitation. She couldn't go anywhere without us. He led the way on all our walks. I stuck my tongue between my teeth and bit until I tasted iron. It was just after seven o'clock. Enough sunlight crept in through the windows to make the electric glow above us obsolete. I couldn't look at Fiona. Instead, I found the sky. Robin's egg dappled with glittering leaves.

"We were considering it as a family," Lena corrected her. "But there are concerns about whether Fiona will be able."

"Dad knows I can do it."

"Fee-*oh*-nuh." She emphasized the second syllable, the roundness of exasperation. "He wasn't with us when you blacked out in the P-oh-conos. He didn't look over his sh-oh-ulder in Denver just in time to see you barely miss breaking your neck on a b-oh-ulder the size of this house." Lena was not okay.

Fiona and I studied different spots on the ceiling. Her leg went still. "I'm fine now, aren't I? Besides, five-year-olds have done it." She was retreating to a place for which I did not have a map. "Dogs have done it," she added. Maybe she had factored Cedar into her plan.

"Something tells me those five-year-olds and those dogs were sensible enough to eat."

Eleanor poured Lena more wine. "Well, I'm sure there are plenty of more relaxing vacations for y'all to try instead."

Lena's voice tilted when she thanked her. Their glasses clinked. But our mothers never became friends. Any intimacy they came to share was a side effect of whom they'd spawned. We were all they had in common, and even then Lena disapproved of the raccoon makeup I was allowed to smear on my face and Eleanor objected to how Lena performed the role of the Sick Kid's Mother Who We're All Pretty Sure Is To Blame. Eleanor's culottes—white linen—and Lena's pussy-bow blouse—yellow silk—could never emulsify. They were a batch of broken mayonnaise. I really wanted something to eat.

The game in front of us was all but abandoned. Fiona placed her palm on my mother's as they both folded with indifference. Eleanor had her wedding ring on.

Lena called to match my bet.

Fiona furrowed her brow, silently tallying the calories in the alcohol on the table. No, she was wondering what it was like to fall in and out of love. She could have been thinking about mineral deposits in the Rockies, or whether her left shoe had just come untied, or when she'd last shaved her legs. Maybe her mind was blank. It killed me not to know.

I showed Lena my cards.

"You won!" She squeezed my pinky and she smiled. With veneers. Things made a little more sense then. Surely the way she treated Fiona was a front for the sake of something. Surely, she had a good reason. That's what I told myself: I'd understand soon.

—

[27]I didn't ask Fiona about the trip she'd planned without me. I couldn't trust whatever she would've had to say for herself. One minute I was her oxygen, the next she was ready to abscond without me. But true to Lena's word, there was no separation that summer. Truer, I realized, to Fiona's, she really did need me. It was terrifying, intoxicating, secondary to Matty.

He and I stuck to my usual stupid questions about how long he took to brush his teeth and if he always started from the same spot in his mouth. My intensifying longing was not subtext but supertext, and his decision to ignore it made it that much more conspicuous. He knew I'd stalked Fiona, was stalking him, was possibly psychotic, thought The Get Up Kids were overrated. But he always wrote back. I asked what the name of his dorm was. I could come to him, I offered. I would only go, I told myself, if Fiona got banished to a treatment center again. Or tumbled off a cliff. I awaited his answer. My phone chimed. Fiona asked when I was coming over. Eleanor came down from upstairs and uncorked a bottle of wine.

"Do you want to start your own band?" my mother asked.

"No thank you." I would miss her when I was gone. Maybe I'd invite her to the wedding.

He still hadn't responded. I logged off.

I read an oral history of a band I hated. An hour later, I let Eleanor kiss me on the cheek before she went to bed. Cedar followed her. I logged on. No response. He wasn't even typing. I printed out every word of our love story and brought it to my room. It was a difficult read. A mortifying read. I'd been so naive. I was one of the guys, but worse, I was a child. A distraction from an unfulfilling semester. My organs squirmed. I tore his poems off my walls. I slammed my hand into the newly empty spaces. To my surprise, it was very easy to puncture something. I moved a flyer over to cover the holes. I shoved the mass of papers into my backpack and ran to Fiona's.

She steadied me. I wept atrociously. I was jagged. Full of long vowels. I dripped phlegm onto her sundress and porch.

"Oh, Olive, I promise you'll be okay." She escorted me to her bedroom before I woke Lena up.

"I need him," I told her. "We were made for each other."

"You have me," she said. "Besides, do you really know him? He could be anyone, dear."

We sat in her bed. Her hand fit nicely around my knee. She stroked my hair. I wanted her to be enough. She wasn't.

"You wouldn't say that about him if you really loved me. If you loved me, you would love him. You don't know anything about love. Clearly." I opened my bag and squeezed the papers to my chest.

"Reminders make things worse." She pried them from me. "We don't need these anymore."

"Yes we do!"

"I'll get rid of them for you. I won't even read them. Promise."

I didn't care; everything he and I said to each other was beyond her comprehension. She got up. The floor creaked beneath her. I flopped onto my back. Her voice was moving, quick and quiet.

"Fiona, are you *praying* for me? Please get up."

"I'm almost done."

I rolled onto my stomach, half hoping a pillow would suffocate me. It was so soft. How was every textile in that house so soft?

"Here you go, dear." She handed me a pen. "Take this too," a postcard with an illustration of a wild plant. One you could eat in a pinch. She said it was time to say goodbye. Forever. I wiped my nose and wrote.

> *Matty, if someone ever asks you to describe me, please don't. Can you keep me to yourself? Because I think you can see me so well—without even looking—that I never need to be seen by anyone else. Hey, I still don't believe you can get splinters from the hairs in your beard.*

I dictated his address to Fiona. She pressed a Statue of Liberty stamp into the corner. Fifty-four words. A forty-one-cent finale. She told me not to move. She was going to drop it in the mailbox around the corner so her parents wouldn't see.

"Okay," I said. "Just be fast." Eyes closed, I imagined what I'd never hear. His voice. Was it coarse or cream? I didn't know; I'll never know.

She returned with Merricat. "Almost all orange cats are male. Did you know that?"

"I did not know that." I sat up. She explained the genetics, the math. When she sat next to me, Merricat leaped away.

"Fiona, is that story about you attacking Hannah true?"

"Which Alison told you that? Oh, never mind. Olive, don't you ever get angry?"

"I do." Now that Matty was gone, maybe I could marry my favorite feeling. "I do." I got so angry all the time and had no idea what to do.

"Good, then I'll tell you the truth."

On the night in question, Fiona had spent another day fidgeting and making excuses (half the room believed her; half would parody her later) every time a bowl of pretzels was passed around. They poured so much soda, ordered so much pizza, freed so many cupcakes from their wrappers. She didn't. She was hungry, but worse than that, she was the only one who couldn't want to change something about her body in one moment and genuinely smile for a picture the next. The only one for whom calorie counting was quicksand. She was furious. She lashed out at a girl who happened to be healthy.

"Do the things people say about you bother you?" I asked.

"The true parts or the lies?"

She thought the cancer rumors were a kindness in their own way. With cancer came pity, whereas rich white girls who starved themselves were ungrateful. Attention-seeking. Shallow. I tried to look at her objectively. Shallow, sure—if she were to lay down on her side, among other people in the same position, she might not measure up. Shallow, sure—there were spots in which her body sank toward itself.

"Sometimes," I said, tears streaming again, "I feel like I was made for anger. Like I could kill someone if I had to. If someone hurt you, I would—"

"Oh no, that wouldn't be necessary. Who could hurt me more than me?"

I would have taken Fiona's place if I could have. Not that she'd have allowed it. Not that it would have done anyone any good. A few weeks earlier, when the heat insisted I take off the sleeve of black bracelets I'd been wearing since spring, she deflated. It took hours of nagging before she would say what was the matter. She'd thought I'd started cutting myself too. She swore, with a frown, she was happy I hadn't.

"Don't cry," she said now. Her arms bent around me. The angle was acute.

"But usually, I feel like I was made for love."

"Me too."

I pulled away. Something orange was peeking out from beneath the bed. Not Merricat. One of many disposable cameras we were always picking up and putting down. We got the film developed only after we could no longer remember which memories they held.

I wound the dial. Merricat appeared. I captured them both.

"What if Mary Katherine's tail was what everything was made of?" Fiona posited. I put the camera down and asked what she meant. "Like the bed—one big tail. The books—all tails, and each page a tail, and each letter a tiny tail. What if the universe were made of tails instead of atoms?"

I played along. "The tail clouds rain tails. It hails tails?"

"Each blade of grass is a tail!"

"Each hair on the tail is another tail!"

"When you mow the lawn with a machine made of tails . . . do the tails bleed?"

"They do. It sprays everywhere. It's awful! But it's not blood, it's just more tails."

We were slumping sacks of laughter, gesticulating, declaring ourselves unable to breathe.

Then she asked if she could take me somewhere. Yes. It was just to her backyard. We could sleep there, she said, half on thin blankets and half on rough grass. When we woke, we'd be covered in dew.

I listened to her map the stars. I forgave her for everything she had done and everything she might someday do.

"There you are, my December love," she said, like a movie star whose legacy might soon be lost. I tried to figure out what she was pointing at. "The center of the Milky Way is in Sagittarius—did you know? There's too much light pollution for us to see it."

"Are you close by?"

"It's a clear shot across to Gemini. Point your arrow straight ahead and you'll hit me." She acted it out. I could borrow one of Cupid's if I wanted, she said. A wound in the name of love was still a wound.

I had another question for her. I drifted off before I could ask it. It was a selfish kind of sleep; I knew she wouldn't be able to rest for more than a few hours. At least she wasn't alone. She could talk to the plants in her garden. Maybe they could tell her what I couldn't. *Fiona, this is how to grow.*

—

MAYBE YOU COULD HURT ME

FEBRUARY–APRIL 2011

28

Fiona still believed in God. Her faith was heresy, a crime I witnessed from the tiniest holes in the heartiest concrete, from the other side of a thing I had no business peering through. I asked how God fit into her anorexia, which by our senior year had nearly bored me to death. According to her, he had nothing to do with it. She didn't pray for it to go away. According to her, no one else should be held responsible for it. Especially not him. His grace would be wasted on her.

She'd recently moved into her attic—in solidarity with Rochester's first wife—and covered each wall of her new bedroom in a different vintage wallpaper. Gaudy carousel horses, suspended in front of golden stripes, gazed at curling pastel flowers across the room. The room sloped on two sides, slanting yellow and yellowing pin dots toward blue and white sailboats stamped in perfect formation. The effect shrank the space.

"You deserve grace," I said. "You deserve whatever you want."

"You just said you don't think I deserve believing."

"You know what I mean. I just don't want you to need it."

Her beliefs were everchanging and currently Unitarian Universalist, Quaker, and pagan in parts. She had a soft spot for Catholic rituals and drama. She couldn't get enough of the book of Revelations. The Great Schism, she marveled, was so perfectly petty.

She asked if I remembered saying, years ago, that she was strong. I shrugged from where I always sat, with my back against the door. Her perch was the radiator beneath the window. We cranked up the air conditioning all year round in case someone was listening. She layered wool and cotton against the cold.

"Well, I remember you saying it," she said. "But I am the weakest person I've ever met. Really. Sometimes I feel like I can't take it any longer. But you believe in me. So I suppose that helps. Olive, are you paying attention?"

I was thinking about Matty. I'd never stopped. I'd never kept anything else from her. As of late, the thoughts were lengthening, multiplying. I rearranged my mind. I buried him and salvaged something for her from the remains.

"I don't have to believe in you, you're sitting right here. How could I love someone who wasn't real?"

That made her burrow deeper backward: I'd once told her she was like a make-believe girl come to life from a book, *from long ago and far away.* A witch or a princess, it was all the same to me. I had to convince myself she really existed. That someone lonely (me) didn't invent the perfect companion (her).

"I've never stopped thinking about it," she said. "It's like this pressure on my chest. I don't think it was a compliment."

"I just meant you're surreal." Or that most of what comprised her persona was suspiciously affectatious. "Surreal," I repeated.

"So is faith, you know. I don't see why you find it so offensive. I bet you've said a tiny prayer before. I bet you say things out loud when you're alone *because* you know someone else might hear and be able to help."

"That doesn't mean anything. It's like saying 'bless you' when someone sneezes. No one actually means it."

She asked how I knew when someone did or didn't mean it.

"I don't. And there are plenty of things you don't know either. Like you don't need God. You can just believe in people."

Her foot distractedly skimmed the edge of her desk. "You can't understand if you don't want to." Merricat slinked toward her.

I touched the walls, feeling for bumps in the patterned paper. "I understand it, Fiona. I just can't comprehend it." Or I simply didn't care.

She loved seemingly synonymous word pairs with fundamental differences. I'd spent hours with her, teasing out where jealousy ended and envy began, where prideful people diverged from the proud and the courageous from the brave. Sometimes it was as simple as looking up the definitions of pottery and ceramics. Now we sat in silence, which was better than her telling me that she didn't understand what I was trying to tell her: that she and I were fundamentally different. We were not fated for forever.

She awkwardly crawled onto her desk. Was she exercising? She grabbed a book from the shelf above it, where Merricat was curled. Art, Fiona said, was better than real life. As long as it was fiction. She spent most of the year prior reading to me from *The Collected Stories of Flannery O'Connor*. Each time she came across *nigger*, she pronounced it as a three-second pause before moving right along. "Song of Songs" was another favorite. This time it was *Franny and Zooey,* the cover deliberately plain. Her yellow highlights illuminated the insides. She began to read. Zooey was, she said, so clever.

Matty was shrewder. Probably. Fiona had made me delete the digital record of our correspondence, so I didn't have proof. I could barely remember anything he'd said.

"Reading this sucks me even deeper into my circular thoughts, but it's not the worst place to be trapped because, see—" According to Zooey, having very strong likes and disliked was ill-advised. A recipe for disaster. One needed to be able to talk to people they did not like. Or love. "Maybe that is part of my problem," she said. "Everything is good or bad."

Food was bad, fasting was good and St. Catherine had done it, but Fiona would never be canonized. If we were excluding three minor relapses and two month-long stints in inpatient treatment, she had maintained her weight for most of high school, including the entirety of our senior year to that point. She was still banned from the soccer team. She tried to escape into books and me and maps and movies. She traveled in place. She was spiraling.

"Do you think we'd like more people if we had more friends?" I asked.

She laughed. We had acquaintances. *Where is she?* they'd ask when they spotted one of us alone.

The book cast a shadow over her lap. "Listen to this," she exhorted, waving her hands. Maybe she could make it as a cult leader. A nun? Zooey's next lesson was that nonconformity was often its own kind of convention. That was hardly radical; I could've played her at least twenty songs with that sentiment.

Soon, Lena's footsteps and the last minutes of the sunset would signal dinnertime. Those were my cues to leave Fiona to face it alone. Her recovery, major undertaking that it was, seemed to consist solely of tedium. Of little things. Really little, because although she was eating more, it's not as if we ever had to go shopping for bigger clothes.

"It's been dreadful the past three days, but I need to practice feeding myself," she told me. "With college pending and all."

She unwrapped a piece of gum and said she didn't think she was going to make it through her bachelor's. "I shouldn't be allowed any freedom. I'll just waste it. I imagine it's quite easy to when no one's there to stop you."

"No it's not," I said. "We won't slip back." I feigned complicity. If I'd invented her, I hadn't done a very good job.

She hadn't asked me about the extremely important show I was going to that night. Each year, between Christmas and New Year's Eve, Eleanor budgeted for a single one of The Bouncing Souls' annual Home for the Holidays shows—three consecutive dates at the Stone Pony, each with different openers. Some years forced me into difficult deliberations; other years, the choice was easy. That December, The Menzingers were the deciding factor. I'd chosen their night and counted down the days. Then the sky brought ceaseless snow, then sunshine to melt it, and cold air to freeze it into "dangerous weather conditions." Fiona and I took Cedar out to play in it.

The shows were rescheduled for February. The new date had finally arrived. That was my valentine.

She tapped on the window. She called the rain outside anemic. She wanted a tempest. When Lena shouted up both flights of stairs, asking if I needed a ride home, Fiona reeled herself in from whatever she saw on the other side of the glass.

Earlier that month, I'd overheard Lena griping to Fiona's father. *I gave up my body for a girl who doesn't want one. Isn't that funny!* That was what her daughter was to her. Disease, treatment, and patient had merged. That was what her daughter was to me. It seemed the more we loved her the more she disappeared behind the saddest kind of—*stubbornness* wasn't the right word. If her mother and I had started at the same time, I wondered which one of us would have been the first to stop meaning it when we told Fiona *I'm proud of you; It's okay; It's not your fault.*

I yelled down to Lena that I could walk home. I said to Fiona, "Good luck, I love you." I told Merricat goodbye.

"Wait!" Fiona yelped. "Are you going to miss me when you leave for college? Promise you'll come back home and visit me."

I didn't know what she was talking about. She was leaving too.

"Yes, Fiona. I promise."

—

[29]Eleanor was waiting for me at home. She'd been there only a few minutes. I recapped the trivial parts of my day for her. As my reward, she relinquished the car keys. When this all began, I'd been forbidden to go to shows alone, no matter how close they were. When Off with Their Heads played the Meatlocker (8 Park Street; underground), equidistant from our apartment and my school, she'd chaperoned me. For a time, she was my

constant companion. She'd work a nine-hour day in Manhattan. I'd meet her there after walking Cedar, feeding him and myself. From Penn or Port Authority, she and I'd continue, usually to Brooklyn. I walked ahead, leaned against the train car doors, pretended not to know her. She hoped wherever I was taking her would have a place in the back for her to sit with her earplugs and flashlight and Iyanla Vanzant book. The third time we did this, she stopped trying to keep an eye on me. I was not in harm's way. I was just one of some people who counted chaos an amenity at high volume. (No matter how much I screamed, my voice only scratched the next morning; I could not lose it.) When our destination was in Manhattan, she never betrayed her obvious relief.

A jovial drunk man slammed into her at the Glass Door on the night I heard Cheap Girls for the first time. She granted me independence a week later. *Come straight home* was the rule. Off I went, to the Knitting Factory (361 Metropolitan); Shea Stadium (20 Meadow); Europa (98 Meserole), where BtMI! was always playing; the basement at Suburbia (30 Melrose). I got my learner's permit and off I went. Down the Parkway, at exactly the speed limit, to a beachside bowling alley (exit 10A to 18 South to 66 East), or down the turnpike, a little over the speed limit, to New Brunswick crevices (exit 9; Meat Town; Drucker's; ask a punk). If I missed the last bus or lost the keys, I was on my own until the morning. When I told Fiona that, she dropped emergency funds into my wallet. Sophie went with me sometimes. I didn't tell Fiona that.

I looked forward to the inevitable emergency. At 538 Johnson (apartment 208; take the L to Jefferson), it finally extended its invitation. The woman running the door scribbled numbers on attendees' hands. In the hallway behind her, kids melted into pearls of smoke. A dog barked in an adjacent apartment. The poor thing's ears. Guilt blitzed me. I still went inside. I passed the merch table and, wanting to be taller, stood on an overturned wooden crate against the back wall. The man next to me clapped during all the right parts. He turned to me during a break. *Did you know this used to be a paper factory?* I felt like I was being spoken to for the very first time. I said, *No. I didn't know.* I was in love. He was a twenty-two-year-old from West Something, Connecticut. With my titled ear to his mouth, I pretended I could hear. I was already planning to spend the next day online, indulging my newfound interest in the state. He drank from a reusable bottle. I asked him for a sip and was relieved to taste water. He told me about the bicycle crash that morning that had swollen his ankle, leaving him wary of the crowd, leaving him on that crate with me. Someone on the loft landing spilled something on our heads. More relief; more water. The new love of my life shook his head dry the way a puppy would. The bandana in his hair was dirty anyway. I was too enchanted to move. I tried not to stare. A band I didn't know was playing a cover I didn't recognize. My ignorance gutted me. He sang along and pumped his fist. I couldn't decipher the patch on his pants. He wasn't there, he said, to see The Menzingers but to see Lemuria. Unenchanted, I moved to the front of the room. My reason for living was about to begin, and by the first chorus I couldn't dam the swell at my back. Greg's mic stand fell over. I picked it back up. They covered "Straight to Hell." Everything was perfect. I checked the time. One, maybe two more songs, if I wanted to make it home. Where else could I seek shelter for the night? The former love of my life was flirting with the woman behind the merch table. Three songs later, I decided to stay. I watched Lemuria, I made the 1:22 train from one Penn Station to the other, and I missed the last bus home from there. Fiona's money covered a cab. When it dropped me in my driveway, Cedar bolted from behind his favorite window and came to greet me at the foot of the stairs.

That February night, I said goodbye to Eleanor, just as I had to Fiona and Merricat, and drove to Asbury Park. Parkway South to 10A to 66 East to Ocean Avenue, all with Salinger stuck in my head. I arrived early and got a place at the front of the floor to watch Dirty Tactics for the first time, then The Menzingers for maybe the tenth. I hadn't seen them since September, and May before that; they weren't so local that they felt overexposed. They fit my predilection for groups with two vocalists and lyrics rife with literary references to discuss with Fiona. *Either way, Ophelia will cry.* The late adolescent phase of their career aligned with the same era of my life such that older songs were vanishing from setlists. The title track off their debut became a requisite finale—better yet, the last song in the encore, a beacon of nostalgia when it was only a few years old. "Straight to Hell" was soon lost to time constraints and artistic growth, and maybe increasingly legitimate shows came with increasing attention to licensing fees. Regardless, I accepted whatever they wanted to perform. I did not have it in me to shout out requests. That night, I didn't have to. A group of people who I dressed like but did not look like, and I got the finale we wanted, we got to belting, *and nothing stays gold,* then got to stomping when the guitars cut out in the final seconds.

Strike Anywhere was next: Iron Front iconography; contributions to compilations raising funds for good causes;

pro-animal; anti-police. A good political song was a hard thing to write, but they managed, and maybe that was why no one gave too much of a shit about the politics of Thomas's hair.

Then came the Souls. They led a chant of *East Coast! Fuck you!* They had us wrapped around their fingers. The climate in the crowd forecasted March, April, May's forthcoming weather. June, July, August, Fiona and I were almost out of time. A hand enveloped mine. It was not the heat, nor the humidity, but the humanity of it that clogged my throat. It was romantic. To be touched. By a stranger. We liked the same music. It wasn't strange at all. My shirt slid from my shoulder. I'd cut the neck wide. I'd worn plenty of slack into the remaining seams. I'd left my coat in the car. If I lifted my arm, the bottom half of my torso was bare. He traced the underwire in my bra. The physical contact I was normally afforded in such situations had all the sensuality of getting the back of your seat kicked at a movie theater. He was different. It should have been different, December, February, maybe it didn't make a difference. His hand strayed. I couldn't bring myself to turn and look at his face. The only light was trained on the stage. The hair on his skin was on my neck. He hit the point at which my thighs met. He smelled like sap and maple resin. Everything was static. There was a moment of collective calm. A slower song, maybe "Night on Earth." Maybe some things were meant to be. Maybe with the lights out it was, in fact, more dangerous, in a room throbbing with warmth in an unending winter and I could not turn around and face him or choose how he made me feel. He had me until the music stopped, and when it did, I panicked. I wanted? Him. To take me—where?—to the back corner of the bar, beneath a pier on the beach, across the upholstery in the back seat of his car? I ran to the parking lot and honked at every pedestrian obstruction. So many of them still took their time getting out of my way.

*

My mother. I wanted my mother. I froze at the threshold of her bedroom door.

"Have a nice night, sweetheart?" she asked. Her room was dark. Cedar didn't wake up to welcome me. Her curtains weren't drawn. Light from the street caught on the ring on her finger. I didn't want to be like her. I wanted?

I was on the floor, still by the door, with my knees to my chest. My tampon, my underwear, my jeans were soaked through with blood. I'd let things get out of control. My reproductive matter, his fingers, my heart.

"Yeah," I told her. "It was really good."

I chewed the black off my nails. I wasn't going to ask Eleanor for relationship advice. If she'd been on a date since leaving my father, she'd been discreet. If she hadn't, it wasn't for want of options. She had a new admirer every time we went to the grocery store. A man in an ugly blazer, a lone porkchop in his cart, might look her up and down, right next to the artisanal cheeses. Or she'd riff with the butcher as he leaned over the counter. They were on a first-name basis. She put her hand on a few forearms. Tossed her braids over her shoulder. She didn't give out her number. She didn't bring them home. I received no attention—perhaps because I was not outgoing. Perhaps because I looked nothing like her. Eleanor: an hourglass. My silhouette: six o'clock sharp on an analog clock.

"Mom, what do you think the worst thing that will ever happen to you will be?"

If she'd been there, she would have been too far away to make out the minutiae that the people next to me must have judged unremarkable.

"Well," she yawned. "I'd like to think it's in the past. Is something wrong, honey?"

"No." I switched on the light. I asked if she would recognize my severed hand if it came addressed to her in the mail. She side-eyed me, her eyes still adjusting. "What! I'm just trying to settle an argument with Fiona." I was trying to settle an argument with myself about whether men were truly dangerous.

"How is Miss Fiona? She hasn't come over in a while."

"She's fine. So the worst things happen when you're young?"

"No, those hurt the most in the moment and the least in the long run."

"So you mean Dad—never mind. Why don't you ever go on dates now? I wouldn't care."

"I could ask you the same question."

She couldn't have known about him. She was grinning. It was a joke. It woke Cedar up.

"Come on," I said, and took him out to pee. I apologized for the gap in our togetherness. "You wouldn't like it. It would hurt your ears." He kicked up grass, then surveyed the new smells on me. "I told you I'd come back. I'd never leave you." We went back inside. He chose my room over Eleanor's.

I woke up to him sitting dangerously close to my head. Slivers of fur settled in my eyebrows. He flogged the air with his tail. I nudged him aside and kicked through a lump of laundry. My new Dirty Tactics shirt had a spot of blood on the collar. I must have thrown it on top of my jeans. I picked them up to see if I could get away with wearing them to school. A bar napkin popped out of a pocket. I smoothed it between my palms. A phone number hid in a crease. An area code from two counties over. Then what? An eight? A three? I couldn't calculate the weight of his premeditation. Our sweat was sure to compromise, if not ruin, the ink. Did that encourage or discourage him? What was I supposed to think?

I held it out to Cedar. A sniff. A tentative lick. "You're right," I said. "We can't spend the rest of our lives wondering." I pressed my forehead into his. He didn't look away. That could have been approval.

Green Day looked down on me from the wall, just one of at least a hundred sheets of paper, in various sizes and weights. They were with me always and never actually there and was it really possible that no one saw or cared about the way that man—

That eight was a three. I started typing.

I think we met last night?

—

[30]He didn't ask who I was. He said his name was Matty. Not Matthew or Matt. I asked. A coincidence, of course, but for a moment, I believed in Fiona's God. I wrote his name on every piece of paper I encountered. Forward, backward, upside down. *MattyMattyMatty.* My handwriting looped so uproariously that I almost threw up in the middle of class. My desk rattled when I got up to the bathroom.

Every stall was empty. Serendipity. I leaned over the toilet.

I wasn't sick. I was giddy. I faced away from the mirrors and brought Matty's words up on my phone. He'd just asked, for the third time, to see me. The first time he asked, I misunderstood. He did not want to descend upon the school and rescue me from AP European History. He wanted a picture of me. The second time, I ignored him. I found my face unimportant between glances, but when I managed to really look, there was always some surprise: I was more grotesque or I was more palatable than I remembered, my esteem so malleable it became inconsequential.

Now I asked if he was sure about the photo. He was. He was unflappable. I gave him what he wanted so I could go back to making him rank every Black Flag vocalist. I stared in the mirror while I waited for his next message. My body fussed with a familiar longing. I had to see him again, or for the first time. It would have to be a weekend, under the pretense of spending the night at Fiona's. She would faint upon hearing how we met. *Finger?* she'd say and look skeptically at her own.

I walked the ninety-six steps back to class. I took my seat and took notes.

<u>*1869–1914: New Imperialism: Motivations and Methods*</u>

- *Motivations: political power + territory; belief in own cultural supremacy; $$$*
- *Methods: new technologies in travel, warfare, communication, medicine, admin*
    - *Imperial nations turned dependent nations into*
        - *suppliers of food + raw materials*
        - *consumers of industrial products*

- *Matty has never left the country*
    - *has been to all fifty states*
        - *Grand Canyon = overrated*
- *Dependent African and Southeast Asian nations controlled by colonialization (direct)*
- *Dependent Latin American nations controlled by aide + trade (indirect)*
- *Matty = libertarian*
    - *always felt too "clean" for the anarchists*
    - *can't remember if registered to vote*
    - *broke 2 ribs stagediving at a Bane show in late 2004*
        - *in 2004 I was 10 or 11 with 0 friends; spent recess kneeling by the fence, with my back to the playground, sneaking bits of soil into my mouth, savoring when a tooth caught on a pebble, like a tiny unripe pear, because I'd do anything for the sake of a secret*

Tim Shapiro nudged me. "Is it weird for you to sit back here? Surrounded by a bunch of white guys?"

I flipped my notebook over. He'd been adopted from South Korea as an infant. He clearly wanted to say something whenever I wore my Asian Man Records shirt, though I don't think he knew what. He was obsessed with Fiona, who claimed not to know who he was.

"So Tim, the thing is you aren't white."

He had a point, though. We weren't totally surrounded, but it was close. I tallied their number and carved the count into my desk. Someone else's inscription read OFWGKTA.

*

Fiona and I took all the same subjects, taught by all the same teachers, but were scheduled to sit in their classrooms at different times of day. This detracted from our education, because in our last year together, they'd placed us in different lunch periods. They forced us into truancy. Early afternoon walks weren't easy to come back from. Trees on both sides of the streets came together in arches above us. The final scenes of our childhoods were framed in lurid green. We borrowed *The Wall Street Journal* from mailboxes whose owners were on vacation. We took turns reading the headlines. We watched *The Magic School Bus* at my apartment and fed Cedar popcorn. We took the train into the city to walk around there instead, hoping not to run into any parents who'd recognize us. We window-shopped for leather luggage.

We waited to cross the main street downtown, a ten-minute walk from school, between a Dunkin' Donuts and a combatively curated furniture boutique. Fiona was supposed to be in AP Language and Composition. I'd gone to it in the morning. Eulogies were the topic of study that week. We each had to write one for a topic of our choosing. I penned a requiem for letter writing, in an epistle, to her, of course. She wrote hers to herself.

"I mean, I wrote it to being a real person," she said, "who could keep her food in her stomach and keep her wrist skin intact. But I couldn't turn that draft in. Obviously."

"Obviously." She hadn't cut herself in a very long time. "Can I read it?"

"I can summarize. It was silly, really silly. Something like, *If I were a real person, I'd want to eat ice cream, and my jaw would be stronger than a carrot, but ever since my humanity malfunctioned, all I can think about is how I might manage a look at my insides to see what in there is so messed up that I can spend hours looking in the mirror, just staring, just supposing something on the outside could point me in the direction of what I need to cut out in order to function, and then I'm bleeding and the teacher notices but it's only study hall, and he's a sub, so I say it's paint from art class and he believes me.* Something like that."

"Something like that." A bus whipped through a yellow light. I wouldn't have minded going back to school.

"I'm so tired, Olive. I can't say I've had an okay day without my therapist being called. Every day has to be *good.* If I take a nap, or I don't want a snack or to get a manicure with my mother, I'm suicidal. Heaven forbid I'm not feeling well, I mean the plain old regular kind of unwell. Call the paramedics! Fiona has a runny nose."

She had therapy that night. Her parents had just added a second weekly session. I held her hand and pretended it was Matty's. He'd left me a voicemail. She'd mobbed me in the hallway before I could listen to it.

"Then they tell me to talk to them about temptations but how could I? Asking for permission to eat the stupid 'mid-morning portion of protein' by myself is 'a declaration of depression'? I bet you they never let me go to college. I think they want me to let it run its course. Maybe I will."

"Fiona. Fiona, I think it hurts me more that you keep willing yourself dead than it would if you actually did it."

I'm horrified at the casualness with which we treated that kind of utterance—baffled that no one who passed us on the street paused and slapped us—toward or away from our senses?—before they ran their next errand or took the next bite of their bagel.

"I don't want to be like this. You know that. I just am."

I didn't want to disbelieve her. She knew that. But I did.

"I'm just hungry," I said. It wasn't something I usually said. She enjoyed it a little too much. She would have loved to chase down a wild boar with a spear and set the corpse at my feet. "Let's get pizza."

We walked westward, climbing the hill that divided the town into north and south, into mostly white and mostly black, mostly rich and mostly making it work. I lived in the middle. We turned onto a street with adjacent pizzerias. I chose the one I knew she hated because of something that happened at someone's third-grade birthday party. She sat on stool near the door while I ordered. She stared out the window. She was very good at that.

I paid, with my own—Eleanor's—money, then pressed my phone to my ear.

"First-year students at Swarthmore default to an unlimited meal plan. That's a bit extreme, don't you think?" There went her pointy chin on my shoulder.

I put my phone away. "It's extremely extreme." I retrieved my phone, started a text, checked after every third word that she couldn't see the screen. I asked Matty if he would ever possibly consider the concept of wanting me to maybe come to his house. He would, he said, do whatever I wanted. And he wanted more pictures. I wanted to thank him for communicating so clearly.

"Sorry I'm boring you." Before I could deny it, she began explaining the rare phenomenon in which embryos develop outside of the womb, attaching to the mother's fallopian tube or somewhere else they weren't supposed to be. "Isn't it strange," she asked, "how many ways a body can go wrong?"

"Yeah." Even stranger was that a doctor had told her, when she was thirteen, that she'd never be able to give birth, as if that was the most pressing piece of information in her chart. She then took it upon herself to learn the list of other animals that died after they gave birth. Octopuses and mayflies.

My order was ready. The slices were arranged across overlapping paper plates.

"Can you take that to go? I need to stop somewhere else."

I finished my food before she finished her coffee. Then I followed her a little more west. In a cosmetics store, she held out jars for me to smell. Patchouli, musk, whatever didn't recall anything edible.

I checked my phone. *Would you like that?* I didn't thumb up to read what *that* was.

"Do you like this one?" she asked. And then she bought it, and she probably never used a drop. I told her I really needed to go back to school.

After my last class, I holed up at home. Cedar chewed a toy and intermittently snorted. It was just us, and Green Day, and all the futures I imagined with Matty, who soon interrupted.

If I wanted to come over, he said, he needed to get to know me better. First, we needed to talk, and though I thought we were talking already, he informed me that we needed to speak on the telephone. *Like adults.* According to him, he shouldn't have had to explain this to me. I apologized. I could repent on my knees. I could not untangle fear from desire. He called. I picked up. It wasn't fair, he explained, for me to toy with him. He laughed in sharp spurts. I felt fireworks. I prattled. *Of course, yeah no, yes, totally, obviously, of course you're right*, until he said I could stop. My jaw locked when he took too long to respond, loosened when I got him back. He imparted his life's banalities upon me. The errands he had to run, the plans he had to solidify with friends, his favorite living bassists. I was, he said, a good listener. I wondered when he'd snap again. If I could make the next snap crisper. If I could break him. Give myself a splinter. I figured out the rules: don't interrupt, don't disagree too often, don't be too quick to tell him yes. He spoke at me until I fell asleep.

We filled weeks. His monologues. My provocations, purposeful and inadvertent. My atonement withheld until he was sufficiently fuming. He never said please and I never said thank you and I started sleeping so well that I stopped dreaming. Soon, I had a single picture of him: a shot he'd taken of a years-old photograph in a nondescript frame. His arm was around a woman just out of view, his fingers hidden in her long black hair. After a week, I deleted it. His appearance was beside the point. It was in an entirely different quadrant. I scribbled his name on my calculus homework.

*

In chemistry, Tim asked me if Fiona was still single. He'd sprouted a small patch of grey hair at his right temple. A sugar bloom on a candy bar in a forgotten cupboard.

"Fiona is busy . . ." I drew out my pause, "like digging up pottery shards and fossilized bones and shit."

She'd unearthed something the year before. It didn't take much before she hit bone. It just took a box cutter, and she wouldn't show me the gash until it was safely a scar. I still had the letter she wrote me. I still have every one.

> *I touched it. I couldn't not. I don't want to freak you out. I got stitches. I don't want you to think I'm a monster. Oh well. It's done now. I can't change anything. How was your Spanish test?*

I flinched at the slightest commencement of my imagination. I could not begin to conceive of that kind of pain. She promised it wasn't a suicide attempt. I couldn't exactly argue.

"Are we talking paleontology or archaeology?" Tim wanted to know. Mr. Farley called him up to solve the new problem on the board.

I stared at the periodic table poster by the door. Iron. Oxygen. Sodium. I looked away. The non-calcium-deficient scapula of the girl in front of me was a sight to behold. And if it had been her, if it had been anyone else in the library, then maybe— She turned around. It was Alison. She asked me to stop breathing so loudly.

*

Fiona wasn't in school the next day, or the next day, and when she resurfaced, she gave me not an explanation but a list.

> *Coffee, milk*
> *Mint*
> *Pear*
> *Rice cake*
> *Mint*

I didn't read to the end. I couldn't remember if food diaries were encouraged or prohibited in her current course of treatment. That was between first and second period on a Wednesday. She came and went throughout the week, seemingly at random. I nearly fumbled the next one when she pressed it into my pocket because Matty had left me a new voicemail and I kept forgetting to ask what he did for a living and nothing she did could get my attention.

The good news is I'm beginning to feel very clear, every sense is sharp, and I'm hyperaware. You'll think this is weird: I want to hold my brain. I'm very close to God now. Do you think he's ever held a brain? Do you think he could hold his own? I just texted that to you. Hah. I'm sitting outside now. It's very brisk. I hope you're nice and warm.

Love always,
Fiona

Letters leave you with only half the story. That's enough of a reason to not write them. Imagine an email account with no sent folder, no previous messages quoted in the replies, a string of text messages with a wordless right side of the screen.

Khaki my dear,

I'm in calculus now. How much do you think it would cost to buy up everything the pharmacy has in stock? The boy next to me keeps trying to strike up a conversation but I certainly can't ask him to weigh in on the matter! Ha. I'm not allowed to practice driving anymore. I was supposed to have my test a week or so ago . . . Did you forget or did you not bring it up because you didn't want to upset me?

What's your favorite color these days? Let me guess, you still think black counts? It's the turquoise-y color of the Statue of Liberty for me, well not that exact shade, but very close. I will show you sometime. We could go on a field trip.

They're going to weigh me tonight. They won't let me see. I thought it didn't matter! Isn't that what they say? Well, it seems quite important to them, and yet they insist that I shouldn't concern myself with it. It's very silly, isn't it? As if I haven't got a scale at your house. The Nicorette gum they gave me tastes like . . . I am afraid somebody is going to ask for a piece of it and discover

I think I do want to get better. I want to live if I'm alive. But I don't want to live how I am now. How I am now is

Do you think I'll be able to sleep in a dorm?

I wish you'd tell me who you've been texting. Is it Tim? I think you have a crush on him. Are you waiting to tell me because it's a surprise? I could use some good news. I've been thinking maybe I've never been in love because I—I don't love myself, exactly, it's more like I'm extremely self-obsessed.

I've been thinking that if you truly love me then you will never truly trust me. Because I lie so often

Can you guess the difference between concrete and cement?

Love always,
Fiona

—

[31]He agreed to see me. He was going to pick me up and drop me off a few hours later. A trial run. A test. I had to tell her he existed. She waited with me in the park, though she didn't know that's what she was doing.

"The person I've been texting is— I have," I said to my palm, ". . . an old boyfriend."

The sun was out and setting after weeks of rain. The flowers tiptoed taller. Her skirt skimmed a puddle. "What, like an ex? No you don't." She knelt on the pavement to inspect a half-dead worm and crossed herself in reverence.

"No. Old like elderly."

"Not like *elderly*, as in hoary or retired?"

"Yes, Fiona, AARP. How fucked up do you think I am? He's only like twentysomething. Like post-college but pre-dad. His name is Matty."

She tensed her forehead. The freckles danced. "*The*—"

"Of course not." I stopped her before she could say his name. "But I think it's a good sign. And you can't get jealous again. I'm serious. I really like him. But never more than you."

"Jealous?" She picked at something under her sleeve. "What's he like?"

Tall and polite, I said, but not too kind. His hair was auburn. More brown than hers. "He's kind of needy," I added, carefully. She asked what he needed. "To see me all the time. Like, pictures of me." Pictures of me doing what, she asked, and I didn't know if she was messing with me or really that innocent.

Eventually, her eyes widened. Her jaw dropped. "Oh."

A cop car idled on the other side of the pond. Six geese swooped up from the surface. I squinted into every passing car. A woman and her children. That kid who graduated three years ago and still worked at the movie theater uptown. A truly hoary man with a beagle in his passenger seat. If Matty didn't show up, I assumed Fiona would help me fill my pockets with stones and see me off as I waded into the water.

He arrived just in time. The gold paint on his car was so somber it was beige. I felt like half-treated sewage. Fiona tucked a curl behind my ear and said I was perfect. We'd decided that him taking me to his house was to mitigate the risk of our being seen together. We'd decided that he did not intend to maim me. I made her an accessory to whatever was taking place. She was the only person who I would have let stop me. If she were to try, I would never speak to her again.

"I was waiting to tell you about him until it was real," I whispered when I kissed her cheek goodbye. "He's not that great, anyway. I think I just want to fuck him," I added. I didn't know if he was sharp or blunt, only that he was a weapon.

She gagged.

"Grow up." I dodged the guano on the ground and made my way to him.

The car was locked and running. I couldn't open the door. He jammed down the button to unlock it. Before I could try again, he tried again, relocking it. *You can still leave, Khaki. No thank you!* We persisted and prevailed. I took my seat by his side. The interior was spotless. American leather, air conditioning on. I fastened my seat belt and checked my phone. He hadn't said hello. I didn't mind. His eyes were stupefying.

"Somewhere you'd rather be?" he asked. I told him no. Then came the tic of his laughter. He watched my hand migrate toward his. He didn't react when it landed. The Germs were playing. With his free hand, he drove. He seemed to have nothing more to say.

I considered crawling into his lap or into the glove compartment, but either course of action would have stymied his focus and likely caused us to crash. I picked at a run in my tights. Fiona's tights—she gave them to me when they'd ripped. I sat on my hands and got to memorizing the right side of his face. He was impeccable. What was it about him? Nothing, everything, nothing.

For some reason, I told him I didn't like his shirt. Iron Maiden. Metal? Really?

"Would you like me to pull over?" He laughed and reached for my chest. I told him no.

Roadkill peppered the Parkway with increasing frequency as we moved south. We went back to silence. Exits passed. My excitement advanced. Per the plan, Fiona had made a note of his license plate number. *Just in case!* My excitement retreated.

A penny slid forward from beneath my seat. I put my foot over it, convinced that the sight of it would upset him. There was nothing else in the car. The cupholders were free of wadded receipts. No gym bag in the back seat. I waited until he was switching lanes to lift my foot. Fiona had been collecting pennies and telling me they cost more to manufacture than they were worth. I tried to read the number on the coin face. She wanted to collect at least one from each year she'd been alive. She thought it would help time feel more right. The time, place, and body she was in never felt right. There'd been a day, or many days, that I'd sucked the dirt from my nails while she pointed and flexed her toes and told me, *I think Joan Didion and I would have hit if off if we'd met in kindergarten. I think Truman Capote would have taken a shine to me. He'd like my essence.* She was positive her essence would peter out at twenty-five. *Peter out* meant die. *How do you think I'll die? If I knew the answer, it might change how I decide to live until then.* She'd hurried the words. I didn't want to think about her dead. I could not live without her. I told her and told her and told her. And she said, *I can't live without you either, but who are we to stand in the way of fate?*

"How much longer?" I asked Matty.

"Say that again."

The music wasn't even that loud. I repeated myself anyway, only for him to say he'd heard me the first time.

"Why did you make me—"

"I wanted to hear you again." He parked on the street. He lived in a condo. "Are you going to thank me?"

"Thank you for . . ." I searched everything in sight. This was it. We were here. I felt like someone had just pulled a sack off my head. "Thank you for . . . the . . ."

"I gave you a compliment, babe. I like the sound of your voice."

"Thank you for liking the sound of my voice." I undid my seat belt and let it return to its resting position.

"Hold on," he said. I fastened it back. We were near the water. Not the Atlantic but Raritan or Sandy Hook. Some lesser shore. "I can take you home. You know that, right?"

"No, you can't. You cannot do that. If you make me leave, then I'll—die." On the other side of the windshield, a new shade of night dimmed the sky.

"Okay," he said. "Okay! Let's go then."

I walked up four flights of stairs with his hand on the small of my back. He removed his shoes at the door. I did the same. He latched and locked it and then went on with his day like I wasn't there, like I didn't matter at all. Or like I belonged in his life so completely that of course he'd never think to treat me like a guest. Maybe I'd passed the test. Maybe I lived there now. That cabinet, of course, was where the glasses were. And yes, we drank the tap water, and we used paper napkins.

"I wish you'd been here for the snowstorm," he said. His nose had that crooked charm. And, as I would come to learn, it twitched when I made mistakes.

"Really?" I was still standing by our shoes.

"Come here."

He cringed when I climbed onto the kitchen counter. I sat with one leg swinging and the other pulled into my chest. He didn't tell me to get down. "Like we could have gotten cabin fever and done a whole Donner Party thing?" I asked.

"Who'd eat who first?"

That was a stupid question. I assumed he'd sacrifice himself. I had much more of my life ahead of me. I told him that. He wouldn't stop chuckling; I wasn't joking. I offered an alternative: we could eat each other at the same time. His hip, then mine. My left big toe, his left big toe. A brain for a brain and hearts then swapped, the best saved for last.

He put a hand on his stomach and tipped forward. Apparently I was hysterical. He gathered himself. "Well, the snow melted, so what are we going to do now?"

Fiona had lent me a dress. I'd put a dirty flannel on over it. The microwave clock read 6:53. He went into the next room.

"Come here," he said. I did. He handed me the remote for his strangely small television. I gave it back and waited. He turned it on.

"Now we're going to—" I said. But he already knew. My mouth, his mouth.

It was paramount, absolutely imperative, to remain placid. I did no such thing. I had to stand on my toes to reach him. My arches began to ache. He still smelled like pancakes. That was my first kiss.

"Okay. Okay!" he said when he was sated. I never would be.

I flung myself on the couch and looked at the screen. The contestants were in double jeopardy. He put my legs over his lap and kneaded my calf.

"Should we say 'what is' before our answers?" I asked. I felt very cared for. That feeling felt like a fact. The board of blue clues gave way to a spinning wheel and he turned the television off.

His mouth, my mouth. Maybe it was a competition. His Adam's apple bulged from the branch of his neck. I wanted to puncture his throat. To hold what it held. He brushed my breath from his ear and me from his lap.

"Slow down."

I kneed him in the ribs, harder than I meant to. He got up and disappeared into a room I couldn't see. A second bedroom, maybe, though that idea upset me. He was supposed to be alone. I returned to the kitchen. A takeout menu sat on top of the microwave on the counter. It had been set, not tossed, there. I flipped it back and forth.

"What are you doing?" He was back. Did he look the same now as he had five minutes ago? Why had he left? Why had he come back? I told him I was hungry. That he had to feed me.

"I have to feed you? You're not a dog, babe."

"I know I'm not a dog. You, though . . ."

"Hah. I what?"

"You need to be adored. Very badly, I've noticed."

His hand found my cheek. He pulled his thumb down my oily skin, moving with whatever the opposite of force is. Ha, ha, ha, he said. He refused to be insulted. "There's a diner down the road. Why don't you go pick us up something?" He tossed me his unadorned keys and some cash and told me to make a left and two rights. I'd see the neon sign. He disappeared again and shut a door behind him.

I could pass this test too. I went out to the car. Somehow, he would know if I called Fiona or investigated the contents of his trunk. The penny, it turned out, was ineligible for her collection. It was from 1985. With that settled, I coaxed the seat closer to the pedals and did not adjust the rearview mirror and probably forgot all about the headlights. What had I done? What had he done? He'd told the truth, he'd given good directions. That was all.

I parked at the restaurant and went inside to review the menu. The waitress at the counter smiled at me. I returned the gesture. She scribbled in her notepad as I spoke. Chocolate chip pancakes and a grilled cheese sandwich and a cheeseburger and a slice of red velvet cake and two orders of disco fries. I spun around on a vinyl stool for twenty minutes while I waited.

I decided not to let myself be overwhelmed by the unfamiliar things—his face, having sat in multiple seats in his car, having sat in multiple rooms in his home—that he'd thrown at me, all of which contained smaller, equally unfamiliar new things. The stool spun very rapidly. Shari called me sweetheart when my order was up. I made my arms a cradle. She fit the food in. The paper bag, without handles, was inside a plastic bag with handles.

Matty pretended my return was a surprise. He took the buckling bag from me before I could get my shoes off. He'd been scrubbing his hands. There was no oil left on them. His place was, I realized, more empty than clean. He'd changed into a plain white shirt. The table was set for two. He arranged the foil-covered food and the cardboard containers and sat down. I sampled everything except the burger, which he unwrapped and ate without looking. He said I could sit down. I remained vertical and ate while looking mostly at him.

"Don't forget to breathe over there."

I flung down a fry. "Why am I here?"

He picked up the potato and threw it away. "I'd really like it if you sat down." I sat down. He came around to my side of the table and squatted, bouncing on his heels. "I think you're overthinking it."

"I think—"

"My point exactly." He went back to his seat. I went back to the food. I couldn't think of anything to say to him. He watched me eat for half an hour. I expected my stomach to swell when I stood. It didn't then, or when I bent over to put on my shoes.

"I'd really like it if you took me home now."

A strange pressure snaked around my neck. The difference between a chain and a necklace eluded me. He spun me around. A mouth and a mouth. Frosting and ground beef and provolone cheese.

"Take me home, I said." Why was I aggravated? Because I'd already lost count of how many times we'd kissed.

"Okay. Okay!"

I regret, deeply, that I cannot remember what was playing on the drive back.

*

He deposited me at the park. I walked to Fiona's house from there, but she said she didn't want to stay. We went to mine. It took forever. She insisted on crossing only at crosswalks. We stopped twice so she could rest. She was cold to begin with. The breaks from moving made it worse. In the second interlude, she told me about a tornado outbreak sweeping certain parts of the country. I couldn't stop touching my lips.

"Ready to start again? We're almost there."

I told her Matty had cooked dinner for me. The actual events were too disjointed to convey. I told her things, both true and not. I made myself the object of many of his many transitive verbs. She reacted with enthusiasm, with overwhelming support, akin to the way she might, on my birthday, bake more cupcakes than I could eat.

At my front door, I paused. *Why*, I wanted to ask her, *do you think he even likes me? Why do you even like me?* I didn't. She'd chalk it up to fate. When I let us inside, Cedar nearly knocked Fiona over. Eleanor didn't appear to be home. I kept my voice at a whisper. Fiona spoke at a high volume in the kitchen. She started brewing the coffee she kept above the sink.

"Will you be gone longer next time? Are you going to, you know? *It.* Wait, no, don't tell me." I threw a stuffed duck for Cedar to retrieve. She asked what Matty's house was like. Did he have any plants? Had he been a Boy Scout of America? Was he *prepared*?

"Your dad says hello," Eleanor said. She was just beyond the kitchen, phone in hand. Glowing. "Who y'all talking about? Someone have a boyfriend?"

Cedar ran to her side. No one said anything. My mother's mouth was forming the first words of an inquisition. Fiona crafted a sentence about a movie we'd been watching earlier. She'd fallen asleep during part of it. Now she needed coffee and I needed to fill her in on what she'd missed.

"Which movie?"

We were already halfway to my room.

Fiona wouldn't let me thank her. I told her I'd be right back. I caught my breath in the bathroom. I could not stop checking to be sure I'd locked the door. There were so many of me, in the mirror, and on the screen of my phone, in the new collection of photographs I took and sent Matty in succession.

Caution and curation were no longer necessary. I was almost hostilely calm.

I went to the kitchen. Eleanor was gone. Fiona was, however, still in my room. Was that where I wanted her? Face up in my bed. Limbs straight. Statue still. Eyes closed. On top of the covers. Was that who I wanted there?

"Hey!" I tapped her wrist with my foot. "Here's your coffee. It's getting cold." Still on her back, she took the cup.

—

[32]It felt like overnight that they—they, they, they; who were they!—set Fiona up with a new psychiatrist and some other overeducated woman who worked with, maybe at, our school. The latter looked at Fiona funny when she asked to spend their session discussing the difference between an obligation and a compulsion. This woman cared only about her own questions:

You find a letter, stamped, addressed, but dropped on the street, so you—?

Three things you would want on a desert island are—?

If you could be an animal, it would be—?

You are given three wishes, so you wish for—?

When Fiona asked me the same things, I indulged her. I would read the letter before I mailed it. Food, water, and music. I wanted to be a boat, not an animal. The answer to the question about wishes went without saying. Fiona, for some reason, allocated all her wishes to Matty loving me.

She paced the carpet in my bedroom. I had not yet seen him again. I'd been with her all day. It drove her crazy that the only window I had was stuffed with an air conditioner and blacked out by a poster. IN ALL OUR DECADENCE PEOPLE DIE.

"The things you say about him are so sweet," Fiona sighed. "If I see a shooting star or one of my eyelashes falls out or I get the long end of the wishbone or look at the clock at 11:11 or find a genie in a lamp, I will wish with every fiber of my being that he falls in love with you too. You deserve it more than anyone." I told her to stop wasting her wishes on him. "But it's not for him, it's for you!"

"Okay, fine, whatever." I should have raised my voice at her. Just once. *Your selfishness is really outstanding. Just wish to get better so I can have my friend back. You'll still have two wishes left.*

"I am so happy you found him," she said. "The way you met is so romantic. I might never get to love someone. Or have someone love me. But romance doesn't have much to do with love, does it?"

What was she overcompensating for? She had to know I knew her smoking was back in full swing. She never did it in front of me, but I saw the packs at the bottom of her bag. Marlboro 27s under her pillow. I kept meaning to tell her that the smells of black coffee and peppermint and smoke couldn't cancel each other out. She was a walking bowl of failed potpourri.

She had to know I knew what else she'd gone back to. "I saw your arm, Fiona. How can I be happy if— I didn't think I'd ever have to see that again."

"It barely counts. I did it with my nails. I didn't notice I was doing it, and it's not like I can take it back."

"I don't want you to take it back, but maybe—"

"My new therapist, when we were talking about not cutting too deep and being sterile and scarring, she said someday my kids will see the scars and they're going to ask. She said to stop worrying about the past and start worrying about the future. Someone should tell this woman I don't have a future. Which of course I don't mind, but what she said made me cry until I was gagging. She sat watching me like a robot until I was finished and then she asked if my heart ever hurt. Well, of course it does, lady! It's a muscle. It hurts whenever anything happens."

I handed her a sticker I had lying around. CHEAP GIRLS SAY RELAPSE. The wax paper was still on the back. I could rarely commit to sticking them anywhere.

She read the white square and tucked it into her bag. "Thank you, dear, but I'm not going to relapse." She had to know it had been years since I stopped believing everything she said.

Cedar wandered in and stole our attention. I spent the better part of an hour clipping both of their nails.

"I'm just so happy you're finally happy," she said among the flurry of keratin shards, almost to herself.

"Will you stop saying that? I've been happy the whole time! Ever since I met you," I said. "Nothing feels like you. As good as you."

There was a time when I meant it. But the way she so nakedly needed me became obscene at some point. The predestination of it all—the hushed, literary beginning; the unthinking bonding, no questions asked—was adolescent. I had outgrown it, and her. There was only one way it could end. I didn't want to be around when it did.

*

A few weeks later, I found myself riding around in the back of a Toyota being driven by some guy named Cai. Sophie was up front, skipping around a RVIVR EP, not knowing or caring that I found her older not-boyfriend and his (ironic?) Municipal Waste hat marginally repulsive. His hand never brushed against her leg when he reached down to change gears. He punctuated every aimless drive with reminders that we could always just go to his friend's bar. My sanity was contingent on believing Matty was superior to this person, and to his friend, and to the Prawn-obsessed classmates of ours who spent a lot of time milling around the basement in the art wing at school and would soon be off to Philly, to private and public universities, where they'd get caught tagging and rack up small debts to the city and maybe go on to be pediatricians and would ultimately get to see Algernon far more often than I would.

"Where do you want go to?"

"I don't know, where do you want go?"

We could go to a diner two towns over, because Quick-Chek would be full of people we knew but did not want to know. White Castle wasn't an option because Sophie was vegan that week, and she wanted to go somewhere nicer anyway because three years later stealing silverware was still a large part of her life.

"But *where* do you want to go?" Cai repeated. His car climbed a hill. He was headed to where we could stand next to a 9/11 memorial and study the revised skyline across the river.

"People are at Marcus's," Sophie announced. We murmured our assent. Cai made an illegal U-turn.

At Marcus's, people were in the backyard shed. Cai banged on the door, pretending to be police. Marcus looked petrified, but when he saw who was actually there, he pretended to be glad.

"I told Cai it wasn't funny," I whispered. Marcus didn't hear me. Cai and Sophie greeted everyone.

I took my hands in and out of my pockets and waited for a hit of whatever was being passed around. Either no one or everyone was thinking about how I'd hung out with them three times three years ago, and then never again. Back then, our interactions also revolved around blunts. There were worse things, I knew now, than listening to them talk about anime or that one French teacher's ass. Teenagers are disgusting. These teenagers skipped school on Thursday mornings to line up at Supreme. Watching the wet on their tongues as they showed off their rolling skills was—*Khaki, there are worse things.*

I knocked over a rake. It fell over again as soon as I tried to set it back in place. Marcus told me not to worry about it. When the weed ran out, we went inside. The question of whether his parents were home ate away at me. Greg left to go to the bathroom. I took his seat, and I would have gotten up when he got back but he didn't ask me to get up; he instead picked me up and set me down somewhere else. There were worse things. We ate bowls of cereal topped with ice cream. I asked Marcus if I should put the ice cream back in the freezer. He told me not to worry about it. I asked John P. if I could share his seat. He scooted over. He still had braces, but I'd seen him ollie a six stair once. Sophie and Cai played pattycake across the marble kitchen island. I was high, if not happy. Marcus's parents, as it turned out, had not been home. We dispersed out the back door when they came in through the front. I had Cai drop me off at Fiona's.

She was sitting behind her house, half awake, in the bed of her vegetable garden, contemplating the scratches—no, those were festering gashes—on her arms. She reeled when I tried to stick my finger inside one. Like she was a cat and I'd pulled her tail.

"You never responded to my last letter," she hissed.

"Of course I did."

She'd slipped me something on Monday. I was going to read it during chemistry but Tim wouldn't stop talking and Matty was taking something that had nothing to do with me out on me and there was a pop quiz and it was possible that her note could have gotten mixed up with the paper I'd handed in, but that was impossible because then the teacher would have seen it and read it and recognized her handwriting and seen her signature—she really didn't have to sign it, I knew who it was from—and given it to the guidance counselor who would have given it to that new doctor or whatever whose name I couldn't remember and then Fiona's parents, who had no business reading her private thoughts, would put her back in the hospital for telling the truth about how she felt.

"Fiona, you're probably misremembering. I know that happens when you haven't been eating and I know you haven't been eating but I don't know why you haven't been eating because you won't tell me. I've never not responded to a letter, have I? Did you just forget to give it to me? Did you check the secret pocket in your bag?"

"I don't like your tone right now, Olive. It's rather condescending." She swore she remembered giving it to me because my hair was in a bun and I was wearing that shirt with the giant hole in it and it was a Wednesday. "How could you do this to me? What if—"

"I didn't do anything to you. No one's going to find it. It's probably under your bed. Just, like . . . chill out. For once. It won't kill you. Or sorry, it will. That's the goal, right?" She watched me step on a sprout. She was briefly speechless. "Anyway, like I said, I never had your letter." I drilled my foot beneath more dirt.

"That's too bad, because I told you why. In the letter. So, I'm sorry, I suppose, that I never gave it to you."

I sat by her side. "Forget about the letter. Tell me now. I'm here. I'm listening."

"Never mind," she barked. "I forget what it said."

"Fiona, I'm sorry. But please—"

"No."

The single syllable was hollow. It was like we'd just met. I was relieved. If she was lonely, I didn't want to know.

When I asked her to show me a constellation, she didn't hesitate. Leo Minor, she said, and I asked what the myth for that one was. "Some things just are," she said in her best Katharine Hepburn voice. "We just point and give them names." There isn't always a story.

We listened to the insects chatter. Before long, she turned to whisper into my hair. "My mom said I'll never find someone to love me if I don't recover because they'll lose patience eventually and the only reason she hasn't left is because she can't legally abandon me. I told her she was wrong. She's wrong. You love me unconditionally, right? You'll love me even if I can't do it."

I told her I'd love her forever if I ever loved at all, loved her more than I'd ever loved anyone before, more than I'd love anyone to come. And she had no idea I was just smushing together a couple of songs.

*

Her last day of high school was five days later—the same day she surprised me with an entire pineapple in the hallway between seventh and eighth period. I could barely look at her. The yellow flesh I ate at home that night was perfectly ripe. It stained the first page of the first letter I'd send while she was gone. I finished writing it the next morning and dropped it in the mailbox on my way to school. She'd been sent three states away this time, but otherwise it was all the same. She'd endure another place where everything she relied on to get through the day was forbidden. She'd barely be able to respond to my ramblings. That was okay. I wrote to her every day, sometimes twice, once four times, knowing better than to expect an answer. Which one of us was lonelier then?

—

YOU MIGHT HAVE BEEN MY SUNSHINE

MAY–AUGUST 2011

33 fter a day in which I sat through all my classes—three hundred and ninety minutes of classes—I sat on the ledge of a rooftop parking garage, facing east. Behind me, Sophie and her age-appropriate friend Caroline were arguing over whether the two halves of a new couple the grade below us were in the same league of attractiveness. I swung myself around and tried to join the conversation. It didn't happen. I just stood and looked at the three of us reflected in the back window of a hybrid SUV. We all had dark hair and eyes and otherwise asynchronous faces. The scissored hemlines of our secondhand floral dresses flipped back like tensed lips. Loose threads drooled halfway down our thighs, and we relished the safety afforded to us by the black spandex shorts we wore underneath.

"Did you tell her?" Caroline asked.

I was lost in their sea of ambiguous pronouns. I sat on the concrete behind Caroline and considered picking apart her matted hair. I was, Sophie revealed, the *her* in question. She'd heard Fiona say she wanted her dad to marry Eleanor.

"You don't want to be sisters?"

That was funny. I didn't think there was a word for what Fiona and I wanted from each other. "Wait, when did Fiona tell you that?" As far as I knew, the last time Sophie and Fiona had spoken, Eleanor and I lived on the other side of the country. Though now that Fiona was gone, I had trouble with time and space and specifics. For all I knew, Fiona was back. Fiona was done consorting with me and she and Sophie were consorting behind my back and I was still writing her letters daily, apologizing without admitting what I'd done.

"She said it a long time ago," Sophie confirmed. It had been a half conversation over a cigarette, when I was still the new kid. "Before you two started—"

Caroline refused to believe Fiona and I were platonic. She pointed to Sophie and said, "We've had sex." she said. "Sort of," they then said at the same time. I didn't know what that meant.

"If you haven't, then . . . that explains why both of you look so morose all the time," Sophie added. She was wearing glasses and I wasn't sure they were prescription.

An ant crawled across my ankle. On the other side of the lot, a Jeep backed into a spot. Caroline chugged iced tea from a plastic takeout container, then began contemplating different types of beauty. She was going to art school next year, and her makeup was always flawless regardless of the relative humidity. Logically, that lent her ethos on aesthetics.

Sophie suggested we analyze the guys' appeal before they got there. I had no idea who the guys were. I was afraid to ask. Caroline suggested we categorize Fiona, but then John P. arrived, his skateboard in tow. He explained that the others were looking for a place to park.

"This is a parking garage." Caroline pointed to the empty

spaces we were taking up. Busted backpacks and discarded hoodies straddled the painted borders between them.

He said, "This is expensive."

I could not endure any more of it. I gathered my stuff and told Sophie I might see them later.

I tried to call Matty during my walk home. He didn't pick up. Cedar greeted me at the door with a mangled pen in his mouth. The blue ink on his blond paws looked like frozen berries folded into pancake batter. His tongue was mostly pink; regardless, I was fairly confident the ink wasn't toxic.

"Cool. You're trying to kill yourself too." I reached for his leash and he reared on his hind legs. He almost reached my shoulders. "For this walk," I told him, "let's avoid anywhere we might run into Sophie and company."

We succeeded. I fed him after that and had nothing else to do. His jaw snapped around his late bite of food. I savored the texture of each phone key as I wrote Matty a message. Cedar rolled onto his back. I passed my hand mindlessly over his stomach. His leg spasmed in bliss. I saw the coffee above the sink. I sprinted downstairs and back outside and lifted the lid of the mailbox. Cedar was right behind me. A yellow envelope was caught in a supermarket circular.

It was her second letter in however many weeks. "Cedar, sit. Stay." I read it where I stood.

Khaki, my dear,

Sunday: I have not yet found out why he is here (Green Eyes). If I do I won't be allowed to tell you. We aren't supposed to give names or that kind information.

You must forgive me for my delayed reply; it's difficult to get anything private or personal done here, not to mention the complicated procural of stamps. To answer your question, I am not even the least bit bored of your letters. But you'll be off the hook soon. We have begun to discuss, but have not decided upon, my discharge date. That was fast. Maybe I was never supposed to be here and they've realized their mistake!

Monday: I'm not mad at you. Honest. As long as you promise you won't forget me. I am terrified of getting better, that when I do, you'll realize I am very dull.

Tuesday: Do you know the difference between venom and poison? It's poison when you put it in your own mouth. Venom is from their mouth to you.

Wednesday: I just got off "program hold," which means door alarms on, no going off the unit/ward. It was because I

Should I not tell you this? There must be something else I should tell you.

Friday: I do, despite that hiccup, think this is helping. I am trying, really, to be helped and help myself.

Saturday: Can you go check on Mary Katherine for me?

Wednesday: I, Fiona, am in a mental hospital. It's strange to put it in my own handwriting. It's strange when I realize that I won't always be in a mental hospital. It's strange to be supervised when using scissors to cut pieces of string to weave a bracelet for a boy whose name you aren't supposed to know. It's strange to see myself accounted for acronymically on the reports and forms. Fiona is a mental patient with . . . well you all the diagnoses. All that angry shorthand they use. All their capital letters.

Thursday: I'm glad I waited a few days to send you this! I did something against the rules with Sean! It was nice but I think that he's too good for me. I think I am going to tell him I don't like him at all.

Friday: I had a feeling to wait just a bit longer. Now I'm ready to send this, and Olive, listen, look (?) to (at?) this! He loves me. I want to sleep with him every night. Just sleep! But if he wanted to, well, sleep, then I would do that too. I think God would approve.

Fiona,
Love Always

Wait . . . I got that backward!

*

Matty picked me up from school on a Friday. We went to bed. He handed me a tissue. I didn't know what for. Was I crying? "Wipe your mouth," he said. "I don't like that."

The lipstick was Fiona's. I didn't really like it either, but I'd found it behind my bed that morning and decided it looked better on me. "I don't care what you like," I said. Did I know the difference between a joke and a lie?

His laughter cascaded. My beloved avalanche. When he caught his breath, he declared, with the utmost precision, that he wasn't going to have sex with me. "And you know exactly why not," he said just as clearly. But AP classes were college-level. He didn't care. But I was on the pill. He was indifferent. "I'm not," his nostrils protracted, "going to have sex with you," the promise not to me but to himself.

His mouth, my mouth. The way his word bent. He didn't break it. My eyes latched on to the crown of his head as it slipped away, which was strange because I was sure the room was shrinking, and that should have brought us closer together. He wasn't going to, he was going somewhere else, where hands hovered and something creaked and something parted. It was flat—a palm against me against the sheets flush with the mattress on the even plane of the bedframe on the flat, flat floor. There was the width of shoulders. Legs; length. Another dimension. The cool of a wristwatch burned a circle on a knee. Time tangled, unfurled, he tripped back into his jeans. I looked at the floor. He was leaving and he had hair on his feet.

The lock on the bathroom door clicked. I had time to text Fiona a message she wouldn't see for weeks. I'd need more than a decade to figure out what to say. I opened a drawer and put his Iron Maiden shirt on. I ignored the sting of the sock slouching down my ankle. I exited.

He found me sitting on his kitchen table. Chewing. "These pretzels are stale," I said. He turned his back to me to sneeze. I burst into tears. It was too much abandonment.

"Hey, it's okay. Okay?"

"Okay. Tonight, I can—I want to stay."

He engulfed me. "Well, then, I guess it's time for bed."

He'd changed the sheets. He cooed at me in broken French. When he fell asleep, my heart decided to thump. He didn't snore, or sweat, or kick, or stir. I reached across him. The nightstand held his phone. I deleted every photo: of me, of Cape May, of a power drill.

"I could've done that for you, babe. Just ask next time." His eyes were still closed. Of course, I could not speak. He rolled over and faced me. "I've never made you do anything you didn't want to do, right?" he rasped. I was conquered by the sound.

I tried to climb on top of him. He rolled me over. We were spoons again. I wish I could say that the strangeness of his night light or of his erection pressing against the base of my spine made it impossible to sleep. But I passed out without thinking—that night, and the next weekend, and the next, parking lot, bed, parking lot, and so went the last days of spring.

I tried, once, to get him to commit. To promise to take me to the Fest.

"Florida in October?" He took my hand. "You'll be long gone."

I got out of the car without saying goodbye. Parking lot, bed, parking lot, walk home alone. Fiona's house was only a few minutes out of the way. I went. I stared at her yellow door from across the street. She wasn't in there reading a field guide to North American plants or baking me lemon bars. She wasn't going to walk me home, where Eleanor wasn't going to insist on driving her back to her house, and the three of us and Cedar wouldn't all get into the car and listen to *Songs About Leaving*, the only pretty music I knew.

I left before her parents saw me. My cold fist curled open and closed. I caught the air, released it. I maxed out the volume on my headphones. Do I have to say what was stuck in my head? *I'm not going to have sex with you.* And he didn't. We were careful, he was so full of care, like the time he ended up inside me and removed himself so quickly that for all I know I imagined the sharp suffocating pain. How it felt like my lungs were full of vinegar. For all I know it was just wishful thinking.

—

[34]He kept me late one morning. Cedar wasn't at the window when I got home. Eleanor's car was in the driveway. Whatever business trip she'd taken or spontaneous spa weekend she'd treated herself to had ended ahead of schedule. I attempted a subtle entrance. Her suitcase was tipped over on the floor. Her voice was weirdly taut.

"I didn't hear a car drop you off."

"I walked." I took a step upstairs.

"Don't," she whispered. Had I met her eyes, I would have seen something wrong.

"Why? I need to take a shower."

"Where were you last night?"

"Sophie's. I told you that." I was halfway up the stairs. My mother knew.

"I tried to call you."

"My phone died. Where's Cedar?" She had turned him against me, trained him, in just an hour, to not come running at the sound of my voice.

"Baby, I need to talk to you."

"Just let me get my charger." I made it all the way up the stairs. I made it into the hallway. My bedroom door was open. He was dead on my pillow.

She was behind me, ready for when I buckled. "He was cold when I got home. There was nothing I could do."

I squeezed her wrist. My nails sunk through her skin. She bled. She kept asking where I'd been.

"Nothing you could do," I repeated. He was bloated. Jaw slack. "Did you try?" His gums receded in a listless snarl.

"How long have you been gone? When did you leave him?"

I couldn't go near him.

She called a neighbor to help carry him down the stairs.

In the bathroom, I cowered. The window opened to the roof. The sky was a slate of unbroken blue. I climbed outside and gripped the shingles. I'd seen the writing on the wall. On the fences at dog parks. *No dogs without people. No people without dogs.* I went back inside. Eleanor returned, without an explanation. The cause of death was inconclusive.

*

I slept in my mother's bed for days. When she got too close, I reverted to weeping. I couldn't hold him; she couldn't hold me.

She took the couch downstairs. When I returned to my room, I found foreign bedding. My old sheets were in vacuum-sealed bags at the foot of the bed. There were smaller bags too. A worn-out chew toy trapped in new plastic. The corner of his favorite blanket. Her hand on my back. I didn't let myself buckle.

"Only open the bags when you have to. His smell will fade." She motioned to the marks I'd made on her arms. "The vet asked about our cat."

I think I was supposed to laugh at that. "Please leave me alone."

She did.

I wrote:

F—

Cedar died in the middle, the end, I don't know, of the night, in my bed, while I was in someone else's. It's just you and me now.

—K

And Merricat.

*

I stopped speaking. I started eating faster than Eleanor could cook. My neck swelled with lymph. I inhaled potlikker with enough hot sauce to draw out the last of my tears. I made it a third of the way through most days of school before walking out and wandering for miles. I ignored Matty until he started cracking threats like jokes.

Before bed, my mother braided my hair. I asked her to redo it, more tightly. She served ice cream for breakfast. She left the red, white, and blue rope Cedar and I played tug of war with—he nipped my fingertips without malice; he won—halfway under the washing machine. His leash hung on its hook by the door. I stopped wiping his fur from my clothes. At a quarter past seven on weekdays, he didn't gallop around until I was awake. On weekend mornings, I slept in, woke up, and yelled his name. She bought me an alarm clock. I broke it in half.

"I love you," she told me over breakfast the next morning. Cornbread and a cookie. "And I need to know where you really were."

I tried to cork my mouth with food. To my chagrin, I had to swallow in order to breathe. I inhaled, exhaled, resumed speaking. "I woke up early that morning and Cedar seemed like he was having a nice dream so I walked to Fiona's house by myself because I forgot she isn't there and I felt like an idiot and I looked like an idiot so I turned back around." My voice was rusted over. My fork clanged on my dishes. "She was fine for so long and I was an idiot for believing that it was for good this time, or any of the times." Guilt polished my pupils. "It's so boring to spend all your time worrying, so I stopped bothering, then I—"

"You didn't do anything wrong," she said. "And you don't have to hold everything inside." She got up to open a bottle of wine. "Can I tell you some news? It's good news. I saw your father while I was in Portland. We're working on, you know, working things out. I think we could get back to how we used to be." She filled two glasses. A drop of burgundy spattered the floor and there was no one there to come lick it up. "I might go back there again. My heart just isn't here."

"What is wrong with you?" I spurned the glass she gave me. "I thought you would be happy, for me. For us."

"Why on earth do you think anything's going to be any different? You're so ridiculous. Both of you."

"You need to watch yourself."

What did I have to lose? "I'm glad you lied about where you were too."

"Excuse me?" she said, harsh and hushed. I thought she might break the stem of her glass. Her shoulders tensed over the counter.

"You weren't at a business conference. I wasn't at Fiona's house. Or Sophie's. I spent the night with a man. Like you." I traced a divot in the leg of the table.

"Khaki Anita Oliver, you better mean a boy."

"Yeah, a boy, whatever. I'm going to go now."

I ran outside, betting, correctly, that she wouldn't try to stop me. I put one foot in front of the other until I was hacking pale vomit into a rosebush. Half the flowers were in bloom. I kept going. Twenty blocks away, a dog ran the length of their fence. I crossed the street. If I touched one, breathed on one, looked one in the eye, the entire species would go extinct. My mind began to quiet until the blankness was too like snow, and I was back to trying to understand how Cedar knew what it was, how the first time he looked outside and saw white falling, he went instinctively wild. Like he'd been waiting for exactly that. He turned in circles, his mouth wide open like Armageddon was approaching, and as he spun, I swore I heard him say *Let me out.* I did. The morning he rushed into was hazardless, still serene. My father had taught me not to call for Cedar to stop if he ran into the street. It was safer, he said, to let him reach the other side uninterrupted. He hadn't mentioned that he could die safely indoors.

I was back at our porch. I'd conjured an eerie composure. Eleanor had lit candles in the living room. If Cedar had been there, she wouldn't have risked the open flames. He wouldn't have allowed her such a stretch of peace. I sat next to her on the couch, careful to leave space between our knees.

"Mom, I need to talk to you." She stayed in her pose. "When Cedar—the boy I told you about is named Tim. You picked me up from his house freshman year when we were working on a bio project. I don't know if you remember. But we're not hanging out anymore. There's not really a point. He's moving to Canada for college. I'm not holding anything else in, there's just nothing else I want to talk about. I'm really sorry. For lying."

"Thank you," she said. I couldn't stand the smell filling the room. "But! I'm not condoning you running around behind my back. Or that damn disrespect. You can be so sweet sometimes. And other times . . . I have to give it to you—you know just how to hurt me."

"Did I hurt you more than you hurt yourself by leaving Dad?" She looked at me like I had a knife to her throat. "Sorry," I said. "Forget I asked."

"No. I just didn't see that question coming." She reminded me that I'd never asked anything about the divorce while it was happening. "We practiced what we would tell you so many times and then," she snapped her fingers, "it seemed like you couldn't care less." She laughed for a second, her lashes damp.

"It didn't feel like any of my business. But if you'd wanted to tell me about it, I would have listened." I put my head in her lap and looked up. I memorized the way her neck met her chin. There were thirty-five years between us and I'd never thought to fill them in. "You can tell me now if you want to."

"Where should I start?" she asked.

"I guess with you."

The candles burned down. She started to fade when she reached her high school years. We said we'd finish later. We never did.

—

[35]I didn't bother acting grateful the last time I saw him. He didn't try to touch me. He let me look at his things. The only book he owned was *Dune*. He'd become an animal I visited at the zoo, except he was in charge of the keys.

"What's all this?" I asked.

"Those are records."

"Yes, these are," I pointed to the ones I recognized. "What are these?" Mississippi John Hurt looked like someone from a sleeve in my father's attic. Maybe I had seen him before. I told Matty that my father stopped listening to new music the year I was born. He grunted in response. I did not ask Matty when he was born.

"Is this one . . . electronica? Do you, like, like to dance?"

"I contain multitudes," he said. His nostrils flared into bells. The shape of foxglove flowers.

"You really don't." We locked eyes. I tried to find his repulsive. "Don't worry," I told him. "No one does."

He plucked the record away and filed it back in place.

"Have you ever been in love?"

"Yes," he said. No further details were volunteered. I just wanted to erase the strain on his face.

He stood and walked away. I followed so close that my nose grazed his back. I couldn't think of anything better to do, and he was still coming up with new things to do while I stared at his ceiling. I emitted no noise. My silence seemed to please him, and I wonder if it was not in fact a choice I made but an instruction of his that I'd absorbed. Or, worse, a new preference of his I'd anticipated and complied with preemptively. He left me in the parking lot after that.

*

I hadn't seen him in ten days; he hadn't texted me back in four. I called him nine times, from the floor of my kitchen. He was working. I sat with Cedar's empty dishes. It was the middle of the afternoon. He picked up on what I promised myself would be my last attempt.

I had the first word. "Just tell me what I did wrong. Please? I love you."

"Whoa! Yeah, no. We both know you don't mean that."

"But I want to. What's the difference?" I asked, in shambles. "I really want to. Why isn't it working?"

"Because you know you deserve . . . not this." He sounded like he was making an appointment for an oil change. "Look, babe. You're very . . . important to me. But we shouldn't be friends anymore. Let's just get it over with before you leave. Okay?"

"No. Fine. Maybe. But first, just say—" The rest wouldn't leave my head. *That you watched me watch a band and then you tried to take me away from that; you tried to take that away from me.*

"Say *what*, babe? I don't have time for games."

He hung up, as one does when there's no sound on the other end of the line.

Let's say love is what compelled me to keep calling. Nine rings. Again. Nine more. Twenty-seven. I got to eighty-one. I hung up before it went to voicemail. One hundred and seventeen. I threw my phone in the dog dish and grabbed Eleanor's laptop. I searched for him there. I typed in the name I'd seen a hundred times on the mail on top of his microwave. He was many years older than I thought. Never married. No arrest records. A graduate of TCNJ. I cleared the search history and called him again. *Hey, it's Matty,* he laughed on the recording. *Leave a message—*

Fiona's house was the only place I could think to go. I blasted angry bargaining into my ears. *I would die to not care anymore. I would die to hate you.* The mile and a half felt like ten, so I ran. Humidity hung over my head. The clouds refused to rain.

I walked, entirely disheveled, through the Davieses' front door. I kept my shoes on. That was strictly verboten. Her dad didn't notice. He half knelt over an enormous puzzle on the coffee table. His Cornell T-shirt caught on his paunch. His crystal glass of meticulously aged bourbon rested, without a coaster, on the planks that made up the lacquered floor. *Did you know,* she had written in her first letter, *that it costs them a thousand dollars a day to lock me up in here? A day! What a waste!*

"Hey, kiddo."

I said I'd come to borrow a book from Fiona's room. He waved me past. I didn't know why I was there, only that I wanted to sit with my back against her door, smell the lotion on her dresser, read the notes we'd scribbled on the wallpaper in homemade invisible ink. The stairs were inexplicably difficult to climb. The sweat on me showed no sign of drying. The attic was on the far side of eternity. I made myself reach it. The doorknob didn't resist. Where was Mary Katherine? I'd probably killed her too.

I went to the window by the desk. Lena was out back. In a chair. Fiona would have been in the grass, begging the earth to subsume her or willing herself to sprout roots that would tie the land to her. She and her mother had the same chin on their sleek, plucked faces. I turned back around and scanned the room. *Franny and Zooey.* That was why I'd come. Fiona arranged her books at random. I might be here for a while. I searched three times, two shelves top to bottom and back again. I checked her drawers, under her bed, behind her mirror. She might have had it with her. I knew it wasn't in the closet. I went over there anyway.

Her wardrobe hung from white velvet hangers. On the floor below the fabric, I found a box the size of rainboots. She'd sketched an ornate *K* over the brand name on the lid. I wiped my hands on my shirt, which only made them damper. I opened it. It was just an archive of everything I'd written her over the years. I closed the box and toed it back to its place in the corner. It wouldn't sit flush with the wall. I pushed a few ankle-length dresses to the side.

An unmarked manilla envelope, absolutely stuffed with paper, was causing the blockage. I broke the seal and dumped the contents onto the carpet. I recognized them too. Every word Matty—the first one—and I had ever exchanged. The goodbye postcard that she made me write that she promised to send that she promised not to read. My awe beat the anger. I wiped at a new wave of sweat. One page of the transcript was folded into fourths. I pried it open. It was from her to him.

I was, she warned him, obsessive, controlling, possessive. She couldn't blink without me trying to hold a symposium on it. *Woah*, he said. *Fuck. Good to know.*

She'd warned me too. *Are you sure you want to love me? I lie so often. There must be something else I should tell you.* I hit my skull against the wall. I hoped the house would collapse. My hair caught on a peacoat button. The tedium of detangling it slowed my heart down. I put everything back how I'd found it. The day I met Fiona, she'd tricked me into thinking that it was okay that I was the way I was. She was outlandishly cruel.

The chair at her desk was handsome and so uncomfortable. I slumped into it. Her laptop had been charging without interruption for over a month. I opened it and tapped each key. Matty couldn't be too hard to track down again. The truth would be a weight off his shoulders. It had all been a misunderstanding. He'd be relieved! I still loved him; still didn't want him to love me back. He was probably in California now, and somehow my soul had known it, and I would be there very soon, and the two of us would be blessed with wide open possibility. We would flourish. We could flee. We—

I smelled smoke. The door groused open.

"Khaki? We weren't expecting you this evening."

Lena stepped into the room and put out her cigarette in an empty coffee mug on the dresser. Orange pollen clung to her shirt collar. It brought out the ocher in her eyes. She looked like a worn-out mannequin. "You look . . . distressed," she told me, her voice at a loss for luster. "Is something wrong?" She came closer. Merricat stayed at the threshold.

Yes; a grenade or two had gone off inside me. Triage was in motion. "I got dumped today." I shut the laptop. "I thought I was in love, but I didn't know them at all."

She leaned forward. I half stood up from the chair. She pulled me into a strange embrace. Our body odors mixed, though hers was perfumed and pleasant. "Dumped, huh?" She let go and took a few steps back. "Anyone I know?"

I sat back down. "Not really." She wasn't close enough to touch anymore, but she was close enough to kick. In a way, she was to blame. Fiona was her creation.

"Well, I'm sure he's a twit," she said, because the Davieses never cursed.

"A twit, yeah. I miss her more, though." It was true. I reconsidered Fiona's cruelty. She and I were predestined; Matty had to recede to make room for her. Romance was obsolete. Fiona was who I wanted to wake up next to every morning. Friendship was cleaner. Simpler. Superior. She saved me the pain of seeing who he really was—someone who took a stranger at her word. Someone who left, no questions asked. And unlike her, he didn't come back.

"I miss her too." Lena took out her next cigarette.

"I feel like it's my fault that she had to go away again." My knuckles rocked across the desk.

Lena was strangling the cigarette in silence. She produced a match out of nowhere and inhaled while she spoke. "Well, no, that was all me."

"It was?" I wasn't sure how literal she was being.

She told me things Fiona never had, or that she'd never told Fiona. When Lena first realized Fiona was sick, she made appointments with preeminent doctors, joined every support group, took insightful notes on cryptic scientific journals. She told Fiona it was her fault. She didn't know how, but it was. She rammed apology after apology down Fiona's throat.

"She didn't want to eat those either," she laughed.

I joined her. It drained me. She told me to stay put. Her steps resounded on the stairs. Two years earlier, when Fiona was getting a new roll of paper towels from the basement, I overheard Lena on the phone. She didn't know whether to be ashamed or embarrassed. *My failures are written all over her. She's telling the whole world how badly I failed her.*

Lena came back to the attic with a glass of water. Condensation already covered the cylinder. "You're dehydrated," she said. "You're sweating like a pig."

I laughed at that too. A train horn blared in the distance. Eleanor would be home from work soon. Lena half glanced at her watch. Diamonds lazed around her wrist. She said it was time for me to go. I followed her to the kitchen and placed my empty glass in the sink. Her husband hadn't moved since I arrived. *Monty Python* flickered on the television.

"Hey, kiddo," he said, "don't be a stranger."

—

[36]Fiona came back in June. She didn't look different. She swore that she was. I listened to her pontificate about metamorphosis. What else did I have to do? *Look what they've done to me,*

look what they've made me do to myself, it's not so bad now but surely I won't be able to stand this forever, surely progress can't go on indefinitely, I've lost and gained my entire body weight back throughout the years so if you think about it I've already died and been reborn. Call me Theseus's ship! I nodded non-committally. We started watching documentaries to pass the time. She traded *Breakfast at Tiffany's* for *In Cold Blood* and *Play It as It Lays* for *The White Album*. I still preferred things that were pretend. Like the envelope in the back of her closet. Surely that had been a dream.

She got to do all her schoolwork from home. I had to spend the first three weeks of June at school, going through the motions, finishing out the school year, handing in tedious documents and showing up to painful meetings like I was finalizing a passionless divorce. My last final exam was in Spanish. Ten minutes into the test, Sra. O'Brien (née Alvarez) answered a knock at the door and stepped into the hallway. The room took the chance to chat, but not cheat. It quieted when she reappeared.

"Maya Brooks passed away in her sleep last night." She repeated it in Spanish, as if in a trance. The test would have to be rescheduled.

I watched everyone react. An Alison made eye contact with me. Her face had become blotchy at an impressive rate. She was sniffling in wet, hot bursts. People were speaking in platitudes. Sra. O'Brien was patting backs. Unstable expressions oscillated across faces and I really didn't like Alison's. Her tears were like a puddle of pothole water splashed onto a pedestrian by a passing truck. I was the pedestrian. She was the truck. I just wanted to finish the test. "It doesn't make any sense," Alison managed to say. I agreed until I realized she meant an eighteen-year-old's sudden death.

"Isn't it awful?" she asked. "Don't you feel so awful?"

How I felt didn't strike me as important. But she seemed to both want and not want me to answer her questions. They weren't rhetorical, they weren't literal. I didn't know what I was supposed to do. The situation was sad, abstractly. People died every day for all sorts of reasons and in all sorts of situations, and the thing was, I had no idea who Maya was.

"Awful," I said.

Sra. O'Brien dismissed us. We could stay if we wished. For support. Not to finish the test.

Eleanor had let me drive to school that day, though the distance didn't warrant it. I drove to Fiona's and called her from the driveway. The Wild was playing. I had the windows up, the banjo trapped in. She traipsed out a minute later, antique sunglasses eating her face, and plopped into the passenger seat. With her came the smell of a recovering addict's last vices. Tobacco stung by peppermint, covered in coffee. I rolled the windows down.

"Everyone who bet on me being the obligatory pre-graduation death must be devastated," she said through tears.

"That's fucked up, Fiona." I laughed.

"I know."

I drove in a random direction and hoped she was crying for Maya rather than herself. I hoped that by then Alison was no longer crying, unless she found extended crying productive, in which case I hoped she was going strong and had found someone with whom to make eye contact and discuss awfulness.

"Can you describe Maya to me?" Fiona couldn't, but she

held her phone up to my face at a stop sign. Facebook was little help. If I'd ever seen Maya, she'd never stuck. I tended to have tunnel vision.

Fiona wondered if, come graduation, someone from Maya's family would accept her diploma on her behalf. I'd assumed there wouldn't be a diploma; she'd probably missed a test or two by dying, so if any of her grades were hinging on passing a final, then she might have been shit out of luck.

"I think you're missing the point, Olive."

I knew I was. I always knew I was missing something, but never what it was. I told Fiona I didn't know what a dead person needed a diploma for or if anyone wanted to be told *happy birthday* or *good morning* when those occasions came around. Or if they enjoyed having brunch with their cousins when they randomly came to town, or if they only did so out of some sort of unspoken obligation, or if it depended on the cousin and the restaurant and the time of year. "Have you noticed how much people complain about having to do things that they don't actually have to do? Why don't they just say no to doing them to begin with? It's not that hard."

"It's very hard, actually, to not do what's expected of you." She turned off the air conditioning and rolled the windows up. "I wish you weren't so disturbed by the things that make us civilized. But there's something admirable about it, I suppose."

"Thank you?" I stole a glance at her. Cloth-covered buttons ran down the length of her scarlet romper. She'd bared her legs for the first time in two summers. The sleeves hid her arms. Beneath them, raised scars scattered from her shoulders to her hips. There were stacks of them in places, like toothpicks caught beneath her skin.

"And what else disturbs you?" she asked.

I gave my eyes back to the road. "When two people trip over themselves to be the one to hold the door open, I think they're just showing off, trying to prove they're good people who understand how people are supposed to be. And no one actually likes when someone gives them flowers, right?"

"I do." I knew she did. Purple ones.

Since leaving her driveway, we'd left our town and crossed through two more. It didn't take long to reach somewhere much poorer or much more right wing. Some were both. I followed a sign for the Parkway. I got on it, going north. She passed me money for the toll. For the first time since I'd met her, her chapped hand was warm.

I asked how many calories she'd been tasked with eating that day and what she wanted to do instead. She didn't want to do something instead. She wanted to do that and something else. Have a picnic and engineer a kite. Rent a boat and bring a baguette and bite into it and swallow the bite and let herself absorb the nutrients. Explore the abandoned insane asylum after a bowl of spaghetti. It was too late in the season to harvest ramps, but she wanted to go to High Mountain. She thought we might find some mushrooms and she thought she would maybe have some ice cream sometime soon. Was that okay?

No, waiting around for you to cross over into the real world only to retreat a month later is not okay with me anymore. We both know you're never going to eat ice cream again. You have no idea how much I've forgiven you for and you're not even going to have the decency to stay alive and keep me company. Are you finally going to kill yourself tomorrow or are you going to wait a few years? Choose wisely because I'm not coming back home just for your funeral. Maybe I should kill you myself.

"Of course that's okay." We never really told each other no. *This is too much* and *I think this is a bad idea* were not in our vocabulary, at least not when it came to wanting what we wanted.

I took her to High Mountain and followed her around the woods as it got dark. There was slate and there were logs and buds and decay, and all I could do while she stopped every half mile to bring her nose to the mud was hope that when we reached the lookout point, I'd have a happenstance dalliance with a William Paterson senior. I couldn't help it. I was set in my ways.

She got up from her knees. "Do you still miss him?"

I did, and I had for three years, and I would never stop, especially now that I knew our relationship had ended under the false pretense of her barbarous design. But that wasn't who she was asking about.

"I only missed him for like a week. He was kind of mean to me. And I didn't really like him to begin with. I told you I just wanted to fuck him."

"Did it hurt? Not *it*, but when you broke up? And before that, he didn't ever physically hurt you, right? He just wasn't the right one, right?" She waved to a middle-aged couple trekking across the way. "Hello? Olive!"

"What?"

"Did he hurt you?"

"No, he just wasn't the one. And I don't think he's very well read. His whole name is David Mathieu, did I tell you that?

He's like the French-Canadian Dave Matthews, so yeah, he's actually the most embarrassing thing that's ever happened and he's not even hot, so let's never talk about it again."

"My dad likes that band."

"Oh my god."

I was not going to ask her about Sean. I could neither care less nor convince myself he existed. She was not going to confess any of the things she was supposed to confess. We walked the rest of the trail in silence, without any more botanical investigation breaks. When a branch caught on her sleeve and made a small rip in the fabric, she was oblivious. Beatitude shone through her sunglasses. She pressed the crucifix on her necklace against her thumb. Ladybugs landed on her and alighted away. Her hallowed sublimity was unavailable to me. Everything I wanted was unavailable to me.

We should go, she said. She didn't want to overexert herself. When we got back to the parking lot, she said we should get something to eat. I couldn't fit the key into the ignition. It kept scratching just shy of the hole. My elbow knocked hers as she tried to help.

"I've got it, thanks! Put your seat belt on." Her seat belt was already on.

I drove to the Parkway, going farther north. I didn't know where. I was causing traffic to back up in the left lane.

"Well," she said, "I always thought Matty was sort of a creep. From far away, anyway." She tipped her sunglasses, which I hated, down the bridge of her nose. "But I'm a creep too. So are you. If we were boys, they would take us away! Well, they already took me—but for different reasons."

"He's the stupidest thing we've ever done."

"You never told me his license plate number. Oh well!"

I remember this as whispered, but we would have had to shout over the road noise. And I never turned off the jangly music. "I can't believe I asked him to prom."

"Can you imagine?" She laughed. I did too and it made my driving even worse. Honks abounded. "I really think you should get out of this lane, dear."

"Fiona, I have to ask you something. It's important. While you were gone, I came over to borrow *Franny* and—"

A passing truck splattered mud across the windshield. The wipers couldn't move it. I couldn't see ahead. I gripped the wheel. The wipers continued their ineffectual flailing. The other car lights peeked through the mess, faraway reds and whites, out of focus. I slowed down, sped up, hit the brakes again. We were going to die—two more deaths before graduation and they'd accuse us of lovers' suicide, of trying to upstage the girl whose name I sort of recognized but face I did not know—and people to whom we were completely irrelevant when we were actually alive would get themselves all worked up about our deaths and I wouldn't get to ask them why. She cut the music. For a fraction of a moment, I could stare right at her without having to worry about what was going on around us. A busy highway was going on around us. Her sunglasses bounced off the seat and disappeared beneath it.

"Olive, you have to breathe," she said. I shook my head no. "For me. Everything's going to be okay." She stuck her head out the window and talked me through moving over two lanes to an exit. "Just put your hazards on and keep the speed steady. One, two, wait . . . wait . . . now!" She directed us to a gas station like it was nothing.

I pulled into the first open pump. I couldn't make further movements. I doubted I could speak. My foot couldn't leave the brake. I left the car in drive. She touched my jaw to remind me to relax it, then grabbed her purse. She told the attendant we didn't need any gas, then ran inside. She returned with a jug of blue fluid and a bottle of seltzer. "I need you to turn off the vehicle, dear."

My limbs were back under my control. I turned the car off and joined her in front of it. She had the hood open. She unscrewed something and sent the blue liquid down a small well.

"Was that expensive? I can pay you back. Is my mom going to know that something was wrong? What is wrong? How are we going to get home?"

Without looking up, she told me to take a deep breath. "You ran out of wiper fluid. We're good as new now." She screwed the cap back on the bottle and left it at the foot of the pump. "See—no evidence!"

She tried not to laugh. She surrendered when the sky cracked to suddenly pour. Our makeup streaked into mayhem. I worried she might dissipate, with the wet weighing her down.

"How did you know what to do?" She couldn't even drive.

"I've been teaching myself things. The real world is so wonderfully mundane. Who knew how important it is to establish a good credit history as early as possible? Do you know your social security number? I sure didn't! I learned both of ours. I'll teach you yours. And how to change a tire. I swear, Olive,

I swear to God, I'm not going to be helpless. You should be learning this stuff too."

Her blush was wayward. Her hair was plastered to her head. She was not a mess. I knew I should just stop it with her. I tried. I really did. She pulled my hair into a bun and tried to pat me dry with her sleeves.

"I love you."

"I love you."

We never said *I love you too.* That would suggest we were only saying it because the other person had said it first. It was better if we arrived at the same conclusion independently. That meant it was meant to be.

I took my place in the car and waited for her signal. She stood on the passenger side, where she'd left her door and window open. Rain ran into the car. She poured the seltzer on the windshield to loosen what might be stubborn.

"I'll be right back." She ran toward the store. She stopped. "Don't move!" As if I would go anywhere without her. She kept moving. She took her time coming back, chips in one hand, a napkin in the other.

"Do you know," she asked, "the difference between agency and control?" Free will had something to do with it.

—

[37]We graduated. Maya's mom walked across the stage on her daughter's behalf. Alison bawled. Fiona stayed home. The next night, Fiona sat stiffly on my bed while I got ready to go to a show. I braided my hair in front of the mirror, compacting it as

much as possible, making it less likely to get ripped out. I was leaving for California in fifty-six days.

"Can I come with you?" she asked. It was the most insane thing she'd ever uttered.

"If you want to hang out with me that badly, I guess you can ride the train with me. But you can't come inside."

"Why not?" She was not herself. She wasn't picking at her skin or bouncing her feet. The elastic I was twisting around my hair snapped. I found another one under my dresser and started the whole process again.

"I think it's sold out."

"Aren't there scalpers or something like that?"

"Even if you could get in, it wouldn't be safe. You might legitimately get broken."

"Olive, I eat more than you now! I'm a perfectly sturdy person. And I've been listening to Title Fight."

"You've been what?"

"Don't laugh! Not all their songs are fast. I think 'Safe in Your Skin' is nice. How dangerous could it possibly be when they're playing that?"

I finished corralling my hair. "You actually aren't wrong." I considered putting more deodorant on. I decided not to. "But let me tell you a story. Once upon a time, the kids convened and someone said, *Hey, you know Title Fight?* and his friend answered, *Yeah, they're great—why?* Then another boy chimed in, *I know they aren't the hardest band out there, but they can be pretty heavy . . .* A small crowd began to gather. *I think what we need to do is . . . Go. As. Hard. As. Possible. Whenever they play.* The one who said it was wearing a Trapped Under Ice long sleeve. A girl in a Wonder Years beanie nodded. *Even during*

'Shed'? she was dense enough to ask. *Especially during 'Shed.'* They each put in a hand, many of which were attached to wrists wrapped in straightedge watches. *Go Ned!* They yelled on the count of three, then broke the huddle. And no one ever spoke of it again. It just was. The end."

She said she couldn't tell how serious I was being.

"As serious as you getting your nose broken during '27' and me getting in a lot of trouble with both our moms!"

"I can go hard!"

"Can you, though?"

"I can break someone's nose before they break mine!"

"That's not how it works. You aren't playing offense."

"Well, then fine, I'll just stand on the sidelines."

"What's the point of even going then? Do you want to take the train with me or not?"

She pulled a glossy magazine out of her bag. "I'm not *that* lonely." I sat with her. My head went on her shoulder. "Help me look through this," she said. It was her college course catalog.

I didn't help, I just listened. The words streamed together as she read them to me. AstronomyLabEcologyReligion&Food MechanicsOfSolidsPlato&SocraticIrony. I tried to cram more of her into my long-term memory. Two, then ten, then twenty passing minutes were palpable. I grieved each millisecond. I knew I was late. It was very hard to stand up and leave.

*

She made me miss The Menzingers. I got there while Touché was taking a breath. What remained of Jeremy's voice was a medical miracle. On the floor, hats and single shoes sprung up from lighthouse limbs, shining dimly for their owners to retrieve them. The next song started. A blow to the head knocked my left contact lens out. No problem. Whatever was happening around me, I'd seen it before. With half my vision, I shouted about Los Angeles like it already meant something to me. Maybe at the end of the night, the band would take me with them, to Pennsylvania, the Midwest, and Canada before Europe, where we'd meet up with La Dispute, and we'd be back in LA for FYF, which would be only a few weeks after I was supposed to start school, and that way Fiona and I would never have to actually say goodbye.

While Title Fight got set up, I looked for Sophie. She'd said she might be there, but she'd also said something about having to bail Cai out. Her word choice could have been euphemistic or literal. I texted Fiona, *Maybe we'll meet again.* She asked if that meant I wasn't sleeping over tonight. I put my phone in a zipped compartment inside a zipped compartment in my backpack. Guitars fed back. The lights went down. Applause picked up. The fabric of my shirt touched the fabric of my neighbor's shirt. My nerve endings were somehow interwoven with the threads. He was so close. It was starting again. Six guys climbed on stage and, with no regard for each other, all tried to dive into the same two parts of the crowd. They all incurred different injuries. I held tight to my backpack, thumbs pressing down on the insides of the straps; I wasn't going to asphyxiate where I stood. *Beneath the sheets you buried me.* Arms wound like windmills. The noise was locomotive, speeding or not. Bodies barricaded the bodies that needed a second to recover.

Ned sang roughly but entirely decipherably, with heavy

hints of defeat. The reaction that the band inspired wasn't as absurd as I'd made it seem. Converting every emotion to anger made everything easier. How like or unalike were manipulation and magic? I tried to turn my brain off and let the next song make me into a loon. Something barreled into me. I blacked out between the first and second choruses. A hand, a hip. I turned and found narrows of air. Something brushed the back of my neck. I couldn't tell where he was hiding. I caught an elbow to my side and understood I was going to die there. I felt the tears coming. The kid next to me asked if I was okay. My pulse was in a dozen places and I wondered if it mattered that none of them were my wrist.

I pushed through the crowd, found the bathroom, and dry heaved to the muzzled sound of "Evander." *He's not here, Khaki. He can't hurt you. It didn't hurt.* I splashed water on my face and pressed my hips into the counter. When I'd walked into my first show three years earlier and the bass made its way inside my chest, I'd come close to combusting. Some reflex I had said I was in peril. I'd looked to the rest of the room. No one else had panic written on them. No one else had been invaded. I realized it wasn't sinister. And I wasn't the only one who could feel it. I'd just never heard anything that loud before.

I went back to the floor. The sweat on us was sexless. *What if Fiona snuck in? She's not here, Khaki. No one can hurt her.* My hands, their hands, were open-palmed. We shoved each other away. I tried to figure out if there existed a kind of violence that didn't cause harm, or if that was something else altogether. They surfed and they dove and I accidentally floated. My stomach fell when I dropped back to the floor. At the end of the encore, I was barely on my feet. I was so glad it was over.

I went without headphones on my way home. The train was a test—a time and place to confirm the fact of an absence. He wasn't there. Apprehension was at my back. I was where? I was heaving? My tongue skid in my spit. I wondered which distant flaps of butterfly wings had set it all in motion, if it would have killed Fiona to just let me have what I had with him—it was just words on a screen—why she had to annihilate it and leave me to supplicate affection from someone whose Black Flag vocalist ranking was satisfactory at best.

I handed my ticket to the conductor and curled up in my seat. I pulled the two new shirts I'd bought on top of the one I was already wearing. That morning, Fiona had told me *When I gain weight it's like someone has altered me without permission. By that logic, losing weight should feel the same. But it doesn't. It doesn't feel the same.* Our friendship must have altered her. I wouldn't ask. I didn't want to know what it had felt like. I took out my phone and looked at a picture of her. She caught me by surprise, the way only something you've memorized can. She was beautiful to me because I loved her, not the other way around. She was really rather plain. A canvas hoping to hold paint and stretch across a frame. We both were.

Tomorrow, I'd get her flowers. I'd get her flowers for the next fifty-five days. I'd remember which she liked best. Lavender, lilac, a lily? I'd once written *lungwort* on the back of an envelope; that could've been the name of a band. She'd mentioned false goat's beard and bear's breeches. I wasn't sure if those were real things, or where they grew. She'd want me to forage, not purchase. Heliotrope. That might be it. With whatever was in bloom, I'd make her an arrangement that was good enough to keep her eternally unhurt. She could listen to Title Fight all she wanted but she'd never go to her first show. The one I'd just left would be my last.

—

[38]Her future ended in August. She wasn't going to college. The mechanics of solids would have to wait. It was best, it was decided, that she defer for a year, to ensure she was fully committed to recovery. Her parents could not be swayed or reasoned with. They didn't care about the nonrefundable tuition deposit.

The day before I left, we wandered onto someone's lawn. We made a pact that we'd never buy a house that was less than one hundred years old. She lay, fetal, in a striped hammock. I was sprawled on the grass. It was an unannounced contest to see who the bugs would bite more. It was a shapeless conversation. I told her Sophie and I had once gotten in an argument about pears. She said they tasted sandy. I thought it was more like dirt.

Fiona said she'd never had a pear. "Did you know they're related to roses?"

It turned out she was over purple plants. I'd never gotten her any. I bit the inside of my cheek. I was fresh out of unbroken lip. She started listing things with thorns. I caught on. We volleyed in rapid succession: porcupines, cacti, Jesus's crown, sea urchins. The Statue of Liberty had spikes, which can also be found in the chokey, and maybe we would watch *Matilda* later. She stuck out her jaw and blew upward, fanning her new bangs across her forehead.

"If you've never had a pear, then why do you write down *pear* on those lists?"

She killed a minute looking confused, then blurted out that she was sorry.

I didn't say a thing. After many weeks' worth of sleepovers, I'd ended up in her father's Ivy League T-shirt. Matty's Iron Maiden shirt hung down her chest. She'd been making me wear sunscreen all summer. She said we needed to start taking better care of our skin. I sat like a petulant child while she rubbed it onto me every morning.

"I said I'm sorry!"

"Are you sorry? I'm not a nurse and I'm not your mother. I'm not a hospital chart. You can't lie to me about that. What is even the point of lying to me about that?"

"I didn't lie exactly, it's just that when I go in now, I have to do the IV again. I converted the calories from that into real foods because I was embarrassed about how I got them. But I didn't lie about the numbers themselves."

The first time she ever told me it was her umpteenth consecutive day without food, I was literally dumbstruck. More than usual. I'd known the basics but never assumed she did anything that extreme. Frankly, I had no idea why she wasn't dead. The question still stood. The worry still weighed on me: not if, but when. The why was clear. But the how—?

"When your esophagus explodes, that's going to be a very stupid way to die. You do realize that, right? You must realize that you don't want to get better. Or you would have done it already. You're clearly like this because you like being like this."

No one passed us on the sidewalk. The woman whose

property we were on peeked through the blinds, decided we weren't a threat, and went back to whatever.

"Olive, you know you can't—how could you say that?" She took off her sunglasses and eyed the patch of shade on the ground. "I want to stop, truly, honestly. Of course I want to stop, but I'm too pathetic and too scared to. It's compulsive now, an addiction, a very strong habit, a result of my altered brain chemistry. It's very complicated."

"Chew and swallow. The food goes in your stomach. You shit it out. It seems pretty simple."

"My stomach isn't the problem and you know that. You know it's all in my head. The pills and the shock treatments can cure my brain, but my mind's a lost cause. No one can really tell you what a mind even *is*. I can't really tell you what's my fault or what's a side effect from the antidepressants and the antianxiety pills and the antihistamines to increase my appetite. I don't even know who I am or remember if I'm on mood stabilizers right now, so why should I care if 'I' end up my own casualty? No one treats me like a person. I'm a toy and I'm a payday for the people my parents throw money at in exchange for more labels. Guess what? My therapist wants to 'explore the possibility' of me having a personality disorder. There's a whole galaxy's worth of things about me for them to gawk at and not know how to conquer. Gosh, maybe my parents can donate some money to NASA and they'll name the next satellite after me."

"You don't want them to name a satellite after you. You want them to rename the sun in your memory. You can't wait to die and for us to start mourning. You don't care about me.

You only care about other people in relation to how much you can get them to care about you."

"How on earth do you come up with these things! What will it take for you to believe that I am still trying *for you*? How much guilt do you need from me every time I get stuck? Just because I want to stop trying that doesn't mean I'm going to. I haven't yet, have I? Sometimes it physically hurts to take a single step out of bed—and did I or did I not make you breakfast every morning this week?"

"You didn't eat it with me!" A welt erupted on my earlobe. One on my calf. I was not going to scratch them. "A piece of toast isn't going to kill you."

"Do you know how lucky you are to believe that? What if I told you that starting right now you would barely be allowed to eat? And that it was the only way for you to survive? For the rest of your life. Oh gosh, wait, I have told you a thousand times what would happen. You wouldn't even entertain the idea. You'd think I was crazy. That's what it's like to be told that I have to eat thousands and thousands of calories every day for the rest of my life. I'm supposed to believe it's going to save me. I'm supposed to believe other people over myself and I do, I start to, but it never lasts and I don't want to be Sisyphus. I can't."

"If you're so sure it's your fate, then why not?"

"Because the pity is the worst part. *Poor thing, pushing the boulder up the hill.* I just need someone to care without being so condescending. Whenever someone starts to care, I can see where it's going—nowhere good! So I start to hate them and then—"

"You don't hate me."

"You're right. I think I love you, but if I love you so much, then why can't I get better? I'm going to keep trying, just don't give up on me yet. Please? I almost—I just wish you could understand it without having to suffer through it yourself."

Sweat breached the barrier of my eyebrows. Maybe I was crying. I watched her watch a bug land and take off and I stopped myself from asking its scientific name.

"I gave up on you already. I don't care if you stop going to therapy. Just don't stop eating however much you're supposed to eat. And don't keep pretending you've eaten pears when you haven't."

"I know you gave up. I'm not stupid. I already forgave you and I forgive you for whatever else you have to do. But if the only thing that means anything to you is me putting food into my mouth or whether it's a certain piece of fruit, then I don't know what you've been doing all these years but you haven't been listening. It's not about a pear or a banana or a carambola."

I had no idea what a carambola was. "You don't have to follow their rules anymore. They clearly don't work for you. You should make your own decisions now."

"It was my decision to stay here, not theirs. I didn't want to tell you because I knew you'd—I'm sorry that I still need help. I don't know why you hate me for it. I thought you loved me for asking for help when I need it. Nothing about me has changed since you helped me just by being there and holding my hand. That's all I need, but you're . . ."

The hammock swayed with the force of her tapping her foot.

"I'm not going to apologize for leaving. Is that why you let me get in Matty's car?"

"Let you? As if anyone can stop you once you're fixating on something. I let you go with him for the same reason you never got in my way when I hid food in napkins and the same reason you stood watch for me at the bathroom door."

"And the same reason you told my first Matty to stay the hell, sorry, the heck away from me. Right?"

Her foot shook faster. There weren't any bites on her legs. "Oh, Olive, I am so, so sorry. I was just trying to—I could not sleep at night knowing you might give him the chance to hurt you."

"Fiona! You can't sleep because you're literally psychotic. How could he, how could anyone, possibly hurt me more than you?"

"I'm sorry, I'm sorry, I'm sorry, I'm sorry, I'm sorry!"

"Shut up. I'll only accept your apology if you leave here when I do. Stop being so scared to grow up." I scooted toward her. "You'll be fine. You know about bank accounts and shit."

"Are you listening to anything I'm saying? If I moved out by myself next week, I think I'd be dead in a month. I wish you could stay with me forever and be my eyes. That's the only workaround I can come up with. It would make me so happy, but I know you have better things to do."

"I don't care about you being happy anymore. I just want you to be alive."

"I'm sorry." How many ways could the same word color a conversation?

"I'm sorry too."

"Anyway," she said, "I've been meaning to tell you that I don't think you'll like it in California. It's not like the city here, where you can walk right up to the edge. No one really knows where Los Angeles ends. And who wants a single coastline when you can have a whole island? They built their buildings out instead of up, you know."

"I know." I nodded. "But I have to go. It's only for a little while."

"Four years is a long while. That kind of time is so daunting when you have nothing to work toward and I still have that thing where I know I'm not going to be here long in the long run. That I'm not meant to."

"You aren't meant to do anything. You don't have a destiny. Or a fate. And thinking that you do is more dangerous than accepting that you're free."

I took the stud out of my nose and flung it into the grass. It no longer seemed to fit.

"Don't throw that at me," she shrieked.

"Calm down!" It hadn't landed anywhere near her. I knelt beside her, level with her knees, and brought her finger to my skin. I lowered my voice and asked her to look. "Do you think it's going to leave a scar?"

"No." She pulled me into the hammock.

It was hot enough without our body heat mixing. I curled up with her and waited for the swaying to stop.

Then I waited for something to close the gap between sympathy and empathy. But she'd never had a needle through her nostril and I'd never had one pump supplemental nutrition into my veins. I wanted to understand her more than I wanted to help her, though at the time I saw no difference. What we had was not something that could or should endure. We didn't say so but we knew. That's why we never considered facing adulthood together. Anything else was just a story we liked telling, a way to pass the time until I walked away. If I'd stayed or she'd gone— I should stay away from speculation. I was gone the next day. It was a while before she could go. But she went.

Having met her feels more destined than getting sick does, or perhaps one necessitated the other. That isn't to blame her for who I am now. These are just things that happened. That doesn't mean they were meant to be.

—

PART FIVE

Unfortunately I have a body and I'm the only
one in charge of it you know what I eat the bones too
I'm in the world I'm in the world

—Morgan Parker
"Magical Negro #217: Diana Ross
Finishing a Rib in Alabama, 1990s"

YOU DON'T KNOW WHAT'S GOOD FOR YOU

MARCH 2022

39

When Cedar was a puppy, stairs confounded him. My parents said this was good: fewer rooms to keep free of choking hazards; fewer things lost to teething. They said he could wait until he was older, which they also often said about me. One day, they were away—I don't know where—and I lifted the baby gate at the foot of the staircase. I crawled to the second floor, knowing Cedar would copy me. He did. But when I started back down, he was still at the top, one leg extended toward the first step. I returned to comfort him. His ribs were shaking, his ears pinned back. No barking, no baring of teeth. Fear, I figured, was rooted in ignorance. I tried to explain that he had to trust me. That I would take his first step for him and not let him fall. His limbs were unpliable. He was unreasonable. I had to push him. I thought that him not knowing was worse than him getting hurt. I threw myself down after him and I forgot my own pain when I saw his confusion veer to comprehension, then forgiveness. He licked my tears. Our foreheads pressed together. *I'm sorry I love you*, I said. The separate sentiments ran together. He rolled over. I patted his stomach. He was unscathed. A month later, my parents removed the blockade, and up and down the stairs he went. I realized that I was very proud of him and that I would make a terrible mother.

Fiona looks good. Child in her arms. Badge-of-honor exhaustion in her smile. I should leave them to it. I put her invitation and her letter in their respective envelopes and drop them in the trash. I count to ten before retrieving them. I toss them on the table and consider pouring water over them, to seep the ink into nonsense. If I were to do it, she'll somehow know. She'll feel a shiver up her spine. I can still hurt her.

I plug in my dead phone. The date and time that fill the screen are news to me. It's after 9:00 p.m. and the party's in three days. I check my bank accounts and wince. My search for a baby shower gift produces bespoke, miniscule items that evoke nothing in me. I don't know if adopted babies need different kinds of gifts. I put a set of hand-carved alphabet blocks, in the darkest shade of wood available, into my cart, gag at the price for overnight shipping, and close the window. The cuts on my hands have healed just in time for me to hold Flannery. Will she burp? Will she thank me when I reprimand Fiona for naming her that?

I return to my magnum opus, which is unfortunately nearing completion. The moment I cement the tracklist, order a tape recorder and blank cassettes, fill said cassettes, and declare my project complete, I'll have to go back to work, at which point the nothingness of my life will finally obliterate me. And what will I do with the thing I've been laboring over? Let it rot on my shelf, never to be listened to, because it's helped me remember things I never need to think about again. Maybe it was meant for her all along, despite her nonexistent taste, unless this is the thing that will finally convert her, though wasn't the point aways that music was the part of me she couldn't eclipse? I'm delirious. I turn whatever I'm listening to up and move empty wrappers, which I've apparently turned inside out, and records around. I find my phone. Fiona isn't the only one who can beckon old friends out of the blue. I type in ten numbers I can't seem to unlearn. The empty text bubble I send is basically an accident. I turn my phone off. Bright batters me when I flip the lights on. I feel reborn.

I get in the shower. A colony of mold is encroaching on the faucet, but it's okay—the water is clean and I can be clean. It hurts, but I detangle my hair. Then I try to shave. The razor clogs after the first stroke and cuts after the second. I put a different album on while I wait for the steam on the mirror to clear. My face has sprouted things I should remove. I take my time with it. I scrape my tongue until it feels recently scalded. Blood marks where I drag floss between my teeth. I slather on lotion. All of this just to don a shirt advertising a band I never liked. I turn my phone on and the record over.

What's up?

I tell him I'm wearing his shirt. He asks if he can see.

Why can't you just believe me?

One of us calls the other and though he's always made me feel like I'm in trouble, this is the first time I understand what I'm doing wrong. I turn off the music. He asks me if I'm okay and I ask where he is.

"Home."

"Alone?"

"Are you?"

I ask where he lives now. "Uh-oh," I laugh, while I braid my hair and undo it and do it again. "That's racist." I wait for him to hang up.

"Living here is racist?"

"They took redlining and really ran with it, David."

"Whatever you say, babe."

I tell him I haven't talked to anyone else in a very long time. I tell him that no one else is very good at what he was always very good at. I don't tell him that I despise how much easier he is than a first date. How he is electrifying, but I'm in the tub. How he is a very large candy bar bought on a whim at a gas station in the middle of the night, ultimately sickening, though he seemed like such a good idea at the time.

He asks me to remind him what he's good at. I tell him only if he'll do it again. He inhales, trying to be stoic. I worry he's outgrown me. The call has been disconnected. I barely have time to sob before he's downstairs asking me to buzz him in. There was a moment at the beginning, in the middle, at the end, when I could have said no. There is another one now, but I can't leave him out in the snow. Silver flecks my field of vision when I unlock the door. A ring is wrapped around his finger. Otherwise, he is the same, if I ignore the grey in his hair and the fact that he no longer scares me.

I go sit in the far corner of my bed and point at the ring. "What's that?"

"What's what?" He assesses my environment and shakes his head. At least I hid the mouse. "Do you need money? Are you okay? Have you been crying?" After taking off his farcical sneakers—I highly doubt he's been on a skateboard this century—and hanging his coat by the door, he gets on his knees and creates order. I'd forgotten how he likes a home to look not lived in.

"Hey," I bleat, "please come here."

His nose twitches while he inspects the floorboards. "This is not okay." He puts down the pile of records in his arms, without bothering to comment on them, and sits on the floor with his back against the bedframe, winded.

This was never okay. He dusts himself off and joins me in bed. And for what? When I wrap myself around him, he smells like leather on an ocean breeze. He's different, and for a moment it's the worst thing he's ever done. I run my thumb over the bend in the bridge of his nose. A terrible grunt leaves his lips when I kiss him. This is not okay. His mouth slumps away.

"You gonna tell me what happened here, babe?" He flicks the wet spot my hair made on his chest.

"Well . . . I— Fiona—"

"Who?"

I ask him to get the envelopes from the kitchen table, half of which is visible from where we are. There's no room for him here. He makes a big show of getting up—presses his palms against his knees and braces himself. The floor squeaks under him until he's back in the bed, this time in the corner opposite me. "Of course there's blood on this." He studies what he's fetched. "So she what? Adopted a kid and wants you to come meet her. You said this is your ex?"

"Not that one, the other envelope."

"Are you gay now?" he asks before tossing the first envelope aside.

"Be careful!" I sit up.

"Okay. Okay!" He squints at the letter. "Didn't think I'd need my glasses for this." He pats his empty shirt pocket, then holds the first page ten inches from his face. I lie down and slide my head into his lap.

"*Dear Olive*," he starts. "Who's that?"

"Just read!"

My hair hangs off the side of the mattress. A puddle's forming on the floor. My lips move in sync with his as he reads what I've memorized. Her words do not sit right on his tongue. He gets further than I have been able to on my own.

I know I said I didn't want to talk about it, but would you mind terribly if I asked just one question? Is it all my fault? I always thought that my mistakes would keep you sane. When we first met, you promised you'd never be like me. Remember? Did you even hesitate before you—? Did you think of me? Whoops! That's more than one question. You were the strong one. You were supposed to be better than me. I'm sure you are again. You must be back to normal by now.

"Please stop." It's the first time I've said it or the first time he's listened. "No—keep going."

He does and starts editorializing. He says it's overwrought. She's written too much or not enough. She isn't really saying anything. Her logic's impossible to follow. The writing is so small and she keeps saying she loves me.

I've changed a lot, you know. I'm not going to hurt Flan. I am good at love now. Like you.

I make a sound, strangled and wet. He pauses for further instruction.

"You don't have to read it out loud anymore. Just tell me if she ever says she's sorry."

His eyes trawl every line. I poke my finger through a hole in the hem of my, no, his shirt.

"Nope."

"Oh."

What was I expecting? *I'm sorry I didn't try to stop you, but I* am *all better now, so in a way, your crazy plan worked! Love you! See you soon!*

He checks his watch and retires the letter. "So you forgot to eat because this girl broke your heart? Happens to the best of us. You'll get over it. You just have to stop trying to control everything." He seems oblivious to the fact that he's stroking my thighs. "I should get home soon."

"Will you please just fuck me?"

"You're a very funny girl," he says without laughing. He asks if I'm comfortable. If he can get me another pillow or blanket. Things I clearly don't own.

"Go fuck yourself, David. Don't wear your seat belt and I hope there's ice—"

"Oh, babe, I hope you don't listen to them anyone. Haven't you heard what he did? Haven't you stopped making all those references?" No, I think that thought was my own, but some things are so deep in there that I can't know what's original and what I stole. "Besides," he says, "you invited me over here."

I ask him to stay. Maybe he kisses my cheek, saws open my skull, and pries every poached lyric out of my neural network. I don't know. I can't keep my eyes open anymore.

—

[40]I wake up alone, both envelopes restuffed and resting on my pillow. It's before sunrise. Every hard surface stinks of bleach. I steep in the symmetry of the neatly shelved and alphabetized records, then in the sanctuary of the spotless shower tiles. Takeout waits in the kitchen: chocolate chip pancakes and a grilled cheese sandwich and a cheeseburger and a slice of red velvet cake and two orders of disco fries. I stick my finger in the frosting and try to bring it to my mouth. He's dead to me. I will never see or speak to him again. And so what if I do? And so what if everything I tell myself for the rest of my life is a lie? So what if I don't mean it when I say I ate his horrible diner provisions. They went down without a hitch. I'm at peace now, definitely not wishing I could remove my epidermis and hook it by the door. I'm not at all hung up on the bone I have to pick with my skeleton, not shouldering a modicum of inexplicable rage at the fact that it holds me together and still—somehow!—is not the most important thing.

So I mean it when I say: I'm going to work today and back to therapy tomorrow and to work again the day after that because recovery is always only one step away, and then a trillion more steps, a death march to make sure you live enough before you die, and I can live without it, can't I? The way Fiona would say *Olive*, the way she used to switch the letters around. *I love.* I can live if she's dead to me too. I look at the photograph on the invitation, unsure if she was ever beautiful or if we were simply young. The invitation, the letter, they go in the box with the rest of what we used to have. *F—K.* The most or least perfect union. I find the mouse and name her Jennifer-and-June and balance her on top of the lid. I banish them and us to the closet's farthest corner. Never to see the sun stretch or sink again. Dead, dead, dead.

One record comes back off the shelves, but after that I'm going to work. And if not there, then somewhere. My shoes will crush soil and grass. I'll call Georgia and I'll tell her everything she doesn't know about me. I'll take her advice when she tells me what she would do if she were me. I'll be a person again. I just need to pick one more song before I can. Something for the present. Something before the hour gets away from me and then the day—well, every song still strikes my soul, so the days get away from me too.

—

[41]The train doors clamp closed. It took a few days, it took a mountain of music, but I made it out. The lids and sockets of my eyes feel shrunken. Is decomposition commencing? No, this is insolvency, an account overdrawn, then over-overdrawn with a penalty fee, and that's without the return ticket I don't want to need. I hope she's still worth it. My pharynx, my larynx, my trachea, my bronchial tubes, my lungs and I, we're having a tough time now. I blink with athletic deliberation until I'm so focused on letting the late morning light in, then shutting it out, in and out, that I can breathe.

The train ride is a train ride. A mistake. I fidget with my headphones, but I suspect there's no soundtrack for this. I scan the half-empty car for someone to silently dote on. No contenders. I count down from a random number, until my brain sticks on *777*. Out the window, wooded highways smear past. I was a moron to abandon my perch at the reception desk, to forgo lunch breaks languishing with Stuart in the basement for this. I don't want this candy-apple red and rotten-apple brown leather seat at my back. I want a rickety stool beneath my sacrum while I look over his shoulder and count the frowzy white hairs on his weathered neck and knuckles. David was a bust, but Stuart? We could spend the last years of his life together. *The last great taxidermist's lovely young wife*, they'll call me. Then they'll say, *There goes the last great taxidermist's crumbling widow.* I can be good to him. Fiona can tell him: I'm far too loyal, I'll slice our fingers open to exchange some blood, slit to slit, in your backyard. Maybe that's why I'm going back to her now. Not because she asked me to, but because I want my platelets back. Or because I never wanted a husband. I just wanted a best friend.

The conductor patrolling the aisle chants each upcoming stop. Mine isn't for hours.

"Ticket please," he greets me. For some reason, he smiles. It's clear nothing ever goes wrong on his watch. I show him proof that I'm authorized to be here. "Thank you much," he says, still smiling.

I wait for him to fill in the gap, to disclose how much he wishes to thank me.

"Thank *you* much," I parrot at his back. He's already leaving. Now his cratered phrase is all I can I think. *Thank you* so *much, seventy hundred and seventy-seven times* so *much, seven hundred and seventy-six*— I nestle my phone back in my pocket alongside my lucky charm of a long-dead rodent. It gives me something to do with my hands. The grain of the fur is like a lullaby I absorb through my thumb and first finger. I want the train to rattle roughly on its tracks, to consider just a little derailment, a slight delay. My foot slugs a rhythm into the empty seat in front of me. I can't wait to see her. I just need more time. In the meantime, I worry myself toward tight-jawed sleep. I want the whispers of my scattered fellow passengers to rise up, to mute my latest thought. But in my dream, they're all thinking what I'm thinking. *Fiona never loved you. Not much. Not any much at all.*

*

The train station is a train station, and I've never been to this one before, but I have a plan. I intend to arrive last and by bus. I'll be not the grand finale but the thing after that, the understudy's postencore, prepractice improv for the empty auditorium. And what are my lines?

You seem healthy. [Sucks low-key rotting teeth.]
That must be really hard for you.

No, no one deserves that.

Hiiiiiiiii!!! You don't have to apologize, really. I
don't even remember what we were fighting about.
Do you? Just give me a hug. I missed you so much.
I don't have to apologize either, right?

No, she'll have her hands too full of pacifiers to embrace me.

Um I'm going to need you to explain why the fuck,
sorry, I mean hell, sorry, I mean why the heck
you thought it was okay to let me think you were

dead. It doesn't matter if it was only for a fraction of a second! And by the way, I kind of assumed you were going to get your dad to pay my medical bills. I mean, the offer still stands if he's down, and by the way, can you spot me for my train ticket? And where's your bathroom? I'm three coffees and two Diet Cokes in but I didn't want to piss, sorry, I mean pee on the train. No, there was nothing wrong with the train, I just didn't want to walk around and be looked at. Actually, come to the bathroom with me. Like I said, it's just caffeine and aspartame, so don't worry, I'm not going in there to— Yeah, I guess the baby can come if you really want.

That'll do.

A boy sprinting down the platform bumps into me and continues on without a word. I'm stuck motionless. Did I touch him? Shame cements me where I stand. *Olive*, I think, turning my inner voice into Fiona's outer voice, *you're going to be okay.* I manage to step out of everyone's way. I keep moving. I'm already broke, so I order a car. It arrives with haste.

I consider telling my driver that I'm going to a baby shower and the baby is already here. The baby is fresh from the Continent, and my driver, he could be from the other side of it. Maybe he's Liberian. Senegalese? But it's not a baby shower. It's more of a baby lake. The water's settled and slightly polluted with Fiona's white tears. I let him drive in peace. I respect what he's got on the radio.

What I can see of myself in the window is disconcerting.

I had every intention of wearing makeup and clean, intact, properly sized clothes, to signal to everyone that for Fiona I'm willing to go above and beyond. But I know she'll know my current state means more, means *Honestly, this is the first time I've left my apartment in maybe months, and I won't be surprised if there's an eviction notice being stuck on my sticky door as we speak, and I'd prefer not to open the quickly accumulating messages from my boss, who probably isn't my boss anymore, because when I got your letter I got on the floor and got lost in a few things that I was probably misremembering.*

The car stops moving. "Thank you much," I say like an asshole as I exit. I tip him 77 percent and somehow don't projectile vomit on the short path to Fiona's front door, which is the only one on the block without a camera recording its porch and perimeter. My fingers coil around the handle. My arm, or wherever the next motion should originate from, isn't working. I search for a way out. It's futile. *You're going to be okay, you're going to ring the doorbell, you're going to step inside the home. Okay? Okay. Okay!*

I ring.

Sam greets me, their arms full of the baby. They introduce themselves, first and last name, like that's the information I came here for, like that what's been keeping me up at night, not the question of who they even are and if they're good enough for Fiona or if Fiona's good enough for them and what their game plan is for when she does what she does to their heart.

I step.

I'm given a hug I didn't ask for. I really don't need to know what these people—Sam and this baby—smell like. They smell nice, but that's beside the point. "Welcome," Sam says. "Make yourself comfortable," they add, adorably unaware of the kind of person I am.

I catch the door and ease it closed behind me. Sam and the baby go mingle with people who are capable of existing at ease. I keep my coat and shoes on and camouflage my gift among the pile of gifts. My name isn't on it, so it doesn't matter if she—I'm not sure if I'm thinking of Fiona or the baby—doesn't like it, though I have to admit they are good blocks. As good as blocks can be. I count a dozen other wrapped and bowed offerings, one of which my mother sent in her absence.

I wonder where Fiona's mother is and then I remember she's dead, which we obviously haven't discussed, though I'd considered, at many points, breaching the silence, to say what, something, anything, but didn't breach anything because even though it's Fiona, in this case, I wouldn't know what to say. But Fiona's not dead and she will emerge at any moment and we can talk about anything she wants to talk about.

A jumble of chairs arcs opposite the sofa in the living room. I should go wait there. There are four matching dining chairs, plus one that looks stolen from a psychiatrist's office, a strangely attractive lawn chair, and some motley others. The furniture is as diverse as the people using it. Someone glances at me and absentmindedly pats the empty cushion next to her. She seems a little drunk, on joy or something else. I sit on the floor in front of the seat I was offered. My coat makes a petty ruckus as I hug my knees to my chest. "It's so chilly in here," I mutter, before someone offers to whisk my outwear away. But by the grace of some god, I seem to be invisible.

It's the baby, I realize. The baby is the god. They worship her. Her holiness Baby Flan Davies the First sits in Sam's lap.

She stays still like an angel while Sam holds up a baby photo of another baby—there are party guests, celebrities, and nineteenth-century philosophers in the mix—for us to guess who the baby grew up to be. They're all talking over each other, and sometimes they get so distracted cooing over Flan that they hurl guesses at photos they've already identified.

A stray balloon invades my sightline. Fiona? No. My mouth goes dry. I look for a drink I can grab without getting up, though I really shouldn't. My bladder is about to burst. The good news is there are plenty of drinks lying around. The bad news is they all contain plastic babies suspended in ice. Little half-thumb-sized babies clinking around in big ice cube wombs, melting slowly in everyone's cups. Oh my god. They aren't cups. They're bottles. They're drinking ice-cold baby beers and iced baby teas and chilled baby wine out of baby bottles. At least most of them have removed the nipple tops and are drinking rather than suckling. I'm too stunned to cackle. I've never felt so sane. Sam passes Flan around to all the hungry hands. The congregation goes wild.

"Cake!" someone announces. Not Fiona.

In it comes, on a white cardboard platter balanced between Not Fiona's outstretched ulnas. And on the white platter sits a white cake in the shape of a diaper. Also Not Fiona flounces in with a knife and saws the diaper open. Beneath the white frosting lies chocolate cake with lemon jam filling, and these maniacs go to town, licking shit-and-piss-colored diaper cake off their fingers, trading scato-urological banter between licks.

I think I've seen enough. I find the bathroom and pee for an amount of time that seems inhuman. I am finally comfortable. I am empty and my freedom is back within reach. I flush,

I wash, I return to the hallway and head to the front door. I get it open. Something seizes my other hand. Someone is trying to shatter my palm because they know that the pressure helps me remember to breathe.

"I'll come with you, Olive."

I forget my lines. "Good!" I pull Fiona out to the porch without turning around. "So you and Sam are—" I start. I gather the nerve to look at her. "Fiona, go put your shoes on."

"Whoops," she lilts. "You know, it's really not that cold out." She has Flan in one hand and cake in the other. She feeds herself with her left hand, which I remember my mother saying is something all good parents learn to do, because childrearing is quite the imposition and all one can do is enthusiastically adapt.

I tell her, "There's snow on the ground." And it's not unlike the polka dots on the green dress covering her from wrist to shoulder and hanging past her knees, but even then it's not low enough to protect her toes.

"I don't want to go back inside."

The baby wriggles her limbs beneath Fiona's limbs. The baby moves her inchoate facial features around. I think she has dimples but maybe we're all born with dimples and lose them along the way. "You don't even have socks on." The baby has socks on. The baby has a lot of clothes on. If anything, she's probably too warm. Her clothes are also green.

"Fine," Fiona says to me, but it feels like she's talking to the baby. "If you really want us to leave—"

"I don't want you to leave."

"Good! So, to answer your question, yes, Sam and I spend a lot of time together."

"So they live here?" I ask. Fiona nods. "And you live here?" She bobs her head again. "And is the baby just your baby or is the baby also their baby?"

"The baby is just my baby, on paper. But we take things one day at a time. And we're not subscribed to the concept of ownership. Do you have any more questions?"

I say, "You must really be happy." It's not a question. I think now the baby's asleep.

"And you—"

"Oh, you know me. I like to be alone," I tell her. She snorts. It's been years since someone got my jokes. "By the way, are you aware of what everyone's doing in there? The games? The decorations? Everything transpiring in your home is grounds for institutionalization. Please tell me you didn't approve any of that in advance."

She grins. "Well, some of it I did."

My stomach settles the more she speaks. I ask what exactly she does out here. She says she talks to people, mostly.

"What they need," she says, when I ask about what. It was hard at the beginning, when they had no idea who she was and no reason to trust her. "The gaps between people are really awful," she explains, and starts to pace in a neat little polygon. "Especially here. There's so much money, and they won't share it, except with each other. So first I ask people with not so much money what they need, and I really, really listen. Then I put on a dress that would make Lena, God rest her soul, proud. And I convince people like Lena, God rest her soul, to part with things they only think they need." I wonder how many coffees in she is. "You have to make them feel like they're making a noble sacrifice, you have to basically vow to canonize them for it. And then I take what they give and give it to someone else. That's it."

"That's it?"

"Oh, and I send them a prayer candle for their troubles. Pure white, and the jar is transparent. The atheists love it more than the Catholics. Oh, and I hand paint their initials and the initials of the person they helped in gold on the underside of the glass. That's it! It's pretty easy."

I ask a clarifying question about the logistics of her non-profit. She corrects me. They don't do that particular paper-work. It's all under the table. It's none of the government's business. She sounds like Stuart, so I tell her about him and the rest of the nothing I've been doing this year, though David gets elided. I'm in the middle of recapping something boring when I remember her real gift.

One mouse, stiff and stuffed, with a second mouse head sewn on the first head's neck. Two peas in a pod. "Here." I thrust it at her.

She screams and clutches the baby, now freshly awake, tighter. She doesn't drop her. I think if it were me, I might have dropped her. If it were me, I might be nervous, not malevolent.

"I couldn't tell if it was cute or weird." I shrug and place the mouse, or mice, on the ground between us.

"It's perfect. I love it. Flan loves it. Wait, I have something for you too." She pushes a loose greasy lock of hair off her neck to reveal a gem of a pimple. I squeal my gratitude for the satisfaction of pinching out the pus. The high fades as fast as it came. She doesn't have other blemishes. I wipe the mess off on my knee and Fiona laughs at my disappointment until she cries and I do the same until she pulls out a cigarette.

My eyes dart between it and the baby. She rolls her eyes and gestures at the open air we're standing in. She flicks her lighter, her fingernails painfully short, and lets the flame peter out, to prove there's a substantial breeze and no substantial danger from the secondhand smoke.

"Fiona."

"Fine!"

Through a window, I watch the people applaud as Fiona hands the baby wordlessly to Sam. The baby gulps and gurgles but doesn't seem displeased. Fiona curtsies and exits.

"Thank god we got rid of her," I say when Fiona gets back. "I understand the urge to eavesdrop, but she could be a little less obvious about it."

"You'll love Flan once you get used to her. Trust me," she says with erratic inflection. She's pacing again, being careful not to step on the mice or mouse.

"So you love her? You're used to her?" I ask. Her answer is a very stern look. "Okay. I trust you. But I might need like thirteen years to get used to her. Or to have any idea what her life is like. Sometimes I can't remember anything that happened to me before you did."

"Don't say that, Olive. Other people have happened to you. You've happened to a lot of other people." She's either forgotten about the cigarette or thought better of it. "I wish you would tell me about it."

"I know," I say, and she says, "I know."

Maybe that's all there is to say. After that, there's silence. There's the noise of the party inside, yes. Grating. Booming. Unable to infect what she and I have brewing. I listen to our quiet, which is miraculous, until I'm afraid it's just more of the same, more of the bullish abandonment she put me through for ten years and four months, and then it's clear, for somehow the first time, that I abandoned her too. Sweat pricks the skin at my temples. This is it. I'm going to swing. I'm going to break something. No, I'm going to soften. I'm over anger. I'm going to tell Fiona that I'm sorry, but my stomach is empty, and it's not her fault, but it means I can smell everything: her hand on my hand, and the car exhaust in her neighbor's driveway, and the fact that I'm not going to sleep here tonight, no matter how many extra rooms she does or doesn't have, but I want to come back when it can be just the two of us and we can do something arcane and dicey and dumb, and in the meantime, I'm going to need something other than cake to eat, and I'm going to need her to keep her hand on mine while I eat it, and if that's too much, if that's not something she can do or something she wants to do, then I need her to tell me the one thing we've never told each other before. *I don't think that's a good idea.*

But that's not what I say. That's not what we tell each other, at least not yet. Her gaze flutters across my face. I shut my eyes, though I've never minded looking right at her, or being looked at by her. I think she shuts hers too.

"You seem—" one of us says.

"—alive."

—

a Khaki Oliver mix

I'M ENCLOSED NOW

#	Song	Artist
1	Reach Out to You	Adventures
2	Shed	Title Fight
3	Introducing Morrissey	The Ergs!

WHAT I MIGHT DO IF I WERE LET LOOSE

#	Song	Artist
4	Time Tables	The Menzingers
5	Facet Squared	Fugazi
6	Housebroken	The Hotelier
7	Drug Lord	William Bonney
8	Me + Genine	Glocca Morra
9	220 Years	Hot Water Music
10	Holy Cannoli	Walter Mitty and His Makeshift Orchestra
11	Lvl. 2 Pidgey in a Masterball	Free Throw
12	Important Things (Specter Magic)	Snowing

TO SUFFER FOR YOU LIKE I DID

#	Song	Artist
13	Peacock	The Sidekicks
14	Calendar	I Kill Giants
15	Autonomously	The Measure [SA]
16	For Want Of	Rites of Spring
17	To Friends Old and New	Titus Andronicus
18	Coca Cola	Pity Sex
19	Chase, I Hardly Know Ya	Marietta
20	Wise People	Lemuria

WE'RE ALL CLOSE TO THE END

21	Busy	Jawbreaker
22	Planning Is Easy	Punch

A LONELY RAGE

23	Intransit	The Lawrence Arms
24	You've Got So Far to Go	Alkaline Trio
25	Spirit Desire	Tigers Jaw
26	Concrete	Spanish Love Songs
27	Our Love Will Last Forever and Ever	The Mr. T Experience

MAYBE YOU COULD HURT ME

28	I'm Gonna Deck Your Halls, Bub	Dikembe
29	All Ages Shows	Bomb the Music Industry!
30	Tell Me So	Bikini Kill
31	What A Dump	Swearin'
32	Hiding	Pianos Become the Teeth

YOU MIGHT HAVE BEEN MY SUNSHINE

33	Benediction	The Weakerthans
34	Honeybee	Seahaven
35	Augusta, GA	Into It. Over It.
36	Walking Is Still Honest	Against Me!
37	Cadence	Touché Amoré
38	Sunshine State	Frank Turner

YOU DON'T KNOW WHAT'S GOOD FOR YOU

39	Bring It On	The Gaslight Anthem
40	Uniform	Loma Prieta
41	Vampires Are Poseurs (Song for the Living)	Ramshackle Glory

Author's Note

While every show described herein did take place in the real world, some details, including but not limited to dates, locations, lineups, and setlists, have been adjusted to fit the world of the text. Inaccuracies and anachronisms may be intentional. They may also be mistakes. Forgive them.

Works Cited & Referenced

The title of the novel is taken from the song with that name by Jawbreaker.

I'M ENCLOSED NOW

The phrase "I'm enclosed now" is taken from the song "Reach Out to You" by Adventures.

Shed by Title Fight

The quotation "Love seems with them to be more an eager desire, than a tender delicate mixture of sentiment and sensation. Their griefs are transient . . . In general, their existence appears to participate more of sensation than reflection" is taken from Thomas Jefferson's *Notes on the State of Virginia*.

WHAT I MIGHT DO IF I WERE LET LOOSE

The phrase "What I might do if I were let loose" is taken from the song "Housebroken" by The Hotelier.

Housebroken by The Hotelier

The essay about gender and emo is Jessica Hopper's "Emo: Where the Girls Aren't," from *Punk Planet*.

TO SUFFER FOR YOU LIKE I DID

The phrase "To suffer for you like I did" is taken from the song "To Friends Old and New" by Titus Andronicus.

Autonomously by The Measure [SA]

The passage about marriage is taken from Emma Goldman's essay "Marriage and Love," from *Mother Earth* magazine.

For Want Of by Rites of Spring

The refrain of "I love you" is delivered by Sissy Sullivan, as portrayed by Carey Mulligan in the Steve McQueen film *Shame.*

Wise People by Lemuria

The Home for the Holidays announcement is taken from bouncingsouls.com. (I think.)

WE'RE ALL CLOSE TO THE END

The phrase "We're all close to the end" is taken from the song "Busy" by Jawbreaker.

A LONELY RAGE

The phrase "A lonely rage" is taken from the song "Intransit" by The Lawrence Arms.

Intransit by The Lawrence Arms

The quoted description of the high school is taken from nemodkdkld's *Urban Dictionary* entry "Montclair High School."

Spirit Desire by Tigers Jaw

The various news headlines are taken from punknews.org.

MAYBE YOU COULD HURT ME

The phrase "Maybe you could hurt me" is taken from the song "Tell Me So" by Bikini Kill.

YOU MIGHT HAVE BEEN MY SUNSHINE

The phrase "You might have been my sunshine" is taken from the song "Sunshine State" by Frank Turner.

YOU DON'T KNOW WHAT'S GOOD FOR YOU

The phrase "You don't know what's good for you" is taken from the song "Bring It On" by The Gaslight Anthem.

The seventy or so musical references and allusions not listed here are yours to find, if you're into that kind of thing.

Acknowledgments

Thank you,

Joe Meno,

for *Hairstyles of the Damned*. Thank you especially for Dorie's Iron Maiden shirt, and for my favorite sentence of all time, the one about the kids in matching Minor Threat shirts.

Kevin Dettmar,

for the assignment "Write about a song."

Rodney Jackson and Gibb Schreffler,

for the education.

Stephanie Steiker and Mensah Demary,

for getting this published.

Abby Barce, Laura Berry, Zoë Bodzas, Betsy Carlson-Burkhart, Tobias Carroll, Wah-Ming Chang, Christopher Combemale, tracy danes, Sue Ducharme, Rachel Fershleiser, Megan Fishmann, Cecilia Flores, Vanessa Genao, Donovan Griffin, Markus Hoffmann, Tajja Isen, Stephanie Jimenez, Zain Khalid, Dustin Kurtz, Loan Le, Rachel Letofsky, Lena Moses-Schmitt, Ivan Ngo, Jack Smyth, and Chris L. Terry, and Kira Weiner,

for your attention, help, and encouragement.

Mary Offutt-Reagin,

for talking so much, and for listening so much.

Alex Cromidas and Jennifer Renick,

for marathoning meals with me, and for driving me to shows.

Mom and Dad,

for everything.

Calvin,

for being first.

Zeke,

for loving and for being beloved.

Every artist whose work informed this book, every label who put out their music, every venue that put on their shows, every fan who made more fans, and everyone else who does anything to keep it all going.

Jarred,

for love a song could never capture. And for not caring about Jawbreaker.

© Jarred Stanford

MARIAH STOVALL has written fiction for the anthology *Black Punk Now*, for *Ninth Letter, Vol 1. Brooklyn*, *Hobart*, *Minola Review*, and *Joyland*, and nonfiction for *Los Angeles Review of Books*, *Full Stop*, Hanif Abdurraqib's *68to05*, *Paris Review*, *Poets & Writers*, and *Literary Hub*. *I Love You So Much It's Killing Us Both* is her first novel, and *24 Hour Revenge Therapy* is her favorite Jawbreaker album. She lives in Newark, New Jersey.